DETROIT PUBLIC LIBRARY
P9-DNM-428

DEAD GIRL RUNNING

CHRISTINA DODD

DEAD GIRL RUNNING

HQN™

HQN™

Recycling programs for this product may not exist in your area.

ISBN-13: 978-1-335-01743-7

Dead Girl Running

This edition published by arrangement with Harlequin Books S.A.

For questions and comments about the quality of this book, please contact us at CustomerService@Harlequin.com.

www.HQNBooks.com

Printed in U.S.A.

With gratitude to Arwen and Todd,
a fabulous couple who come to help when called, who love to cook and eat,
who like fine wine, who pull enormous weeds, who help bring
the Christmas tree in and pack the decorations away.
You're always welcome in our tree house and on our zip line.

And thanks to their borador for her unending vigilance
in keeping the deer out of the yard.

1

Washington State's Pacific Coast
Yearning Sands Resort
September of last year

Before Priscilla Carter came to Yearning Sands to be the resort's assistant manager, she supposed her life here would involve a blend of poetry, nature and wealth. She imagined long walks among the towering pines, evenings spent in the luxurious lobby, sipping a cocktail while watching the sun set across the restless Pacific, and a wealthy, interesting man who would catch sight of her and rush to her side, drawn by the rhapsody of their souls.

That hadn't happened.

When a wealthy, interesting man did show up—and they did, on a regular basis, because Yearning Sands was a destination resort—he was usually married to someone smart, pretty and young. If a single guy caught her gazing at the sunset, he would inevitably tell her his room needed to be cleaned. Her two seemingly good prospects bought her a couple of drinks, gave her a quick grope and rushed for the finish line, and when she demanded romance and promises, they couldn't be bothered. Every viable candidate treated her as if she was a slave, and not the kind they wanted to handcuff and spank and have wild sex with, either. More like a faceless vehicle who lived to make their lives easier. That was *so* not her.

The man she considered her best prospect, actor Carson Lennex, had reported her brazen behavior to the resort owners. In forceful terms, Mr. Di Luca had reminded Priscilla that her role here was to assist Mrs. Di Luca, the resort's manager. He'd used words like *probation* and *trial period* and suggested she might consider chasing her dreams elsewhere.

Elsewhere? She didn't have another position—or a runaway marriage—lined up. So she went to work and got her chores done…mostly.

Priscilla was in training to take over from Annie Di Luca when Annie had one of her sick spells—Annie was *really old* and suffered from rheumatoid arthritis—or when the Di Lucas went on one of their rare vacations.

The main hotel building resembled a European castle with towers and turrets, and 592 rooms. Forty-eight cottages were scattered around the property. The resort hosted whale-watching tours and fishing expeditions off their dock, hiking trips to the nearby Olympic Mountains and expertly led scientific treks seeking local flora and fauna. They rented all-terrain vehicles, bicycles and small launches. They had four bars, twenty-seven miles of running paths and a beach access that led to the second-longest beach in Washington State. Luxury-inclined guests indulged in the infinity pool, the fine restaurants and the top-notch spa services. When the hotel was at capacity, they had two thousand guests, and ordering and organizing for the resort required hours and hours. Priscilla got tired and impatient and sourly commented that it seemed as if all of the guests were complaining all the time. But surely no sane person could expect her to do it all and do it all with a smile.

Apparently someone did, because that someone complained about her sullen attitude and Mr. Di Luca called her in *again* and gave her another tedious lecture about being polite to the guests and even the rest of the staff. Like *they* mattered. He made Priscilla so mad she couldn't sleep.

That was the night it happened.

The resort had lodged her in a rustic cottage at the farthest end of the property, supposedly so when she was off duty, she'd have privacy. Priscilla suspected it was to keep the lowly employees away from the privileged guests.

She went upstairs to the bedroom to try to sleep. No luck. At midnight, she got up and poured a glass of wine. She went out to the front porch and paced and drank. She got another glass, sat in the porch swing and rocked and drank.

She got madder. She put her foot up on the arm of the swing, looked at her silver toe ring, at the Celtic knot with a purple topaz. That ring was the only memento she had from her mother. It kept her safe.

Finally, she abandoned the wine and headed along a path toward the beach, walking fast and angry and muttering curses on the entire Yearning Sands Resort staff.

Off in the distance, she heard a motor, a boat on the ocean. Probably someone illegally fishing…

But it wasn't illegal fishing.

A person clad in dark clothing ran the path from the dock and toward the wind-warped pine the locals called the One-Finger Salute. Belated caution made Priscilla duck into a nearby pile of boulders. In the moonless night, she couldn't see who it was or if the person was male or female. She only knew whoever it was bent to place a package at the base of the tree and then ran back to the dock. The motor started again and the boat raced away.

She saw no one lurking in the darkness. Fueled by curiosity, recklessness and wine, she scurried to the tree and groped for the package. She found it in a shallow hole—an oblong box wrapped in paper. For its size, it was heavy; she knelt in the dirt and lifted it free. Hugging it to her chest, she got to her feet and ran toward her cottage. She arrived out of breath and out-of-proportion excited, as if she had been given a late birthday present. She scurried inside, locked the door and hustled through the cottage, closing the blinds as she went. She climbed the stairs to the bedroom, turned on a lamp and placed the box on the bedside table.

She stared at the dirt-smudged package and wondered what she had gotten herself into. Whatever this was, someone had smuggled it onshore in the middle of the night. Logically, someone was now scheduled to pick it up. So it was valuable, and she was an idiot for sticking her neck out to grab it.

But her hopes of a rich husband had been crushed, she'd been working hard and gotten nothing for her labors but a reprimand, so why not open this in the hope of finding treasure inside?

Tearing off the paper, she lifted the lid. Inside, she discovered Bubble Wrapped packages of various sizes, and when she unpacked the largest and heaviest, she discovered the red stone figure of a man squatting on his haunches, an immense penis protruding between his legs. She was so startled she dropped the grotesque thing. It landed on the mattress, and she stood breathing hard.

What was *that*?

She opened another, smaller package and found a similar stone carving of a woman's naked pregnant body. Then a series of broad-cheeked faces with glaring eyes and ferocious scowls. Finally, a flat stone carved with weird symbols. She lined everything up and looked at the hideous things.

Someone was sneaking around for *this*? Her knees were wet and dirty for *this*? For a bunch of ugly rocks?

She went into the bathroom and brushed her teeth. She intended to go to bed, damn it, go to sleep, and... Okay. Those statues looked old. They were worth something to somebody. One quick online search and she found photos of those very statues in an article about Central American tomb looting. In Guatemala, armed thieves had held archaeologists at gunpoint and stolen statuary worth millions on the private collectors market.

"Holy shit," she whispered. She stared at the ugly statues lined up on her nightstand. *Millions.*

She double-checked to make sure the blinds were tightly closed.

One of the archaeologists claimed the symbols on the flat piece of stone were a tomb curse that had been chiseled out, and whoever possessed that would be doubly cursed.

Yeah, sure. Cursed with *money.*

She should turn this find over to the authorities. Maybe there was a reward. Or maybe she'd be in trouble for...for stealing the statues.

Millions. That meant someone around here was going to be plenty mad not to find the box by the tree. Better return these at once.

Except...she'd never before been this close to anything worth millions. She deserved something for knowing about the smuggling and keeping her mouth shut. This was her opportunity. If she had the guts.

Getting the resort stationery and the resort pen, she wrote, "Leave $2,000—"

She threw that note away and started again. "Leave $5,000 in a—"

She threw that note away. She took a photo of the stolen tomb treasures. She printed the picture, put it in a plastic bag and wrote, "I know what they're worth. Leave $25,000 in cash here in an envelope on Sept. 12. When I have the money, I'll return the box to Ocean Notch Park beside the high schoolers' painted rock." She'd make the drop-off in broad daylight, on her way out of town, when there were people around. She'd be safe.

She reread the note. The handwriting was shaky, but she sounded clear and tough. She knew the smuggler—who could it be?—would follow directions. Because...*millions.* All she had to do was put the letter in the bag with the photo, return to the tree and drop them off, and not get caught by someone who… Briefly, she shivered. Someone who might be violent.

She would not chicken out. Better do it now. She donned dark clothes, pulled a dark wool hat over her blond hair and ran in a crouch back to the tree. She put the plastic bag in the hole at the base and a rock on top of it. She raced back to her cottage, and every moment she felt the back of her neck crawl. When she was inside, she locked the doors, checked the rooms, sat on the bed and stared at the collection of statues.

They stared back, solemn, angry, cruel.

They gave her the creeps, so she packaged them up again and stashed the box in the closet.

The next morning, the sun was shining. She went to work and apologized for being late. Annie was, as always, a sweetheart. That skinny exercise freak and spa director, Mara Philippi, invited her to attend the new self-defense class. One of the pilots who flew guests into the airstrip confided that he was a war hero and hinted at a tragic disposition that only a woman's true love could cure.

As Priscilla worked on the resort's supply orders, she began to think she had a future here. She began to have second thoughts about demanding money from a smuggler who, well, might be willing to kill for a fortune. *Millions.* Maybe she shouldn't have sucked down that entire bottle of wine…

At noon, she returned to her cottage, got the box, brought it to the resort and stashed it. But now what? She couldn't give those statues to the authorities. She had incriminated herself by writing that note. She needed to retrieve the note. Then she would take the box of horrors to Mr. Di Luca and tell him…tell him what happened, but say she forgot about it. Or she didn't realize what was in it.

No, not that. Better to pretend she hadn't opened it.

Whatever. She'd figure it out.

She spoke to Sheri Jean Hagerty, the guest experience manager, and volunteered to lead a tour of the property. Sheri Jean was surprised, but civil. She gave Priscilla a stern lecture about how to behave to the paying guests, then anointed her official Yearning Sands expedition guide.

Priscilla promised to do everything precisely right. She put on the charm for the guests, made a point of taking them to the tree and explaining why it was called the One-Finger Salute and glowed when they laughed. She directed their attention to the nearby stack of boulders and explained it was called the nut sack, because the rocks were shaped like walnuts, and she pulled a disbelieving face. They laughed again. With some surprise, she realized she could be good at this. She directed them to the path leading to the Butler Lighthouse Viewpoint, told them it was a great spot to watch for whales. While they were off exclaiming about the panorama, she checked on the plastic bag.

It was gone. In its place was something that looked like... She leaned down and brushed at the dirt. Something mostly buried... She brushed a little more.

A finger.

A hand.

A woman's hand. With polished nails. And a ring.

A hand. Dear God, a hand, a hand, *a severed hand.*

Priscilla didn't scream or throw up. She had enough sense for that. Head swimming, she stood, wanting to get away from the vile thing. That threat. That promise of death and dismemberment. What should she do?

Run away. Now.

"Are you okay? You look ill."

She jumped, looked up at the older woman, a guest with concern on her plump face. The hand in the ground was revealed, crumpled in death's agony, so Priscilla made eye contact with the woman and started shoving dirt into the hole with her shoe. "I don't feel well. A sudden sickness... Flu season has started..."

The woman took a step back. "You should head back."

"You're right. I should. I'll call the other guests..."

"No!" The woman took another step back. She didn't want to be infected. "Send somebody from the resort for us."

"Thank you. I'm sorry." Priscilla must look bad. White. Sweaty with fear.

She was going back to her cottage to pack. Now. Put everything in her car and run away. And whoever found that box of cursed statues could keep it.

I have three confessions:

1. I've got the scar of a gunshot on my forehead.

2. I don't remember an entire year of my life.

3. My name is Kellen Adams…and that's half a lie.

2

Washington State's Pacific Coast
Yearning Sands Resort
January of this year

On January 27, a low tide revealed ocean caves normally submerged by water, Leo and Annie Di Luca left on vacation, a woman's mutilated corpse was found on the grounds and it rained.

The rain was business as usual.

In early November, US Army veteran Kellen Adams had accepted the position of assistant resort manager. Annie had warned her she had arrived at the beginning of what the locals called the Monsoon Season.

Kellen had chuckled.

But they weren't kidding. In winter, on the Washington coast, wind blew. Rain fell. The sun rose late and set early. Every day was an endless gray. The holiday season had been busy and full of guests and lights and cheer, but when the decorations came down and January trudged on, their few guests came for discounted prices on meals and rooms. The resort used the downtime to paint, repair and clean, and Annie practically pushed the hospitality staff out the doors, telling them to go somewhere sunny and come back refreshed and ready to face the Valentine's

Day rush. Everyone snatched at their chance to vacation elsewhere, and they knew where to find deals. They were, after all, in the hospitality business. They had connections.

Kellen told Annie she had nowhere to go, no relatives to visit and no desire to smell coconut-scented sunscreen. She stayed, reveling in the isolation, determined to learn everything Annie could teach her, and kept so busy she fell into bed at night and rose early in the morning. She loved the schedule; it left her little time to think, to remember—and to not remember.

Then on that dark, cold, rainy morning of January 27, Annie followed her own advice. She and Leo prepared to fly to warm and sunny Bella Terra, California, to celebrate their family holidays at the original Di Luca family resort.

Under the hotel portico, a group of elderly tourists climbed into a tour bus, so Annie rolled in her wheelchair through the rain toward the limousine.

Her assistance dog, a black Lab named Hammett, trotted beside her.

Kellen walked on the other side, holding an umbrella and protecting Annie from the windblown blasts of rain, her brain's little quirk kicking in, her mind subconsciously scrolling through its catalog of data on the elderly woman:

ANNIE DI LUCA:
FEMALE, WHITE, ELDERLY, HEIGHT UNDETERMINED. TOO THIN. CURLY WHITE HAIR, GREAT CUT, BROWN EYES. WHEELCHAIR BOUND. RHEUMATOID ARTHRITIS. RESORT MANAGER. BRILLIANT WITH STAFF AND GUESTS. KIND TO A FAULT. FRAIL. HUSBAND: NAPOLEONE (LEO) DI LUCA, MARRIED "SINCE THE EARTH'S CRUST COOLED."

"We'll be back in two weeks," Annie said. "After my last experience with an assistant, I was determined not to hire a replacement. But Leo insisted, and you know the only reason I relented was because you were a wounded veteran."

"I wasn't that wounded." Kellen rotated her shoulder.

"Enough that the Army discharged you!"

"Men were killed." *I was unconscious for two days. Had an MRI to discover the cause of my coma. Tricky things, land mines. Woke to find myself being discharged; I hadn't realized the military could process paperwork that fast.*

"I'm sorry, dear, about the deaths. I know how you feel about your comrades in arms."

They reached the car where Mitchell Nyugen waited to drive the Di Lucas to the airstrip. Again her mind spun and Mitch's info popped up, like a little index card:

MITCHELL NYUGEN:
MALE. VIETNAMESE AMERICAN, SECOND-GENERATION, 26, 5'9", 160 LBS., EXCELLENT PHYSICAL CONDITION, NEEDS LITTLE SLEEP. NO AFFECTIONATE ATTACHMENTS. ARMY VETERAN, HONORABLE DISCHARGE. EXPERT LICENSED DRIVER—MILITARY VEHICLES + COMMERCIAL DRIVER'S LICENSE (CDL) (TRACTOR TRAILER). EMPLOYED 79 DAYS—DRIVER, MECHANIC, ELECTRONICS. FRIEND.

Mitch was one of Kellen's men. Skilled woodworkers, electricians, maintenance and handy workers didn't have to come to Washington in the wettest, darkest, most miserable time of the year, so when Annie appealed to Kellen for a chauffeur, Kellen had in turn appealed to Mitch. Mitch, who had been driving long hours for a trucking company, leaped at the chance to work at the resort.

He was the first of her people to arrive at Yearning Sands.

Now he opened the door and Hammett hopped onto his cushion on the floor. Mitch dried the dog, then picked Annie up and deposited her on the seat.

"Thank you, Mitch. When Leo comes out, will you help him with the bags?" she asked.

"Of course, Mrs. Di Luca." Mitch backed out of the car.

"That boy is so formal," Annie said to Kellen. "I've told him to call me Annie, and he won't."

"He's from the South. Houston. Things are more formal there. He still calls me captain."

"Half of the staff call you captain." Annie patted the seat. "Won't you come in and sit for a minute?"

Kellen shed her rain poncho and handed Mitch the umbrella before easing inside. She took a second towel and dried Hammett some more, then scratched him under the chin. As she stroked his soft head, the anxiety she felt about taking charge of the resort faded.

Mitch shut the door, encasing the two in quiet leather luxury, and walked around to put the wheelchair in the trunk.

Annie shivered, and Hammett abandoned Kellen to snuggle closer to Annie's legs.

Annie took Kellen's hand in her cold, fragile fingers. "Every day you've been a blessing. I never dreamed anyone could pick up the hospitality business so quickly."

Kellen couldn't explain. She didn't even understand herself how she could meet a person and forever after see them as a list of attributes, or view two timelines and mentally integrate them, or take four spreadsheets and shuffle them through the circuits of her brain and instantly come up with ways to improve operations. It was a gift.

She touched the scar on her forehead. A gift that had come at a great price. "Business I understand," Kellen said. "The guests and the staff are the challenge."

"You are very private."

For good reasons.

"Yet you handled people when you were the officer in charge of moving men and goods around a war zone," Annie said. "No one's shooting at you here. This has to be easier."

"The people I managed in the Army had one thing in common—they were soldiers. We were united in one goal—to come out alive."

Annie laughed. Probably she thought Kellen was joking.

"We—my military friends and I—are all of us grateful that you've welcomed us so generously."

"Leo says I take in strays." Annie looked startled at her own insensitivity. "I'm not trying to say that you're a..."

"It's all right. I understand. Since my discharge, I have been adrift. It's difficult to go from being part of a close-knit military community to being...alone."

"I can promise, you'll never be alone again."

Another odd statement from the normally diplomatic Annie. Perhaps leaving on vacation made her lose her usual delicacy. "The staff we left in place for you to manage is well trained. Everyone is up-to-date on their first aid certifications, and they can handle all the jobs—although some better than others. We have very few scheduled guests incoming, so hopefully difficulties will be few and far between." With an expression of dismay, she knocked on the limousine's rosewood interior. "Now, why did I say that? I've doomed you to difficulties."

Kellen shook her head. "I'm not superstitious." *I'm simply afraid of the darkness that stalks me in my own mind.*

"At least there are not too many children scheduled as guests," Annie said. "That will make it easier for you."

"Wrong time of the year. Not many school vacations. But it doesn't matter. I don't mind children. I've just never learned how to handle them." *No point.*

Annie asked, "Who do you foresee as your greatest challenge?"

Kellen promptly said, "Sheri Jean."

"Ah, yes. Sheri Jean." Annie sighed softly. "The best way to handle Sheri Jean is to accord her the respect she deserves."

"As I always do."

"Her personality is split between her mother and her father, and the two halves are constantly at war. She terrorizes her staff, yet no one makes the guests more comfortable than Sheri Jean."

"She's good at her job, but it's hard to decipher when she's going to take offense. Most of the time, I don't know what I said, and I was raised by my aunt and uncle, and my aunt is a delicate flower."

"Really?" Annie's eyes gleamed. "So you *do* have relatives?"

Mistake. Uncomfortably, Kellen admitted, "My uncle and cousin are deceased. My aunt and I don't communicate."

Annie's kind face grew distressed. "I am sorry. Family can be a blessing and a trial. Like marriage."

Kellen's strained smile faded. Why had Annie introduced the topic of marriage into the conversation? Kellen never wanted to talk about marriage.

"When I hired you," Annie confided, "Leo didn't trust you."

Oh. This was about Leo. "I suspected he didn't trust me when he demanded my records—" birth certificate, undergraduate degree from University of Nevada and business degree from Vanderbilt, honorable discharge from the Army "—be examined to see if they were original and investigated their authenticity." He had uncovered no deception, of course, but even when he was satisfied, he had continued to watch Kellen like a hawk.

"It was because of that girl. A nice young woman, but misguided."

Was Annie rambling? "What girl?"

"The girl I hired first. Priscilla Carter."

Kellen had heard mutterings about Annie's first attempt to hire an assistant manager. "The one who left without notice?"

"She didn't have to do that. We had already realized she was unsuited for the job and intended to help her find another position. We're not without heart!" Annie's cheeks flushed.

"You're lovely!" Kellen pressed those cold fingers.

"Leo says I give too much. I don't think that's true, but I did hire Priscilla..." Annie stared out the side window at the wide spread of lawn and the ring of rhododendrons that tossed with each gust of the storm. "Priscilla imagined the resort would be her stepping-stone to a life as a rich man's wife. Leo reprimanded her twice. I should have reprimanded her myself, but I'm a coward. Then she volunteered to take guests on a tour of the property—and left them out there on the cliffs. It's one thing to make the resort look bad, but she abandoned elderly guests out there. No compassion!" Annie sounded so hurt.

Kellen barely knew what to say. "She sounds like a piece of work."

"The guests said she fell ill, promised she'd send someone out after them. Sheri Jean didn't realize the guests had been left until one called. They were worried about Priscilla! We were all worried about her until Leo discovered she had packed her bags, gotten in her car and headed south. She never even contacted us for her final paycheck."

"I promise I would never do that." With a fair amount of humor, Kellen added, "I like my paychecks, and anyway, I don't have a car."

Annie's brow knit fretfully. "So I should worry when you buy one?"

"Not even then."

"Thank heavens. I… I don't know what I'd do if you disappeared, never to be found, and I hadn't told…" Annie seemed to drift off.

"Told…?" Annie's rambling was so unlike her, Kellen was concerned.

"Told him… He's suffered so much. He's fretted. He's searched…"

"Who? Who's searched? For what?" Kellen leaned forward, her eyes fixed on Annie's, and in her brain, a new slot lit up, empty of information and hungering to detail this new person.

In a normal tone, Annie asked, "Do you have any final questions?"

"Um, I… I don't think so. Just, you know, what you were talking about before. Or who you were talking about."

Annie brushed her hair off her forehead. "I didn't sleep well last night. So excited. To go to California, to see the family.

But I want to make sure you feel comfortable in your role as resort manager."

Because Annie suddenly seemed to need reassurance, Kellen said, "With Mr. Gilfilen to handle security, with the tight staff and the small guest list, this is a great way to introduce me to handling the job of resort manager."

Annie fussed with the folds of her long black velvet skirt. "Yes, Vincent Gilfilen. He's a difficult man, you know. Obstinate. A little odd."

"I do know that."

"He does things his own way. He'll always do the right thing." Annie avoided Kellen's gaze. "You go along with whatever happens. It won't be so bad."

"I'm glad to hear that." Kellen felt as if she'd missed something. Like the point.

Annie leaned forward and affectionately took Kellen's face between her palms. She looked into her eyes, and in a dreamy voice, she said, "I told Sarah and June about you. They could barely believe you'd come back."

"Came back?" Kellen pulled out of Annie's clasp. "Came back from where?"

Annie blinked as if trying to clear a fog from her brain. "What?"

"What did you tell Sarah and June about me?" Sarah and June were Annie's sisters-in-law and best friends. But Kellen didn't know she'd been the topic of discussion and she didn't like the sound of *They could barely believe you'd come back.* "Is this to do with the man you didn't tell about me?"

"What man?"

"You said you didn't know what you'd do if I disappeared and he hadn't been told..." Kellen trailed off enticingly, exactly as Annie had done.

"My head aches." Annie closed her eyes and rubbed her neck.

"I'm so old and creaky." She opened her eyes. "Could you hand me a bottle of water?"

Kellen realized Annie's eyes were too bright. "Are you all right?" Kellen placed her hands over the top of Annie's. "You feel warm."

Even with the heated seat, even with Hammett pressing close, Annie shivered. Yet she sounded sensible and prosaic when she said, "Don't make trouble, dear. I just need water."

Kellen pulled a bottle out of the cooler, opened the top and pressed it into Annie's hands.

"I've looked forward to this celebration for months." Annie took a small sip, then put the bottle in the cup holder. "It's the Di Luca family Christmas, you know. We're a large family and all so busy with the resorts and the wineries, this is the only time we can get together."

"I know." Kellen got a throw out of the warmer and slid it around Annie's shoulders. "But you feel as if you're running a fever."

"I'm fine. Look, there's my darling Napoleone headed our way with our overnight bags rolling behind him. The dear man will not let the staff do their job. He is so stubborn."

"Like someone else I know," Kellen muttered.

"Hmm?" Annie raised her eyebrows. "Dear, we can't leave him standing out in this weather. I'm not the only one with creaky bones!" She offered her cheek.

Kellen kissed it. It was warm, too. "Have fun."

"Believe me, we will. We Di Lucas always have a riotous good time."

Kellen slid across the seat and put her hand on the door handle.

Annie stopped her. "When I was interviewing you, I asked what your goal was in coming to Yearning Sands. Do you remember what you said?"

Kellen met her gaze. "I said I wanted a home."

"Do you feel as if you've found what you wanted?"

Kellen's mind produced the globe of the world and spun it like a top. She saw where she was now, on the far edge of the North American continent. She saw those places she feared and avoided: not Afghanistan, not Kuwait, but Maine, New York and Pennsylvania, black holes that swallowed every ray of light and joy. On that day five months ago when she was told she would be released from the Army with an honorable discharge, she had gone looking for a position that would fit her unique talents. At first she had hesitated to come back to the United States. But her first job as a civilian had proved that nowhere in the world was safe. Yearning Sands had proved to be a shelter, and the terror that had once driven her to always glance behind had diminished. She had grown comfortable here in the job. "I could live here forever."

"We would like that. And your friends?" Annie gestured toward Mitch. "The ones we've hired. Are they happy?"

"I can't speak for them, but I think so. They came back from combat in need of employment and they found it here, where they could use their skills to make a living. That's a great thing."

"I want to keep my staff for years. I like to make sure they're happy." Annie squeezed Kellen's arm. "I'm so glad you told me you'll stay. The resort needs you. I need you."

"Wow. That's...great." Kellen broke her hold, snatched up her yellow plastic poncho and leaped into the blustery weather. She pulled the poncho over her head and flagged Leo down.

LEO DI LUCA:
MALE, ELDERLY, FORMERLY 6', NOW 5'10". 190 LBS. SHOULDER-LENGTH GRAY HAIR, GANDALF EYEBROWS. MARRIED "SINCE THE EARTH'S CRUST COOLED." RESORT OWNER. AMERICAN WITH STRONG ITALIAN ROOTS. SUSPICIOUS OF NEWCOMERS.

He bent to hear Kellen when she said, "Keep an eye on Annie. I think she's ill."

He sagged. "She won't ever take it easy. The arthritis has

weakened her immune system, and…" He gestured toward the car. "Thank you for letting me know. I'll do everything I can to protect her."

Outside, the downpour increased. The wind blew. The tourist bus moved on. Some early guests arrived, and Russell, their doorman, welcomed them and carried their luggage inside.

Kellen lifted her face to the cold, rainy sky. To be bound by the iron constraints of need and affection Annie put upon her… so foolish. She knew better. *Yet…need.* Being needed was her weakness.

She could hear Gregory's voice in her head, courting her, winning her. *I need you, my darling Cecilia. I need your vitality, your warmth, your smiles, your youth.*

Young Cecilia had fallen at his feet—and into a marriage of horrors that she had barely survived.

Her cousin, the real Kellen Adams, had died.

3

"How long has it been since you've been outside?"

Cecilia wet her lips, and the wind off the Atlantic Ocean blew them dry again. "Winter is hard in Maine. I couldn't leave the house then."

Her cousin, Kellen, slashed the air with the flat of her hand. "It's July."

Kellen had always been like that. Older by three years. Decisive. Bossy. Pretty, blonde, manicured even in jeans and a jacket and hiking shoes.

"I was ill."

The two cousins climbed the granite cliffs, braving the oncoming storm to speak in private.

"You were hurt," Kellen said. "Gregory is hurting you."

"No. No." Don't make me admit anything. *"He…he… I frustrate him. He's my husband, and I'm not very bright."*

Kellen stopped walking. Took Cecilia's shoulders. Turned her and looked into her eyes. "You're brilliant. You were accepted to Vanderbilt, no small feat."

Cecilia couldn't maintain eye contact. "I'm not a good wife. I don't always understand what he wants."

Kellen shook her. "He's thirty-eight years old. You're twenty. He should understand you."

Cecilia wasn't used to climbing. Her ribs hurt when Kellen shook her, hurt where he had kicked her. "He doesn't hit me. He, um, disciplines me when I need it."

"Disciplines you? When do you need it?" Kellen could not have sounded more incredulous.

"I... I didn't cook his eggs right. So he...he... That night, he had me kneel in the corner, and he cracked all the eggs over my head, the ones in the refrigerator, and opened the window."

"In winter? That's sick. That's criminal." Kellen couldn't contain her outrage. "Is that when that sister of his contacted Mama and Papa? After a year of not hearing a word? Said you had pneumonia and weren't expected to live?"

"I'm lucky he chose me. He's one of the Lykke family. They're wealthy, influential." The wind off the Atlantic blew hard, ruffled Cecilia's hair, blew her own words back in her face. "They've been here since the country was founded."

"What is all that worth? Nothing! They're so self-important they won't let me in the house, and your Gregory can't bear to look at me."

"He's busy." Feeble excuse. But it was all Cecilia had.

"Busy ignoring the only relative you've seen in two years!" Kellen took a breath. "You graduated from high school. You wanted to see the country. You were afraid to fly, so my folks gave you a car and said go for it. What the hell they were thinking, I'll never know. First place you get to, you stop and get married to some old guy—"

"He's not old. He's in the prime of life!"

"That's what he told you! He married a girl half his age!"

Cecilia looked down at the cracked granite that formed the cliffs. She inched closer to the edge, wanting to see the waves pounding on the rocks below.

Kellen caught her arm. "You're not committing suicide on my watch." She looked back at the estate, at the mansion nestled into the cup of the hill and Cecilia's tiny home on the edge of the cliff. "You're not even in the main house. You're living in the...in the maid's quarters."

"Honeymoon cottage."

"Honeymoon-from-hell cottage! One bedroom, one bathroom. Built in the 1950s with all the ugly styling still in place."

"The house isn't awful. When the storms blow in, we lose power. But the Lykke mansion is historic. It would be unkind for me to…to impose myself as Gregory's wife." With the backs of her hands, Cecilia whisked away bewildered tears.

"Unkind. That's bullshit. You are his wife. You should be first." Kellen looked around. "I'm your cousin, and you can't even invite me in, can you?"

"I…"

"I couldn't come up until you called and gave me the all clear. You didn't want me to drive my own car up here. You didn't want your Gregory to know you had a relative arriving to support you. Did you even tell him I was coming?"

"I did! I told him." Because she was afraid not to.

"What did he say?"

"He, um, asked if you were coming to take me away." Cecilia bent her head and stared at her own skinny hands. "I said no."

A pause, then with impeccable logic, Kellen said, "That's because I can't take you away. But I can help you get away."

"I said no, you weren't going to take me away," Cecilia repeated. She had said no, over and over, while he harangued her, accused her, grabbed her wrist and squeezed and twisted. Finally, in a flare of temper, she had shouted, "Yes. Yes! I'm leaving with Kellen!"

Gregory had released her and backed away. In a low voice, he'd said, "If you leave me, I'll kill you and I'll kill myself."

Cecilia hadn't cared what he threatened. She'd curled protectively around her wrist, wondered if the bones were cracked, realized she would have to wear long sleeves for Kellen's visit. For all the good that did, as soon as Kellen had stepped out of the cab into Maine's summer sunshine, she had seen through Cecilia's poor attempt at concealment. Kellen had slid up the sleeve and looked at the bruises, and right away she had known the truth.

"His sister is a problem, isn't she?" Kellen asked.

"Erin is older, an important part of the family business." Honesty caught Cecilia by the throat, and she confessed, "She doesn't seem to like me much."

"She sounds as if she loves her brother a little too much."

Cecilia winced. "She feels as if she needs to protect him. She thinks I…seduced him."

"What does she think about him hitting you?"

"I don't know." That I deserve it.

"They're all sick. He's sick."

"No. Really, Kellen Rae…"

"Honey. Sweetheart. You're my cousin. When your parents died and my folks brought you home, you were so timid, so sad. I tried to make you strong—"

"You did! You made me so much braver. But I'm not like you. I'm not—"

Kellen's interruption was brutal and direct. "A lesbian?"

They had never spoken of this before. "No. I'm not a lesbian."

Kellen looked out to sea, seeking something on the horizon: understanding, solace…something. "I came out of the closet to Mama and Papa. They threw me out of the house, told me I was going to hell unless I repented."

Cecilia heard a world of pain in Kellen's voice. Putting her arms around her, she said, "I didn't want that for you."

For one moment of weakness, Kellen leaned her head on Cecilia's shoulder, and they stood together, hugging, cousins and sisters of the heart.

Cecilia had always known Kellen was a lesbian, and she wondered how Aunt Cora Rae and Uncle Earle failed to see the truth. Probably because they didn't want to know.

"I would have kept quiet," Kellen said, "but my partner…she deserves to be recognized as part of my family."

"Is she lovely?"

"She's a dear. So smart. So kind. You'll like her. She says we can be married, have children and love them, let them be who they want to be."

"Is that why you came here now? So we could talk about your love?" Cecilia teared up. "All we've done is talk about me."

Kellen's smile disappeared. "No. No guilt. I won't have it. You're already swimming in guilt. Tell me about last year when you broke your leg."

Weary and heartsore, tired of confronting the truth and being confronted, Cecilia collapsed onto a rock. "I… I got lonely. Gregory was at the main house. I went in search of him and I…fell down the stairs."

Kellen sat next to her. "Fell down? I'll bet he was standing behind you."

More tears leaked from the corners of Cecilia's eyes.

Kellen put her arm around Cecilia's shoulders. "Look at us. Look at you." She held out her phone, clicked on the camera, took a picture of them in selfie mode. "We look alike, but you were always the beautiful one. Your hair—" she caught the length in her fist "—had that burnished gold look. Now it's rough, tangled, and the ends are split. You know Mama would be shocked."

Split ends were the ultimate sin in Aunt Cora Rae's house.

"Your mom gave you that perfect skin, that natural kiss of terra-cotta to your skin. Now you're so pale you're almost a ghost."

Cecilia looked away, trying to see across the ocean to a different place, a place of comfort and of warmth. "The Lykkes have never had a, um, Western American, um…"

"Western American…? You mean, Native American? Part Cherokee?"

"When I told them, they were shocked." Cecilia had overheard Erin saying plenty to Gregory about adding a savage to their family tree.

Kellen's voice rose. "What did they think you were going to do? Scalp them?" When Cecilia didn't answer, Kellen's voice gentled. "Your eyes are so big and blue, and your lashes—you always had the most beautiful lashes. And they're gone! Have you been pulling them out?"

"They fell out when I was sick."

"You're too thin, and, Cecilia, you can't even look at yourself."

Kellen was right. Cecilia couldn't look at herself, into her own haunted, shamed eyes.

Kellen continued, "We used to resemble each other so much people thought we were sisters, called us by the other's name. Now...you're haggard, old before your time."

Cecilia sighed, a feeble whimper that made her ashamed. Again. So much shame.

In that distinctive, decisive tone, Kellen said, "Cousin, here's what we're going to do. You're leaving him today. Now."

Fear grabbed Cecilia by the throat. "I can't. I need my...things. My..." Cecilia struggled to think of what was important. "My photos. Of my parents."

"Don't you have them on digital?"

"I don't have a...phone or a..."

"He doesn't let you have electronics. Okay. First I'll put you in a cab and send you down to my hotel in Greenleaf." Kellen called the taxi. Because Kellen did what she said she would do when she said she would do it. "You'll have the same cabdriver I had. Talkative, but really nice. You'll be safe with him. I'll walk to that pissant little house you call a home and get your photos. I'll meet you at the hotel. We'll drive to my place in New York. I'll take care of you."

Cecilia felt as if she was fighting a spiderweb, trying to free herself yet caught ever tighter. "I should tell him. Explain."

"I'll tell him. I'll explain. I'd like to do that." Kellen's relish weighed her voice with pleasure.

Cecilia had to tell the truth. She didn't want to. Kellen would despise her. Who wouldn't? "You don't understand. He'll come after me. I tried to leave once and he was watching me." If you leave me, I'll kill you and I'll kill myself.

"He has cameras in that house?"

"I'm so clumsy. He wants to make sure I don't hurt myself."

"Can you hear yourself? Hear the things you're saying? You're so terrified and battered you're brainwashed."

Cecilia stared at Kellen, mute with terror.

Kellen knew. Kellen saw. "Honey, I won't let him get you."

"He'll be angry. He's strong."

"I know. But you'll be safe. That's what matters. You can live with me. Heal. Be yourself again. Come on." Kellen helped Cecilia to her feet.

Kellen was so brave. Bossy, of course. She always had been. Cecilia had never been like Kellen, but she knew, too, her marriage had changed her from a hopeful girl on the edge of womanhood to a trembling leaf in the frigid wind, always waiting, fearing that shocking moment of violence.

Kellen towed Cecilia down the hill toward the road and in a bracing voice said, "It won't take me more than a half hour, then we'll be outta here. We'll drive down the highway, windows down, and laugh at the world. Remember how we used to travel together?"

"Yes." Nevada roads. Battered old barns. Long straight stretches of desert roads with no turns or kinks. "Those were…good memories."

"We'll have them again. Today." Kellen dug money out of her jeans pocket, handed it over. "Here's twelve dollars for the cab, then a few bucks for something to eat out of the gift shop. Here's the key card for the room. Don't let anyone in except me. Wait here for the cab."

Cecilia sat in the grass on the side of the road and watched Kellen stride toward the honeymoon cottage. Honeymoon from hell. She wanted to laugh; she sobbed instead. It had been so long since she had been down to Greenleaf, over a year since her trip to the hospital. The town wasn't three miles from the Lykke estate, yet she didn't want to leave. Because she loved Gregory, even when…he hurt her.

She gripped the clumps of grass, her fingers aching. She did love him, didn't she?

She had once, two years ago during that brief warm summer when he had seen her walking the rocky beach. He told her she delighted him with her laughter, that he wanted to spend his life making her happy. He bought her flowers, candy. He tried to buy her jewelry, and when she rejected it, he said he respected her. It was the courtship she had read about in books, the gentle wooing she had imagined. He begged, and she had married him. He had made love to her, a glorious experience of worship and respect.

She hadn't wanted to live in the main house with his mother and sister; clearly, they weren't enamored of her and she thought the concept of living in the family home was weird, a guy in his thirties living with his mommy and sister. She had put her foot down—or so she thought—and Gregory had been glad to move into the cottage at the edge of the cliff. He called it their honeymoon cottage and Cecilia was gloriously happy.

Slowly, gradually, the atmosphere had darkened. A cold dark winter such as Cecilia, desert girl that she was, had never imagined.

She talked about inviting her aunt and uncle and cousin; Gregory wanted to be alone with her.

He pointed out the things she did wrong; she argued.

He didn't care for her tone of voice; he was older and knew better.

Eventually, she found it easier to concede…to everything.

He arbitrarily changed his mind. She pointed that out, and he brutally corrected her.

She got bored and asked for a job.

He laughed at her, asked her what she imagined she could do, her, a high school graduate without an exalted family background or a higher education.

She walked to the village, went to the bookstore, bought lofty tomes to improve her mind, a few paperbacks for fun reading, an e-reader so she could grab a magazine while the northers blew in off the Atlantic…

In a humiliating scene, he came and got her, dragged her out, took her home and spanked her. He hadn't cared about sex, not since the first month, but when she cried, he consoled her. Then she was pregnant. When she realized—oh God, she had always wanted children—she rushed to the main house to tell him.

That was when he had pushed her down the stairs—broken bones and a baby's life that faded before it began.

The doctor said there wouldn't be any more children.

Gregory said, You and me, together forever. The two of us, alone.

Now, as she waited for the cab to take her to the village, she tried to think how Gregory would react when Kellen confronted him, what he would do when he discovered Cecilia intended to leave him.

I'll kill you and I'll kill myself.

That was what he had promised, and she believed him.

But first...he would kill Kellen.

Cecilia scrambled to her feet.

He would kill Kellen.

She ran through red-leafed huckleberry patches.

Why hadn't she told Kellen about the baby? Why hadn't she told Kellen about the cruelties?

Because she was embarrassed to be so stupid as to pick an abusive man, humiliated to be so weak and afraid. In withholding that information, she had sent Kellen to her death.

Cecilia reached the rise half a mile above the cottage and stopped, gasping, holding her broken ribs. The sun shone on the old tar-and-gravel roof. Yellow daylilies surrounded the foundation...

Gregory walked around the corner of the house holding something metal, long and cruel-looking.

He would hurt Cecilia. He would kill her.

Cecilia froze, gasping, fear and chills holding her in place.

He would hurt Kellen. He would kill her.

Desperation and guilt fought to send Cecilia forward.

Gregory knelt at the gas meter, using something—a pipe wrench?—to fiddle with the connection.

Cecilia scanned the area, looking for Kellen, and she spotted her. There she was, inside the house, sitting on the couch, facing the front door, her back to the picture window, waiting to confront Gregory.

Gregory stood, dropped the wrench onto a clump of golden daylilies, wiped his hands on his dark trousers. He was handsome, tall, strong. And so cruel... He walked briskly around the house, as if on some kind of timetable.

Without him in sight, Cecilia was able to move. She ran toward the house. Through the window, she saw him come through the front door—with a pickax, its long spike lethal and shining.

"No!" Cecilia ran faster. "Kellen! Come on!"

Kellen didn't budge. Maybe she was afraid.

No, not Kellen. Even if she was afraid, she would react.

As Gregory approached, Kellen slumped forward on the cushions.

What had he done?

Gregory walked around the couch, behind Kellen, lifted the pickax, slammed it into her head.

Her skull split. Gore…blood…death. Oh God, death!

Cecilia screamed, stumbled to a halt, covered her face with her arms.

Then…a whiff of gas. And she knew. She looked.

Inside the house, Gregory walked to the drawer where they kept the lighter for the fire.

I'll kill you and I'll kill myself.

That was what he intended. But he hadn't killed Cecilia. He had killed Kellen and now—

He clicked the lighter a few times. No spark. No flame.

Something drew his gaze up and out the window. He saw Cecilia standing there. He looked down at Kellen's body. Looked up again, his face twisted by a too-familiar fury.

The house exploded.

4

"Captain? You okay? It's really rainin' out here. You want to come inside?"

At the sound of Russell's voice, Kellen shed the grim memories like rainwater. She looked at the man who stood outside the portico, holding an umbrella over her and staring anxiously.

RUSSELL CLARK:
MALE, 46, 5'11", 220 LBS., AUTISTIC. YEARNING SANDS DOORMAN SINCE HE WAS 16. GOOD AT HIS JOB. WILL NOT GO ON VACATION EVEN IN WINTER. LIKES/NEEDS ROUTINE.

She looked down at herself, at the yellow plastic rain poncho that draped her to her knees and protected her from the worst of the rain, and at the soggy hem of her long black dress and the damp leather of her fashion boots.

She mentally checked her schedule, made sure she had her top-security-I'm-the-acting-manager pass card that would open any room in the resort and said, "Yes, thank you, Russell. It's time to go inside."

"Captain, you're an interestin' woman," Russell said.

"A lot of interesting people work at Yearning Sands Resort." As if the fires of hell pursued her, Kellen hurried into the resort. A familiar feeling—she'd been pursued by a devil before.

She walked into the tall, warmly appointed lobby that glowed with golden, color-washed stucco, a lush plant wall, an eccentric floor-to-ceiling gas fireplace that produced flame from artfully arranged metal rods, and comfortable seating areas where, every morning, the resort served a full complimentary breakfast. She was, for the first time, on duty as resort manager.

As Kellen walked through, she accepted a cinnamon roll bite from the servers who were cleaning up the meal and replacing it with platters of cookies and bowls of fruit. The lobby's comfort and the warmth were dwarfed by the two long window walls. Drawn by the panorama, Kellen walked over and looked, first to the west at the thrashing ocean and gray clouds rimmed with gold, then to the north, toward the towering Olympic Mountains. In every mood, even in this unrelenting rain, the view was stunning. Breathtaking. No wonder Yearning Sands was one of the world's most exclusive, expensive, out-of-the-way resorts.

A critical voice sounded behind her. "Taking a moment, are you?"

"There are no words to describe this setting," Kellen said and turned to face Sheri Jean Hagerty.

SHERI JEAN HAGERTY:
FEMALE, AMERICAN/ASIAN/POLYNESIAN, 40, 5'2", PROPORTIONED LIKE A CLOTHING MODEL FOR PETITE SIZES. EMPLOYED 18 YRS. GUEST EXPERIENCE MANAGER. SHAKES HANDS TOO FIRMLY. RIGID SCHEDULE. STAFF FEARS. GUESTS ADORE. **WANTS MY JOB.**

Sheri Jean gave the roiling Pacific a cursory glance. "Yes, it's pretty."

"Pretty?"

"Grand, epic, blah blah." Sheri Jean waved a dismissive hand. "I know how to do the tourist spiel—I simply choose not to waste it on you. Don't you have something more important to do than look out the windows?"

Kellen's teeth were suddenly on edge. "Sheri Jean, when we

meet this afternoon at two fifteen, if you wish, we'll discuss Annie's decision to hire me as assistant manager."

Sheri Jean's eyes narrowed. She looked like a small tiger ready to pounce. "It should have been me."

"Yet it was not, and perhaps you should consider why."

"I could have assumed the role with no training."

"The employees would have fled the resort." Kellen watched a man in a suit walk toward them, then step back, away from the confrontation.

Sheri Jean followed her. "No one would be challenging me now."

"Ladies, excuse me."

Sheri Jean flung herself around.

The data scrolled in Kellen's mind.

CARSON LENNEX:
MALE, 64, IRISH/SPANISH, 6'3", 200 LBS., IRON GRAY HAIR, HAZEL EYES (CHANGEABLE), TANNED, SWIMMER, AMAZING WHEN SEEN IN A BATHING SUIT CLIMBING OUT OF THE HORIZON POOL. ACTOR, MOVIE STAR, FORMER ACTION-ADVENTURE HERO. MARRIED TWICE. DIVORCED TWICE. LIVES ALONE IN A YEARNING SANDS TOWER SUITE. LEAVES CAPRICIOUSLY. RETIRED. ALOOF.

Sheri Jean smoothly made the transition to guest experience manager. "Mr. Lennex, good to see you back! I hope you enjoyed your vacation."

"I had never visited Machu Picchu. Words cannot express the magnificence." Carson nodded coolly to Kellen and spoke to Sheri Jean. "The Shivering Sherlocks are arriving this afternoon."

"Yes, Mr. Lennex. We look forward to them every year."

He included Kellen in the conversation. "The Shivering Sherlocks are six ladies from Alaska who come to Yearning Sands for a murder mystery weekend."

His deep, Irish-accented voice melted away Kellen's irritation with Sheri Jean. "They have a lovely reputation here at the resort."

"I've grown to know them over the last few years, and this year I'm the author of the murder mystery script." He laughed a little, a laugh so warm and smooth Kellen wanted to bottle it. "I'm nervous." He turned back to Sheri Jean. "I'm hosting the welcome party in my suite. I wanted to make sure we have appropriate killer foods."

"I've spoken to the chefs, Mr. Lennex," Sheri Jean said, "and they assured me they had the appropriate hors d'oeuvres in mind."

"Wonderful." Mr. Lennex rubbed his palms together. "I can't wait to see what they concoct." With a nod to them both, he strode toward his private elevator.

Kellen realized she had been holding her breath. She let it out slowly. "He's never spoken to me directly before."

"Don't let it give you ideas," Sheri Jean snapped. "The last assistant manager got reprimanded for thinking she would make him a good trophy wife."

"Sheri Jean, do you see this?" Kellen circled her own unsmiling face. "This saw combat in Afghanistan and Kuwait. This has no illusions left, and you do not comprehend what you're challenging."

Sheri Jean took a step back.

Kellen continued, "In fifteen minutes, I'm scheduled to speak to Chef Norbert about tonight's menu and I know he, also, will be testing my fitness to run the resort in Annie's absence. After that, I speak to Chef Reinhart, who will be irritated that I spoke to Chef Norbert first. Both of those gentlemen will also have to be reminded that after several tours into the world's war zones, I was wounded and then honorably discharged from the US Army as a captain, and I am fit to lead this resort."

Sheri Jean's mouth opened, then closed without a word.

"It's a good thing we're currently running only a skeleton

crew. If I had to repeat that too often, I would grow irritated. I'll see you at two fifteen." With military precision, Kellen turned back to the view and waited while Sheri Jean's heels clicked away across the tile.

The men and women Kellen had led could have warned Sheri Jean not to challenge Kellen's authority. In Afghanistan, in her first deployment, superior officers and soldiers had taken one look at her and assumed she would be a pushover. They hadn't realized how fiercely she would push back, and why.

She would never be abused again.

When Annie had interviewed her for this position and asked about Kellen's goal, her answer had been "A home." But it wasn't as simple as that. The deaths of her parents had left Cecilia orphaned at nine. Her aunt and uncle had taken her in and given her stability, but they weren't her own mother and father. Only Cousin Kellen had made her feel a true part of the family with wholehearted generosity of spirit.

Then Gregory happened; he had successfully dug into her psyche and undermined her strengths. Looking back, she recognized that and knew, too, that Cousin Kellen had saved her; Cousin Kellen had died for her. So that was what *this* Kellen wanted, to find a place in this world where she could be safe, where she could bring her friends, raise them up and give them security. She wanted to be to her friends what Cousin Kellen had been to her: the person who had the strength to make the world better, the person who created a safe haven for lost souls… like herself.

With two minutes to spare, Kellen strode into the restaurant kitchens. The two chefs' hulking forms stood opposite one another.

CHEF NORBERT/CHEF REINHART:
BROTHERS, 47 AND 46. WHITE, BOTH 6'5", 240 LBS., BLOND, BLUE EYES, VIRILE, IMPOSING. RECENTLY IMMIGRATED FROM GERMANY.

MASTER CHEFS. FIVE-STAR FOOD IN TWO RESTAURANTS. LOUD. ARROGANT. *RIVALS.*

Kellen's appointment with Chef Norbert ran over by five minutes and cut into her time with Chef Reinhart. Chef Reinhart was irritated, throwing a fit that included pacing and arm flailing. With knives.

Chef Gabriella arrived holding a restaurant-sized cake pan. She paused and glared at Chef Reinhart.

He subsided and backed up, muttering what sounded like prayers.

CHEF GABRIELLA:
FEMALE, PORTUGUESE, APPROX. 35, 4'11", 125 LBS. MASTER CHEF IN RESORT'S LARGEST, MOST CASUAL RESTAURANT. PLACID UNTIL PROVOKED. NORBERT/REINHART COWER.

The conference between Gabriella and Kellen took five minutes. Kellen approved the layering of pecan cookies, vanilla cream cheese pudding, chocolate cream cheese pudding and whipped cream covered with chocolate shavings. Gabriella slapped Chef Norbert's hand when he reached in to steal a bite, and sent an ample portion with Kellen when she moved on to her next meeting with the roofing contractor.

Obstructive jerk.

Within five minutes, Kellen lost her temper with him, enough so he made calls and discovered he *could* get the tile to match the resort.

Note to self—Shout at the roofing contractor.

At noon, she went into the spa. The waiting room was immaculate, a cradle of soothing music, low lighting, comfortable chairs, a luxurious oriental rug, the scent of bergamot wafting from reed diffusers and a trickling copper wall fountain. Old leather books, never read, lined the bookshelves, and their gold decorations provided ambience and distinction. At this hour and in this season, the room was empty, and as always, the atmosphere made Kellen want to sit down and meditate.

Instead, she was scheduled to exercise with Mara Philippi. With the enthusiasm of a game show host, Mara asked, "Are you ready to work out?"

MARA PHILIPPI:
FEMALE, WHITE, AGE LISTED AS 29(?), TANNED, 5'6", 130 LBS. AGGRESSIVELY PHYSICALLY FIT. EAST COAST STREAKED-BLONDE PREPPIE, DORIAN GRAY PERFECTION OF SKIN TONE, LASHES, LIPS. EMPLOYED 8 YRS., SPA MANAGER. UNCLEAR ON DIFFERENCE BETWEEN WAR ZONE AND GYMNASIUM. DO NOT LIKE. **NO GOOD REASON.**

"Because I have the most exciting news for you." Mara's blue eyes glowed like jewels in her smooth skin. Even now, even in winter, she wore tight workout capris and her black sleeveless T-shirt displayed her toned arms, clung to her taut abs and showed off the jut of her perfect boobs. Her only bow to winter was her mottled black-and-brown fashion hoodie, tied around her waist.

"Wow. Exciting news?" Kellen suspected she wouldn't agree.

Like her own cheerleader, Mara jumped and clapped her hands. "I've applied to compete in the International Ninja Challenge!"

"Yay?"

"You were a soldier. Do you think we can get in shape together?"

Several answers came to mind—

You're not in shape?

I'm not in shape?

What is the International Ninja Challenge? Are you comparing some reality show to getting shot at while running up a mountain in Afghanistan?

And—

When you get that aggressive gleam in your eyes, you're scary.

"Sure," Kellen said. "Sounds like fun."

"Great. I'll start right now." Mara bounded toward the stairs that led to the gym. "Get changed!"

Kickboxing. Kicks. Punches. Sweeps. Before the hour was over, sweat soaked Kellen's hair, dripped into her eyes, stained her workout clothes. She stood before the full wall-length mirror, hands on her knees, gasping in agony.

"You always give me such a good workout!" Mara dabbed at her glowing skin with a towel.

"You, too," Kellen wheezed. She couldn't help working as hard as she could. Mara's boundless enthusiasm shouldn't be irritating...but it was. Everything about Mara—her toned figure, her fitness, her excellent management of the spa and gym—brought out Kellen's competitive spirit, and every time Mara opened her mouth, Kellen wanted to contradict her, argue with her, prove her wrong.

And why? It didn't make sense. When Kellen arrived, Mara had studied her injury, given her a physical therapy regime to ease the pain in Kellen's wounded shoulder. Mara had advised her stylist on a short, easy-to-care-for cut for Kellen's dyed brown hair, and her cosmetician on the right program for Kellen's Native American skin tone, sculpted bone structure and blue eyes. Mara was perky, cheerful, and she never overtly challenged Kellen. Yet Kellen felt hostility in every smile, in every upbeat word.

Probably it was her own hostility reflecting back at her.

5

Washed and dressed once again in a calf-length black dress with the resort's signature blue scarf, Kellen combed her wet hair off her forehead and hurried through the gym.

Mara stopped lifting weights long enough to look Kellen over. "Wow. You still look tense!" Grasping Kellen's hand, she pulled her to the mirror and they stood shoulder to shoulder. "Stop worrying. Look at us! You're so much like me, I know you can do anything you set your mind to!"

Standing together, the two were almost identical in height and weight, but as far as Kellen was concerned, there the similarities ended. She was the opposite of bubbly. Her stint in the Army had finished off whatever vanity remained after Gregory and her time on the streets. She worked out to be healthy, to be strong, and could not comprehend the concept of training to win a television show competition. Most of all, she suspected one of them, either Mara or Kellen, was out of step with the world.

She knew it was her.

"What *really* brought you here?" Mara asked.

What did that mean? "The job."

"No boyfriend?"

"No."

"Girlfriend?"

"No."

"Got a bad relationship in your past?"

Kellen faced Mara and moved close enough to make her point. "Not that I discuss."

Yet Mara wasn't done. "You came here to feel safe."

Kellen flinched.

"It's okay." Mara tossed her hair and headed back to the weight rack. "All of us out here are running away from something."

What should Kellen do? Tell Mara to mind her own business? Deny she was running away from something? Ask what Mara was running away from?

No. She hadn't come to Yearning Sands to exchange confidences. That left her with no good choices, and one more reason to dislike Mara Philippi.

Like a waif from below, Xander appeared.

ALEXANDER RISCHARD:
MALE, WHITE, 41 (LOOKS 30), THIN, SHAVED HEAD, PALE BLUE EYES, BROAD PALMS, LONG FINGERS, BIG KNUCKLES. YOGA, MEDITATION, MASSAGE. REIKI SPECIALIST. VEGETARIAN, ALL ORGANIC.

Yet—Kellen liked him.

Like an East Indian guru, he put his palms together and bowed. "I regret to report the universe has presented us with a challenge." He picked up a pair of binoculars from the windowsill and handed them to Kellen.

Through the veil of rain, in the distance, two coyotes fought over a bone while vultures dived and scolded. Kellen texted Temo. "Someone in maintenance will go out and pick up the skeleton."

Mara took the binoculars and looked, too. "Do you know how upset guests get when they see scavengers cleaning up a dead deer or a raccoon or whatever?"

"Some people are not meant to appreciate the fullness of an outdoor life." Xander spread his fingers above Kellen's shoulder and let them hover there. "You're in pain. I have time on my schedule for a massage."

"Thank you, Xander, but I've got another couple of appointments, then I need to see where we are on orders and bookings."

"You will have time later for a run, won't you?" Mara asked. "Not far—we'll race each other back to our cottages."

"You'll win," Kellen said. "My cottage is the last one."

Mara smiled brightly. "I *know*!"

Xander's hands settled over Kellen's SC joint and massaged. "Something long denied is fighting to erupt from your spiritual center and to ignore it would have dire results on not only your well-being, but the well-being of the resort, which you now lead."

Kellen questioned Mara with wide eyes and a pursed mouth.

"Better go for a quick massage," Mara said. "Last time he said something like that, Destiny spilled a bottle of lavender massage oil on the rug and we had to have it cleaned twice before it stopped exuding inappropriate amounts of serenity into the air."

Kellen stared at them both. "Inappropriate amounts of serenity?"

"The scent of lavender creates a tranquility of the spirit," Xander explained.

Kellen realized again why she needed to succeed as the resort's assistant manager. Mara might be a competent spa manager, but she knew nothing of real life and real combat. And a woman like Kellen, who didn't realize lavender could exude inappropriate amounts of serenity, needed to stay on the practical side of the business.

Kellen followed Xander, eased herself onto his massage chair and put her face into the cradle. "I've got fifteen minutes. No more."

"Time has no meaning in the boundless eternity of the universe."

By which she guessed he meant she should set an alarm. So she did.

He applied a heating wrapping on her neck and worked his fingers into the rigid muscles of her shoulder. In that calm, soothing tone, he said, "Dismiss those thoughts that disturb you, and breathe with me."

Thoughts that disturbed her… *All of us out here are running away from something.*

What did Mara mean by that? It was not like she knew Kellen had been running for the past seven years, from a past corroded by guilt and a year that had vanished from her mind.

"Breathe with me," he said again. "In… Out… In…"

She concentrated on the slow breaths, blanking her mind as she relaxed…and dreamed.

Through the darkness, she could hear him calling her. "Ceecee. Ceecee. Where are you? Come back to me…"

She loved his voice. Unlike Gregory's, this voice was deep and warm, loving and despairing.

"Ceecee, I love you. Come back."

Who was he? Memory came in flashes, like a night sky split by lightning. Deep brown eyes surrounded by long dark lashes. Tall, over six foot. Fast, smooth, physical, accomplished.

"Ceecee…" His voice grew fainter, like a spirit's fading into the gray lands.

She strained to open her eyes, but the darkness would not yield. The lightning was moving away, over the horizon.

She was alone in the night. Alone…

Kellen woke and sat straight up on the massage chair.

Her pocket was vibrating, her alarm going off.

She pulled out her phone and silenced it, then placed a hand over her racing heart. The dream. The man. The dark. Again.

On a stool across the room, Xander sat balanced in the lotus position.

"Did I say anything?" she demanded.

"You were silent, but your soul walked in a far, dark place where combat rages and death holds sway." His large, sad eyes watched her as if he could see her pain. "You've returned from war to find your own battlefield still waits."

"The war is over. Only the shadows remain." Enough of that. If she hung around Xander much longer, she would start talking like a guru, too.

"Every hour, do one thing. Take a moment to stop and breathe." He lifted a hand and breathed in, lowered his hand and breathed out.

"I *do* know how to inhale and exhale," she snapped.

He looked a reproof.

Right. He didn't deserve to have her snap at him. "I'll do it. Thank you, I feel better. You are a magician." She checked her texts.

Nothing back from Temo about the animal carcass. If she didn't hear back soon, she'd give him a call.

She strode to the door, opened it and halted, her head cocked toward the commotion down the hall.

"She's one of my best masseuses. She's got appointments!" Mara shouted.

Mr. Gilfilen's deep, distinctive voice sounded as if it was coming from the depths of a crypt. "She has stepped over the line."

Beneath the sound of conversation, Kellen could hear a woman crying, and she headed out to intercept what sounded like a rip-roaring fight.

In the spa waiting room, Mara and Mr. Gilfilen had faced off, Mara furious, Mr. Gilfilen austere.

Mr. Gilfilen inclined his head. "Miss Adams, we have a security situation." And just that quickly, her mind produced his information.

VINCENT GILFILEN:
GENDER UNDEFINED, POSSIBLY MALE, OF AFRICAN DESCENT, FRENCH ACCENT, 38, 6'1", 145 LBS., FIT. FORMAL CLOTHING, ALWAYS BLACK. ECCENTRIC FACIAL HAIR CHOICES. MILITARY/SECURITY BACKGROUND, SPECIFICS UNKNOWN. OBSESSIVELY PRIVATE. POSSIBLY A VAMPIRE?

Today he wore a black turtleneck, slacks and loafers. His thin face started at the top with carefully styled curls and ended with a curling goatee that emphasized his long chin. His brows looked as if they'd been shaved and drawn back on to point at an angle toward his hairline. His deep voice rolled out like the clap of doom. "Miss Longacre left the outside door to the spa unlocked to allow a friend access."

"Her boyfriend," Mara said. "He's from town. He's not much. Of a threat, I mean." The nearby town of Cape Charade was nothing more than a bump in the two-lane highway: eight hundred people, a ten-room motel built in the 1950s and one grocery store that sold food, swim gear and souvenir sweatshirts. But it did supply the resort with about half of their staff. Destiny Longacre was from Cape Charade; that alone guaranteed she would continue working at the resort until she'd saved enough for college.

Mr. Gilfilen offered not a shred of empathy. "*Accidentally* leaving the door unlocked is a violation of resort policy and warrants a reprimand. *Deliberately* leaving it unlocked could result in the loss of supplies and equipment and, most important, is a danger to the guests and the staff. Miss Longacre must go."

"I can't replace her right now," Mara said.

"You'll have to work around that," Mr. Gilfilen answered.

Mara got on her toes to get into his face. "This is stupid. Did Destiny or her boyfriend steal anything? Did they threaten anybody?"

"I believe their intention was to have intercourse in the comfort of the spa." Mr. Gilfilen appeared to feel bilious. "Regardless of her relatively innocuous intentions, she caused a security breach and she must. Be. Fired."

Mara looked at Kellen in appeal.

Kellen shook her head. When it came to security, Mr. Gilfilen was clear in his rules, and on the rare occasion an employee challenged those rules, there was no appeal. Not even Annie or Leo went up against Mr. Gilfilen.

"All right. But she's a nice kid. Losing her will put a kink in my schedule, and it's going to devastate her. Plus I have to fire her!" Mara flounced away.

Kellen felt sorry for Mara and Destiny...

...Until Mr. Gilfilen said, "Miss Adams, I have an announcement. I am leaving on vacation."

"What?"

"There's no need to shout."

She modulated her voice. "What?"

"I'm leaving on vacation," he repeated.

"When?"

"Now."

His audacity took her breath away. "You are kidding."

"I never kid."

"Does Annie know about this?"

"Yes. She did object on your behalf, but Leo and I agreed now was the time for me to take this action."

Men. Men who made decisions without thought to preparation or convenience or plain, simple courtesy. "Take this action?"

"If you were not capable, the Di Lucas wouldn't have left you in charge."

"Damned with faint praise! Who have you lined up to replace you?"

"You will replace me."

Kellen was speechless. Then her brain snapped into gear. "Me? I'm to run the resort and be head of security? These are two separate jobs. Two people fill those two separate jobs. One person cannot fill those two separate jobs. Certainly not one person who started one of those jobs today!"

"The resort is almost empty of guests, and, Miss Adams, I wouldn't leave if I hadn't assessed you as being competent."

"Competent!" Kellen almost danced with rage. "I demand you appoint one of your people to take over!"

"That's not possible. When it comes to staff, I suffer exactly the same problems as Miss Philippi and everyone else at the resort. I cannot hire enough competent, experienced security personnel. None of my subordinates are capable of overseeing the entire operation. You are."

"You're not being rational."

"Miss Adams." He lowered his voice. "I'm trying to tell you I don't trust everyone on my own staff. It is very possible my absence will provide some insight into who is causing problems with the resort's security."

"Oh." Her indignation faded…just a little. "You're setting a trap."

"Indeed."

"Who do you expect to catch? What do you believe they're doing? Are we talking simple theft, or am I facing potential violence?"

"I'm handling the matter and no one will be in danger."

Her indignation rekindled. "Who's going to apprehend these untrustworthy members of the staff? You're not going to be here!"

He acted as if she hadn't spoken. "Follow me. I'll acquaint you with the inner workings of security procedures and the resort video room."

6

After her security tour, Kellen should have grabbed lunch. Instead, aggravated and with a nagging worry about those bones moldering out on the plain, she bundled up and fought through the worsening wind and rain to the maintenance buildings to spend a few minutes with her friends. Or, as she called them, the real people.

The resort had a three-bay garage complete with hydraulic lifts, air compressors, welders, tire storage and enough steel tool cabinets to work on jeeps, ATVs, vans and the old-fashioned tour buses used to convey guests and staff. Maintenance for everything else—heating, air-conditioning, plumbing, electrical—was next door in an equally spacious and well-supplied area. A long table, chairs, benches, stools, vending machines and two small, old refrigerators separated the two trades. All was housed in a structure that mimicked the castle's architecture and included a loft that overhung the back of the shop with storage for vehicle and operational manuals, light bulbs, Christmas decorations and odd tools they occasionally needed but that were too fragile to leave on the main floor.

Adrian Wright stood at a workbench filling grease guns. He glanced up and gave Kellen a half-assed salute. "Hey, Captain, want to get dirty with me?"

"Hmm." Kellen pretended to think. "No."

ADRIAN WRIGHT:
MALE, WHITE, 23, 5'9", BROWN HAIR, BLUE EYES, BURN-AND-PEEL SKIN. BORN NEW ORLEANS: PICKPOCKET + STREET GANG. ARMY VETERAN, HONORABLE DISCHARGE. GOOD WITH WEAPONS, ENGINES. MOUTHY, BRASH, EDGY. EMPLOYED 49 DAYS. FRIEND. POSSIBLE TROUBLE?

He lifted his greasy hands and wiggled them. "Admit it. You want me. You love me."

"I do love you," Kellen said. "Like a disgusting, loud, gross younger brother who deserves to have his head stuck in a toilet and flushed."

"Sweet talker."

"Where's Birdie?"

"She's getting dressed." Adrian went back to work. "Someone has to go to the landing strip to pick up guests."

Kellen called up the schedule in her mind. "Right." She checked the housekeeping schedule. "Rooms will be ready. Where's Mitch?"

"He's not back from taking Leo and Annie to the airstrip."

"Really," she said flatly. She checked her device to see when their plane had taken off.

Mitch should have returned an hour ago.

Temo sat at the cluttered table. His prosthetic leg leaned against his chair. He was massaging his thigh and talking into his cell phone in rapid Spanish, none of which sounded like a compliment.

TEMO IGLASIAS:
MALE, HISPANIC AMERICAN—SECOND GENERATION, 25, 5'7", 150 LBS., BLACK HAIR, BROWN EYES, FIT. SPANISH SPEAKER. ARMY VETERAN, HONORABLE DISCHARGE. PROSTHETIC LEG. BORN EAST LA. FATHER DEAD, DRUG-ADDICTED MOTHER, BROTHER TO YOUNGER SISTER, REGINA. EMPLOYED 62 DAYS. MECHANIC, HANDYMAN, LEADER. FRIEND.

She had tempted Temo, Birdie and Mitch to the resort with the offer of a job, and they had all taken her up on her offer.

Adrian had come by a different route. One day, he'd appeared, told her he'd hit the skids, offered his services doing anything. She knew him pretty well; she'd served with him for most of her deployment in Afghanistan. He never knew when to shut up and lately, when she caught him glancing over his shoulder or jumping at an unexpected noise, she suspected his big mouth had finally caught up with him.

Temo got quiet; he sat listening to whoever spoke at the other end. He met Kellen's gaze and rolled his eyes, then launched into another tirade in Spanish that ended with him slamming the phone on the table, picking it up, hanging up and slamming the phone down again.

"Those phones don't grow on trees, you know," she said mildly.

"It's not broken." He flung it on the floor.

She picked it up, examined it. The tough case had saved it. "This is why we call you... *Lucky.*" She tapped his artificial leg.

"Call me by my real name... Cuauhtemo."

She laughed. "Like I could."

In Afghanistan, when Kellen met Temo, he had been belligerent; he hated her for being white, in charge, an officer and a woman, and he let her know it.

She hated him for being smart, mean and tough.

Then on a dark mountain road, he spotted a trap.

She rerouted the convoy, got them in a defensible position and saved his sorry ass.

They made a great team.

He lost his leg on his next assignment, in Peru, to a car bomb.

When she offered the job in maintenance for the resort, he took it sight unseen. In the first month, he discovered his boss was siphoning materials to a construction firm south of Portland. Temo went from flunky to manager of a thirteen-man crew, fixing whatever needed to be fixed: HVAC, leaky toilets, fire damage caused by a cigarette smoked in a nonsmoking room. In the spring when the guests arrived, that crew would double.

Kellen wasn't surprised at his fast promotion. Temo's near-fatal injuries, his long recovery, his rehabilitation had put fire to his already iron ambition. Before it was over, this guy would own the resort. Which made this display of temper unlike him.

She wiped the phone clean on her skirt, handed it over and asked mildly, "What's up?"

"None of the new room controls for the gas fireplaces are working and those bastards who sold them to us are ignoring us. Smart controls, my ass."

She'd been the one to recommend they try something more than a timer. "Are you going to be able to make them work soon?"

"If I had a manual written by someone whose first language is English!" Temo's Spanish accent was fierce, but he had been educated in American schools and he had no sympathy for foreign firms who used a translation program for their communications.

"Okay," she said in a bright tone. "About the animal carcass..."

Temo stuck his phone into his pocket. "I haven't had a chance to get out there."

"I'd bet none of the guests will venture out in this weather, but now that I've said that, some intrepid soul will go exploring. Can you send one of your guys?"

"*My guys?* The guys I inherited from the *last maintenance man*? The guys who can't *scratch their own balls* without an instruction manual?" Temo's color rose. "Too bad none of them can read a manual, English or Chinese or Spanish or any other language known to man. Maybe Klingon!"

"*All* of them are idiots?"

Temo sighed and subsided. "Two of them are okay. The rest of them have to go, but not until I find someone to replace them."

"Have you checked in town?"

He eyeballed her evilly.

She backed away. "I just asked!"

"I'm looking around the US, trying to find old friends. If you don't mind, I'll go to LA and check on...friends."

The way he said the word *friends* made her think he was trying to tell her something. But while she remembered every chart and schedule she'd ever seen, she couldn't understand the unspoken words of a man who had faced too many challenges. She took his hand. "Go when you need to. Just...come back."

"Sure. I can't stay down there. There's nothing for me there. My mom...and that guy she calls my stepfather."

"What about your sister?"

"Poor kid." He shook his head. "Poor kid." He attached his leg, shoved his arms through the sweatshirt hanging on the back of his chair, got up and stretched. "I'll go rescue that carcass from the scavengers. I could use a ride in the fresh air, plus it's the only way I know to get Smart Home to call, so they can complain I was out of touch." He headed toward the coatrack, wrapped himself in a muddle of scarves, hats and the warmest gloves he could root out. Yep, that was Temo. Add the slightest touch of winter and the guy froze. You could take the boy out of LA, but you couldn't keep him warm.

Birdie walked out of the changing room.

BIRDIE HAYNES:
FEMALE, 24, 5'10", 130 LBS., AMERICAN OF COLOR—HISPANIC, AFRICAN AND FAR EASTERN. BIG RAW HANDS, LONG FINGERS, CONSTANT BAND-AID ON AT LEAST ONE KNUCKLE. BEAUTIFUL SMILE IN A NOT-BEAUTIFUL FACE. ARMY VETERAN, HONORABLE DISCHARGE. RECENT WIDOW. EMPLOYED 70 DAYS. LEAD MECHANIC, GARAGE MANAGER. **BEST FRIEND.**

Birdie wore a starched white button-up shirt, the resort's blue scarf and black slacks, and she held keys in her hand. When she spotted Kellen, she headed right for her. "I'm off to the landing strip to pick up the guests. I've got nobody to ride shotgun. Can you come?"

"I'm not dressed." In the appropriate outfit for welcoming guests, Kellen meant. Then she looked around.

Temo was gone. Mitch had returned and slipped into greasy coveralls. Adrian was dirty, and due to his big mouth, he was never appropriate to greet guests.

Kellen ran through the working roster in her mind; in the whole resort, everyone was either on vacation or trying to cover for everyone else. She was stuck. "Only if I can drive."

"Feeling out of control?" Birdie asked.

"Driving would help." Driving always helped. Feeling the vehicle respond to her command promptly, smoothly, efficiently gave her a measure of peace. "Do you have the hors d'oeuvres?"

"I ordered them. You get them from the kitchen. I'll bring the van around."

"Give me thirty minutes. I'll change and meet you at the kitchen door." She grabbed an ATV and drove fast toward her cottage at the farthest corner of the resort's property. She had to hustle; it had been her idea to serve hors d'oeuvres to newly arrived guests. Invariably, the travelers were tired, hungry and crabby, and a prompt application of salmon cakes, tofu bites with chai tea crema, and prosciutto-wrapped artichokes never failed to put them in good humor. Kellen had implemented a successful strategy: a pain in the rear, but successful.

At her cottage, she jumped into her hospitality costume: like Birdie's, a starched white button-up shirt and blue scarf, black slacks. Then she did as Xander advised; she looked around and took a moment to breathe.

She loved her cottage. Its rustic exterior blended well with the wildness of the coastline, its blue door gave it a shocking pop of color and the interior was pure Pacific Northwest: comfortable furniture, an efficiency kitchen and a bedroom loft that had sloped ceilings, gable seats and a bed so comfortable the resort sold them to enamored guests. The decor was a blend of Asian, Native American and local artists. After a day dealing with suppliers, staff and guests, she relished the coziness and the isolation.

Kellen reached the resort kitchen as Birdie pulled the van under the portico. She nipped into the kitchen. The pizzalike boxes waited for her on the counter; as she picked them up, she realized she'd interrupted a violent scene.

Chef Reinhart was shaking blood off his hand while Chef Norbert roared with laughter. The kitchen staff continued their work as if this madness was an everyday occurrence.

Kellen ducked out, placed the boxes in the van on the floor behind the driver's seat and climbed in behind the wheel. "Chef Reinhart was bleeding, Chef Norbert was laughing and no one seemed to care." Kellen put the van in gear and drove.

"I would never date a chef," Birdie said. Which seemed like an odd thing to say, especially in a voice that ached with loneliness. During four years of deployment, Birdie had never been wounded. Then she came home, got married, and within two months, her husband, a Detroit police officer, was killed in the line of duty, ambushed outside their home. He had died in her arms.

"How's it going?" Kellen asked gently. "Parents talking to you yet?"

"On the phone. My mom and my father-in-law, while my dad and my mother-in-law yell in the background." Birdie's parents and in-laws hadn't wanted the new widow to take a job so far away, but she'd been looking for work when her husband died, job prospects in Detroit hadn't improved and at Yearning Sands she could do what she'd been trained to do without the constant reminders of what she had lost. "I only remember at night."

Kellen wanted to scoff at the idea of an eternal love. But although the welter of bitterness and pain tainted her marital memories, she knew most wives had never lived through hell, and no other woman had watched Gregory murder her cousin in her place…

★★★

The gas explosion sent a blast at Cecilia that lifted her, then slammed her into the ground. She lost consciousness, then came back, panicked. She smelled burning cloth. Burning flesh. Sweet Jesus, smoke drifted past her face.

Someone threw a coat over her head, blinding her, panicking her.

She fought.

Suddenly she was free. Her ears were roaring with some…sound.

A man leaned into her line of vision. He was shouting at her, gesturing toward his own head, then hers. She read his lips. "Lady, your hair was on fire!" She turned her head away from the direction of the house, coughed. Smoke clouded the air. A cab was parked haphazardly at the end of the drive where it met the road.

He was the cabbie. Not Gregory. The cabbie.

She lifted her head, looked toward the house.

Nothing was left but the foundation and burning pieces of wood, charred plaster and singed insulation dancing on the wind.

Off the cliff. Gone.

The roaring in Cecilia's ears diminished. She could hear the cabbie's voice now; she couldn't yet distinguish the words, but he had his jacket in his hands, offering it to her, and he was averting his eyes and peeking at the same time.

She looked down at herself. Her linen slacks and cotton blouse had been shredded by the blast. Her panties and bra still covered her, but barely. Cecilia wrapped his jacket around herself. The arms were too long, and the hem barely reached her thighs.

Kellen was dead. Cecilia felt nothing but shock. Kellen, who had been so alive, so brave… How could she be dead?

And Gregory…was gone? Dead? Blown to bits? Cecilia felt shamed relief. And guilt. So much guilt.

The cabbie was still talking.

She could almost understand him. She stared, watching his lips.

"Are you hurt? You, uh, you were standing so close. You okay?"

She nodded. A lie. She wasn't okay. Her lungs hurt. Her head hurt.

She had blisters on her belly and blisters on her shoulders, and they burned like live coals. It didn't matter. She was alive.

"I was called to pick up a passenger," the cabbie said. "Saw the explosion. Was Mrs. Lykke in the house?"

Cecilia. The cabbie didn't know she was Cecilia.

"I'm sorry, wow, what a tragedy, but the Lykkes always were a scary family with lots of 'accidents.'" He did air quotes. "I should call this in. Right? Call the police?" He looked toward the main house. "Maybe not, though, because his mother and sister are coming to the site."

Mother Sylvia Lykke and sister Erin raced toward the place where the house had been, and even from this distance, even with the ringing in her ears, Cecilia could hear them screaming.

In a panic, she said, "Drive me to the hotel."

"But you want to stick around. You saw everything. Even more than me." The cabbie was agog, thrilled at being on the front line of a breaking story. "The cops will want to talk to you. Get your testimony."

"I want to go to the hotel." Heart pounding in fear, she grabbed his arm, dug her fingers into his skin. "Take me to the hotel."

"Right. You're in shock. Let me help you—" He tried to support her.

She yanked herself away.

"Shock. Right. Don't touch you. I'll call, tell the cops I'm dropping you at the hotel. You can…do whatever you do for shock."

"Lie down. Elevate the feet. Keep warm." She had been a Girl Scout. She knew this stuff.

"Hospital!" The thought seemed to startle and thrill him. "Want me to take you to the hospital?"

"Hotel."

"Right." He hurried toward his vehicle. "I'll get you down there, come back and give my testimony."

Cecilia stumbled away, not from the explosion, but from Gregory's family. The cabbie beat her to the taxi; he opened the back door. She slid in and huddled down on the seat, hiding from Sylvia and Erin, hiding from the events of the past hour.

The cabbie leaped into the driver's seat.

"Go. Go!"

"Okay, lady! Hang on." He started the car, pulled a U-turn and headed down the road.

She looked out the back window.

Sylvia stood immobile, staring at the crater where the house had been.

Erin stared after the taxi with a gaze both intelligent and vengeful.

The driver glanced at Cecilia in the rearview mirror. "Like I said when I dropped you off earlier, you're a lot different from young Mrs. Lykke, poor thing. Word was, her in-laws hated her and her husband was out to beat her to death. I would never mistake the two of you."

He really did think she was Kellen. Should she correct him?

She should correct him.

He kept talking. "I'll drop you off and head back up there, see if I can do anything, but that house, it lifted right off the foundation and blew off the edge of the cliff. I've never seen anything like that. Knocked you ass-over-teakettle, too, bet you flew ten, fifteen feet. You must have cracked your skull a good one."

Her neck ached. Her head hurt. "Yes," she whispered. What would it hurt if he thought she was Kellen? If she could pretend to be Kellen for a little while, leave Greenleaf in a rush, she could get out without—

"Here they come. The cops!" The cabbie pulled over to the side of the road.

Sirens blasting, lights flashing, a fire engine raced past followed by the fire chief and two police cars.

Cecilia flinched. Yes, if she pretended to be Kellen for a few minutes at the hotel, she could escape without talking to the cops, without having to face Sylvia and Erin, who would tell her the explosion was her fault.

The cabbie pulled onto the road again, then back onto the shoulder while the county sheriff raced past. "They're all going up for this one. Prominent family, huge tragedy. Say, are you sure you don't want me to take you to the hospital? You're looking sick."

"Hotel." She felt like she'd been saying that for hours. "Faster."

As he entered Greenleaf, he slowed to a crawl, complained about the twenty-mile-an-hour speed limit, stopped in front of the hotel and opened the door for her. "You look bad, burned all over. Want me to get you in there?"

She shook her head. Which hurt. "Go back up to the Lykke estate and give your report." Her lips felt cracked. The heat, she supposed.

"That'll be eleven dollars..." He seemed to realize she didn't have any money on her. "I'll stop by and collect it later."

"Yes." She moved as fast as she could into the lobby empty of everyone except for two desk clerks talking excitedly. At the sight of her, their heads swiveled and they openly gawked.

Cecilia groped for Kellen's key.

It was gone. Her whole pocket was gone, burned away.

7

Cecilia had to talk to the Greenleaf Hotel desk staff and hope they, like the cabbie, identified her as Kellen. She approached, kept her voice low, avoided eye contact. "Can you tell me my room number? I hit my head and can't remember."

The desk clerk went into a flurry of activity, clicked keys on the computer. "Of course, Miss Adams. I'm sorry about your… That is, I heard that… Mr. and Mrs. Lykke…"

"Yes. Thank you."

"You were there? You saw it?"

She lifted her gaze and stared him in the face. "Yes."

She didn't know what was in her eyes, but he shrank back and offered the key card. "Room 323. Let us know if we can do anything to assist you."

"No." She took it, turned away, turned back. "Yes. Can you tell me where I parked my car?"

"Of course." He clicked more keys. "You're in space eighteen in the parking garage. Below the hotel. Garage level on the elevator." He scanned the screen. "You're valet parked. When you're ready, they'll bring the car around."

Realization hit her. "I need the car keys." Of course she did. In the past couple years, she had had so little real experience with the trivia of life, she had forgotten she needed keys to drive a car. God. What had she become?

The desk clerk took her comment as a command, lifted the phone and called the valet. "Miss Adams wants her keys." He hung up and spoke to her with a combination of avid curiosity and real concern. "He's bringing them now, but you shouldn't be driving in your condition. Let me call a doctor."

"I'll see a doctor as soon as possible." The valet appeared at her side and handed her a key ring. She stared stupidly at it. Five keys. So... car keys, keys to Kellen's apartment, and...she didn't know what else. "Thank you." She limped toward the elevator, pushed the button, and when the doors opened, she entered. She pushed the button, faced front. The doors closed. She collapsed against the railing and clung there until the doors opened on her floor. She pushed herself upright and walked out, studied the signs and moved toward room 323. She stopped at the door. She swiped the card, walked into a narrow, old-fashioned room. She wanted to crumple onto the chair, sleep on the bed, hide...

In the distance, she heard the wail of another siren, spurring her to movement. She staggered to the closet, pulled Kellen's clothes off the hangers, threw them into the open suitcase on the luggage rack. She shrugged out of the cabbie's jacket and stripped.

The blast's heat had branded and blistered her shoulders where her metal bra adjustments rested. And why? She wasn't busty enough to worry about a bra. Gregory had insisted she wear one. For decency, he said. So men wouldn't stare at her. What men? He never allowed her around other men. To hell with him.

She eased her wedding ring off her finger, his grandmother's wedding ring, and stared at the blisters raised by the heated platinum. Even his family wedding ring had burned her. Yes! To hell with Gregory. She flung the ring into the trash can.

Willy-nilly, she chose an outfit from Kellen's wardrobe. She sat on the bed to pull on the jeans. When she stood, they slipped off her skinny hips. She had to notch Kellen's belt on the last hole and it was barely enough to keep the pants up.

More sirens.

Panicked, she ran into the bathroom for the toiletries. She flipped on the light and— No wonder everyone stared and wanted her to go to the hospital. She put her hands to her head. Strands of hair cracked off in her hands. She rubbed her face. Her eyebrows...gone, burned off by the blast. Her skin looked thin, mottled, as if the explosion had slapped her. Her blue eyes...were haunted.

Leaning over the sink, she used Kellen's brush and gingerly brushed what was left of her hair. In Kellen's overnight bag, she found a pair of scissors and cut off the random long strands. Now she looked like a Halloween monster in June. But not so wounded, more like a fashion statement gone bad.

In the bedroom, she tossed the toiletries into the suitcase. She swooped down to get two pairs of shoes off the closet floor—and came face-to-face with the locked room safe. She froze. She had no money. Like the key, the money had disappeared with her pocket. She sank to her knees. She needed what was in that safe. But she had no way in. She couldn't break into a safe...

Wait. Maybe she didn't have to break in. Aunt Cora Rae and Uncle Earle had always used the same password for everything—ECKC. Earle, Cora, Kellen, Cecilia. 3, 2, 5, 3. The family knew the code. Maybe Kellen had used the code.

With shaking fingers, Cecilia pressed 3, 2, 5, 3.

Nothing happened.

She dropped her head into her hands. What other code would Kellen use? Maybe her girlfriend's name...but she didn't know it. If Cecilia and Kellen had been able to drive away from Greenleaf, roll down the windows, let the wind blow their hair...then she would have known. She would have rejoiced in their relationship. Instead, Cecilia was grief-stricken, and Kellen's girlfriend remained a mystery.

Desperate, Cecilia punched in the same code. 3, 2, 5...2.

The safe sang a little song and the door opened.

She'd done it wrong the first time.

Gregory's voice sang in her head. You're incompetent. You're not fit to be out on your own.

"Shut up." Inside, she found Kellen's credit card, five neatly folded

twenties, a black velvet box with a blue enamel wedding band inside... Cecilia stared at that band. Kellen had wanted to marry her girlfriend, and...the young woman Kellen loved would suffer a loss she would never comprehend. With a snap, Cecilia shut the box and placed it in a side pocket of the suitcase.

At the bottom of the safe, she found Kellen's computer. She smoothed her hand across the black matte finish. She hadn't been allowed to touch a computer for so long, to communicate, to discover, to learn. A tear dropped onto the lid. She wiped it off. She was glad to be alive, glad that Gregory was dead. That didn't mean that she was glad Kellen was dead, but...she was grateful. Kellen had sacrificed her life to give Cecilia her life back.

Cecilia placed the computer on the bed. She emptied the dresser drawers into the suitcase. The underwear and bras would never fit; she and Kellen had looked alike, but they had never worn the same size. Not the point. Somehow, it was important not to leave a trace of Kellen in this room, in this town.

The suitcase bulged; Cecilia sat on it to close the zipper. She slid the computer into the side pocket, did a last, rushed search of the room and dragged the wheeled suitcase down the corridor to the elevators. In the elevator, she pushed the button for P1 three times. When the doors opened, she entered a concrete cavern filled with cars, vans and freedom.

Kellen's car surprised her. Kellen had always liked fast cars; a Mini sat in the spot. Cecilia hadn't driven for two years, yet she remembered how to unlock the door, stow a suitcase, start the car. Everything in her screamed, Hurry! Hurry! *But she needed out of this town without incident, so she would be cool...*

In the rearview mirror, she saw someone walk out of the hotel elevator. Panic clutched at her. She backed out too fast, squealed the tires, took too long to figure out where Drive was located, found it, put the car in gear and ripped out of the garage without looking. She drove out of town and onto the highway, heading south. She didn't know where she was going. But she knew where she'd been, and she swore she would never return to Greenleaf.

★★★

The van's steering wheel jerked in Kellen's hands.

With far too much acuity, Birdie said, "Whatever it is, it's not worth all that."

Kellen was here, now driving through Washington. But… "Sometimes it is."

The woman who had been Cecilia had kept her promise to herself. Greenleaf was nothing but a nightmare she visited when sleep came hard and darkness held reign.

Birdie sighed, a soft breath of sadness. "Yes. Sometimes it is."

8

At the airstrip, Kellen parked the van and she and Birdie got out their ponchos—every Yearning Sands vehicle was always equipped with dry ponchos—and donned them. They turned on the runway lights and prepped to receive the plane, then climbed back into the van to wait. "It's good to be busy," Kellen said. "When the memories hover like bat wings."

"This is a different kind of busy than the holidays." Birdie handed her the roster. "We've got newlyweds from Wenatchee. Six ladies from Alaska. A single guy from Virginia."

Kellen knew. In her brain, she had already started an entry for each guest, and as she met them, she would finish filling them out. She said, "The single guy. Nils Brooks. I took his reservation. He asked for an isolated cottage with a view of the ocean and the mountains. He wants to be alone to write his first book." She looked sideways at Birdie. Nils Brooks was not the first author to arrive and demand privacy to write.

Sometimes they even did it.

"So he's going to want someone to haul room service out to him through rain and snow and wind?" Trust Birdie to see the practical side of things.

"Figure on an ATV parked at the kitchen door all the time." Kellen's phone rang. She answered.

Sheri Jean said, "I've got this afternoon's three receptionists from town who slid off the road into a ditch. One of them is hurt, the other two tried to push the car out and are covered in mud. I can transfer one of my people to the front, but the concierge has a dentist appointment and Mara says she can't help me with coverage."

Someone beeped in. Kellen looked. No kidding. It was Mara.

Kellen ran the employee schedule in her mind, hooked the two of them into a conference, smoothed their ruffled feathers, presented them with a solution that both could live with and got off the phone.

Birdie gave Kellen the side-eye. "Have you always been able to do that?"

"Do what?"

"Know the location, schedule and qualifications of every employee and juggle them around until they fill the needed space. You don't use a computer. It's in your brain."

"It's a gift." With her fingers, Kellen circled the round scar on her forehead.

"That thing looks like you were shot."

Kellen took her hand away. "It's a birthmark."

"Sure. What dumbass would ever believe that?"

"The doctor who did my Army physical."

Birdie did such a double take Kellen was glad they were parked. "You convinced a doctor that *that* is a birthmark?"

"I told him that's what it was. He convinced himself. He couldn't believe that anyone could survive a gunshot to the skull, much less be walking and talking. He couldn't find any problems like seizures or schizophrenia or, you know, outbursts of maniacal laughter." Kellen remembered the terror she'd felt during the military doctor's staccato interrogation. "Most important, he couldn't find an exit wound."

"Whoa. There's no exit wound? *Is* it a birthmark?"

"I guess." It wasn't. But when a person couldn't recall a whole year of her life, that threw a lot of stuff into doubt: memories, skills, maybe even sanity.

"You don't know?"

"If you'd been shot in the head, what would you know?"

Birdie nodded thoughtfully. "Good point. Speculation is that your lover shot you."

"I wouldn't think so." Pause. "Dunno." Pause. "There's speculation?"

"You know how the boys and girls are. Gossip is their life's blood."

"The boys and girls?"

"The boys and girls at the resort who spend too much time making beds. The staff who stand around waiting for guests to arrive and have nothing to entertain them until—oh God!—everyone arrives at once, all the crises need to be dealt with now and no one has time to catch their breath. Same shit as in the Army, only without all that messy death."

They both nodded. Birdie might be maligning "the boys and girls," but Birdie and Kellen had both been there, in the military, doing the most boring grunt work day after day until the moment the mortars started raining down, the enemy advanced and suddenly there weren't enough seconds in a minute. Resort work was usually less dramatic, but the atmosphere was comparable.

Birdie grinned at her. "Want me to make up a big lie? Entertain them?"

"Ick." The idea of speculation gave Kellen the creeps.

"Your husband caught you with your wealthy lover, shot you both and turned the gun on himself. They both died, but you lived, and in your despair, you joined the military."

Too close for comfort. "The wealthy lover and the husband? That's so done."

"You're right. I could make it juicier." Before Kellen could tell her no, Birdie drew a quavering breath. "I want people to talk to me again, to meet my eyes and forget my husband died in my arms."

"I swear I didn't tell them."

"You didn't have to. It was in the news, and inevitable someone would… Anyway, they feel so bad for me all the time they make me remember Daryl even more."

Damn it. Kellen didn't want the staff gossiping about her, but if they were going to do it anyway, why not allow Birdie to use her? It couldn't hurt. Not really. "Well, I always say, if you're going to tell a lie, tell a big one."

Birdie grinned, a bright smile that lit her long, thin face and made her beautiful. "Let me work on it. I'll get all those folks hopping!" She pointed. "The plane just dropped out of the clouds. We'll be on duty soon."

The plane came in fast, hit the runway and skidded on the wet asphalt.

Kellen closed her eyes.

In a patient, amused tone, Birdie said, "You're really afraid of flying, aren't you?" Kellen's crew were eternally entertained by her horror of leaving the ground.

"I'm not afraid of flying. I'm afraid of hitting the ground too hard and exploding into flames." Kellen sneaked a peek as the pilot straightened out the plane. "Also, it makes me want to throw up."

"You can take Dramamine."

"How's that going to help with the impact and the flames?"

The plane came to a halt. The pilot opened the door, lowered the steps and secured the plane while Kellen parked the van as close as possible.

Birdie gathered rain ponchos. Kellen got the first box of hors d'oeuvres, and together they hurried up the stairs. Inside, they found the passengers gathering their belongings.

Birdie did the honors. "Welcome to Yearning Sands Resort. I'm Birdie and this is Kellen."

Kellen smiled and waved, scanned the faces and completed her roster.

JUSTIN AND JULIA FLORENCE:
NEWLYWEDS. YOUNG. REALLY YOUNG. HIGH SCHOOL?

SHIVERING SHERLOCKS:
SIX FEMALES FROM ALASKA. DEBBIE, CANDY, RITA, NANCY, TAMMY AND PATTY, LATE 60S–EARLY 70S. ANNUALLY VISIT YEARNING SANDS FOR MYSTERY WEEKEND.

NILS BROOKS:
MALE, 30S, 6', 180 LBS. DARK-RIMMED GLASSES. CUTE. NERDY.

Kellen didn't recognize anybody and nobody appeared to recognize her. She relaxed a previously unnoticed tension in her shoulders. She'd been thinking too much about Greenleaf, making herself jumpy. Because Xander had told her to, she breathed, and because she was in the hospitality business, she smiled.

Birdie continued, "We'll be transporting you to the resort. We've parked the van at the end of the stairs. As you can imagine, in this weather, our goal is to keep you as dry as possible."

Some chuckles.

"It's too windy for umbrellas, but if you need a poncho, I have them. One size fits all!" Birdie raised the yellow plastic over her head. "But first, Kellen has some hors d'oeuvres to sustain you until you get to the resort. Help yourselves to one on the way out the door, and don't worry—we have more in the van."

The promise of treats got the group moving in a hurry. Everyone took one, descended the steps, gasped at the lash of the wind and rain and headed for the van.

Out of the corner of her mouth, Birdie asked, "Are those two old enough to be married?"

Kellen knew exactly what she meant.

Justin and Julia held hands and smiled at each other. When the ladies from Alaska asked about their love story, the two of them gushed that they'd met as freshmen at Wenatchee Valley College, dated until they both graduated, and gotten married in January because it was the cheapest time of the year.

The pilot unloaded the luggage onto a cart and pushed it toward the back of the van; when Birdie started to lift the suitcases, Justin leaped forward and took over. Nice kid. Julia waited patiently, then the newlyweds crawled into the back of the van and snuggled and kissed.

"The Shivering Sherlocks ladies are a hoot," Kellen said to Birdie.

They were. Tammy White seemed to be in charge; she herded them toward the seats, consulted her clipboard and told them their room numbers and who their roommates would be. When she was done, the other ladies saluted, laughed and teased her, then talked over each other in rapidly increasing volume. Debbie had no-nonsense iron gray hair, Candy had dyed hers a soft blond, but they were obviously twins. The ladies helped themselves to the hors d'oeuvres and pried into Kellen's and Birdie's backgrounds.

Nils Brooks came down the steps late, holding his computer case to his chest like a child he needed to protect. He ducked to get into the van, smacked his head, backed away and took off his rain-smeared glasses. He slipped them into his pocket.

Kellen caught a glimpse of his eyes. Brown, with thick black lashes.

Kellen took a long step back. She knew him. *Didn't she?*

"He's an *author*," Mrs. White told Birdie and Kellen, as if that explained everything.

Kellen watched from behind as he climbed into the seat in the back corner and scrunched away from the newlyweds. Those eyes… She remembered those eyes. But his face… No. She didn't remember him at all.

"He can write in my book anytime," Birdie quietly told Kellen.

Startled, Kellen raised her brows at Birdie.

"I'm a widow," Birdie said. "There's nothing wrong with my vision."

Kellen could hardly argue with that. He was nice to look at. And those eyes… "He's not what I expected. On the phone, he sounded impatient. The way he questioned me about the area—he thought he was the shitz. *That* man has a dimple."

"More than one, I'd imagine."

"I'm talking about the one in his chin." With everybody seated, Kellen got into the driver's seat.

Birdie lowered the jump seat, faced the guests and picked up the second box of hors d'oeuvres.

"Hey, folks!" The pilot stuck his head in the van, startling everyone. "It's getting dark. The weather's closing in. I've got ice on the wings and I'm not going to chance taking my plane out. Mind if I stay at the resort until it clears?"

CHAD GRIFFIN:
MALE, 40S, PILOT, ACCOMPLISHED WOMANIZER (IN HIS OWN MIND). EATS TOO MUCH, DRINKS TOO MUCH, DRAMATIZES HIS (UNLIKELY) MILITARY BACKGROUND. SHIFTLESS, LAZY, IRRITATING TO RESORT STAFF, BARNACLE-LIKE (DIFFICULT TO REMOVE).

Still, Kellen had no choice, so she said, "Of course, Chad, come on in."

He flung in his carry-on, slid into the passenger's seat and turned to face the group behind him. "You're not rid of me yet."

The women laughed and assured him they didn't mind.

As they made the trip to the resort, Birdie gave them a brief history of the area, the Di Luca family's vision for this place where the land met the sea and sky and what they could expect in the way of activities. All the while she passed more hors d'oeuvres.

The newlyweds fell on them with enthusiasm: they were teenagers, this was free food—and they were going to need the energy.

The drive took twenty minutes, and as Kellen turned onto the sweeping driveway toward the portico, she saw something white near the drive under a row of rhododendrons. She knew what it was; one of the coyotes must have dragged a bone away from the carcass out on the grasses to gnaw on in peace.

Kellen interrupted Birdie, and with a broad gesture, she pointed toward the resort. "The main hotel building was built in 1957 and inspired by the royal palace of the Spanish kings of Navarre Olite. The resort was enlarged in 1970 and again in 1999. While you're here, take the time to study the antiques the Di Luca family has collected." She drove under the portico, turned and smiled at the guests. "Here we are! Your luggage has been tagged and will be in your rooms when you get there. Go in, check in and enjoy a complimentary beverage."

Russell opened the van door and helped the ladies out. Chad Griffin grabbed his bag and hurried in. Birdie herded the guests into the lobby.

Kellen waited until they were inside and standing in line at the desk, then she pulled on her rain gear, grabbed a handful of linen napkins out of the van and sprinted down the wet driveway and into the grass. She started to reach for it, then halted, her hand inches from the broad bowl of the well-gnawed bone. It wasn't a shank or a rib, but a hip socket or...or something similar. The femur remained in the socket and that, too, had been gnawed on.

Something about this wasn't right. More than not right. Terribly, horribly wrong. This looked like...

A man's voice spoke behind her. "That's a female human pelvic bone."

She jumped hard and spun around.

Nils Brooks stepped back, hands up.

Right. He had startled her, but she'd overreacted. Feeling foolish, she snapped, "How would you know?"

"Writer. Suspense. I study this stuff. Also, I was in the military. I saw some bodies while I was on active duty."

Rain fell. Wind blew. He kept his glasses in his pocket and those eyes—brown with dark lashes—made her nervous. Made her wipe her damp palms on the thighs of her pants. "What branch?"

"Marines."

No wonder she didn't like him.

"Why are you out here?" she asked.

"I spotted the bone when we drove in, saw you run for it, thought I'd see why it had your attention."

Great. He was observant *and* irritating. "This held my attention because guests are squeamish." Covering her hand with a napkin, she picked up the bones.

The femur wiggled around, grinding in the socket.

"Unless you have gorillas around here, there is nothing other than a human woman that has that distinctive shape." He bent to look more closely.

She covered the bones with another napkin. "I'll show this to the Cape Charade policeman."

Nils Brooks stuck his hands into his pockets. "Let me know what he says." Turning away, he wandered back toward the portico and the lobby, and as he did, he called back, "But I'm right."

Too bad that he probably *was* right.

She sprinted across the soggy lawn toward the hotel wing where the remodelers were working, and as she ran, she called Temo. "Did you get that carcass picked up yet?"

"Not. Yet." She could hear the motor of his ATV, the wind blowing past the phone and his incredible frustration. "First I had to explain to two of the local idiots that, no, I'm not paying them to play games on their iPads. Then Smart Home called. They are neither."

"Smart, nor home? I am sorry, Temo. Let me know what you find as soon as you find the, um, skeleton." She hung up on him, then called Sheri Jean Hagerty. "I have an emergency. Can I postpone for an hour?"

"You had an emergency yesterday."

"Did you hear about the carcass found on the grounds this morning?"

"What about it?"

"One of the coyotes dragged off a chunk and a guest saw it." Which was true. Nils Brooks had seen it.

No one understood the megrims of some guests as well as the guest experience manager. "Let me know as soon as you're free."

"Will do." Kellen ducked under the tape warning guests not to enter, opened the door and walked toward the still-unfinished concierge lounge. Sheets of plastic hung over the door; she pushed them aside and entered a hell of leaning ladders, a roaring belt sander and swirling wood dust.

Lloyd Magnuson stood alone in the middle of the room, wearing ear protection and a filtering mask, and frowning at the cornice board he was smoothing.

Kellen waited until he paused, then shouted, "Lloyd!"

LLOYD MAGNUSON:
MALE, 5'7", 130 LBS., BALDING IN FRONT, DREADLOCKS IN BACK, AGE 46, LOOKS 60. CAPE CHARADE POLICEMAN, DUTIES INCLUDE DEALING WITH: SPEEDING TICKETS, VEHICLE COLLISIONS, UNRULY TOURISTS. MAIN INCOME FROM CARPENTRY WORK + CREATING OBJETS D'ART FROM DRIFTWOOD, SHELLS, FISHING NETS, FLOATS. SELLS AT CAPE CHARADE GROCERS.

He looked up, startled, dropped his ear protection around his neck, wiped his sleeve over his safety glasses and pulled his mask to the top of his head. "Now what?"

They'd had an argument about the size of the cornice board, Annie had taken Kellen's side and he was still irritated.

"I need you to be a policeman." She pulled off the top napkin and held the bones cradled in the other napkin. "I found this in the rhododendrons and I was wondering… That is, I thought it looked like…"

Lloyd pulled a pouch out of his pocket, unzipped it and pulled out a clean rag. He wiped off his safety glasses. "Yep. I'm a hunter, and that's a hip joint." He studied it. "No animal I've ever seen."

"A woman's?"

He nodded. "Yeah. Yeah…"

She put it down, napkin and all, on the cornice board.

"Don't! After all the work I did on that cornice board, I'm not having someone's moldy bones mess it up."

"Then you move it. I'm not holding that any longer."

He stepped back instead.

"Maybe the coyotes had dug their way into the local cemetery?" she asked hopefully.

"Are you kidding? Agnes visits Felix and Oscar every day."

Kellen blinked. "Um…"

"Agnes Juettner. Spinster lady who donated a new fence around the cemetery in return for getting her dogs buried there. This is probably a suicide or an accidental drowning that washed up onshore in the high tide. Let me check in with the sheriff. She's in Virtue Falls, north of here. I swear, Sheriff Kwinault's got connections with everybody in the county, and with the state and Feds. She'll know if anybody local is missing and for how long."

"How did the hip bone get to the resort grounds?" Kellen answered the question herself. "Coyotes." And said, "Oh God. Oh no." She had connected the dots. The carcass she had sent Temo to collect wasn't a deer or a raccoon. It was a woman. She pulled out her phone. It rang in her hand. She answered before the first ring finished. "Temo?"

His voice was tense. "I've got a situation here. We need the cops."

Kellen looked at Lloyd Magnuson. "I'm here with the cop."

"*The* cop. Of course there's only one." Temo laughed harshly. "Bring him—her?—and come out. Now."

9

Kellen was pretty sure she already knew the situation out there in the scrubby grass, and she drove that ATV fast enough to make the rain splat against the windshield and Lloyd Magnuson clutch at his seat. He didn't say a word, though. He, too, knew what they were likely facing.

When they got close to the place where Temo stood, draped in rain gear and leaning against a shovel, she rolled to a stop. Not only because she didn't want to run over any evidence, but also…she didn't want to see this.

My God, hadn't she witnessed enough death in the war zones and…

A pickax, its long spike lethal and shining. Gregory lifting it above her cousin's head… Kellen blinked the rain out of her eyes. It was just rain…

Lloyd leaped out before the ATV stopped moving and hurried to stand over the carcass. Except it wasn't a carcass. Even from a distance, she could see that. The scavengers had stripped away most of the flesh and scattered some of the bones over the landscape. But the bones that remained were concentrated and arranged in roughly a human shape. This was a body.

Kellen got out, the wet turf squishing beneath her black leather shoes.

Lloyd stood over the remains, then backed away. "Gross." Then, "Either of you got a camera?"

"Um. Yes." Kellen pulled out her phone.

So did Temo.

They looked at Lloyd questioningly.

He retreated farther. "I've got a flip phone. Never seen a reason for more."

"Now you have," Temo muttered.

"How do you want this photographed?" Kellen didn't want to take the pictures. She didn't want to look.

"Um, like, all around. From a distance and close in." Lloyd shoved his hands into his pockets. "Do you know the last time there was a murder victim around Cape Charade?"

They both shook their heads.

"Neither do I, and I've been here for over ten years." Lloyd glanced at the body. "I've never seen someone who was dead and…and rotting. That's creepy."

How had Kellen managed to land in the middle of a death investigation with an inexperienced police officer? She asked, "How do you know this is a murder?"

"I'd say her hands have been removed. Wouldn't you?"

"Dear God." She didn't want to know. But for the first time, she looked. Most of the smaller bones were gone or scattered. One hip bone remained, most of the leg bones, one with parts of the foot still attached. The rib cage had been gnawed, the spine had been dismembered and scattered. Wisps of hair clung to the skull…

Don't look at the skull. Don't think of Kellen, helpless under Gregory's pickax.

The arms were there, close to the rib cage as if the victim was holding herself.

"I don't see her hands." Kellen had to hold her hood with one hand to keep the wind from slashing it from her head. "But that doesn't mean they've been removed, only that the scavengers—"

"No, he's right." Temo knelt in the grass taking pictures with his phone. "The ends of the bones show rasp marks, like marks a saw blade would make, and little bits of joint are hanging in there."

That's horrible. She looked around, at the start of the path that led down to the beach, at the rise that led to the cliffs, at the one wind-mangled tree that pointed its defiance at the sky.

"You hope she was killed somewhere besides here," Kellen said to Lloyd.

"Don't you?"

Yes, of course she did. A death here at Yearning Sands Resort created problems she was ill equipped to deal with.

"She's awfully dirty." Temo was zoomed in on a piece of cloth. "Seems like with all this rain, she shouldn't have dirt ground into her clothes and hair."

"If this woman was buried around here, she wasn't buried deep enough, but there's not much in the way of clothing remaining, which means she's been exposed to the elements in a big way. No coffin, no blanket, no care whatsoever for her remains." For someone who allegedly didn't know what he was talking about, Lloyd Magnuson sounded confident. "I'd say whoever did this hated her."

"Or maybe hated all women," Temo said. "There's a lot of that in this world."

Kellen had to say it. "High tide. Really high tide. She could be from one of the sea caves."

"Sure. Wow. Murder. Definitely need to show this to Sheriff Kwinault. If she—" he gestured at the body "—washed out of the sea caves, maybe the murder took place here."

"God forbid," Kellen said fervently.

"Could mean there's a murderer on the loose." With a towel, Lloyd picked up a grubby piece of rubbery material and a torn piece of faded cloth and offered them to Kellen. "Take this and show it to the women at the resort. Ask them if they recognize the shoe or the material and remember who they belong to. Maybe we can figure something out that way."

Kellen looked at the misshapen thing. A shoe. The sole of a tennis shoe. And a swatch of material.

She didn't take it. "I'm not showing this to the staff! It would create a panic."

"If you don't show it to them and somebody else gets murdered, you're responsible," Lloyd said.

She didn't need more guilt to deal with. Yet— "This body has been around for a while and no one else has been killed."

Temo stuck his two cents in. "That we know of."

She looked down at her friend. She thought of all the staff who were on vacation, how some of them had already called to say they weren't coming back. She thought of all the guests who came and went, and never returned. Temo had a point. Still, she argued, "No one's going to know who wore this tennis shoe. It's just…a tennis shoe. I can't even tell what color it is. Or was."

"You have a better idea for identifying the body?" Lloyd was honestly asking.

"A coroner?" she suggested.

"We haven't got a coroner. We've got an undertaker. He's not busy and he likes it that way. But…good idea." Lloyd pulled out his cell phone. "The county coroner is in Virtue Falls, too. Mike Sun has dealt with this kind of thing before—murder and whatnot. I'll drive the bones up, deliver them to Mike, talk to Sheriff Kwinault and see if either one of them can figure out something about the death and who it is."

"It's a nasty drive in this weather," Kellen said.

"I don't mind." Lloyd sounded positively cheerful. "I've got friends in Virtue Falls. Good time for a visit!"

"Go on, Kellen," Temo said. "I'll get the photos taken. I'll get her up off the ground. You're not doing any good here."

Kellen knew she shouldn't make Temo do something she wouldn't do herself. But it wasn't so much *wouldn't* as *couldn't*, at least she couldn't without vomiting. "Thank you. Really. Thank you." Gingerly, she took the towel by the four corners, carried it back to the ATV and drove back as fast as she'd driven out. She didn't want to go in the front lobby and face the guests, so she parked by the back door to the spa, the one Destiny Longacre had left open for her boyfriend. Before she got close, Mara swung the heavy metal door open.

The wind caught it and slammed it against the wall.

Both women grabbed it, fought with it, got it under control and got inside.

"What a wretched day." Kellen meant more than just the weather.

"I heard." Mara had that significant tone in her voice.

Kellen turned to her. "How did you hear?"

"Lloyd Magnuson called Sheri Jean and asked for a storage box. Said he had to drive something out to Mike Sun in Virtue Falls. She knew you were picking up something the scavengers brought in. She figured it out. A natural death?"

Kellen shook her head.

"Damn it." Mara looked around at her determinedly peaceful domain. "Damn it," she said again. "Do you know who the body is?"

Kellen held up the towel she had twisted shut. "That's what we're supposed to deduce using a piece of cloth and part of a shoe."

"This way. *Don't* drop it, and *don't* make a mess."

She led Kellen to the spa waiting room, where nine anxious employees waited.

Sheri Jean + three concierge staff:

FRANCES:
34, CONCIERGE/FRONT DESK, CHICAGO NATIVE, TOUGH, SARCASTIC. EMPLOYED 7 YRS.

GERALD:
MALE, 42, FRONT DESK. GUATEMALAN, FLUENT IN SPANISH. EMPLOYED 16 YRS.

TRENT:
37, DESK STAFF. CAPE CHARADE NATIVE. EMPLOYED 7 YRS., THEN SERVED PRISON TERM FOR BREAKING AND ENTERING, REEMPLOYED 4 YRS.

Mara + four spa staff:

ELLEN:
23, BEAUTY PROFESSIONAL, CAPE CHARADE NATIVE. EMPLOYED 4 YRS.

DAISY:
67, CLEANING LADY WITH APPARENT SANITATION FETISH. EMPLOYED 42 YRS.

DESTINY LONGACRE:
19, MASSAGE THERAPIST. CAPE CHARADE NATIVE. BLOTCHY FACE, RED EYES. SILLY GIRL, PROBABLY DIDN'T DESERVE TO BE FIRED. EMPLOYED 13 MO.

Xander sat cross-legged on the floor in the lotus position, his hands resting upright on his knees.

Mara turned up the lights. "Kellen wants help identifying the body."

Sheri Jean sucked in her breath.

Destiny gasped. "The body?"

Every eye was fixed to the towel.

Mara shook her head violently. "No, I don't mean… That's not the body. It's clothes."

Kellen pushed magazines off a low table, placed the towel in the middle and opened it. She stepped back and gestured. "It's not much. We think she was wearing a dress and the white rubber thing is a tennis shoe sole with some of the canvas attached." Her hands didn't shake; being here with these people helped her get a grip on herself.

In a voice that sounded as if it was coming from far away,

Mara said, "I never get used to seeing the sad scraps of another person's life."

Kellen looked at her in surprise. How many "scraps" had this pretty, competitive female looked at?

"So it was definitely a lady?" Destiny asked in a wobbly voice.

Kellen thought of that hip bone. "Definitely a lady."

"She was a guest?" Destiny's voice got higher.

"There's no one missing from the area that I've heard," Mara said. Which was no answer.

But Destiny said, "Good. I mean, not good, but I don't want to think that's one of us."

Heads nodded.

"That cloth was against her skin?" Ellen dragged a table lamp over to the table and knelt on the rug to study the scrap. "It was sky blue at one time, cotton or lightweight wool, a natural fabric and probably worn in the summer. There's a lot of disintegration here, but exposure to dirt, wind and rain will do that. There's a lot of salt in the air here, too. That should actually preserve the color."

Kellen stared at Ellen. The woman was talking like a CSI investigator.

Ellen looked up and saw the general wariness. "I'm a colorist. I'm a hairdresser. I understand how color fades, and hair is a natural fiber, too… You didn't get any hair? Did you see hair?"

Kellen had captured a mental snapshot of the skull. She didn't want to review it…but she did. "The hair was wet. It looked brown. Maybe ash blond?"

"But the hair could be dyed, and that doesn't get us anywhere." Sheri Jean was impatient.

Even more impatient was Frances. "How are we supposed to ID a body based on a scrap of cloth and a piece of tennis shoe?"

Mara disappeared and came back with a pair of large tweezers. She used the towel to pick up the rubber sole. She poked around inside.

Sheri Jean continued, "We could pull this apart and still it would be the same shoe that every woman wears when she's—"

Mara jerked out the insole.

A silver ring flew out, landed on the rug, bounced to rest at Destiny's feet.

10

Mara dropped the shoe.

The room settled into a profound silence, marred only by the soothing harp music that played in the background. Then—screams, high pierced and terrified.

Like a cartoon character afraid of a mouse, Destiny jumped onto a chair and shrieked and pointed.

Xander stood in one smooth movement and stepped away.

Kellen tried to calm them down. “It’s a ring. It’s okay…”

Heads shook wildly.

Kellen got it. There was something about this ring. “What? Tell me. What?”

The screams died down. Shock quivered in the room.

Destiny visibly trembled, and her voice trembled, too. “That’s Priscilla’s ring.”

“Who’s Priscilla?” Kellen asked. Someone they knew, obviously. Then she remembered. “Wait. Priscilla, the assistant manager before me? The one who left without notice?”

Destiny nodded her head, up and down, up and down.

Xander went to the pitcher of lemon-infused water and poured glasses full. He put them on a tray and started around the room, offering them like fine wine.

“I never thought…” Mara took a glass and tossed it back like a shot. “That woman was such a—”

"Don't speak ill of the dead," Ellen warned.

"Right." Mara gathered her thoughts. "She disappeared one day and we all thought... Well, her car was gone and her cottage was cleaned out, and we thought... But that's her ring. Her toe ring. She always wore it, a Celtic knot with a purple topaz. She said it was her lucky ring."

Destiny crouched down in the chair and covered her face with her hands.

"She hid it under the sole of her shoe. She must have done that when she knew she was in trouble." Sheri Jean waved Xander away and turned to Kellen. "*What* did you say killed her?"

Kellen thought about those hands cut off at the wrists. "I don't know. I'm not a coroner."

"The question isn't *what* killed her, but *who*." Mara leaned down, wrapped the shoe in the towel and placed it on the table again. With the tweezers, she picked up the ring and placed it beside the shoe.

"Why do you think it's murder?" Frances asked.

"Kellen said it was," Mara answered. "She said it wasn't a natural death, and I have to say I agree. Why would Priscilla hide her ring in her shoe if she wasn't trying to send a message?"

"Definitely murder." Kellen accepted a glass of water and sipped, a wonderful dampness in a mouth that had been dry for too long.

Destiny lifted her head out of her hands. "Was her other shoe out there?"

"I didn't see it," Kellen said. Because she hadn't wanted to look. "But as gloomy and wet as it was, I didn't spot this one, either."

"I wonder if she hid any messages in the other shoe," Destiny suggested.

Kellen had her phone pulled out before Destiny finished speaking. "I'm texting Lloyd Magnuson and Temo right now. If it's out there, they'll find it."

"Good thought, Destiny," Mara said.

"The killer can't be one of us!" Ellen said. "It must be a stranger. A vagrant! There are always weird people floating through town."

"It could be a guest." Destiny took a glass, too. She tried to take a drink, but her teeth chattered on the edge. "Some of them are not nice people."

Kellen's phone chimed. She checked the message. "Temo's got the other shoe. When Lloyd gets back with his car, it'll go to the coroner with the other remains."

"Shouldn't we examine it?" Frances asked.

"It's evidence in a murder investigation. I suspect we shouldn't have messed with the first shoe." Kellen saw the look on Frances's face. "I know. I half want to look, too."

"How did it happen?" Sheri Jean was working it out in her mind. "Priscilla came in, all smiles, volunteered to take the tour. I sent her off with the group. One lady said she got sick out there, that she was white and sweating. She dumped the group, went to her cottage and…"

"Someone was there and abducted her!" Ellen said.

"And packed up her bags and drove her car?" Sheri Jean scoffed.

"So she packed and got ready to leave, and he jumped her?" Ellen was on the trail now. "Forced her in the car, forced her to drive, took her somewhere and killed her?"

"Or she stopped in town on the way out and he grabbed her there," Destiny whispered.

"Maybe it was your boyfriend, the one you left the door open for," Frances taunted.

"It wasn't!" Destiny straightened out of her hunch. "In September, he was in Seattle at community college. He didn't come home until Christmas."

"Flunked out," Frances told Kellen.

Xander placed the tray with the extra glasses on the table within easy reach and sank back into his meditative pose.

"Where was the body found?" Mara asked.

"On the grounds above the beach." Kellen would never forget the scattered bones, the shattered remains of a life. That image would never fade from her mind, and yet, how could she have survived a whole year—and forgotten?

"Maybe she washed in from somewhere else," Destiny said hopefully.

"Or out of a cave," Mara suggested.

"We cannot solve this crime." Kellen stood, legs apart, arms folded over her chest, and spoke the way she had in the past when facing an impossible battle. "We're not going to waste our time trying. Speculation will get us nowhere. None of us are experts. The body is in an advanced state of decomposition. In all likelihood, this will remain an unsolved murder."

Mara and Sheri Jean agreed with her.

The others were uncertain, groping for a way to make this come out right.

"What horrible person would kill Priscilla?" Destiny's voice wobbled. "Priscilla wasn't happy. She was always trying to make up stuff about herself, trying to make herself interesting."

"Then she'd forget and contradict herself." Sheri Jean laughed shortly.

"She didn't have anyone who loved her. No family. No friends. Then to be murdered..." Destiny jumped off the chair. "I hope the killer's face is devoured by flesh-eating bacteria!"

"I hope the killer discovers his lover in bed with his best friend," Ellen said.

Nervous laughter rippled around the room.

"And they both have the clap and he's slept with both of them," Daisy said.

Laughter died. They all stared at Daisy with wide eyes.

"You kids." She shook her head. "I'm old. But not older than sex."

Kellen broke the icy crust of shock that held them in place. "Everyone, we've got work to do, and that includes reassuring the guests, who will undoubtedly hear this news in the most lurid way."

"I wish Mr. Gilfilen was here," Ellen said.

"I do, too—" the understatement of the year "—but he left a solid security system in place." What a lie.

Mara stepped in to support her. "You know Vincent Gilfilen. He's totally without empathy, but he would never leave us unprotected. Now—my staff has the six Alaskan women coming in for a group spa experience, so, ladies and gentlemen, let's get to work."

"The guests will be talking to each of you, so let's keep the gossip low-key," Kellen said. "Be encouraging. The death was months ago, we're horrified and grieved, but we go on as a family. Right? Because we will watch out for each other, won't we?"

Fear bound the group like glue.

Xander came to his feet again in that don't-touch-the-floor maneuver that made him look like a cobra rising from a basket. In his overly serene voice, he said, "The universe watches out for us, and we trust the universe to keep us safe."

"The universe didn't give a damn about Priscilla," Frances said.

The employees separated reluctantly, moving toward their stations, arms clasped around their middles. Each of them glanced back as they left the room, and Kellen nodded encouragingly as they did.

Sheri Jean shooed her staff out the door, too.

The last to leave was Destiny. She came to Kellen. "I wouldn't have left the door unlocked if I'd known a killer lurked close. Captain, I'm so sorry." She wasn't asking for her job back. She was apologizing and acknowledging her mistake.

"You understand now. This could happen at any time and to anyone."

Destiny blew her nose.

Kellen threw caution to the wind. "Mr. Gilfilen will take me severely to task, and he'll probably override me when he returns from vacation, but for the moment, you can stay."

"I've got my job back?" Destiny's red-rimmed eyes lit up. "Thank you. If I don't make money, I won't go to college next year. My mom works here as a housekeeper—she can't afford the tuition, and I'm not smart enough to get a scholarship. But college is my only ticket out, and I promise I won't screw up again."

Kellen noted that Destiny hadn't played the sob story card until she was reinstated. Bonus points to her.

To Kellen, Mara said softly, "I told you she was a good kid." To Destiny, she said, "Mrs. Yazzie specifically requested you for her massage. I substituted a free pedicure, but she wasn't happy. When she comes in, let her know you're back and ready to work on her."

"Okay!" Destiny started to leave but turned back. "What I want to know is—what did Priscilla see out on the tour that scared her so badly she tried to run away?"

11

Good question, kid. Kellen had come here seeking a place to build a home, and now the home had become its own kind of nightmare with friends she didn't know if she could trust and her own mind that led her through logic and programming and abandoned her when it came to her own memories.

Sheri Jean turned to Kellen. "You *are* going to call Annie, aren't you?"

"Right now." Kellen started for the office.

"What about our meeting?" Sheri Jean asked.

Kellen turned and looked at her in exasperation.

"You'll come to me after you talk to her," Sheri Jean instructed. "Tell me what she said." She left Mara and Kellen alone in the spa waiting room.

"She has a very stern sense of what's owed to her." Mara grinned without humor. "Gruesome death cannot change that."

"I get that." Kellen had been in so many countries and so many situations where status ruled and wisdom came second to ego. "But it's hard to bend to tradition when today I've seen a mutilated corpse."

"Mutilated?" Mara bounded to her side. "What do you mean, mutilated?"

Why had Kellen told her that? Something about Mara's competitive competence had lured her into confession. "Priscilla's hands had been severed."

"No wonder you were sure it was a murder. That's sick. That's brutal. What else do you know that you didn't tell us?"

"Nothing. I've seen corpses before, in war zones. This is different. Not combat. Cold brutality. The stench of death is different. Less random. More intent."

"What Lloyd Magnuson knows about police work couldn't fill a teacup."

"That's right."

"Do you think the people here are in danger?"

"I think—" Kellen faced Mara straight on "—it's dark and cold and stormy and we'd all be happier if we do as I said and stick together. I don't think there's any more bodies out there, but I don't know for sure, and in the meantime I want Annie to tell me what to do."

"Sounds good. You up for our run tomorrow and some sparring?"

Kellen stared at Mara in amazement. "No, I'm not up for a run. I'll be lucky if I've had any sleep by then!" She stalked out, muttering, "A run. Really."

Mara hurried after her and called, "See you at five."

Kellen faced her.

"Five thirty?" Mara suggested.

"All right, but if I don't show, go without me."

Mara jumped and pumped her fist in the air.

God, that woman was annoying.

Just outside the spa, Kellen met the Shivering Sherlocks; she flattened herself against the wall and waved them on. To no avail.

The six ladies surrounded her and peppered her with questions about the corpse.

She assured them their safety was paramount.

They wanted to know the gruesome details.

She made her disclaimers, assured them she knew nothing about police work. They drooped in disappointment, managed to catch her in one group selfie and, when she told them they'd be late for their appointments, hurried into the spa.

Kellen sagged. For nice ladies, they had a real disconcerting interest in murder.

She started toward the office, passed the elevator and backtracked. Mr. Gilfilen had suggested often dropping into the second-floor security center; now was a good time. Brief security before talking to Annie. She took the elevator up, used her pass card to unlock the door and found:

AXEL RASMUSSEN:
WHITE, MALE, 30, 5'10", WEIGHT 275 LBS., EMPLOYED AT RESORT 9 MO., CURRENTLY ASLEEP IN CHAIR IN FRONT OF THE MONITOR ARRAY. SNORES—APPROX. 90 DECIBELS.

Obviously, she needed a camera in the security center to make sure the employees were even conscious. She walked up behind Axel and clapped her hands as loudly as she could.

He jumped hard enough to almost fall off the chair, then stood up and whipped around, ready to fight.

She didn't step back. She met his gaze straight on. "What do you see out there?"

He thought better of his belligerence and tried to fake his way through. "Nothing much. Not enough guests to worry about right now."

"If we don't have a lot of guests, we don't need to worry about their safety?"

"No, I mean, there's not much chance for trouble with this guest list. Some old ladies, an author, some newlyweds, the regulars up in the suites..." Mr. Gilfilen had indicated his staff was lacking. She had to agree.

"We found a body today," she said.

"One less guest, huh?" He laughed.

She didn't. "Staff. Priscilla Carter."

He shrugged. "Pretty girl. You want a seat?"

"No." If she sat, he would sit, too, and she wanted him on his feet. She pointed to the monitor for the eighth floor of one of the towers, where a tall shadowy figure slid along a darkened corridor. "Who's that?"

"Him." Axel rubbed his eyes. "Yeah. That's Carson Lennex."

"What?" Incredulous, Kellen leaned closer to the monitor. "No." He lived here in one of the top-story penthouses. She'd spoken to him this morning, seen him head out with his golf clubs into wretched weather, watched him greet fans with dignity and kindness. She had never imagined he would dress up like a ninja and skulk around.

"Maybe he's dreaming of his glory days when he played James Bond." Axel laughed, then changed his mind and coughed.

"Does he ever do anything that's a problem?"

"No. That is, Mr. Gilfilen says to let him alone, and he got that word from Mrs. Di Luca."

So Annie knew. "What is it we're ignoring?"

Axel pulled his belt up over his belly. "He breaks into storage rooms and sometimes he takes stuff."

"Like shower caps and shoe shine kits?" She was incredulous again.

"Can't ever have too many shower caps." Axel laughed again.

She did not like this man. Her gaze slid to the old-fashioned big black bank vault, the one they used to store the guests' valuables and the resort's records. Mr. Gilfilen had assured her the locking mechanism was new, only selected staff could access it and he had made her one of the privileged few. She hoped that was true; she would hesitate to trust Axel with anyone's cash or jewels. "Who do we have on the floor?"

"McGladrey." Axel brought one monitor into sharp focus on a man in a dark suit standing in the gift shop staring at a display of candy bars. "He's a good guy, one of our best security men. He's as faithful as an old dog."

As they watched, McGladrey slid a Twix into his jacket and made a run for it.

"Faithful, but not honest," she said.

Axel broke a sweat.

She studied the monitors, watched a smiling Sheri Jean mingle with the guests, saw the miles of empty corridors and the outdoor entrances.

"This guy's interesting." Axel pointed at Nils Brooks. "He came in from his cottage, looked around the lobby, then wandered the halls taking notes."

"He's a writer." She felt as if she was making excuses for him. "But even for a writer, that's odd behavior."

As if he had heard her, Nils Brooks turned and looked up at the security camera. She studied him, added to and corrected his profile:

NILS BROOKS:
MALE, 30S, 6', 180 LBS., BROWN HAIR (BLOND ROOTS?), BROWN EYES (COMPELLING), LONG LASHES, MILITARY HAIRCUT. NARROW JAW. DARK-RIMMED GLASSES. ~~CUTE.~~ HANDSOME. ~~NERDY.~~ CONFIDENT. CLOTHING: EXPENSIVE, WELL-WORN.

Somehow, he didn't add up. Had she misread him on first sight? If so, how? She didn't miss clues. Watching him now, unobserved, he seemed more the commanding personality she'd first spoken to on the phone. In her experience, contradictions in personality meant trouble. Was he hiding something? Or was she overreacting to today's discovery?

Axel was clearly delighted to have redirected her attention. "I'll keep an eye on him."

"Yes, please do." She looked Axel up and down. "Finding a body has made me aware that everyone currently at the resort, both guests and employees, could be victims—and could be killers."

He frowned. "Hey, look, I'm sorry you found a body, but it's not like someone got murdered."

"It was a murder."

"Oh shit." His face got red and he perspired more profusely. "At least it wasn't somebody from around here."

Sarcastically, she said, "That does make everything better." She thought that he was in a prime position to be the killer. But the problem with having such a gruesome crime laid on her doorstep was—everybody looked like a villain. "Mr. Gilfilen set everything up before he left, so he told me. I'll occasionally drop by, but call me if you see anything suspicious."

"Right." Axel pulled a tissue out of a box and blotted his face, then blew his nose. With sweaty sincerity, he said, "I'll watch, Miss Adams. We don't want anything like murder happening again."

At least he understood that.

She made it to Annie's office without interruption—that was one advantage to being at an almost empty resort—up two flights of stairs to a wide set of double doors. A square glass-covered table with a well-constructed model of the resort and its grounds dominated the center of the spacious room. Annie's desk faced the door. Kellen's desk faced the window. A small, comfortable seating area with a gas fireplace and bookshelves hugged one corner. A dusty CB radio, kept for emergencies, hid in a cabinet with paper clips and typewriter ribbons.

Kellen used the house phone to make the call.

Leo picked up. "What is it?" His voice sounded tired and rough.

"Mr. Di Luca, we have a crisis here at the resort."

"Do your best to handle it."

Not the response she expected. "You don't understand. We found a body. A dead body. A corpse."

"*You* don't understand. Annie arrived here and collapsed. She's got pneumonia. She's in the hospital on oxygen and she's in the middle of an arthritic flare-up. She's suffering, maybe dying."

Pity and grief caught her around the throat. "Mr. Di Luca, I'm so sorry. What can I do for you? For Annie?"

"Take care of her resort." He took a rasping breath. "Annie has complete faith in you. I do, too. Whatever decisions you make, I'll back you one hundred percent. If Annie makes it through the night, I'll talk to you tomorrow. If not..."

"I'll pray for her and you and your family." Kellen meant it with all her heart. She hung up and stared out the window at the vista that had been so glorious three months ago when she had interviewed for this position. Now wind-driven rain splattered against the windows, dark low-hanging clouds blocked the view, and behind all that, the sun was setting, stealing the last vestiges of brief winter light. Kellen could see why Annie had warned her of the difficult Washington winters, of the unending dark and constant rain. Annie...

Sweet Annie. Smart Annie. She had been struggling this morning, saying odd things that meant...nothing, or so Kellen hoped. Annie always put on such a good face, it was easy to forget her age and condition. But not now. Not when death hovered close.

Kellen checked the time. If Lloyd Magnuson had left as soon as they'd finished cleanup, he should be close to Virtue Falls by now, maybe even there, and he needed to know they had ID'd the victim. She called his beloved flip phone. It rang, but he didn't pick up. She left a message.

Mara rapped on the door frame. "Hey. You busy? Did you bring Annie up-to-date?"

"Leo says she's ill."

"My God. What luck. What...timing. In the hospital?"

"Yes, and..." Kellen choked back the words. She could not bring herself to say Annie might not recover. She wouldn't believe it, and she wouldn't say it. "We're going to have to go on as best we can."

"Sure. We can do this. This might help." Mara wandered in casually dropping information like Gretel with her pieces of bread. "I wanted you to know. I have a contact at the FBI. I talked to him."

All of us out here are running away from something.

"Will the FBI show up to investigate?" Which would be a relief, considering the situation.

"Doubt it. They'll wait for the coroner's report." Mara made her way to the model of the resort and looked down at the landscape. "They'll put the information in their files, and they'll say Priscilla's been dead four months and nothing has happened since. If another body pops up, they'll be here." Mara shrugged. "That won't happen, so brief answer—no FBI. They're overworked, you know."

"You know an awful lot about the FBI." A less than subtle inquiry.

"Old boyfriend." Mara used the sleeve of her hoodie to carefully clean the glass over the model. "Listen, the spa girls are upset, so I had them bunk in the hotel, two to a room. I hope that's okay."

"Good idea. I don't want them driving between Cape Charade and the resort. Let's keep them here and safe."

Mara started for the door, then backtracked. "You know, I was thinking. Priscilla's death happened four months ago, and nothing's happened since. I think everybody's overreacting."

"Yes. Possibly. But we have a killer who apparently threatened her, frightened her, managed to capture her and hold her long enough to kill her and cut off her hands. That's...vicious. Maybe the sick bastard is gone from here, never to return, but I think this warrants extra caution."

"Wow. When you put it like that, I agree. If you want, I can find you someone to bunk with, too."

"No." *Nightmares. Flashbacks.* "No, I'm on call all the time now, and I thought being manager was a big job. Being manager and security manager of a resort with a murder is so overwhelming, no one will want to room with me. I'll be up and down all night long."

Mara slapped the door frame, turned, and in that bright, snappish way of hers, she said, "Still, you'd sleep better if you weren't alone."

"I wouldn't sleep at all." *For fear I'd scream in terror or cry in pain and grief.*

"Your call. But remember, Priscilla lived in your cottage. Still, if no one's spotted her ghost in four months, I suppose she's not hanging around."

"I suppose not." Kellen watched Mara walk away and was all too bitterly aware of the obvious.

It wasn't Priscilla's ghost she needed to worry about.

It was Priscilla's killer.

12

Kellen had a checklist of tasks left. Sheri Jean held the number one slot. But when Kellen walked into the lobby lounge, she found Sheri Jean leading the predinner wine tasting.

The newlyweds were nowhere in sight. Naturally.

The Shivering Sherlocks were there en masse, dressed in costumes: one wore a man's suit, tie and fedora; the twins had on flapper costumes complete with fringe and feathers; Rita had tied her red hair in a kerchief for an admirable imitation of *I Love Lucy*'s Lucille Ball; Tammy had painted on high-arched eyebrows and pretend-smoked a cigarette; and Patty had pasted on a jaunty mustache and rocked as a stout Hercule Poirot.

Carson Lennex sat in their midst. He looked every inch of his urbane self, not at all the kind of man who lurked in hotel hallways, abducting rolls of toilet paper. He seemed to be enjoying the ladies' conversation. Since they were all about the same age, Kellen supposed they related on a shared experience level.

Nils Brooks sat off to the side, and when he saw Kellen, he pushed his black-rimmed glasses up his nose and observed her with interest.

Kellen walked into the lounge and smiled. "Are we enjoying ourselves?" She sounded like a manic nurse in charge of recovering patients.

The guests cheerfully returned her greeting.

One of the Shivering Sherlocks twins waved her over. "Dear, is there a problem? I'm trying to call my husband and I can't get cell reception."

The gray-haired twin whipped around and snapped, "For God's sake, Candy, Randy will survive for one night without you checking on him."

"Debbie, when the poor man retired, he didn't know how to turn on the oven!"

"Whose fault is that?"

"It's mine," Candy said softly. "He worked so many hours and I didn't want him to have to come home and cook."

"You worked, too!"

"I was only a teacher. He worked the pipeline."

"I'd rather weld something than care for thirty pimply-faced, angst-ridden adolescents every day." In an aside to Kellen, Debbie said, "I'm not totally heartless. I gave Randy a cookbook when he retired. The man can read."

For the first time, Candy looked ruffled. "Well, he can't follow instructions!"

"Show me a man who can," Debbie said with some humor. To Kellen, she said, "Any word on the communications outage?"

Kellen hadn't realized there was a communications outage, but a quick check on her phone proved Candy was right. "The storm probably knocked out our cell tower. Let me find out if our landline phones are working and I'll get you through to your husband."

Sheri Jean scooted over. "Is there a problem?"

"Cell tower must be down. I'm going to get Candy a phone."

Sheri Jean looked sternly at Candy. "I could have done that."

"You were busy! This young lady was just wandering around. You must be the resort's jack-of-all-trades." Candy smiled kindly at Kellen.

"Pretty much. Let me find you that phone." Kellen walked

over to Frances at the concierge desk. "The cell tower has stopped transmitting. Do we have any communications at all?"

Frances looked up from her keyboard and monitor and glared evilly. "All communications are down. No cable, so no TV."

"Landline?"

"*That* we've got." Frances handed over a cordless phone. "And the CB radio in Annie's office in case of real emergency. That thing always works. The storm's playing havoc with anything satellite related. I'm supposed to be making reservations for a whale-watching tour, weather permitting, for the newlyweds." She gestured broadly. "What am I supposed to do now?"

"Tell them weather is not permitting." Kellen glanced around. "It's not like they're hanging around looking for something to do. If you know what I mean."

"Her great-aunt gave them a whale-watching tour as a gift, and by God, she's determined they should watch whales."

"I wonder how long it's been since she was a newlywed."

"Really." Frances lowered her voice. "You can go out on the ocean, heave your guts up, freeze to death and hope for an orca sighting...or you can stay in bed, warm and cozy, and have sex. What would *you* want to do?"

"I hear sex can cause motion sickness, too."

Frances cackled. "Only if it's done right."

Chad Griffin waltzed up to the desk and said, "Thought you ought to know. Communications are out." Without waiting for a response, he headed toward the lounge and poured himself a hefty glass of wine.

"The pilot's staying here tonight?" Frances said. "I can't stand that guy. Look at him trying to horn in on Mr. Lennex and his harem. Those ladies don't want *him* when they can have a movie star."

Chad had pulled up a chair to the edge of the group and was trying to engage Rita in conversation.

"Of course." Frances exuded disgust. "He's making his moves on Mrs. Yazzie. She's the only widow in the group."

"She's leaning away."

"She's a smart lady. He's a freeloader and he thinks every woman in the place is impressed because he's a war hero and a pilot."

Surprised, Kellen asked, "Is he a war hero?"

"So he says. I don't care. He's *old*." Frances couldn't have made her disdain more obvious. "I've got better things to do, like find out if anyone knows what's happening to our communications."

"Call Mitch. He's good with mechanics and electronics. Have you met him?"

"You bet."

"He can't fix anything outside tonight, but there might be something going on with the server."

"Okay." Frances wore the ghost of a grin. "I'll call Mitch. Want him to check the generator while he's at it?"

"How often does the power go out?"

"Not too often, but when it does, it's nice if the generator is functional. Look out, here comes Sheri Jean and she looks like she's on the warpath."

Kellen swiveled on the balls of her feet. "Sheri Jean, I suggest you organize a movie night."

"We've got no cable? No streaming?" Sheri Jean's voice rose.

"We've got nothing but a bitch of a storm and a long, dark night ahead of us." The rotating front door whirled suddenly. A gust of wind swept the lobby; it knocked petals off the flower arrangements and sent papers flying.

Kellen and Sheri Jean stared.

No one entered. Then Russell popped his head in. "Sorry! I did latch it, but somehow it came loose. Ghosts, I guess."

"Priscilla," Sheri Jean whispered. "She's sending us a message."

Startled, Kellen studied her white face. Sheri Jean really believed, and that seemed so unlike her. "What message would that be?"

Something—a branch—hit the big window facing the sea.

Everyone jumped and laughed.

Sheri Jean shivered. "Priscilla is not going to rest until her killer is brought to justice."

13

The Lykke Estate
Greenleaf, Maine

The computer on the desk released a *ding!* and Sylvia Lykke woke from her light doze, leaped off her bed and scampered to the desk.

The computer was the only thing that roused her anymore, her only link to the real world. Erin said Sylvia was getting senile, that she suffered from dementia, and more and more she locked Sylvia in her room.

Sylvia got lonely. So lonely. When she looked out her window at the Atlantic Ocean, crashing and thrashing and blowing froth about, she felt as if she had spent her life at the edge of the continent without love, without friends, without companionship. But when the computer dinged, when there was a text or an email, Sylvia knew someone remembered her, even if it was only an offer of a penis extension.

This email was different. This was from Debbie, her old friend Debbie. They'd gone to school together here in Greenleaf. Debbie had married at about the time Sylvia married. They both had children. They both lost their husbands…

Debbie had mourned the loss of her husband.

Sylvia had been relieved at the loss of hers.

Ten years later, a man had appeared who swept Debbie off her feet. She remarried and moved to Alaska.

The two friends had drifted apart. Sylvia didn't often hear from Debbie, so this email was a treat. She opened it and read.

> Wish you were here! Candy and I are on our annual mystery weekend at Yearning Sands Resort, and guess what? Remember your daughter-in-law, Cecilia? Remember her cousin who visited right before the explosion? I think I met her here. She looks so much like Cecilia! I almost said something to her, then thought probably she didn't want to remember that awful time. I managed to snap her photo.
>
> I hope you're doing well and can write soon. I often think of how much fun we used to have in school…

Sylvia scrolled down to look at the photo.

She stared. Oh God. How she stared!

She laughed. A small chuckle at first. Then a wholehearted belly laugh.

Cecilia. Cecilia.

Erin unlocked the bedroom door and walked in. "Mother, what's so funny?"

Sylvia had long suspected Erin had surveillance on her. She was sure of it now, but she didn't care. She laughed and laughed. "He was right." She pointed at the photo. "He was right."

"Who was right, Mother?" Erin had been a pretty girl, always tall for her age and big-boned, but with startling hazel eyes, thick blond hair and a wide mouth. Yet no man had ever been interested in her. Or perhaps she'd never been interested in any man other than Gregory, not since that moment when Waddington Lykke brought Sylvia and Gregory home from the hospital, put the squalling infant into Erin's eager arms and said, "This is your younger brother. You must take care of him. He's the Lykke family heir, and very precious."

Now Erin carried an extra twenty pounds, but she was still attractive. She ran Lykke Industries with an iron hand...and Sylvia feared her daughter.

"Mother!" Erin took both Sylvia's shoulders and shook her hard. "Why are you laughing?"

Sylvia's neck snapped, and she sobered. "You're such a bully."

"What?" Erin reeked with annoyance. "What was so funny?"

"That." Sylvia pointed at the screen. "He was right. He didn't kill her. There she is, Cecilia, alive and well. The dear child does look well."

Erin shoved her mother out of the computer chair and sat and stared. In a faraway voice, she said, "I've found her. Gregory, I've found her."

"There's nothing wrong with her being alive. Gregory's rotting in his grave."

Erin looked at her in fury. "He is not!"

"So's Waddington. Nobody ever deserved death as much as your father. He was a cruel man. When I married him, I thought I'd married a prince. But he hurt me. All the time, he hurt me." Sylvia wandered toward the bed. She had forgotten Erin was here, forgotten why she was on her feet. She was lost in the past, in memories that brought tears to her cheeks. "He never gave me anything except two children who were monsters like him. I knew there was something wrong with Erin when I found my kitten with its neck broken. I cried. I thought Waddington had done it. But Erin said I loved the kitten more than her, so she killed it. Until then I didn't know about Erin. But Gregory... I knew from the first moment I looked into his eyes that he was warped, like a looking glass all distorted. When he married that poor girl, I thought... I'm still ashamed, you know? That I didn't stand up for her. But Waddington hurt me so much I didn't have any courage left. He said I was nothing and he made me nothing. I'm nothing."

Erin touched Sylvia's arm.

Sylvia turned and looked at her in surprise. "Dear, what are you doing here? How wonderful to see you. I grow so lonely here..."

"Do you know who this is?" Erin pointed at a picture on the computer monitor.

"Oh! Oh! It is Cecilia! Gregory was right. She lived. How good to know she lived." Sylvia laughed and thought how good it was to laugh.

Erin lifted her hand.

Abruptly sober, Sylvia cowered.

Erin dropped her head, took an impatient breath and said, "Gregory wanted her dead. Don't you remember?"

"I remember."

"When we brought him back to the house, Gregory told me to finish the job that he failed to do. That was what Gregory wanted. Don't you understand?"

"I understand, but, dear, Cecilia was such a sweet girl, and your brother...hurt her. The way Waddington hurt me." Sylvia saw the past, felt the pain of broken bones and cruel taunts. "We can let Cecilia go, can't we?"

"Is that what you think?"

"You did bury him, didn't you? Gregory? You buried him?"

"Where, Mother? Everyone thought he was dead!"

"It doesn't matter where. You didn't keep his body, did you? For so long? That would be—"

"Monstrous? Because I'm a monster created by you and my father?" Erin's hazel eyes blazed.

Sylvia shrank away. "Don't be angry. I didn't call you a monster...did I?"

"Honestly, Mother. You're batty!"

The computer dinged again. Sylvia perked up. "Good! An email. I like emails. I'm not so alone when they come in." She tried to walk toward the desk.

Erin steered her toward the bed and said forcefully, "Mother, it's nighttime. You're sleepy. You should go to sleep."

"I am sleepy." Another *ding!* Sylvia remembered the photo and again tried to walk to the computer. "But I want to write Debbie, tell her that that's not Cecilia's cousin, but Cecilia herself. How good to know Cecilia is alive and well!"

Erin blocked her. "At least the cousin is dead," she said with cold satisfaction. "She intended to steal Cecilia from Gregory. For that, she deserved to die."

"No, she didn't." Sylvia wrung her hands. "He shouldn't have killed her."

"Does Debbie say where they are?"

"I don't remember. I think… I don't know. But Debbie and her sister go there every year with their friends for a mystery weekend. Do you think I might go next year?"

Erin put her hands on her mother's shoulders and pressed her onto the bed. "Yes. You should go next year."

"And see Cecilia? I'll tell her to beware of you." Sylvia's mind wandered again. "You're a monster like your father and your brother, only worse…"

"Such a good idea to warn Cecilia." Erin helped her mother lie on the bed. She pulled up the blankets, tucked her in, made her comfortable.

Sylvia smiled into her daughter's face. "I always knew you were the worst of them."

"Yes." Erin picked up a pillow.

"But I love you anyway." Sylvia petted Erin's cheek. "My daughter. My monster. Tomorrow I'll warn Debbie about you. She'll tell Cecilia."

"That's a good idea, Mother. Tomorrow. You do that."

14

Kellen was exhausted. She should go back to her cottage right now, get some sleep before getting up tomorrow for another replay of today. But she was frazzled, worried about Annie, about the resort's staff, about a gruesome death committed somewhere close, and the body... So many questions about the body. And the killer. Was the killer lurking in the winter's dark and observing as they reacted to the recovery of Priscilla's body, hands removed in some cruel dissection?

Lights gleamed from the windows of the maintenance garage. Someone was there, working or cleaning up. Kellen let herself in out of the weather. And heard a familiar sound: the click-release of a safety on a firearm.

She froze.

Birdie sat at a table with her feet up, a steaming mug before her, a book in one hand and a pistol in the other.

Kellen waved tentatively. "Hello?"

Birdie clicked the safety back on and slid the Glock 21 SF into the holster she had attached to the table leg. "Shut the door behind you. You're letting in a draft."

Kellen let the metal door thud shut. Outside, the storm was roaring, but in here it was quiet and safe. "You heard the news, I see."

"Yes. Poor kid. When I'm here alone at night, I keep a pistol near at hand." Birdie smiled without humor. "Although not usually this near at hand."

Kellen took a moment to breathe in the familiar scents of tires, grease and sweat. Electronics from an ATV were scattered in pieces across the floor.

"Where's your weapon?" Birdie asked.

When the two women left the military, they had invested in firearms, Birdie because her husband was a police officer and that put her in the line of fire, and Kellen because for a brief and harrowing time she went into security. After examining and handling weapons, they'd both decided on the Glock 21 SF, legendary for its accuracy and light recoil and holding thirteen rounds. They'd both obtained concealed weapons permits.

"In my cottage," Kellen said. "Carrying a gun is frowned upon in the hospitality business."

"Are you rethinking that policy?"

Here at Yearning Sands Resort, Kellen had always felt safe, but now she admitted, "I am."

"Here." Birdie shoved a thin black metal flashlight across the table.

Kellen examined it. It was small enough to fit in a pocket or purse, had a concentrated beam bright enough to blind an attacker and a jagged edge around the bulb end that could be used as a weapon. She nodded slowly. "I like this. I like this very much."

"I thought you would. Keep it."

Kellen slipped it into her shirt pocket. For someone like her and like Birdie, trained in hand-to-hand combat, the flashlight was weapon gold. "First day on the job, I didn't expect to find myself dealing with murder and mutilation."

"I remember in Afghanistan when you showed up, all pretty and unsmiling. We pegged you as a typical butterbar. Remember what happened next?"

"We took shelling and we had to move the convoy to meet with reinforcements. Wow. That was a mess."

"You got us through with no loss of life and only one jeep down."

"I appreciate your confidence, but there's no comparison. The resort is different, you know? In Afghanistan, we were soldiers. We were there because we volunteered. We knew full well we could die. Here, we have innocent guests and some nice people who work in a spa."

"Like civilians."

"Except in Afghanistan the civilians could kill you. Although, come to think of it, I suppose one of the guests could be a murderer." Carson Lennex's face popped into Kellen's mind, and his foray into the resort's darkened corridors. Perhaps his movements were innocent. But in these circumstances, she could hardly dismiss them out of hand. She looked around. "Where are the guys?"

"Temo has gone to LA."

"He said he needed to go to see if he could lure friends up to fill the positions for his staff. But tonight?" Kellen's finger circled the air.

"It's not staff he went for. Family shit is coming down. He says he'll be back late tomorrow."

"He's going to be pooped." Kellen was going to need him to clean up after the storm tonight. "Where's Adrian?"

"Bed."

"Mitch?"

"Hot promise."

"A date? It never takes him long, does it? Who's got him now?"

"That snooty girl at the reception desk."

"Frances? Wow." No wonder Frances had smirked when Kellen told her to call him. "That woman…well, she's not as bad as Sheri Jean."

"That's like saying Dracula's not as bad as Hannibal Lecter. They're both going to kill and eat you."

"Think Mitch is in trouble?"

"I think if Frances eats him, he'll be a happy man."

Kellen was tired. It had been a long day. She was worried about Annie, the body, the communications blackout. She leaned her head on her hands and giggled. Finally, she looked up. "What about you? Why are you here so late?"

"I sleep in maintenance most nights, what sleep I get. I had them put a cot in the loft."

Kellen looked up at the spiral staircase, the open-mesh metal floor, the steel railing. "A little industrial up there, isn't it?"

"I feel safe here. Tonight especially. If the ghosts wake or the grief comes on too strong, I can always wake up and go to work. You remember. You used to do that…in the war zone."

"I remember." Kellen did remember leaning against a boulder blasted out of an Afghan mountain peak, watching the sun rise and spread glory across the broken landscape and seeing that hint of something Not Quite Right. An hour later, the unit was hunkered down, taking fire and returning it, and all because of Kellen's sleepless night.

"You were a legend. They said you couldn't be killed."

"And here I am." That general, the way he'd looked at her when he told her of her discharge, as if he knew about her missing year, as if he wondered what she had done and what she could do…and who would die.

Birdie sipped her hot chocolate. "Lately I've been sorting through the old maintenance manuals they store up there. No one has ever thrown one away. If you can believe it, there was a vehicle manual for a 1957 Dual-Ghia D-500."

"Whoa." Kellen felt the awe. "I wonder where the car went."

"I don't know, but I saved that manual. Most of the rest are trash. I fill a box full, recycle it, fill another box full. It keeps me off the streets."

Kellen indicated the ATV. “Can I help you?”

“Not tonight. I’m winding down and you should be, too.”

“I am. But for a few minutes, I need something to do with my hands. It takes my mind off...what’s on my mind.”

“Have at it, then. You have a way with circuitry, and that damned thing has a short somewhere and I haven’t been able to locate it.”

Kellen fixed herself a mug of hot chocolate, pulled on a pair of Birdie’s coveralls, slid an LED lamp onto her forehead and went to look at the mechanics and the wires.

In a conversational tone, Birdie said, “I told the guys you got that scar on your forehead when you were a teenager in Turkey.”

“Huh? Oh. This is your story about me? What was I doing in Turkey?”

“I told them you were raised by a spy family.”

Kellen lifted her head from her work. “Birdie! You didn’t!”

“I said your parents were on a secret mission to free a diplomat’s kidnapped daughter and they got killed. You freed the daughter and got her away, but at the last minute you were shot in the head.”

“That’s the dumbest thing I’ve ever heard.” Kellen groped for her mug and took a drink.

“You miraculously recovered because your parents were part of a breeding program that produced superheroes.”

Kellen snorted hot chocolate. *That* hurt.

“You joined the military to change your identity and escape repercussions. You told the CIA that espionage was your parents’ choice, not yours, and now, despite government pressure, you refuse to return to the life of a spy.”

Kellen leaned back against the seat of the ATV and laughed so hard her sides hurt. “Now *that’s* the dumbest thing I’ve ever heard.”

“They bought it.”

“No. They didn’t. A superhero? I’m a superhero?”

"Adrian said that explained a lot, like how you got through that sabotage in Kuwait with only minor injuries."

"Minor injuries, my ass. I had surgery on my shoulder. I was unconscious for two days. I was discharged!"

"You said you wanted something original, not the same old forbidden love and jealous husband story. So I went for it!"

"You're an idiot." Still smiling, Kellen bent back to her work.

Someone beat on the outer door.

Both women straightened.

Birdie click-released the safety on her pistol.

Kellen went to the door and looked through the camera, realized communications were down and looked through the peephole.

A bedraggled man stood there, and as she watched, he lifted his fist and pounded again.

"Nils Brooks," Kellen whispered. Like a grain of sand beneath the shell she had so carefully built around her, she experienced a constant apprehension about him. Was the thing that niggled at her nothing more than a pair of gorgeous brown and possibly familiar eyes?

Birdie indicated Kellen should allow him in, but she didn't lower the pistol.

Kellen shoved the door open and rapidly stepped aside.

Nils hurried in and dragged the door shut after him.

Birdie clicked the safety and slid her firearm into the holster and out of sight. "Mr. Brooks? What are you doing here?"

He faced them, his overcoat unbuttoned, his golf shirt and jeans dripping, his wet hair plastered to his forehead. He pulled off his glasses and tried to dry them on his shirt, then realized it was impossible and slid them into his pocket. "Hi." He gave a sheepish wave. "I had dinner in one of the restaurants, then listened to some music, then came out and got in the ATV... Now I'm lost. I can't find my cottage, and I hope you don't mind, but I saw your lights and hoped you could help me."

The two women exchanged glances and did a mental rock/paper/scissors.

Birdie slid the Glock over to Kellen, stood and got him a towel. "Sure, come on in. It's really coming down out there. Isn't there rain gear on your ATV?"

He looked abashed and embarrassed. "Sure. Probably. I remember being told that. I forgot... I should have stayed in the cottage." He took off his scarf and shook it, took off his overcoat and shook it. He presented a hapless facade, but those eyes... Kellen felt off-kilter when she looked at them, as if she'd fallen into a wormhole and whirled backward in time.

Ceecee. Ceecee. Where are you? Come back to me...

The voice whispered in her mind. She ignored it. "Nice coat." Kellen watched his face.

Nils looked at his coat. "It *was*. It's Burberry and wool. It's supposed to be water-repellent. But it's soaked."

"Yeah..." Kellen nodded. "Guests usually bring raincoats." Not the most tactful thing to say, but man. Talk about epic unpreparedness.

He tossed the coat over a hook, took the towel and rubbed his head.

The man looked slender until the rain plastered his clothes to his body. Then he showed off muscle definition he couldn't have gotten from sitting behind a desk. Nice butt, long legs, corded shoulders. He even looked good in goose bumps. And those eyes...

Birdie stood behind him, and while he had the towel over his head, she pretended to feel him up.

Kellen grinned.

Of course, he whipped off the towel and both women had to fake *not* being two sex-starved, lascivious females.

Kellen replied to the comment he'd made far too long ago. "Mr. Brooks, you did say you intended to stay in the cottage, but from what I saw, you came into the hotel to wander the halls and take notes." Might as well let him know he'd been observed.

"I'm doing research." He sounded reproachful. "You understand that. You understand what it's like to pay attention, to see things and understand what no one else can see or know."

Birdie and Kellen exchanged glances again, this time with more wariness.

"You've got a gun," he said to Birdie.

"It's lonely out here," Birdie answered. "I'd be a fool to trust to human kindness."

"Yes. Finding that body made everyone nervous." He shivered. "Any word from the coroner?"

"Nothing yet," Kellen said. "I expect I'll hear from our policeman in the morning. Do you want a blanket?"

"What I really want is to get back to my writing." He patted the pockets of his overcoat and plunged his right hand inside.

Birdie and Kellen flinched.

But he brought out a leather notebook, shook water off the cover, opened it and groaned. "The ink's run."

"Happens here in Washington when you don't wear your rain gear," Birdie said.

"I'll take your coat to the laundry tomorrow, see if they can do anything with it." Kellen found a rain poncho and dropped it over his head. "Come on, I'll get you back to your cottage now."

Birdie caught Kellen's arm. "He's in really good shape for a guy who lives behind a desk. Be careful." So even Birdie thought something didn't add up.

"I will. I am." Kellen grasped his arm and led him into the storm.

"I've been watching you," he said as he climbed into the ATV. "You're competent."

"Gee, thanks." Was that supposed to be a come-on? Because if it was, he needed to work on his lines.

She dropped him at his cottage, watched him run up onto the

porch and try to get in, turn and wave his hands helplessly. He'd lost his key card, so she used hers to open his door. She shoved him inside and headed to her cottage. She wanted to brush her teeth, wash her face, go to bed and sleep in peace, quiet and comfort between cool, clean sheets. Instead, she crawled up the spiral staircase to her loft and stared out toward the west, toward the ocean and the place where they'd found Priscilla's body.

Two miles out of Greenleaf, the rain started. Cecilia watched the first drops hit the windshield and exalted in the knowledge that the summer storm coming in off the ocean would erase evidence, muddy the explosion site...

She didn't know how to turn on the windshield wipers.

The rain fell harder.

She poked at the controls on the steering column, turned, pushed, twisted. Stuff happened. The headlights came on. The windshield wiper on the back window started a fast, steady swish. If she'd been driving backward, that would be great. Instead, she was driving blind on a twisty two-lane highway. She was scared, dehydrated—and she couldn't see where she was going. She peered through the sheeting rain, spied a turnout, pulled over and eased to a stop.

She sat, heart racing, eyes full of tears. In her head, she heard Gregory's voice. You're not capable of caring for yourself, darling. You're clumsy. You're incompetent. *He was right. She couldn't even flee with efficiency.*

No! No. She'd find the car book. It would explain how to turn on the wipers. She opened the minuscule glove compartment, pulled out the paperwork, shuffled through it—this was a rental, she hadn't realized that—looked back into the glove compartment. There in the recesses, she found the thin, floppy book waiting for her, and the Table of Contents/Wipers.

So! Gregory was wrong.

Someone knocked on her window.

She half screamed, realized a police officer stood beside the car and knew she'd been busted. She stared, wordlessly pleading for him to understand, to believe that she hadn't known what Gregory intended, to let her go.

Rain sluiced off the cop's coat and dripped off the brim of his hat. Impatiently, he indicated she should roll down the window.

She did. About an inch. Her voice shook. "Yes?"

Middle-aged guy. Stern face. "Miss, please present your license and proof of insurance."

"Sure. Um. License." Kellen's license in Kellen's wallet. "It's in my suitcase."

"You're a tourist?"

Was he trying to trick her? Or did he really not know who she was? He was state police, so maybe… "I am. This is a rental. It started raining. I couldn't figure out the wipers. I pulled over to look it up." She flapped the book at him.

He looked at her, mouth cocked sideways. Then he heaved a sigh. "All right. I'm in a hurry, so we'll skip the formalities. Wipers are the right middle lever, push it up and twist the knob up or down according to how fast you want the wipers to go."

She found the lever. She pushed it up. She twisted the knob back and forth. The wipers swished. "That's it." She smiled at him.

"You bet. Your headlights are on bright. That's illegal when driving into oncoming traffic."

"I'm sorry. I must have done it when I was trying to find the wipers."

"Yeah. Lever on the left. Bring it toward you. The headlights will not be bright anymore."

"Okay. Thank you. You want my license and proof of insurance?"

"No. Next time read the book on your rental car before you run into a rainstorm." He walked toward his patrol car.

She adjusted the wipers, put the car in gear and pulled back onto the road.

She smiled. She had bullshitted the cop. She had won the first battle.

15

The rest of the trip was normal, pretty much. Cecilia ran out of gas—she'd forgotten about trifles like refills—scared a girl at a drive-in who asked, "Are you a zombie?" paid for hotels with Kellen's credit card and got so lost she saw signs that welcomed her to Virginia. Virginia! From Maine! On the way to New York!

That was when she rediscovered the wonders of GPS. As she drove into New York City, the soothing GPS voice guided her over the NJ Turnpike, through the labyrinth of SoHo roads and to street parking two blocks from Kellen's apartment. By now she had read through every scrap of paper in the car, and she knew what to do. She parked, gathered Kellen's belongings, locked the car, took the key to a drop box and inserted it into the slot. Then she pretended she knew where she was going, pretended until she found the right street, then the right address, then used the fob to get into the narrow, empty lobby.

She took a deep, relieved breath of musty air. This building had been an industrial site in the nineteenth century, remodeled with a cast-iron facade at the turn of that century, remodeled again in the 1970s to be lofts and apartments. The manager's office was to the right; the name under the number was del Sarto. Cecilia did not want to meet Mr. del Sarto. Or Mrs. del Sarto. Or anybody who might know Kellen.

So Cecilia eased past and climbed the stairs to the sixth floor. She met no one. She began to experience the euphoria of release, of safety in a cruel world. Unit 62—she unlocked the door, opened it, dragged in her luggage and dropped everything. She slid chains, bars, locks. She secured herself in against the world.

Leaning against the door, she looked at the one room that contained a living area, a tiny kitchen, a bed and dresser—and tall, high windows that let in the light. A door led to a dark hole of a bathroom. Perfect. This place was perfect. Lucky, lucky Kellen.

Cecilia crumpled, dropped to her knees, stuffed her fists over her mouth…and unwillingly revisited the explosion.

Kellen waiting for Gregory in the living room.

Gregory messing with the gas connection.

Cecilia watching from the edge of the hill, fearing, hesitating.

Gregory lifting the pickax over Kellen's head…

Cecilia covered her head with her arms, trying to hide from her memories. The explosion of blood. The explosion of fire. The explosion of life and hope. And that moment when Gregory looked up and saw her.

Cecilia was a coward. She was running from a terrible murder, performed by the husband she had allowed to abuse her—because that was the truth, wasn't it? Gregory had undermined her confidence and her abilities. But seeing Kellen standing tall and strong, Cecilia was all too aware of her frailty and knew she should have fled. At the very least she could have stood at the top of the cliff and flung herself onto the rocks.

Not on my watch. *Kellen had been afraid Cecilia would do just that.*

A key rattled in the lock.

Cecilia's eyes popped open. She rested on the couch, curled up on the cushions with the throw over her. Sunshine rolled through the windows.

The door opened, hit the end of the chains and bars.

A woman's voice said, "Kellen, you're back. It's Brenda. Thank God. Let me in."

Terrified, Cecilia stared at the door, open at two inches.

"Why haven't you been answering your phone? Why haven't you called me? Darling, I know what happened."

Darling? This was Kellen's lover.

"I know you. You loved your little cousin. You always protected her. I'm sorry she died."

Cecilia pushed the throw aside.

The person at the door must have heard, for her voice grew more urgent. "Kellen, please! I know we fought, but I love you. You said you loved me. Darling? Talk to me."

Moving as quietly as she could, Cecilia sat up. She didn't know what to do. She hated for this woman to think Kellen was ending the relationship. But what would happen if she knew the truth? Brenda would be grief-stricken. She would tell someone and give away Cecilia's hiding place. Cecilia would be drawn into the investigation. She would have to confess her own weakness.

Brenda shoved at the door. The chains rattled. The bars held. "Kellen, are you hurt? Do you need help? Please! I'm afraid for you. I'm going to call the cops!"

"No!"

"Kellen?"

Cecilia had to speak. "No. I'm fine. Go away. Go...away."

The awful silence from outside the door stretched out for long seconds.

Cecilia held her breath. Had Brenda recognized the differences in their voices? Was Brenda going to call the police?

"All right, then!" Brenda's voice was both tearful and furious. "I'm leaving. I supported you through your coming out. You used me—now you don't want me. I won't be back. Damn you, you bitch. You'll never find anyone else who will love you as much as I do. I hope you die alone." She slammed the door as hard as she could, a muffled thud accompanied by clanking chains.

Cecilia ran over to the window and looked out, watching the sidewalk, hoping to catch a glimpse of Kellen's lover.

A beautiful black woman came out of the building and walked away, wiping her eyes on her shirttail.

My God. Kellen had gone home, admitted she was gay and in love with an African American. She was not just gay; she loved across racial bounds. Cecilia's aunt and uncle were prejudiced against any person of color, and Cecilia's admiration for her cousin's courage rose—and her own cowardice broke her. Cecilia sank back onto the couch, pulled the throw over her head and wallowed in guilt and darkness.

The darkness was growing...

Kellen woke.

She was still in her clothes in the chair beside the bed, tense, sweaty, cold and cramped beneath the patterned throw.

The darkness was *not* growing. In fact, the room's automatic night-light provided enough illumination to see the outlines of the furniture and walls. She pulled her phone out of her pocket, checked for internet, and when she saw it pop up, she sighed in relief. She stretched her stiff muscles. In the daytime, the window looked away from the resort and the cottages and toward the dock and the Pacific Ocean. Now, on this rainy, moonless night, she saw nothing. Nothing.

Then one single bright light shone in the dark. A flashlight? A lantern?

It blinked off.

She blinked, too. Was that the remnant of a nightmare?

No, someone was out there. Lost? Alone? *Looking for the body they had lost?* She flipped off the night-light and moved through utter darkness toward the window.

The light outside came on again and swung in a circle on the ground, then up in the air.

Kellen stepped back to avoid being spotted.

Ridiculous, but automatic.

She glanced at the time. Two forty-five a.m. Whoever it was either wasn't afraid of being seen or wanted to be seen. Or their meeting hadn't occurred as they expected and they were desperate. Or...or she didn't know.

She did know the night was pitch-dark, rain rattled against the window like sleet and today they'd found a decomposing body out on the flats. Had someone found another one?

The light flashed around again.

Damn it. Annie left and less than twenty-four hours later, Kellen was up to her ass in alligators and it was hard to remember that her directive was to drain the swamp. She watched that light, willing it to go out permanently, and when that didn't happen, she cursed as only an Army officer could curse, got her Glock and strapped it into her shoulder holster, pulled her rain gear on over her clothes and headed out.

As soon as she stepped foot on the porch, the wind caught her breath and whipped it away. Sleet blew beneath the overhang and stung her face. This was going to be one fast trip out to check on…whatever. Maybe she should pretend she hadn't seen anything… But no. She owed it to Annie to find out if they'd been dealt another tragedy. Holding the handrail, she groped her way down the stairs. She took small steps toward her ATV.

A man's voice behind her said, "Don't do this."

Not a moment of hesitation. She whipped around in the turning kick Mara had been teaching her. She should have struck his throat. But she slipped and landed a strike on his hip. She kicked again, aiming high.

He blocked.

She landed a solid strike against his arm.

She attacked.

He parried.

She landed good hits, but somehow she never did enough damage to hurt him. She felt as if she was being toyed with by an expert. Or led through a training session.

No. No one was going to lead her anywhere she didn't want to go. She leaped back, out of his reach. She hoped. She pulled her Glock, released the safety, pointed and asked, "Who are you?"

"Nils Brooks." His calm voice continued, "Your drill instructor said your hand-to-hand attacks were organized, focused and deadly in a way he had seldom seen in a woman."

That knocked the breath out of her like nothing else had in

this battle. This guy, whoever he was, had tapped into her military records as far back as Army basic training. He had investigated her. Not a cheap, simple, superficial investigation; one thorough and seemingly impossible. "It's late. It's been a long day. I don't have time for games. *Who are you?*"

16

"I'm Nils Brooks of the MFAA." He waited a beat, then asked, "Ever heard of the MFAA?"

Kellen searched her memory, came up with the correct title. "Monuments, Fine Arts and Archives?"

"That's it. How did you know?"

"I saw the movie. I read the book. I...found some treasure. The MFAA is the Monuments Men." He wasn't going to fool her. "But don't tell me you're from the MFAA. The group was disbanded after World War II."

"Can you say *secret government agency*?" His voice held a trace of humor.

"No, I can't." She didn't believe it. She didn't believe him.

"Don't blame you. I came here from Washington, DC. The whole place is rife with liars, thieves and politicians. But I'm none of those things."

"You're saying you're part of a secret government agency?"

"Who else would care about a smuggling ring using Yearning Sands Resort as a delivery depot?"

"Smuggling?" She didn't stutter and she didn't shriek. Points to her.

"Those lights you saw aren't UFOs." He was nothing more than a voice in the darkness, but he wasn't trying to circle her or play her. "You've got your sidearm. Come on and we'll talk." He turned his back and headed for his cottage.

She sorted through his options, and hers.

He had been waiting in the dark. When she stepped out of her cottage, he could have attacked her, raped her, killed her. He hadn't. Obviously, that made him a gem of a man.

Her own cynicism let her know she hadn't lost herself to all sense. So she would listen, pistol in hand, and wait to see what Nils Brooks said about mysterious lights on an empty plain where today a body had been found.

She followed him to his cottage. His porch light was on; he ran up the steps, unlocked the door—no fumbling this time—opened it and walked in.

The light streamed out, an inviting square of brightness on the porch boards.

She glanced toward the dock.

That light had blinked out.

She slowly followed, keeping the Glock pointed at him.

He shed his raincoat, hung it on the rack, moved into the kitchen, filled the kettle with water and put it on the stove. He faced her, leaned against the counter and crossed his arms and his ankles.

She stood in the open doorway and studied him.

His act of aimless buffoonery had vanished. Nils Brooks actually *was* smart enough to wear rain gear and keep track of his pass card. His brown eyes were sharp, yet his glasses were nowhere in sight. The well-toned body she noted earlier now seemed less of a surprise and more of a weapon. "You've committed yourself. You might as well come in," he said.

She stepped across the threshold but hesitated about shutting the door. When he sighed, she snapped, "Pardon me if I don't want to be one of those women in the movies who hear a noise downstairs, light a candle because the power is mysteriously out and go to investigate."

He laughed.

Whoa. Those dimples.

"All right," he said. "I'll give you that."

Kellen didn't smile back. "I had never considered the possibility of smuggling here. Washington is so..."

"Wild? Free? Pure? Organic?" He did sarcasm well.

Which made her feel enough at ease to gently push the door almost shut. "Off the beaten track."

"It's Washington. Crazy weather, close to Canada, isolated and insular. There's a Coast Guard station south of here and one north, good guys, but they're spread thin and they've got a lot of jobs—water rescues, port security, defense readiness and that concern of ours, catching smugglers."

"Smuggling...what? Drugs?" Kellen's new security job got more and more onerous by the second.

"That. Immigrants. Anything the bad guys can carry, really. That's what interests the Coast Guard." His dimples disappeared. "But not the MFAA. Not me."

"No, I suppose not. Monuments, Fine Arts and Archives... We're talking about antiques, cultural treasures."

"Exactly. There's a lot of money involved in moving stolen art and looted treasure. Enough to kill for."

"Kill who?"

"That girl you found today. And Jessica Diaz. The MFAA director." The kettle started whistling. He lifted two mugs off their hooks. "What do you want? Coffee? Tea? Hot chocolate? Don't even bother with herbal. You'll need some kind of caffeine. You're not going to get any more sleep tonight."

"What's going to happen tonight?"

"We're going to talk. I'm going to fill you in on the situation."

She latched the door with her heel. Maybe she was that woman in the movie, but she didn't think so. She might not trust him, not yet, but for some reason she didn't yet know, he needed her. She placed her Glock on the end table, peeled off her rain gear and hung them beside his and seated herself in a chair facing him. She picked up her pistol and let it rest on the seat beside her hip, pointed it toward the floor.

He watched from the kitchen. "Your trust in me is touching."

"And easily revoked. I'll have broth. My body needs at least the pretense of nutrition."

"Smart." He used hot water and two dry packets to make two cups of broth. He picked them both up, so his hands were full, and gingerly placed one at her elbow. He backed away and seated himself across the room. "There. Far enough away for you to relax a little, close enough for you to shoot me if you need to."

That smile, those dimples, that *charm* irritated her. "I hope I don't need to. Now—tell me why the government would revive an agency dead for so many years."

"Look it up. You're not going to believe anything I tell you, so look it up."

Fair enough. She pulled out her phone, went online and typed in *MFAA*. Lots of World War II history, a brief note of its dissolution in 1946 and an even briefer note on its recent revival.

So it wasn't a secret agency. It was an underreported agency. Suspiciously underreported.

He leaned forward, elbows on his knees, hands clasped loosely. "Are you aware of what's happening with the world's treasured historical sites?"

"They're being looted." Kellen searched for Jessica Diaz, head of the MFAA.

"More than that. The way it used to work was—local people would search out tombs, archaeological sites, strip them of artifacts and sell them at the market for whatever they could get. The practice supplemented what was usually a poverty-stricken existence, and the pieces of art moved through a chain of resalers to end up on the shelves of wealthy collectors." He made that all sound like a good thing. "The whole operation was inefficient." He paused. "How's the research going?"

"I found Jessica Diaz, first head of the MFAA, but information gives only her date of death in the line of duty." A pretty Hispanic woman, thirty years old, soft-looking and smiling.

He nodded. "Keep researching."

Kellen typed in *Who is Jessica Diaz's MFAA successor?*

He continued, "Terrorist groups realized what a gold mine—sometimes literally—the antiquities trade could be. They could fund their armies with the money they made stripping every historical site of every ancient piece of art, literature and relic. The previously random looting became organized. The locals were either pushed out or conscripted and forced to find valuable artifacts and hand them over to the terrorists."

Google showed no answer to her question, nothing but the usual hodgepodge of internet weirdness. "You, um, don't seem to be a member of the MFAA."

"I didn't choose to post my unfortunate promotion. That would be stupid, wouldn't it?"

It would. But she didn't have to admit it out loud.

"Search for the Brooks family of Charleston, South Carolina," he said. "I'll come up."

She did as he suggested and found an old and formidable dynasty—and there he was, part of a family shot that included an elderly matriarch, a nervous-looking mother, six languid uncles, no father and enough cousins to populate a small island. Which apparently they did and had for generations among varying amounts of scandal.

Kellen flicked a glance at Nils's photo and then at his face.

NILS BROOKS:
MALE, 30S, 6', 180 LBS., BROWN HAIR (BLOND ROOTS?), BROWN EYES (COMPELLING), LONG LASHES, MILITARY HAIRCUT. NARROW JAW. DARK-RIMMED GLASSES (USED AS DISGUISE). ~~CUTE.~~ HANDSOME. ~~NERDY.~~ CONFIDENT. CLOTHING: EXPENSIVE, WELL-WORN. MEMBER OF SOUTH CAROLINA'S DISTINGUISHED BROOKS DYNASTY. GRADUATE OF DUKE UNIVERSITY. LEADER OF NEWLY RE-FORMED MFAA (AS REPORTED BY HIM).

Perhaps her background made her too suspicious.

Maybe she was smart to be suspicious. Her first impression of Nils Brooks had proved to be massively inaccurate. He had set out to deceive, and he had succeeded. In so many ways, he reminded her of Gregory… "You're saying the terrorists don't care how they achieve their goals or who or what is hurt in the process."

"Terrorists are terrorists. They want the world to go up in flames, and they don't care how it comes about."

"As long as their cause is the winner."

"Of course."

"What you're telling me is interesting. Fishy, but interesting. But the job of the MFAA in World War II was to—" she looked at her screen and read "'—to safeguard historic and cultural monuments from war damage, and as the conflict came to a close, to find and return works of art and other items of cultural importance that had been stolen by the Nazis or hidden for safekeeping.' I can't believe the MFAA in its current inception will be terrorist fighters."

"Reopening the MFAA was our idea, Jessica's and mine. The declared intention of the agency is to interrupt the flow of cash. That's the only reason we were able to convince the Feds to green-light the restoration of the agency."

Good, succinct, sensible answer. She wanted good, succinct, sensible answers, because everything she'd looked up so far checked out. But was it possible to manipulate the internet, to make everything conveniently fit? Of course it was. Lies were made truth all the time. The MFAA website was a dot-gov website, so maybe that made it supervised?

Yes, by someone in the US government.

She was so right not to trust this information.

Nils continued, "No one else in the government thought to go at the problem of terrorist funding, but I did."

"Why's that?"

"I'm an art major."

She couldn't help it. The tension in the cottage was so high and the idea of this manly man studying art was so funny—she grinned.

He didn't seem to see the humor.

She swallowed the grin and asked, "So what is *your* agenda with reopening the MFAA? Don't you want to interrupt the flow of cash to terrorists?"

"Very much so. But more than that, I want to save the museums, the tombs, the libraries. Ancient cultures should be preserved, not destroyed." He sounded a little like Indiana Jones in the *Last Crusade*. "When I went for the degree, I knew what I was getting into, job-and salary-wise, so I joined the CIA and got a graduate degree in tough guy."

"What about the Marines?"

"I served time with them on a mission."

That explained a lot. His fighting technique, his ferreting out of her military background, his ability to blend into the crowd and pass himself off as a harmless, bumbling author… Sure. CIA tough guy. He had been trained to deceive. But— "Why are you here?" she asked. "You said this was a smuggling *depot*. That means Yearning Sands Resort is one of many. Why are you here instead of—" she waved an expansive arm "—in Louisiana or Florida or San Diego or Cancún?"

He stood.

She lifted her pistol.

He retrieved a long piece of paper from the stack on the kitchen counter and held it toward her. "Here's a list of antiquities shipments that we've identified over the past five years and, if possible, what they were and where they were delivered."

She stood up, grabbed the spreadsheet, returned to her seat and studied it. "On the East Coast, it looks as if most art and artifacts were European or Middle Eastern in origin and delivered to wealthy collectors across the country. West Coast—Far Eastern and Central and South American artifacts. Makes sense."

He pulled out another spreadsheet, handed it to her. "Here's a list of the bodies we've found and approximate dates of their deaths." He sat back down. "We assume others are undiscovered."

She examined the list. Eight bodies over the past five years, on both coasts, in remote coastal areas off the beaten track. She compared the two lists. "Huh. The center of the action seems to be here."

He leaned back in his seat and radiated satisfaction. "That's what Jessie saw, too. What I saw."

"With shipments coming in on both coasts—"

"Which we at first didn't recognize."

"—and a murder here and a murder there..."

"We couldn't see a pattern for a long time."

"It's not certain."

"It is if we all saw it. That's why I decided to bring you in. I've read your profile. You can put it all together."

Yes, she could. "Who's in charge of the smuggling?" she asked.

17

"That is the question I'm here to answer." Nils hitched forward. "The ultimate end of all looted antiquities is in the home of a wealthy collector or a private museum. The wealthy don't deal with terrorists. They fear, and rightly, that *they* could end up on the auction block being held for ransom. The wealthy want to deal with reputable smugglers."

"An oxymoron."

"Not at all. The terrorists aren't the most terrifying part of the chain. Worldwide smuggling is controlled by one man—or woman—a ruthless bastard who brooks no opposition." Nils looked taut, determined and darned cute when he said, "He is, or she is, called the Librarian."

"The Librarian? That doesn't sound too tough."

"Neither did the Godfather."

She would give him that.

"The Librarian controls a huge network of smugglers on both US coasts. He has a reputation of loving books. Collects all kinds of literature. Antique books. Scrolls. First editions. Hieroglyphics."

"Not to be sexist, but the Librarian seems female."

"The Librarian killed Priscilla Carter."

"And you know that because...the Librarian leaves a calling card." She looked down at her own fingers curled protectively over her palms. "He cuts off his victims' hands. One assumes that's not easy and pretty gross. Which means we're probably dealing with a *male* serial killer?"

"The profile would indicate a male, yes, but not a serial killer in the traditional sense. These are retribution killings, according to the leaks of information from the smuggling world."

"Retribution for...?"

"A person who works for the Librarian decides to set up business for himself and steal a shipment. Maybe she picks up a souvenir for her own shelf. Or someone stumbles into a drop and becomes a witness and a liability." Nils was angry. So angry.

Kellen regulated her breathing, in and out, in and out, slow and calm. It wouldn't do to show alarm. She didn't want to show weakness. Because even now, she didn't quite trust him. "Did Jessica Diaz become a witness?"

"Two weeks ago I was in Pakistan, following a lead. Jessie called to tell me she had a break in the case. She had found an informant. Don't make the mistake of thinking Jessie was weak or stupid. She followed me from art school to the CIA. She was a dangerous woman. Intelligent, a punishing fighter. When I got back, she hadn't been to work. I went looking. I found her at her desk in her home in Maryland with her neck broken."

Kellen had half expected to hear of Jessica's death in some faraway land. But at her desk? In Maryland? Caused by a broken neck? Everything about yesterday and this night had chilled her, but this information brought home all the dangers that stalked the resort.

"Whoever got her was good. Experienced. No sign of forced entry, so she knew her attacker." He pressed his flat palms hard onto his knees. "Her place was swept clean. All technology had been lifted. All online information had been wiped. And her hands..."

Kellen had suspected. Even so, his flat pronouncement gave this whole surreal scene a framework. She watched Nils's face and listened to his voice, dark, deep, menacing, and felt a sick sense of horror.

"The Librarian did this. Or someone who does the Librarian's bidding. Jessica was a friend as well as a colleague and I promise you—I will make whoever did this very sorry."

Kellen checked to make sure her Glock was close at hand, then sought clues, sought truth. "You found her. Maybe *you* were looking for a promotion."

She expected him to get angrier.

Instead, she caught him taking a sip of broth. He laughed, choked, and when he caught his breath, he said, "Art and antiquities get no respect, and art majors even less. The MFAA is on trial, with just enough funding for two people. Jessica won the flip for the title of director. My promotion did not give me a raise, and frankly, getting a replacement for a second person is going to be a bitch. Who's going to work for no money, the pleasure of rescuing lost antiquities and the chance of ending up dead of a broken neck…and minus their hands?"

"Removing their hands sounds like something the Egyptians would have done to thieves so they would suffer in the afterlife."

"Interesting theory." His eyes narrowed. "Possible in a weird way. The Librarian does, after all, deal with antiquities and to all intents and purposes knows their purpose and worth. He most probably has a formidable grasp of history and perhaps is willing to use its lessons."

Kellen's watch vibrated. She looked at it in horror and leaped to her feet. "It's five thirty a.m. I've got to go!"

He looked at his watch, too. "You…have an appointment?"

"Worse than that." Kellen stashed her firearm in its holster. "I'm supposed to meet Mara for our run to the resort."

Now he looked out the window, where he could see nothing. "Are you crazy? It's dark. The weather stinks. It hasn't stopped raining since I got here."

"I know. I won't have time for kickboxing class this morning. Too much to do." Kellen pulled on her rain gear. "Mara will conniption when I tell her."

"Does she conniption often?"

"Only when I have too much work to keep up with her fitness demands. I'm her best sparring partner."

"She wants you to keep her in fighting shape?"

"She's been accepted by the International Ninja Challenge. She's getting in shape to compete."

"So she's a really good fighter?" Nils Brooks pulled himself to his feet.

"Fabulous fighter."

"But she wants to be on TV. Glare of publicity, all that?"

Kellen opened the door. The wind roared into the room, rustling the spreadsheets. "All the publicity. She intends to win the competition."

"I don't know if that makes her more of a suspect or less."

"I don't know, either." She stopped. Turned to face him. "I have a question for you. I'm smart enough. What if it's me?"

"It's damned hard to run a smuggling ring from a war zone with the Army directing your every move and a certain general and his aide keeping you under observation with the intention of using you for code breaking."

He'd heard about that, had he? Nils Brooks knew too much, and she didn't know enough. So she went fishing. "I have another question. If you're trying to crack a smuggling ring, what are you doing in here? Shouldn't you be out in the dark and the storm spying on the smugglers, seeing who they are, what they're doing?"

"I didn't come to disable the smuggling. It's not as simple as that."

"That *would* interrupt the flow of cash."

"Only temporarily, and only at this site. No. My ultimate goal is, must be, to identify and capture the Librarian. He—or she—isn't going to be the one out there collecting the goods or doing a drop-off. That's what flunkies are for." He reached into his pocket, pulled out his black-rimmed glasses and slipped them on with the seeming confidence of Superman disappearing behind Clark Kent's disguise. "I'm the author with writer's block who wanders the resort looking for inspiration in all the wrong places and observing everyone with a profiler's eye."

"Okay."

"Okay?" She'd managed to surprise him.

"That's what I figured. I wanted to hear you say it. I have to go. At this moment, I'm way more afraid of Mara than I am of the Librarian. Later!" Kellen jumped off his porch.

He called, "Think about suspects!"

She lifted her hand. Rain splattered her in the face. Somewhere behind the roiling storm clouds, dawn was breaking. She started down the path to her cottage, thinking, *Race to the resort, shower and change, call and check on Annie.* And Leo. But mostly Annie. Then—

"Kellen!" Mara stood under the light on Kellen's porch, clothed in her close-fitting, water-shedding running gear. "What were you doing out at this hour?"

"Nils Brooks got lost on the way to his cottage." Which was the truth.

"He doesn't seem to be very bright."

"Agreed." Anybody who arrived alone to seek out a murderous smuggler didn't get a gold star for smarts, at least not on Kellen's chart.

"Do you like him?" Mara sounded anxious.

"No." Not him, nor his astute observations and his blunt way of attacking. "Hang on. Let me duck in here and we'll get going." Inside, she shed her clothes and stashed her pistol. She pulled on her running gear, then hurried out to meet Mara. She said, "I can't do kickboxing this morning. Too much to do, not enough sleep. Maybe tomorrow. Let's run!" She leaped off her own porch and headed along the lighted pathways, headed toward the behemoth of a hotel where her day would begin.

After a minute, Mara was running at her heels, shouting, "How do you expect me to win the International Ninja Challenge if you're not dedicated to my cause?"

"Determination!" Kellen shouted back. "Yours!" Today she didn't allow Mara to set the pace. Not today. Today Kellen was in charge.

18

Kellen stomped her way through the morning, taking on the battling chefs and banging their heads together until they promised to cooperate, calling the security idiots on the carpet and discussing the spa schedule with a sulky Mara. She told Chad Griffin the weather was due to clear, so he would want to be on his way, and the thoroughly offended pilot cleared out. Finally, she sought Sheri Jean to discuss the current and delicate employee relations.

In between conferences, she reflected that she should go sleepless more often. Problems seemed to melt away when she ceased trying to solve employee issues and told them to handle their jobs with the competence for which they were hired.

Now if she could just get Lloyd Magnuson to answer his phone, she'd straighten him out, too. Take Priscilla's body up to the Virtue Falls coroner and not call in with a report. Could he be more inconsiderate?

In passing, she glimpsed Nils, glasses on, earnest expression in place, interviewing the various members of the staff for his "book."

She found Sheri Jean in the lobby speaking with two of their guests, a middle-aged black woman from San Francisco and her teenaged daughter.

Sheri Jean smiled at Kellen in a clenched teeth sort of way and introduced her. "This is Mrs. Kazah and her daughter, Jasmine. These two ladies would like to check out two days early. I explained we have a policy of, in these circumstances, keeping the room deposit, but they have expressed unhappiness about the storms. I thought perhaps you could okay the change of policy."

Kellen smiled at the thirteen-year-old Jasmine. "The weather has been ghastly, hasn't it?"

"It's dark all the time, not just cloudy, but night lasts for hours! And hours! The hotel is so empty it's spooky. Is it always like this?" Jasmine asked.

"It's my first year here, but they tell me this winter's storms have been unusually ferocious." Kellen put her hand on Sheri Jean's shoulder and ignored Sheri Jean's flinch of rejection. "Of course we'll refund the deposit."

"I do like the food here!" Jasmine stared toward the lobby, where Frances was putting out a plate of cookies, a bowl of apples and some finger sandwiches, and she sounded a lot more like the adolescent she was.

"Then you'd better go get a little more before you move on with your vacation!" Kellen said.

Mrs. Kazah watched her daughter leave, then in a low voice said, "I appreciate this. We really can't afford this resort at any other time of the year, and we would stay, but news of the murder rattled Jasmine and she had nightmares. After the divorce, she's grown so sensitive to atmosphere—and it is very dark and quiet here. So many empty corridors."

Sheri Jean thawed a little. "I understand. Do you have someplace else to go?"

Mrs. Kazah said, "I saw a motel in Cape Charade and thought maybe—"

Sheri Jean and Kellen exchanged horrified glances. The Cape Charade Motel was known for drug deals and bedbugs and was no place for a woman and a child.

Sheri Jean leaped into action. "We have an arrangement with

Virtue Falls Resort. It's a beautiful place, an old boutique hotel north of here about three hours. If that interests you, we can call and get you a room."

Sheri Jean herded the lady to the reception desk and returned to Kellen. "The Kazahs aren't the only ones to be spooked by Priscilla's murder. I lost Lewis from the concierge desk and Lena from guest services, and it's not as if I was overstaffed to start with."

"What are they afraid of?"

"Rumors are saying Priscilla's hands were cut off."

Kellen had told only Mara. But Lloyd and Temo had known. Maybe they'd gossiped. Or maybe the killer had spread the word to sow uneasiness.

Kellen had to discover the truth about the murder before the staff, minimal as it was, panicked. She had promised Annie she would keep the resort running. She had promised herself a home. Murder and smuggling were nothing more than a challenge. She'd faced worse in her life.

Sheri Jean continued, "It's dark and it's cold. The hotel is big and empty." She shrugged as if trying to dislodge a phantom's cold hand on her neck. "It's creepy. Have you heard anything specific about Priscilla's remains?"

Kellen gave a smile that showed too many gleaming white teeth. "I haven't heard a word from Lloyd Magnuson, and his phone goes right to voice mail."

Sheri Jean made a disgusted sound. "When Lloyd goes to Virtue Falls, he visits and eats and drinks. When Mike Sun calls with the results of the autopsy, Lloyd will sober up. Eventually, he'll get around to giving you a call."

"It's really too bad I don't have him here right now. He'd be sober when I was done with him."

Sheri Jean took a step back. "You, um, don't suffer fools lightly, do you?"

"Not when we're dealing with murder."

"I saw that cloth and that shoe and the ring. But it's so hard to believe." Sheri Jean gestured at the lobby, warm, gracious, the epitome of hospitality. "Nobody liked Priscilla, but she wasn't *that* bad. She wasn't worth killing."

Kellen watched Sheri Jean as she said, "Maybe she got into something she shouldn't have."

"That's possible. She wanted whatever she couldn't have." Sheri Jean looked both impatient and sorry.

Kellen couldn't discern anything from that. "Is there anyone you can call to cover for Lewis and Lena?"

"I need someone to serve at tonight's Shivering Sherlocks event." Sheri Jean eyed Kellen. "Carson Lennex is hosting. Have you been up to the penthouse?"

"No. But I'm functioning on three hours of sleep and—"

"I already told Carson you had agreed to do it."

Kellen could hardly contain her irritation. "You suggested me to Carson Lennex?"

"Actually, he suggested *you* to *me*. I believe he likes you."

Kellen's heart sank. "Likes me?"

"Don't worry. He never plays footsie with the staff—Priscilla Carter tried to get him involved in a romp, and that's one of the things that got her in trouble. But he does have staff he prefers to deal with. I'm one of them." Sheri Jean settled into smug satisfaction. "Apparently you are likely to be another. It's a good thing—I promise."

Kellen was too tired to be diplomatic. "Why?"

"He's interesting, he's genuine, he never asks for much in the way of labor, he has great friends and throws fabulous parties."

And he steals toilet paper. Kellen sealed her lips tightly over that one.

Sheri Jean continued, "Look, this year he's involved with the Shivering Sherlocks and their little game. He's paying for the party, he'll pose for photos with them and Lord knows he's not getting anything out of it except a chance to chat with a bunch of older women. I swear, the man is almost too good to be true."

Sheri Jean didn't often enthuse. In fact, enthusing was the opposite of Sheri Jean's usual behavior, and that alone increased Kellen's suspicions.

Kellen said, "All right. I'll serve."

Sheri Jean indicated Jasmine, who was making inroads into the finger sandwiches. "You'd better have some lunch."

Nils Brooks joined Jasmine at the side table and grabbed an apple and a cookie, then with a glance at Kellen and Sheri Jean, he ducked away.

"Authors," Sheri Jean said in disgust. "I thought he was going into isolation to write a book, but every time I turn around, he's here talking to somebody who could be doing real work."

"Writer's block," Kellen said.

"I don't get it. If you want to write a book, just write it." Sheri Jean shrugged him off. "Now, you—you look like death."

Kellen winced.

Sheri Jean said, "Sorry. But this is the first time since I've been here that we've discovered a body."

Her words brought up the memory of those scattered bones, and Kellen found her knees getting a little wobbly.

Sheri Jean tsked, put her hand under Kellen's arm and steered her toward the food. "Annie and Leo don't expect you to work miracles, you know."

"I know!" Now Sheri Jean was being nice. *So* out of character!

"The resort will get along fine without you for a few hours. You need to find a bed and crash. Lucky you're in a hotel, hmm?"

As Kellen made her way to Annie's office, she considered one simple truth: except for the honeymooners and the Shivering Sherlocks, almost everyone in this resort was a murder and smuggling suspect. While she was serving in the penthouse, she would take the chance to snoop around about Carson Lennex. She thought of the urbane, charming actor and chuckled.

As if someone as famous as Carson Lennex could ever be the Librarian.

Kellen sank onto the couch. She ought to work on tomorrow's scheduling, but she was so tired the world was spinning, and every once in a while, she caught sight of something out of the corners of her eyes that when she looked, wasn't really there: Priscilla's ghost, or a murderous smuggler, or maybe an old memory that refused to be vanquished.

She withered back onto the cushions, tucked a pillow under her head and...

Cecilia knew she needed to go out into the city, to get familiar with the area, to take care of herself. To learn how to be Kellen.

Instead, she hid, avoiding television, internet and, most of all, human contact. Inevitably, she ran out of food. She was used to being hungry—Gregory had sometimes locked the cupboards—but she couldn't die here. Not after the crimes that had been done in her name. She had to go out.

She prepared carefully, gathering Kellen's grocery bags, her grocery cart, using the computer to review the route to the store. For the first time in two weeks, she descended the stairs, and as she did, the office door snapped open. A short, stout woman hustled out, eyes snapping in annoyance, envelopes and catalogs spilling from her hands. Mrs. del Sarto, Cecilia assumed.

"Miss Adams, in the future if you're going to be gone for this long would you please stop your mail so it doesn't clutter up my office and it looks as if Cityflix is still charging you so you'd better call them again and your girlfriend was here every day crying about you so would you please return her messages?" Mrs. del Sarto talked without drawing breath and manhandled the mail into one of the grocery bags hanging on Cecilia's arm. As she straightened, she stared at Cecilia's face.

Cecilia tensed and the refrain ran through her mind, Not Kellen. She knows. Not Kellen. She knows.

Mrs. del Sarto said, "The TV was telling the truth. You were there at that explosion in Maine. You look shell-shocked. You know the police are looking for you, right?"

Cecilia shook her head.

"They want to hear your version. Some of the people in that town say it's a murder/suicide, but that guy's family says you had something to do with it."

"No. No!" Cecilia backed away. "I didn't. Please don't…tell anyone I'm here. I want to be alone."

"I mind my own business." But Mrs. del Sarto wore a pinched, pleased expression as if she'd discovered a vein of gold. "You're going shopping? You could pick up a few things for me. Which store are you going to?"

Vivid scenarios filled Cecilia's mind: the press discovering her at the grocery store, or worse, her return back here to the lobby clogged with police and reporters. "I'm not going out."

Mrs. del Sarto pointed. "You have your cart."

"I need to put this mail away. Then I… I have to go call Cityflix." Cecilia backed toward the stairs. "I'll be on hold for hours."

"That's true." Mrs. del Sarto was patently displeased. "But you'll have to come down sooner or later."

Sooner. Before the police knocked on her door and demanded entrance. Upstairs, Cecilia repacked the suitcase and computer. She gathered cash and credit cards and put them in her wallet, then shoved the wallet into the back pocket of her jeans. She carefully stowed Kellen's important documents—passport, driver's license, diplomas and birth certificate—in Kellen's travel wallet and hung it around her neck. In less than ten minutes she was out the door, on the street and headed toward the rail station.

New York was no longer safe for her.

Next stop: Philadelphia.

19

Kellen gasped, came awake, opened her eyes wide.

Philadelphia.

New York's Grand Central Terminal south to Philly's 30th Street Station. Mugged and lost everything except her cousin's papers—driver's license, diplomas, which she had strapped under her clothes.

No money. No credit cards. Afraid to speak to the police, to make claims on Kellen's accounts. Months on the streets, cold, desolate, her best friend a sharp pair of scissors. Then...then there was the child, the sobbing little girl and the man who was hurting her...

Cecilia got so angry!

Kellen didn't remember anything else. She dug the heels of her palms into her eyes. She did not remember anything else... until she woke in the hospital.

What had she forgotten? More than a year gone from her life. What had she done?

The phone on Annie's desk rang. Kellen stared at it, then leaped to answer.

"Kellen. Kellen, dear, I'm so much better." Annie's voice sounded excessively chipper.

Kellen collapsed onto the desk chair. "Thank God. Leo said you were very ill. We kept you in our prayers."

"Those prayers helped, because I'm fine now. How are things

going at the resort? I trust everything is well!" Okay. Annie's voice was definitely too chipper.

"Nothing we can't handle." Although Lloyd Magnuson hadn't yet called. "Are you still in the hospital?"

"The people at the hospital are *so* nice to me. The family is visiting a lot and Leo is such a lovey-dovey. Aren't you, Leo?" Annie made some kissing noises.

Suddenly Leo was on the line. "Sorry about that demonstration of affection. She is better, much better, so I left to grab a little to eat, her morphine has kicked in and how she managed to dial the phone in her condition..." He lowered his voice. "I'm sorry about last night. I didn't mean to be so—"

"Not to worry. I completely understand."

"Whose, um..." Leo's voice regained volume. "I'm out in the corridor. She can't hear me. Last night you said you found a corpse at the resort?"

"Priscilla Carter."

"She didn't ditch us, she's dead? Of natural causes?"

Kellen swiveled around and looked out at the night that had so swiftly fallen. "Murder."

"Who...? Where...? How...?" Leo couldn't proceed beyond shocked stammering.

"Lloyd Magnuson took the remains to the coroner in Virtue Falls, but I haven't heard back from him and his phone is going to voice mail." Kellen let her frustration be known. "It's dark and it's cold and everyone's looking at each other and wondering who did it. We've lost guests and employees over the news. I had hoped getting the facts from Mike Sun might help ease the tension." Although nothing would ease her tension. Nils Brooks had taken care of that. "Do you think if I called Mr. Sun...?"

"He can't release the information to you. I'll take care of it. He knows me from way back, and they found Priscilla on Di Luca property. I'll let you know when he fills me in. I'm sorry,

Kellen. You know Annie and I would never have left if we had imagined something like this would happen."

"Would it be possible to summon Mr. Gilfilen back from vacation? I'm ill equipped to lead the security team at any time, much less while I'm managing the resort."

A pause. "Mr. Gilfilen can't return. It's not possible."

She voiced her vague suspicion. "Look, if he's somewhere close, could I contact him?"

"No! God, no."

So he *was* somewhere close. "Leo, really. This is an emergency."

Leo said, "Perhaps... Well, let me think. Other security personnel work for the Di Lucas. Let me see if I can find someone to send." Another short pause. "Annie's calling me. We'll get in touch with you tomorrow." He hung up.

Kellen looked at the phone, then placed it in its cradle. If she looked, she could probably find Mr. Gilfilen. He might be somewhere on the grounds, or maybe enjoying the great Washington coast...although that seemed out of character. But what good would tracking him down do? She knew Mr. Gilfilen well enough to know he would do what he would do, and nothing could alter his course.

Hell, maybe he was the Librarian.

The events of the previous day and night had acquired a stained veneer of disbelief and distrust. She looked at everyone—employees, guests, workmen—and wondered who they were beneath their everyday masks.

Her watch alarm vibrated on her wrist. She looked at her scheduler.

Time to pick up the appetizers for the Shivering Sherlocks event and do a little sleuthing of her own.

Max Di Luca walked down the hospital corridor toward Annie's room. Today the news was good; she had survived the night and rallied. At breakfast, the whole Di Luca family had at last begun their late Christmas celebration with scrambled eggs and cheese, crisp bacon, fruit salad—and Aunt Sarah's chocolate chip cookies. Now Max had been sent to remove Leo from his post at Annie's side. Of course. Max was aggressive, decisive and a former football running back, hence when a possible challenge loomed, he was sent to take care of it. The family called him the Di Luca enforcer. They were joking. Mostly.

But as he approached Annie's room, he saw Leo sitting in a plastic chair, elbows on his knees, hands over his face.

Max's heart squeezed in fear. He rushed to Leo and knelt beside him. "Leo? What's wrong? Is Annie…?"

Leo lifted his head. He looked worn to the bone and hopeless. "Annie's better. She really is."

Max sat back on his heels. "Then what's wrong?"

"As soon as we left the resort, everything there went to hell in a handbasket."

Max stood up, pulled a chair close and asked sympathetically, "Another incompetent assistant manager?"

"No, she's great. Efficient, intelligent, wants nothing more than to work all the time. She's taken a huge load off Annie's shoulders and mine."

"So what's the problem?"

Leo looked grimly at Max. "Yesterday they found the *first* assistant manager."

Max leaped to the inevitable conclusion. "Dead?"

"Murdered. Kel… The assistant manager called and told me last night, but last night I didn't care. Today I care. Priscilla, that poor, stupid girl, dead. At our resort. Who would do such a thing?"

Max asked the next logical question. "What does Mr. Gilfilen say?"

"He's sort of on vacation."

"Sort of? While you're gone?" Had Leo and Annie gone senile?

"We're having security problems at the resort."

Nope, obviously not senile. "Murder and…?"

"Smuggling." Leo filled Max in on the details of what Mr. Gilfilen suspected.

"Probably connected, then." Max straightened his shoulders. "So while you're here, you—or rather, your new assistant manager—needs someone with security experience on-site. In this situation, you have to have someone who you trust, and you know I've got the experience that you need." He stood. "I'll go."

Leo straightened his shoulders right back. "Don't be ridiculous. It's the Di Luca Christmas. You have other responsibilities."

"Rae will understand." Max lifted his hand to stop any further objections. "We already had our private Christmas on December twenty-fifth, and when she's here in the midst of the family, I hardly see her. I'll explain it to her, and you know her—she has a generous spirit. She *will* understand."

Leo stood and faced off with Max. "*You* don't understand. It's not that easy."

"Of course it is." Max was used to being right, and to getting his way. "I'll leave today."

"First come and see Annie. She has things to say to you about the new assistant manager."

"So there *is* something wrong with her."

"Max! Stop jumping to conclusions! It's not her. It's *you*."

Max took a step back. Leo was always loud—he was slightly deaf—but never so emphatic. "Leo, what's wrong?"

Leo opened the door to Annie's room.

Annie's happy voice floated out, "Max, dear! So good to see you!"

Leo stepped in. "Max wants to go to handle security at the resort."

"That's a good idea! Except…" Annie's voice lost its euphoria. "Oh, dear."

Max could not imagine what was wrong with Leo and Annie. Of course, he didn't have much of an imagination. "I don't understand."

"There's no way you could." Leo gestured him in. "Go, sit down with Annie and listen."

20

Kellen hurried down to the kitchens, where the chefs were getting along admirably—the calm before the storm?—gathered the two waiting cardboard boxes and walked to the elevator that led to Carson Lennex's penthouse.

Each penthouse had its own elevator. She stepped in and took the direct trip from the lobby to the eighth floor. The elevator doors opened and Kellen stepped out into a small entry. She walked through the open double doors into the penthouse entry, where a curvaceous staircase led to the bedroom level, then went into the luxurious living room. The furniture was minimalistic: leather, steel and stone. Splashes of color lit the paintings on the wall, and on the fireplace mantel, bizarre clay art forms writhed. Shelves with well-read books and illuminated glass art lined one wall. Interesting. Kellen would have never suspected Annie would decorate the penthouses so eccentrically.

Carson Lennex stood behind the bar pouring wine and mixing drinks.

The Shivering Sherlocks were in costume, clustered around him, laughing and talking.

One of them was stretched out flat on the floor in front of the fireplace.

Kellen hurried over and knelt beside her. Patty. It was Patty dressed as Hercule Poirot. "Are you all right?"

Patty opened one eye. “I was just poisoned. Now they have to figure out who did it.”

“Oh.” Kellen settled back on her heels. “Oh. While you’re dead, would you care for an appetizer?”

Patty opened both eyes. “What have you got?”

Kellen peeked inside the first box and read the labels. “Wine-marinated frozen grapes, smoked salmon with capers on pumpernickel, rainbow fruit kabobs with yogurt fruit dip and, oh jeez, toast swords tipped with hummus-cide.” She looked seriously at Patty. “The hummus-cide is made from beets. It’s red.” And a little gruesome, considering the events of the past days, but this was a murder mystery weekend and she supposed the chef was allowed a bit of whimsy.

Certainly Patty laughed. “I’ll have one of each.”

“Let me set up and I’ll be back to you right away.”

Patty caught her wrist. “Me first. I’m dead, and once those piranhas descend, I’ll never get my share.”

Mr. Lennex knelt on the other side of Patty and slid two couch pillows under her head. “She’s right,” he said to Kellen. “Better feed her now.”

“I can always order up more,” Kellen pointed out.

“Then you can feed me later, too.” Patty rubbed her naturally expansive padding.

Mr. Lennex fetched a small square plate and a silver spoon and fork wrapped in a linen napkin.

Kellen loaded the plate and handed it to Patty, then made her way to the copper-topped dining table and created an oasis of artful mystery weekend food. The living ladies descended, and as Patty had predicted, they picked the trays clean.

“Egyptian scarab beetles,” she called from the floor.

Tammy confided to Kellen, “Usually we buy a mystery weekend package that includes the script—who dies, who’s the killer and why, and we open the envelopes as we go. But Carson Lennex has seen us come year after year and this time he’s the one passing out the clues. We're in ancient Egypt. I'm so glad. I do love a good Egyptian mystery!"

Kellen looked at their early-and mid-twentieth century costumes and raised her eyebrows.

"We didn't know our setting until we got here," Debbie explained.

Candy joined them. "The great thing about having Carson in charge is we have lines to read."

From the floor, they heard, "All my lines consisted of *Argh*, and then death."

"It was a very realistic death." Carson went into his study, came out with his Academy Award and handed it to Patty. "And the award goes to..."

"Now she's going to give a speech," Rita said in resignation.

"Damned right I'm going to!" Patty sat up. "I've been rehearsing this my whole life!"

"Lie down," Carson instructed. "You can give a speech, but you're still dead."

While Patty thanked the Academy and all the little people who contributed to her success, Kellen inched toward the bookshelves and examined the contents.

Carson joined her. "No need to listen. I've heard a few of these speeches in my day. Although she is pitch-perfect."

Kellen indicated the swath of hardcovers. "Egypt?"

"Mesopotamia, Greece, Rome, Persia, China, the Mayans and the Aztecs... I love the romance of ancient civilizations, and I came this close to finishing an archaeology degree." He chuckled and with his fingers indicated a short distance.

Archaeology. Really. She looked sideways at him. "What happened?"

"When I was twenty, the department sent me on a dinosaur dig. In the summer. In Utah. My God, what a miserable place. Desert in the middle of nowhere, dirt in my teeth, dried rations, no liquor, certainly no romantic ancient civilizations..."

He stepped back from her. "Are you well? You look a little stupefied."

"I didn't get much sleep last night." *I was listening to the single remaining Monuments Man who is searching for a mass murderer who also might do well with an archaeology degree.*

"You carry the weight of responsibility for the resort, so I hear." He smiled with all the charm of an aging roué. "Leo and Annie have a good staff. Depend on them to do their work and you'll be fine."

"Thank you. I'll remember that."

Patty proclaimed, "And now, the award for best director—Carson Lennex!"

"Excuse me, I'm being paged." He gave a little nod to Kellen and went to accept his Academy Award back.

Kellen stared after him. His face had graced movie screens across the world. He was self-deprecating, friendly in the cautious way of any celebrity, going out of his way to charm the Shivering Sherlocks. Although she had wondered at his decision to remain in Washington for the winter, she had never doubted his intelligence. Staying afloat for forty-five years in the entertainment business required a keen mind and a strong survival instinct, two talents that would serve him well...if he was the Librarian.

"Look!" Rita pointed out the wide window. "The storm is gone!"

"A pristine night!" Carson threw open the sliding double doors.

The ocean-chilled breeze swept in, and everyone, even Patty the Dead, crowded onto the wraparound balcony.

The night sky was absolutely black with a crescent moon and stars so big and close they could hypnotize a romantic.

Luckily, every romantic sinew and nerve in Kellen's body had been transformed to steel, and she took the opportunity to see what Carson Lennex viewed from his penthouse.

This would be the ideal location for the Librarian. From here, the resort was laid out like a map: the marriage grove to the north and east; the ocean, beach and dock to the west; the lighted paths, the wings of the hotel and the cottages scattered like gems across the landscape. She looked toward the cliffs, half expecting to see another flash of light, but all was dark and still.

Then, in the farthest end of the darkened west wing, a door opened, and in the square of light, a thin man was silhouetted. He bent, put something down, stepped back and shut the door again.

Lloyd Magnuson. That damned policeman wasn't just working in the west wing, he was also hiding out there, cell phone off to avoid speaking to her.

He was going to be sorry.

21

Kellen turned on her heel. "I should refresh the appetizers," she said and briskly arranged what was left on one plate, took the empty tray and left. On the way down, she contacted Sheri Jean. "I've done the first shift. Send someone up with the next round of food and drink." Sheri Jean started to object, and Kellen said, "No. I've neglected my security duties and now there's a problem."

Sheri Jean wanted to question her.

Firmly, Kellen hung up and steamed through the occupied part of the hotel into the dark and quiet west wing. She flipped on the tactical flashlight that Birdie had given her, and fantasized about using the serrated head to put a divot in Lloyd Magnuson's chin. The corridor was a maze of old drapes piled beside a stack of new, uninstalled doors, half-used cans of varnish and paint, rolls of new carpet covered by a fine sprinkling of sawdust and irritation. The irritation was her own.

Not only was Lloyd abusing his privileges by staying at the resort—he reminded her of Chad Griffin—but with the resort staff worried about the murder and guests checking out, it was callous of him to leave them stewing about the coroner's report.

She got to the end of the corridor, to the luxury suite that had one door that opened into the hotel and another that opened onto a private patio. That was the door she'd seen open and close from above. The suite had a doorbell; she rang it, pounded on the door, then decided she didn't care if she caught Lloyd in his underwear, she was going in. In fact, she hoped she caught him in a compromising act with a blow-up doll. The embarrassment would serve him right.

She inserted her pass card in the lock.

Before she could turn the handle, the door opened, yanking the card from her fingers, and she found herself staring at dark eyes, hair and skin, bony body—Vincent Gilfilen.

She had jumped to the wrong conclusion.

"Miss Adams, good to see you. I'm on vacation." He extracted her pass card from the door and handed it back. "What are you doing here?"

"I was in Carson Lennex's suite. I saw someone open the outside door and I thought it was… Never mind. You're not on vacation." Shock gave way and her brain began to click. She considered his personality and his habits. She considered the odd way Leo had sounded when she asked about Mr. Gilfilen. And she knew she was right. "You're dressed to go outside, Mr. Gilfilen. What are you doing outside at night? Or should I guess?"

In that coolly polite way of his, he said, "You seem to think you know."

"You're investigating a smuggling ring."

"Investigating? Or leading?"

Not an answer. Not really. He was probing to discover what she knew. And she would tell him…within limits, and with the clear understanding an exchange of information could, and would, be required. "Whoever is leading this smuggling ring must travel extensively. According to your records, you never leave the resort." She gestured toward the suite. "Obviously. You're still here."

He opened the door wide.

She saw a wall of security monitors and a chair with a half-eaten meal beside it.

"You might as well come in," he said. "Let's talk."

* * *

Kellen already knew Mr. Gilfilen was a very peculiar and formal man, but visiting him in this place put the *O* in *odd*.

He gave Kellen a small glass of cabernet port—he had apparently noted not only that she liked a small glass of port in the evening, but also the brand—put a plate of Scottish shortbread cookies by her elbow, sat opposite and waited for her to initiate the conversation.

She asked what had precipitated this investigation on his part.

He explained he had gone to Leo and Annie and stated his belief that one of the Yearning Sands employees was using the dock to conduct a smuggling operation. After they got over their disbelief and dismay, he gave them his list of possible candidates.

"Who?" Kellen asked.

"That is not your concern, Miss Adams."

He'd suggested that, at such time when the guests were sparse and those employees remained at work, he would pretend to go on vacation, hide in a room he'd prepared, sleep in the daytime and go out at night.

He stated he didn't suspect her; although she had the talents, she hadn't been in the United States long enough.

While she tried to decide how she felt about that—apparently her character was suspect, but her location proved to be her alibi—he stood, opened the outer door and let in a cat. A mangy-looking, skinny cat. He dried the poor thing, carried it to a food bowl on the floor in the kitchen and fed it some kibble. "Someone dumped it on the property," he said. "They do that occasionally. When this is over, I'll find it a home."

Kellen nodded. Because of guest allergies, cats were absolutely forbidden in the main hotel building. Mr. Gilfilen was a stickler for following the rules. Yet he'd saved the cat and betrayed his position to her when he'd opened the door.

Fascinating. "You might want to dim the lights before you

open the outer door. Anyone who is looking for a reason to be suspicious will find it in that square of light."

Mr. Gilfilen nodded. "I'll remember."

He wasn't as shocked to hear about Priscilla as he should be, so Kellen knew he'd spoken with Leo. But his narrow, dark face tightened with disdain and horror when she reported Priscilla's mutilation.

He advised her on the handling of resort security personnel and let her know he was watching the monitors both inside and out. Unless he called her on an issue, she didn't really have to worry about it. That was one thing off her plate, and she was grateful for it.

Then he turned to her and demanded information.

She told him everything she should know...if she hadn't spoken with Nils Brooks. She told him what she'd seen the night before and asked if he had investigated. He admitted he had, but he had worn night goggles to help him see what was going on, and the smugglers had flashed a light in his direction and blinded him.

"So they knew you were there," Kellen said.

"I don't know if they knew someone was there, or if that's simply a precaution they employ. In the future, I should expect more professionalism from these people." He picked a piece of lint off his knee. "I originally believed this smuggling was the work of an amateur, and I saw no reason to think it wouldn't be easily handled. I now think I will be handling the situation differently."

"What do you intend to do?"

"I'll position myself in the rocks and watch for a landing. I want to know who's doing this. If I can find that out and pass the information to the Coast Guard, that will simplify their very difficult job."

"Are smugglers there every night?"

"If they were, the Coast Guard would have already arrested

them. They're watching, but—winter weather blasts the coast with one crisis after another, boaters go out in terrific storms, rescue takes precedence over smuggling and the Coasties are spread thin."

"So you're going to sit out in the rocks in the storms and the rain and the wind and the cold until you catch somebody in the act?"

"I do know how to care for myself, Miss Adams."

"Of course you do." She couldn't tell if he was sarcastic or merely austere. The cat came over and wound itself around her ankles. She absentmindedly leaned down to pet it, tried to think how best to warn him of the danger he courted. "Mr. Gilfilen, I think we can make the assumption that Priscilla ran into these smugglers and was murdered. Whoever this is, they're ruthless and cruel. I beg you, be vigilant, and if you need help, please know you can contact me and I will somehow assist you." She found herself making the offer in an imitation of his dry and formal manner. "I also know how to take care of myself."

"I appreciate that, Miss Adams. You will be the one I call." He stood and gestured her toward the door. "Now if you'll excuse me, I need to start my nightly vigil."

Right. She was being invited to leave. She gave the cat a last scratch, gave Mr. Gilfilen a nod and stepped out into the corridor.

In the darkness, surrounded by the rubbery smell of new carpet and the moldy smell of old drapes, she made a decision: her working day was officially over.

Outside, the clear sky had dropped the temperature to below freezing. Kellen went through the employee dining room, located a winter coat that was both too big and not heavy enough and headed across the grounds to her cottage. As she walked, her phone rang. She pulled it out of her pocket and looked at it.

Leo. Good news, she hoped. She answered, "Hi, Leo, how's Annie?"

"She's doing well. Sitting up, eating solids and complaining that she wants out of the hospital so the Di Luca Late and Cheery Christmas celebration can begin. The doctor promises, if she continues to do well, she can leave in the morning."

"That's wonderful. I'll let everyone know. Did you hear anything about our autopsy?"

"That's one of the things I'm calling about. I talked to Mike Sun. He hasn't seen Lloyd Magnuson. He hasn't seen a body."

Kellen stopped walking. "What? Lloyd didn't deliver?"

"I talked to Sheriff Kwinault in Virtue Falls. She hasn't heard from Lloyd Magnuson at all. She didn't know we'd found a body here."

Kellen couldn't believe it. She knew Lloyd was ill suited for the police job, but this was ridiculous. "He said he was going to inform all necessary law enforcement. Where did he take the body?"

Leo spelled it out. "No one's seen him. His phone is going to voice mail. Lloyd Magnuson has disappeared."

Kellen's exasperation turned to dread, and as it did, she pivoted and looked at her surroundings. Beyond her stretched the cold darkness that reached into space and in all directions as far as the eye could see. Yet she stood in a lighted path, a clear target for the enemy. For the cruelly deceptive Librarian. Kellen turned back toward the resort and started walking again, more briskly and with a clear destination in mind. "What do we suspect? That he ran off with the body?"

"I've known Lloyd Magnuson since he arrived in Cape Charade. He's not a master criminal. He's not even a petty thief. He might not be terribly bright, but he's honest. He wouldn't steal Priscilla's body, so..."

"So somehow he was diverted from his destination."

"Yes. Before I called, I sent a neighbor over to check his house. The door was unlocked—"

"Unlocked?"

"Cape Charade's a small town. No one locks the door unless they're having an affair."

"I guess that makes sense."

"Lloyd's not home. No sign of him, no sign of foul play. Sheriff Kwinault has alerted her officers to watch along his route."

"Okay." The situation had suddenly become a lot more tense. "Leo, do you have firearms here at the resort?"

"Yes, of course." His voice turned taut, worried. "But—"

"I'm former military. I know how to handle firearms and I'm not quick on the draw." She didn't mind giving him reassurance; having an armed employee was a serious matter and he had no idea of her shooting temperament. "I've got a Glock 21 SF that I can carry for my own safety and the safety of others at the resort. But it's too big to be easily concealed and I don't want to alarm guests or employees."

He snapped to the situation. "Yes. I understand. You need something more compact. Get Annie's keys. Go to my office..." He gave her directions to his gun safe and a list of the weapons he kept inside. He gave her permission to choose what she wanted.

"I'll be smart and careful," she said.

"I know. I trust you."

His words gave her a comfort nothing else about this day had offered. "You said there were a couple of things you called about. What was the second thing?"

"Annie wants to talk to you."

He must have thrust the phone at his wife, for Annie was on the phone at once. "Dear, I'm *so sorry* to have abandoned you in such a crisis."

"It's been exciting." Kellen kept her tone low-key. "But knowing you're better will make everyone at the resort so much happier."

"I have such a loyal staff, and I have a security solution for you. I'm sending up our great-nephew...or maybe he's our great-

great-nephew…to take Mr. Gilfilen's place until he returns from vacation."

Kellen sighed in relief.

"His name is Maximilian Di Luca." Annie paused momentously.

"I'm pleased."

"Pleased?"

Annie seemed to expect something more, so Kellen perked up her voice. "So pleased! He has experience?"

"In security? Well. Hmm. Yes. He worked his way up through the family hierarchy, including time working security, and in a family crunch situation, Maximilian is always the man to call on." Annie seemed to be fumbling for the right information to impart. "Now he's the Di Luca family's East Coast wine distributor. He has a home in Pennsylvania."

"Philadelphia? That's a long way to come. Why would he fly in from so far away?" From Philadelphia, Pennsylvania, that city of cold and dark, blood and cruelty. "That is, can't you find someone closer?"

"Maximilian's Pennsylvania home is in the Brandywine Valley. He also has a home in Oregon. He came to Bella Terra for the holiday celebration. When he learned about your situation, he volunteered to help. Max is a *wonderful* man."

Kellen knew the fact he was from Pennsylvania was no reason to prematurely dislike him. She knew that, theoretically, most of Pennsylvania was pleasant…

But not Philadelphia. It had taken her a long time to recall anything about Philadelphia, and each of those few memories were jagged shards, broken, never to be assembled again.

Philadelphia. The rumbling train, the 30th Street Station, the river, the mugging. No money. No credit cards. Months on the streets, cold, hungry, desolate, terrified.

Then the child, the sobbing little girl.

Annie's voice sounded in Kellen's ear. "Did we lose our connection?"

"No! I'm still here. I was thinking that it's kind of Mr. Di Luca to want to help, but—"

Annie interrupted, "Maximilian is competent at everything he does. He's powerful, aware, responsible, attentive. You'll see."

Nothing Annie said banished Kellen's disquiet, and in fact her emphasis on his qualities made her queasy.

"Max is taking the red-eye and he'll be there first thing in the morning," Annie finished triumphantly.

So it was too late to turn him back, and really, why would Kellen want to? Even if he wasn't All That, he'd at least take part of the burden. "Thank you, that sounds great."

"Maximilian can stay as long as he's needed. In fact, while he's there, I'm sure he'll also keep up his work for Di Luca Wines, although at this time of year, there's not much happening in the business. Now, dear, Leo says I'm babbling, so I'll get off the line. Say hello to dear Maximilian from me. I hope you two get along."

"I'm sure we will." Kellen hung up, held the phone out and looked at it.

Annie was behaving very oddly, almost guilty, definitely excited. That painkiller must be great stuff.

22

Leo's firearms collection included some real gems: an 1894 Winchester .30-30 designed by John Browning and with the name of every owner engraved on the scabbard, a Winchester model 1873 with an octagonal barrel, a Colt Single Action Army, a Smith & Wesson Model 3. Kellen passed over the antiques and chose a Ruger LC9s. Slim and accurate, it felt good in her hands, and the holster fit well under her jacket. When she had it strapped on, she looked at herself in the mirror and nodded at her reflection. Only someone with combat experience would know she was packing.

Then she ran up the stairs to the office. She turned on the computer and searched for Maximilian Di Luca. She found him on the Di Luca Wines website, with a bio so brief as to be curt. Based on the information, she started a file in her mind.

MAXIMILIAN DI LUCA:
MALE, 30S, ITALIAN AMERICAN. FORMER FOOTBALL PLAYER. CURRENTLY WORKS FOR DI LUCA WINES. STERN FACE, TANNED SKIN, BLACK SHADOW OF A BEARD, CURLY BLACK HAIR CROPPED INTO A BUSINESSMAN'S LENGTH. BROWN EYES...

She zoomed in. Long dark lashes surrounding gloriously light brown eyes... Reaching out her fingers, she almost touched the screen, then clenched her hand into a fist. His face was not familiar, but he was from Pennsylvania. If she'd met him before, she didn't remember.

Annie had behaved oddly about him. Did Annie know something she wasn't saying? Or was the danger that haunted the resort stealing Kellen's precious sanity? She'd always feared succumbing to whatever madness had taken that year from her. Had she not saved that child? Had she instead hurt the child?

That would explain…this… Kellen touched the scar on her forehead.

Oh God. She'd been through this a million times before, plucking at her mind, seeking memories. If the truth hid there, she couldn't find it, only fragments of fear and, perhaps, insanity.

She pulled up the resort employee group email, then sat with her fingers on the keys, ready to address the issue of safety…as soon as she figured out what to say. She didn't want to shout out that Lloyd Magnuson was missing when no one was sure what had happened to him. At the same time, she had to say *something*. Finally, she typed a brief note that let them know Annie was recovering, expressed her sympathy for those who had known Priscilla Carter, gave the assurance that law enforcement would investigate and that they had a new security director on his way. She included a heartfelt request that everyone be extra vigilant and take every care of themselves and others. Finally, she asked them to report to her anything they observed that struck them as peculiar, and thanked them for their continued diligence. She pressed Send, shut down the computer and the lights and sat in the dark room.

She had found herself unable to tell Mr. Gilfilen about Nils. She considered Mr. Gilfilen a trustworthy man, but she wasn't willing to jeopardize a federal sting operation based on her belief.

She knew she would not tell Nils about Mr. Gilfilen. She didn't completely trust Nils.

She didn't trust Sheri Jean. Or Mara. Most definitely not Chad

Griffin. Adrian and Mitch she believed would guard her back in a combat situation, but when it came to making a profit by whatever means? She felt a wobble in her trust-o-meter.

She couldn't even confide in Birdie or Temo. Anything she said would put them in danger. So she would say nothing. She would tell no one what she knew from any source; she remembered her aunt's favorite saying, "Of course I can keep secrets, it's the people I tell them to who can't keep them."

This news about Lloyd Magnuson changed everything. He'd gone to the Virtue Falls coroner with the body of one of the Librarian's victims…and disappeared. Sure, it was possible he'd hit the bars and run into trouble. But no one had seen him, and seriously, who went on a bender with a plastic container of rotting flesh in the trunk?

So what exactly had happened? The Librarian had disposed of Priscilla's body somewhere close to the resort on the coast, it had washed ashore, and when the identity of the body became known, the Librarian had been alarmed. Perhaps having the body examined by a coroner might somehow lead to the Librarian's identity.

Yes. What they'd discovered had worried the Librarian and made him, or her, take extraordinary measures to reacquire Priscilla's body, and what happened to Lloyd Magnuson as a result didn't matter. Except it did. The guy's only crime was being a part-time policeman.

Kellen had, she realized, cratered in on herself, erecting that familiar ice wall between herself and everyone else, the way she had after the explosion, in those traumatic days in New York and on the grim streets of Philadelphia…

Turning on the desk light, she pulled a yellow tablet close, got a pen and in her brain pulled up the files for each person she deemed a suspect. If she believed everything Nils Brooks had told her, and she more or less did, then the Librarian was one of these people. Probably. And if she or he had a couple of flunkies, they'd be on the list, too. Probably.

She jotted down each detail about each person.

Then she checked vacations. She knew when Jessica had been killed, so she looked for the employees who had been gone in January. Which was just about everybody except her, who wanted to hunker down here, and Birdie, who didn't want to go home to Detroit. Oh, and Carson Lennex had been in Machu Picchu, a fact that hadn't mattered before and now seemed grossly ominous. She weeded out a few names, but—the Librarian ran a big operation at multiple sites. What size was the Librarian's organization?

Oh. And a large number of the Yearning Sands staff were still on vacation. What if Nils was wrong and the Librarian wasn't currently here?

So many questions, and none of them easily answered.

Kellen tore off the paper and shrugged into her oversize coat, then headed down to employee dining. It was late; she needed something to eat.

There she found Temo digging through the freezer and loading ready-made dinners into a Yearning Sands Resort insulated tote bag.

"You're back!" she said. "How was LA? Did you find friends to hire?"

"No." He was brief to the point of being curt.

"Did you clear up the family situation?"

"*Sí*. Yes. Everything is fine." He didn't look as if everything was fine. He looked tired, he had two days' growth of dark beard on his chin and his scowl brought his forehead down over his eyes.

More problems in the Iglasias family, she guessed. "How's your mom and your sister?"

He looked back into the depths of the freezer, grabbed another couple of meals without looking and dropped them into the bag. "Fine. Good! Well, my mom's in prison, but other than that—"

"That's something different, isn't it?"

"First time for federal prison, *sí*, but no." He had a bitter set to his mouth. "I've bailed her out of jail more than once."

"Is your sister okay?"

"She is now." He shut the freezer a little too hard. "I placed her with relatives."

"She's okay now? You're glad you went?"

"Sí. Sí." He edged away.

"I could talk to Annie, ask if you could bring your sister to live with you."

He froze.

"You know how kind she is. She would probably say yes." Kellen's mind leaped ahead. "School would be very different for her, and you'd have to cut back on your hours, but—"

"Look, I just got back. I have to go to my cottage. I have, um, things I..."

She caught his arm. "Temo, before you unpack and do some wash, I have to ask—did you see Lloyd Magnuson put that corpse into his car?"

Temo looked at Kellen's hand, then into her face. "I loaded it into that policeman's toy car."

"Toy car?"

"He had a toy car, a Smart car. It looks like one of our golf carts, only smaller. I put the plastic box in the back."

"Then he headed toward Virtue Falls?"

Temo pointed north.

"He didn't get there. The body never got taken to the coroner. No one has seen Lloyd Magnuson."

Temo stood with his mouth half-open. Then, "He wrecked his toy car?"

"Maybe. Maybe not. No one has found him, wrecked or otherwise. Maybe whoever killed that girl went after him."

"I bet they find him wrecked somewhere." Temo sounded oddly certain.

"Why? Did he say anything that sounded off?"

Temo scratched his cheek. "He was very cheerful for someone who was driving a toy hearse."

"That's weird." She looked in Temo's bag. "You're going to eat all that tonight? Did you not eat the whole time you were gone?"

"Not much eating. It was a fast trip. Tonight, Adrian…he came over. You know him. Always hungry. I'll see you tomorrow. You don't have to worry. I'll work." Temo fled.

"I know you will," Kellen called after him. She didn't know if she was looking for trouble or whether Temo was acting weird. Maybe he was having a party and hadn't invited her. That would be so embarrassing. But not surprising, either. Since they had both left the service, the things that had bound them had vanished. They were both Americans, both retired from the Army, yet they were separated by position, race and language. Only friendship held them together, a friendship she treasured. Had she been mistaken in his affections? Did he not support her as she supported him? That would break her heart.

She poked through the freezer, collected a small square aluminum casserole marked "Dungeness crab mac and cheese." In the refrigerator, she found a bag of prepared green salad and a small container of salad dressing. She loaded them into one of the insulated tote bags, checked to see that her holster was in place and her tactical flashlight close at hand, left through the kitchen door and ran, avoiding the lighted paths, all the way to Nils Brooks's cottage.

She knocked, and when he opened the door, she said, "The way I figure it, these killings are the jurisdiction of the FBI. So why is the MFAA investigating them?"

23

Nils opened the door wide and stepped aside. "The FBI claims they haven't got a clue what's going on with these mutilation killings."

She walked in, wiped her feet on the welcome mat, shrugged off her coat, walked through his living room and into his kitchen. "So you do work with the FBI?"

"In cases of domestic crime, which this is."

She set the oven to three hundred and fifty degrees and placed the mac and cheese on the middle rack. "But you don't believe what they're telling you."

"I don't believe they're going to share information with the MFAA. To them, the MFAA is like the upstart child who babbles about its pretty antiques while the world is falling into anarchy."

"Not even when Jessica was brutally killed at her desk?"

"The FBI is investigating her death, even though she worked for the CIA." Kellen thought she could hear Nils's teeth grinding. "But the investigating office is run by a dick who's pissed that we've got a plan to shut down the smuggling depots and he didn't get invited in as the lead. Why would he? He doesn't know jack shit about art or artifacts or anything but brute force."

"O-kay." Bad blood there. "Mara Philippi says she talked to an old boyfriend at the FBI."

"She's pretty. Maybe *she'll* get someone to pay attention." He sounded intensely bitter.

Kellen reached into his cupboard, brought out a serving bowl, emptied the bag of salad into it. She washed her hands, then tossed the greens with her hands. She caught a peculiar expression on his face. "I know where everything is. All the kitchens are arranged the same."

"I have never seen anyone actually use their hands like salad tongs."

"Think about it. Someone in the kitchen used their hands to cut up the lettuce, celery, radishes..."

"Wearing sanitary gloves, one hopes!" Still he looked pained.

She thought about that photo of the affluent Brooks family. She suspected they had a home that included a staff and their own cook, and the idea of anyone actually touching food with their fingers would be an anathema to him. That both amused her and helped convince her of the authenticity of his personal history. "I promise I'll use utensils when I add the dressing."

"What kind of dressing?"

"What do you care? I've seen you. You've been in the resort eating all day. This is for me."

He looked even more startled and offended.

Wow. He was spoiled.

She pulled the list of possible Librarians out of her pocket and handed it over. "Here. See what you think."

He pulled a stool up to the eating bar and looked over her chart and her profiles.

"I like the pilot, too," Nils said. "Chad Griffin. In and out, travel the country, transport the goods, stay here when the weather's bad and check up on everything."

"I'm prejudiced against him because I don't like the man, but that doesn't mean he isn't the Librarian."

"Why did you put Carson Lennex above him?"

"Archaeology degree. The man knows his stuff, he has a huge

book collection, went to Machu Picchu on vacation. Which a lot of people do, but..." She shook up the simple dressing of red wine vinegar, Dijon mustard and extra virgin olive oil, drizzled it on the greens and dug in.

"Fascinating." He pulled a pen out of his pocket and scribbled a note on the list. "I would have never suspected him. He's too old and too famous. So I would have never done the research. Good job."

"Snooping pays off."

"I thought you'd include your local policeman, the guy who took the body to the coroner."

Nils was asking all the right questions. "He's disappeared."

That got Nils's attention. "When did you find that out?"

"This evening."

"Disappeared to where?"

"If we knew that, he wouldn't be disappeared." She waved him to silence and told him about Leo's call. "I was aggravated with Lloyd for not getting back to me, but now he's vanished and no one thinks he deliberately ran off with the body. Not even me, because if he's the Librarian, that would be stupid."

"It would. Foul play is suspected?"

"The sheriff has her men searching for him, but the countryside is wild and includes many places to hide someone who is kidnapped, or to stash a body." She stared into the salad and reimagined the rugged mountains, the dense forests, the long stretches of beach battered by ocean. "As we've discovered."

"So only two men made the list?"

"I do suspect a man simply because in the greater world a man is more likely to command the respect and be in the position to obtain power. But if your suspicions are right, that the Librarian is using Yearning Sands Resort as a base, the possibility exists it could be a female because the hospitality business is predominantly female. We have a lot more choices here." She pointed at the names on the chart. "I'm suggesting these two because they have the physicality to handle the rigors of the job. Pickups, drop-offs, if needed." She paused a beat. "Murders."

"I also had Mara Philippi on the list," he said smugly. "She has a murky background."

That brought her interest into sharp focus. "What does that mean?"

"It means I don't believe the research I was able to assemble about her. There are legitimate reasons for her to have faked credentials. She might have worked at a federal agency that obscured or changed her records, she might be in witness protection, she might be running from an abusive relationship—"

"All of which explains her obsession with fitness and fighting—and none of which explains her obsession with winning the International Ninja Challenge."

"Maybe she's throwing up a smoke screen and has no intention of entering the contest," he suggested.

"She says she's already entered and been accepted."

"Have you seen proof?"

"No." Kellen finished the salad. "You're right—she could be lying and will sadly announce she didn't make it. But I don't think so. I think if Mara is the Librarian, she has such an impenetrable ego this is really *the* challenge—to show herself on television and online, to be seen by the world and make fools of everyone."

"You have quite an unflattering opinion of her."

Kellen struggled to explain. "She's not an easy person to be around. She's demanding. She's selfish. I don't know her any better than I did on the day we met. She has said that everyone here has secrets."

"Do they?"

"No one comes to live at the lonely, battered edge of the continent unless they're escaping a past."

"What are you escaping?"

Her temper crackled. "You tell me. You did the research."

"I've never seen blue eyes spark quite like that." He leaned forward. "May I kiss you?"

She couldn't have been more horrified. "Good God. Why?"

He threw back his head and laughed, and for the first time since she'd met him, he looked carefree. "Because we'd be good together."

"I'm not here for that. If that's the game you're playing—"

"No!" He held up one hand. "This is not some long scene I've concocted to seduce you. Forget I said anything. It was an impulse. I'm not usually given to impulse, but you're an unusual woman. Intriguing."

"And you're nosy. It's not an attractive trait. Try to contain yourself." Kellen pulled the mac and cheese out of the oven and tested it. It was still frozen in the middle, but warm around the edges, and she was desperate. With a serving spoon, she shaved off the warm parts and mounded them into a bowl, then covered the casserole again and put it back in the oven. She took her first bite and sighed with pleasure. "You can keep your crummy lobster mac and cheese," she told him. "Dungeness crab is the clear winner."

"I couldn't begin to say. I've never had crab mac and cheese."

An appeal for a serving, and she ignored it. She pulled a stool into the kitchen and settled across the counter from him. "Adrian and Mitch are on the list as possible assistants to the Librarian. They were good soldiers and I like them, and mostly I trust them, but Adrian got into something bad, I don't know what, but he's jumpy and scared. Sometimes Mitch lacks a moral compass. Both have had problems adjusting to civilian life. I don't know whether they truly could be tempted by the Librarian to be the muscle of the Yearning Sands operation, but I know sometimes money leads them."

He studied the list intently. "Right. You didn't include your other two friends as either the Librarian or assistants."

"No." She didn't have to explain herself, or defend Birdie and Temo.

He went on to the last name on her list. "Sheri Jean Hagerty. Why her?"

"Sheri Jean's father was by all accounts a lovely man. But her mother is the matriarch of her extended family and absolutely the most ruthless human being I've ever met."

He scribbled a note beside Sheri Jean's name. "So she could have learned heartlessness at her mother's knee."

"I guarantee she did. The family has a small truck farm east of here where they grow fruits and vegetables to sell on a stand beside the highway. Everyone in the family works that stand while they're growing up and everyone, no matter who they are, spends part of their summer working the farm. We're talking about high-powered people. Business owners, CEOs, president of a prestigious Midwest college. Every autumn, her mother comes to the resort to negotiate the terms for next year's produce, and on that day, chefs tremble, Annie cries and Sheri Jean hides."

"You're saying her mother is forcing Sheri Jean to be the Librarian." He pulled a long, disbelieving face.

"Not at all. I'm saying Bo Fang crushed her dreams, and a woman without dreams has no hope or joy."

"The old lady's name is Bo Fang?"

"Appropriately." She laughed at his reaction. "Sheri Jean told me that Fang means fragrant, but I wasn't sure she was serious." She slid her spoon into the thick cheesy dish, over and over, filling the empty spaces in her belly.

In a goaded tone, he asked, "Do you mind if I try a *bite* of your mac and cheese?"

"Do you know how to get it out of the oven by yourself?"

His eyes narrowed on her. "I may be a Brooks, but I assure you, I have a Bo Fang in my background. My grandmother Mrs. Judith Irene Brooks does not tolerate idle hands."

She had rather enjoyed provoking him, and her one-shoulder shrug was the polished epitome of indifference. "Help yourself."

He came around the counter and into the kitchen.

She scooted until her back was against the wall. Tonight she might feel more at ease, but she didn't intend to discover she was wrong about him.

Of course, he observed her maneuver, and those glorious brown eyes snapped in irritation. "You don't like lobster?"

"I don't like anything from Maine." *TMI.* She needed to be careful about that; he'd already proved himself able to dig through her past. When he seated himself with his own bowl and spoon, she continued, "Sheri Jean is the youngest daughter. According to Bo Fang, the youngest daughter's duty is to stay close to her mother and care for her into her old age. She sent Sheri Jean to a private high school in Massachusetts, where Sheri Jean excelled and was accepted to an Ivy League college. Bo Fang wouldn't let her go there—or anywhere. She made her come home and learn the truck farm business."

"Sheri Jean didn't go to college? Because of her mother?"

"That's right."

"She could have defied her mother."

"She did. She married the most inappropriate man... From all accounts, Dirk Hagerty was a lazy, cheating gigolo, and it cost Bo Fang dearly to get rid of him."

"Which put Sheri Jean in debt to her mother." He took his first bite. "You're right. This is wonderful. The chefs here are gifted."

"The crabs here are pretty gifted, too." She watched him eat *again* and wondered where he stashed all those calories. "My last point—Sheri Jean was born on this coast. She knows every inch of it. Whoever is in charge of this smuggling operation is intelligent, and Sheri Jean is smarter than the rest of us put together."

"You're pretty smart yourself. She wasn't even on my list."

"That's why you picked me to help you, isn't it?"

"Your military records indicate you have a gift for situational analysis."

"Right." Had Nils discovered the real reason she was medically discharged? If he had, he didn't care much, and that gave her some insight into his character. Not a flattering insight, either. And what was with that request for a kiss? "I thought you were involved with Jessica Diaz."

"We were friends. Old friends, good friends. Friends with common goals."

"Hmm." If that was true, that made his appeal a little less offensive.

Damn him. Why had he introduced the man/woman thing into this mess? Sex was for people who had a future, who could remember all the days of their lives and could live without looking over their shoulder wondering what was sneaking up behind them...and what they had done.

Her appetite vanished. She took her bowls and placed them in his sink, ran some water and left them. Let the bastard load his own miniature dishwasher. She said, "The problem is—I can make a list all day long and my suppositions carry the highest percentages of being correct. Commanders tend to command, and thus I listed the resort's department heads. But while we can play the percentages, we have to face the fact the Librarian could be a resident of Cape Charade. It could be one of the housekeeping staff. The people I have on the leader list could be the assistant and vice versa. And how many people does the Librarian have on the payroll?"

"I figure to make an operation of this size work—ten to twenty?"

"There you go. I don't know how you're going to make this sleuthing work."

He finished his mac and cheese and pushed the bowl away. "In the autumn, a collection of illegally seized South American tomb art went astray."

"About the time Priscilla went astray?"

"Exactly at that time." He pulled out his tablet and passed it over.

Kellen flipped through the tomb art photos. A stone tablet covered in hieroglyphs, stone statues of angry, broad-cheeked faces, a carving of a woman's naked pregnant body and the pièce de résistance, a red stone figure of a man squatting on his haunches with an enormous and well-polished penis protruding from between his legs. "Eye-catching," she said drily and passed the tablet back.

"The private collector paid a lot of money to own those artifacts, and the knowledge of his displeasure spread throughout the art world. It's said he demanded a refund and was told some version of 'Ya pays yer money, ya takes yer chances.'"

"I'll bet that went down well."

"Wealthy people don't take being swindled with any amount of grace. Word spread that the Librarian is losing his grip."

"Who spread that word?"

"I may have helped." He twirled his imaginary mustache. "But I didn't start it. I want to find the Librarian, get him off the streets, dismantle the operation from the inside. It's important to me."

"Revenge for Jessica?"

"Yes, and a fulfillment of our mission."

Kellen nodded.

"The Librarian created this very profitable operation, but you must know everyone would like to step into the Librarian's shoes. He has to deliver Central American tomb art to this collector or be discredited. So—four days ago, another tomb was looted. Two archaeologists were shot. One died."

"You think the artifacts are coming here?"

"Yes, and the Librarian can't afford for anything to go wrong this time."

Kellen thought about Mr. Gilfilen, lurking in the dark outside in camouflage, watching and waiting for his chance to break open the smuggling ring. If Nils Brooks was correct, Mr. Gilfilen faced a danger he could not imagine. How could she tell him without revealing what she knew about Nils Brooks and his operation?

She sagged. Was she ever going to enjoy another full night's sleep?

Nils leaned over the counter. "Priscilla Carter was somehow involved in the theft of those artifacts. They haven't resurfaced. Do you have any idea where she might have hidden them?"

"I didn't know Priscilla. I wasn't here when she was alive. Everyone who knew her tells me she wasn't very smart and she wasn't particularly principled. Assuming my information is correct, she might have taken the art, one assumes because she recognized the potential for profit, and she could have stashed it anywhere. The resort is huge and old, riddled with closets, storage, even some secret passageways."

"I know it's difficult, but—"

"But perhaps she didn't realize its worth, or she wanted revenge on the Librarian and put it in the garbage."

He put his hand on his chest as if his heart hurt. "Why would she want revenge?"

"If she was romantically involved with the Librarian and discovered he—or she—was using her as camouflage… A woman scorned, Mr. Brooks. You may never recover that tomb art. You may never uncover the Librarian."

She was quite enjoying Nils's horror, when out of the corners of her eyes, she saw something move outside the window. Someone was looking in.

Slowly, heart thumping, she turned to face the intruder.

Her husband, Gregory, was there, looking in. Dead and looking at her, a soft green light on his evil face.

24

Kellen gasped and slammed her back against the wall.

"What?" Nils swiveled around.

Gregory had vanished.

She cleared her throat, swallowed, said, "Nothing." Because the cottage was elevated above ground level. No one could stand on the ground and look in unless they were ten feet tall.

"A light?" Nils walked over and looked out into the winter darkness. "Are the smugglers out there tonight?"

"No. Just…an overactive imagination. Mine." She pressed her hand to her forehead over the scar and worked to bring her heart rate down to acceptable levels. Ever since the Army had discharged her, she'd been afraid something like this would happen: optical illusions, madness, another year lost and no idea where it went, what happened, what she had done.

"We don't need to *imagine* anything bad." The big, strong man was *chiding* her.

But right now, she was glad of the company of this patronizing, mansplaining jerk. She was glad she wasn't alone.

In a businesslike tone, he said, "It's all happening *here.* I don't exult in the disappearance of a law officer, but you and I both know the loss of Lloyd Magnuson and Priscilla's body means the Librarian is *here* and taking steps to conceal his crimes. We are so close." His eyes gleamed with radical fervor.

When he looked like that, he made her uneasy. "Nils, you're rocking the boat, and rocking this particular boat will result in someone going overboard. That someone could be you."

He half turned his head, and his profile was sharply etched against the shiny dark of the window. "I'm remarkably well-balanced."

She got to her feet. "Let me be clear. You should be careful, because I won't go over the side with you. I didn't survive Afghanistan to recover a penis statue." She donned her oversize coat, walked to the door, opened it, looked behind her and saw him watching her, his beautiful brown eyes avid, his face speculative.

She stepped out onto the porch and firmly shut the door behind her. Alone and aloud, she said, "I didn't survive Gregory Lykke to take a second lover I don't trust."

She looked around, saw no smuggling lights and no disembodied heads.

She found that comforting. But she'd run to Nils's cottage to avoid being seen as a target. Now...now she was more spooked by the phantom she'd imagined than the killer she knew was out there. So she sprinted to the resort, keeping to the lighted paths, taking her chances with smugglers and knowing in the corner of her mind that she was trying to outrun the ghost of her long-dead and viciously brutal husband.

"Mara. Mara! Did you see?" Destiny Longacre peered out the blinds in Mara's cottage. "That's Kellen Adams, and she's sneaking out of that guest cottage!"

"Really?" Ellen leaped up from the coffee table, where Mara was filing her nails, and ran to the window.

"Wait. Wait! I want to see, too!" Daisy hobbled over, her newly painted toes separated by cotton balls. "Whose cottage is that?"

Xander lifted his hands from Mara's shoulders—he had been massaging her and urging a regime of stress-relieving yoga breathing—and wandered over to look. "That's Nils Brooks's cottage. The author. Nice-looking man and I spoke to him today. Intelligent, insightful and curious about how the resort works."

Mara was hosting a spa worker evening to get their minds off the past two days, and they had been fixing hair, massaging tense knots of muscle and snacking on caramel corn while waiting for the pizza to bake.

Now Mara went over and slapped the blinds out of Destiny's hands. The blinds fell with a clatter and everyone turned to find Mara with her hands on her hips. "It's nobody's business."

"You're right," Ellen agreed. "But he's got good hair."

"How does she have time for this while Annie is away?" Destiny shook her hands as if she had hurt them. "She's been working all day."

Daisy chortled. "But not all night!"

A short burst of laughter. Groans.

When the merriment died down, Xander said, "She has superpowers."

He was so calm, so Zen, everyone stared at him trying to decide if he was serious.

"Frances is dating Mitch, and Mitch said while overseas she saved them more than once from impossible situations. They found out—"

"They who?" Mara asked.

"Her team, the people in maintenance, found out that her parents were spies, bred by the government to have superhero powers."

"Wow," Destiny said in an awed voice.

"That's the dumbest thing I've ever heard," Daisy said.

Mara sighed and used the corkscrew to noisily crank the cork out of another bottle of wine.

The oven timer dinged. Xander swooped in and removed the margherita pizza, sliced it and put it in the middle of the coffee table.

Everyone settled down to food, drink and speculation about Kellen Adams, who she really was and where she had come from.

25

"Mr. Gilfilen, please. Priscilla Carter is dead. Lloyd Magnuson has disappeared. Someone out there is smuggling something they're willing to kill for. Won't you let the government agencies handle this rather than putting your life at risk?" Kellen stood with her hands clasped at her chest, watching Mr. Gilfilen make himself a cup of oolong tea.

He had returned to his suite mere moments before, dressed in military camouflage, frozen to the bone and calm in the face of tonight's failure. "Miss Adams, I appreciate your concern. But I am not without resources. Like you, I've served in the military, and unlike you, I promptly went into security as a way to utilize my training. If these smugglers are bringing in illegal and lethal drugs to distribute to our young people, or munitions that they plan to assemble in an act of terrorism, would I be satisfied to tell myself, *At least I kept myself safe*?" He lifted the tea bag out of his cup and looked inquiringly at her. Politely.

"No, of course you wouldn't." Kellen understood that cutting the umbilical cord of funding to the terrorists would benefit the United States, but Mr. Gilfilen clearly believed he was taking direct action against the evils that threatened society, not stopping the illegal import of ancient artifacts. "Sometimes what comes in isn't lethal in and of itself."

He sugared his tea and took a sip.

She tried again. "I've been doing research." Which was a kind of truth. "The head of this smuggling operation is without scruples, compassion, the slightest shred of humanity."

"Miss Adams, please don't tell me you think someone who would kill a young woman and cut off her hands is not a good person." His humor was so dry it could flake paint off the wall.

Right. She wasn't going to win this argument—the argument with Mr. Gilfilen, or with herself. If Nils Brooks and Mr. Gilfilen worked together, they could possibly find and disable the Librarian sooner. But she had never completely trusted Brooks, so if she told him about Mr. Gilfilen and Nils was a bad guy, she had betrayed a man of honor. She wanted to tell Mr. Gilfilen about Nils Brooks and the MFAA, but did she dare gamble her trust on such an important issue?

She couldn't see a way out of this moral dilemma, so she said, "Please be careful, and please know—if you need help, I will be there for you."

"Miss Adams, I do know that, and I promise, I depend on you."

She couldn't force the man to take care, not without explaining everything she knew, and she suspected even then he would do what he thought best, regardless of his own safety. With a nod, she left him alone with his tea and headed toward maintenance to talk to someone sensible, well-balanced and with two X chromosomes. Birdie.

She took one of the resort's ATVs and drove along the lighted paths. Ridiculous. She hadn't really seen a ghost. What she'd seen had been an illusion brought on by… Well, she didn't know what brought it on. Exhaustion. The strain of so much responsibility. Being pleasant to guests. If she had seen a ghost, could she outrun it in an ATV? It was a question that occupied her mind until she pulled up to the garage. She knocked loudly on the door, used her pass card, and as soon as she stepped into the tall, cool, echoing structure, she was glad she'd knocked.

Birdie stood in the loft above, her Glock in hand. "Come on up," she said. "Bring hot chocolate, two marshmallows in mine." And then she disappeared from the railing.

Kellen made two hot chocolates, and balancing them carefully, she made her way up the spiral staircase. She found Birdie sitting on the metal floor, surrounded by reams of paper. She handed over a mug. "Are we having fun yet?"

"Just for that, you can take that pile of car service manuals—" Birdie pointed "—put them in that cardboard box—" she pointed again "—and take it downstairs to the recycling bin."

Kellen put down her chocolate and did as she was told. When Birdie got that look on her face, it was best to do as she said. When Kellen got back, she sat on the floor and sipped her chocolate. "Are you close to done?"

"I'm into the 1980s. If this is to be believed—" Birdie lifted one leather-bound manual "—someone here at the resort owned a 1981 Lamborghini Countach."

"Some impressive vehicles at this resort. You're saving that?" Kellen reached for it.

Birdie put it on her own desk. "You bet. What's up?"

"Can't I come by just for fun?"

"You can. And you do. But your shoulders are hunched and you've got that pinched-mouth expression."

Kellen straightened her shoulders. "It's cold. We've got a whopper of a storm coming in tomorrow morning. The staff is spooked."

Birdie tossed another manual on the discard pile. "There's more stuff going on than you can talk about."

"Why do you say that?"

"You don't do *uncertain* very often."

"In the war zones, the best I could hope for was that no one got killed and mutilated. Since I've been at the resort, I haven't had to worry about that."

"Until now." Birdie picked up a little mimeographed booklet and flapped it at Kellen. "It's the Cape Charade newspaper. Want to know what happened the week of July 17, 1984?"

"Nothing?"

Birdie looked it over. "Pretty much." She threw it on the discard pile, too.

Kellen glanced around. "Where are the guys?"

Birdie opened her mouth as if to answer, then closed it.

Interesting. "You don't do uncertain very often, either."

"What I know—Mitch is on a date with the girl from the concierge desk, and lately I don't like the way he talks about women. As if they're a commodity."

"Civilian life hasn't improved him." The two women contemplated that truth, then Kellen asked, "What about Temo? I saw him in the kitchen. He was weird. I wondered if he was having a party without me. But he wouldn't have one without you, too."

"I don't know. Maybe." Birdie shifted papers as if she needed to keep her hands busy. "Temo got back from LA, and he and Adrian have been sneaking around, whispering in corners. I wondered if discovering that corpse had disturbed Temo. He's Hispanic and there's that Day of the Dead thing..."

"It's not that much different than Memorial Day," Kellen pointed out. "They visit the graves, remember their dearly departed..."

"Are you kidding? Have you seen how they decorate the skull cakes?" Birdie shuddered. "I wouldn't eat one of those things!"

"Sounds like Temo isn't the only superstitious one." Kellen thought of that pale face floating outside the window, and a quick, sharp shudder ran up her spine. "Did he tell you what happened in California?"

"A little. He was terse. I think with his mother in prison, he has to support his sister and you know how much it costs to live in California."

"So...money problems?"

"Maybe. But what's that got to do with Adrian? Why are they teaming up? Why are they avoiding me? And you."

Temo would do anything for his little sister. He needed money to support her. Maybe he could bring her to Yearning Sands. But if Adrian was the Librarian's assistant—he wasn't smart, but he was good with heavy lifting—and if he had brought Temo into the operation, they'd have one smart guy who could fix anything. All of the logic worked. That didn't mean it was true.

Birdie said, "We have so much work to do to get the resort and the vehicles ready for spring, and the guys are just…not here for me."

"I'll speak to them."

"No. No. I think maybe it's me."

"You?" Kellen's indignation rose. "Why are you blaming yourself?"

"I'm lonely and I'm sad. It makes them avoid me." Birdie leaned her cheek against a stack of manuals. "The trouble with being a widow is you bear up at the beginning and tell everyone you're okay, and eventually they believe you and go away. Then you're alone and there's nobody…forever."

Kellen scooted over and rubbed Birdie's back. Birdie had always been thin, but now every vertebrae felt as distinct as a piano key. The guys weren't the only ones who had not been there for her. Kellen hadn't realized, hadn't thought, that Birdie had barely begun to grieve for her husband, that the shadow of his death would weigh on her for months and maybe years. "I'll tell you what," Kellen said. "When Leo and Annie get back, we'll go on vacation, someplace warm and sunny, maybe one of the Di Luca California resorts. It would be good for both of us." Kellen remembered tonight, and that flash of a white, dead face at the window. *I don't remember an entire year of my life.* Perhaps Annie was right; Kellen needed to go somewhere else and relax. Right now, Yearning Sands wasn't the safe haven she had hoped. "Does that sound good to you?"

Birdie nodded. "Maybe we can get Carson Lennex to drive us down."

"What?" Kellen stopped rubbing.

Birdie lifted her head. "We store his car for him. He came by and asked if I'd tune it up, make sure it was road ready. He doesn't fly, and he's leaving soon on a trip."

"Is he?" Kellen thought she kept her tone neutral.

But Birdie glared. "You don't have to sound that way. I didn't really mean to ask him if he'd drive us. That would be embarrassing, to treat a movie star like a cabdriver."

How to warn her without giving offense? "I don't know that I'd accept a ride from Carson Lennex even if he offered."

Birdie's thin spine snapped straight up. "Why not? What's wrong with him?"

"He's an actor." Kellen waved a cautiously dismissive hand. "He's always wearing a mask, and no one can see beneath it."

"He was nice and genuine! Honestly, you act like everyone's out to get you. You're not that important!"

Kellen caught her breath. That hurt. The tension, the death, the weather—it was eating at them all. "You're right." She tried for a little humor. "Only in my own mind."

The outer door flew open, slammed shut. Temo called, "Birdie, are you here?"

Birdie looked at Kellen.

Kellen shook her head. She didn't want to talk to Temo; in the kitchen, he had been dismissive of her.

Birdie stood and went over to the railing. "What do you need?"

Kellen heard him rattling around the worktables.

"I've got to pick up my tool belt, grab a few things and go to work."

"Now? It's dark!" Birdie leaned farther out. "Can't it wait until morning?"

Kellen hunched down and waited in terror for the answer.

"I was gone. Things need to be done, and I have to keep this job."

"Kellen won't fire you for taking time for your family!"

Temo stopped rattling. "She doesn't have family. She doesn't understand what they are worth." The rattling started again. "From now on, I'll work as much as I can, when I can. That's what has to be done, and I'm not stopping for anyone."

Kellen wasn't family to Temo. It sounded as if he didn't even consider her much of a friend. And a shiny edge of Kellen's fantasy crumbled away.

26

In the morning, Mara sat staring at the house phone. As if of its own volition, her hand moved toward the receiver, then back, then out again and grasped it. She lifted it to her ear, dialed the number and fidgeted while the phone rang.

Annie answered, and she sounded cheerful and strong.

Mara relaxed. "Annie, this is Mara. You sound good."

"I'm wonderful! This morning, I got out of the hospital! I'm back in Bella Terra at my sister-in-law's house and we're celebrating Christmas and Hanukkah and every good thing."

"That's great. That's...great. Listen, I feel funny making this phone call, but I've been working at this resort for too long to let something go wrong without saying something."

"What is it, dear?" Annie's voice became warm and concerned.

"Kellen is behaving oddly. I don't know what she's doing exactly, but I've twice spotted her leaving a guest's cottage late at night."

"Oh no!" Annie whispered. "Not that."

Hastily, Mara said, "I'm not saying she's doing anything wrong. Not a good policy with a guest, of course, but she's handling the resort really well. Especially considering the, you know, body and the way it disappeared with Lloyd Magnuson and all."

Silence from the other end.

"Maybe I shouldn't have said… You did know about the, um, body? Priscilla's body?"

"Leo told me. Not everything, I'm sure, but enough." Annie sounded sorrowful. "I feel awful that my first thought of Priscilla was that she abandoned us. To think the poor child was murdered!"

"Yes. The poor child."

"I'm sorry this happened while I was gone."

"Bad timing," Mara agreed. "As to the Kellen thing, I thought you ought to know…"

More silence from the other end.

Mara added, "Maybe I should have kept quiet…"

Annie rallied. "No, dear, thank you for keeping me up-to-date. Of course, that's disappointing to hear. While Kellen's in sole charge of the resort, I'd prefer she concentrate on the job. But these things do happen."

"They do." Mara burst out, "But, Annie, they're out in the middle of the night in the most awful weather, in the cold and dark. I don't know whether it's a romance or something illegal!"

"Luckily, we have already handled this. Leo and I have sent a security manager to relieve Kellen of that particular part of her duties, a member of our family, Maximilian Di Luca."

Mara cheered up. "That will help! This Maximilian, he'll watch her really closely, right?"

"I guarantee his focus will be on her and her alone."

"That's good, because I don't understand what's happening here, but I don't like it."

27

That night, when Kellen slept, she dreamed of running away in the dark from something terrible. When she woke and stared into the darkness, she remembered what Temo had said. *She doesn't have family. She doesn't understand what they are worth.* And *From now on, I'll work as much as I can, when I can. That's what has to be done.*

God, Temo. What have you gotten yourself into?

She slept again and dreamed about a man with brown eyes and long black lashes who pulled her close, kissed her, tasted her, lingered over her lips until she kissed him back. She slid her hands into his hair. He pushed her gown aside, cupped her breast, slid his thumb across her nipple, his skin rough from digging in the dirt…

He spoke her name in longing and need. *Ceecee…* She looked up at him—and his eyes were blue, and he killed her.

She woke on a gasp.

Madness? Memory? Meaningless nightmare?

Yes. The latter. Her subconscious was a sick son of a bitch, and what she'd seen last night didn't exist. Gregory was dead and gone, over the edge of the cliff by his own hand. He wasn't here in Yearning Sands. He would never bother her again.

She didn't remember a year of her life. Why couldn't she forget Gregory?

She rolled over and looked at the clock. Six a.m. Good enough. She got ready for a jog and stepped out her door.

No rain. No wind. Not yet.

No Mara.

She went to Mara's cottage. It was dark and empty. She went to the gym to work out, figuring Mara was there.

Mara wasn't answering the door.

Kellen lifted weights, punched bags, practiced the turning kick. And cursed. She was never going to get that damned maneuver right.

Still no Mara.

She showered, dressed in the resort's calf-length black gown and blue scarf. The resort might be short on guests and the staff might be skittish, Kellen herself might be sleepless and afraid, mostly of herself, but right now, at least, Yearning Sands was her home. She would exude excessive amounts of serenity. She would do as Xander urged; she would breathe. To Mara, she wrote a snarky note on the dry-erase board—

DETERMINATION

She ate breakfast in the lobby bar with the resort guests, who straggled in and out. The Shivering Sherlocks came in en masse, not yet in costume but consumed by this year's mystery and by Carson's clever script. After a little chitchat, Kellen excused herself and started toward the stairs and Annie's office.

Frances flagged her down and in a gleeful voice said, "Something got delivered for you. A gift. Gorgeous! Lavish. Come on. We're all dying to see who it's from."

"A gift?" Kellen followed Frances to the concierge desk. *Who* would send her a present? *Why* would someone send her a present?

Frances gestured at a wide, shallow bowl of fruit wrapped in glittering cellophane and tied with a wide red velvet ribbon. "A new delivery lady showed up in a town car, brought this in and asked that it be delivered to you. May I?" Frances held the end of one red ribbon.

"Go for it."

The Shivering Sherlocks came out of the lounge. The desk staff moved closer. Sheri Jean appeared out of nowhere. Xander took a look, disappeared down the corridor toward the spa and returned with Destiny, Ellen and Mara.

If this was the entertainment of the day, Kellen reflected sourly, the resort needed more guests and hustle and bustle. She wandered over to Mara. "Where were you this morning?" she asked.

"I had a party at my cottage last night for my spa people. I slept in. Then I had some calls to make. Did you come by?" Mara busied herself arranging her hoodie to display more of her off-the-shoulder crop tank.

"I've already run and lifted weights!" Kellen toned down her indignation. "Did you see my note?"

"I am determined to win the International Ninja Challenge, on television, in front of the whole world! But first, I want to keep my employees safe and happy. I know you understand that." Mara fixed her clothing to her satisfaction and smiled at Kellen. "Hmm?"

Nothing created as much teeth-grinding hostility as Mara Philippi telling Kellen something Kellen knew was the truth, something Kellen should appreciate. She smiled back. "Yes, of course. Thank you for thinking first of the resort." *And next time you're not going to work out with me, could you let me know ahead of time?*

Frances gestured Kellen back, and Kellen went gladly. "No card that I can see," Frances said.

Kellen managed a smile and a sensible "I'd say that's creepy, but probably the card fell off, right? Can we call the delivery person and ask who sent it?"

Chad Griffin wandered over, orange juice in hand. "No card?"

When had the pilot returned to the resort?

"Ooh, a secret admirer." He sang, "Kellen's got a lover. Kellen's got a lover."

This man was obnoxious, on her list of probables for the Librarian and on her list as first to be slapped for being an ass. She snapped, "Don't be stupid. It's a lost card, not a secret romance. What suitor sends a stupid bowl of fruit, anyway?"

Kellen supposed she shouldn't have said that. The guests and staff were eyeing her askance, and Patty in the Shivering Sherlocks group said, "I like fruit!"

Kellen reined in her irritation. "I do, too." She pointed at a decorative tin visible behind the cellophane. "Especially when the fruit is covered in chocolate."

The Shivering Sherlocks laughed.

Crisis averted.

Until Chad Griffin stuck his nose in again. "Sorry. You don't have admirers, secret or otherwise. I didn't know that was a tender spot."

She maintained a reasonable tone. "There's another storm coming in. Shouldn't you be getting that plane off the ground?"

"Okay." He held up his hands. "PMS, much?"

Mara put her hands on her hips. *"Really?"*

Sheri Jean said, "Your job's on the line, mister."

Kellen stepped up to him, nose to nose. "Get. Out."

He marched away, trailing tatters of offended dignity. But he didn't get sympathy, and he didn't put down his drink.

Kellen hoped she hadn't made a mistake. Nils Brooks wanted to keep his suspects close. But while the events of the past several days had convinced her Nils Brooks told her the truth about the Yearning Sands Resort smuggling depot, and probably the truth about the Librarian, she still wasn't convinced that Nils

Brooks was telling the truth about *himself.* And that increased her apprehension and her suspicions…about everyone.

Or maybe she was simply sleep deprived.

Frances smiled after Chad Griffin's retreating figure. "You know, Kellen, I didn't know if I liked you before, but you're getting to be almost human."

Murders. Smuggling. Obnoxious men. Handsome men. Missing law enforcement. A fussy generator. A quirky communications system. Sure. The whole equation added up to a much more likable Kellen Adams. "Thanks," Kellen said.

"What's in the package?" Sheri Jean asked.

Kellen poked at the artistically arranged mounds of tangerines, gold-foil-wrapped pears and apples and plums. "It's cold."

"They refrigerated the fruit," Sheri Jean answered.

"You're not supposed to refrigerate bananas." Kellen pulled them off the top and started taking the array of fruit apart, searching for the card. "Are you sure it's for me?"

"The delivery woman specifically said it was for Kellen Adams," Frances said. "That is you, isn't it?"

Mostly. "I can't eat it all." Kellen didn't want to eat any of it. A mystery gift made her remember that disembodied head floating outside Nils's window, made her think about the Librarian and the people who died in agony, their hands cut from their bodies, their pleas for help unheard. In this place, at this time, she had to wonder if someone with less than honorable intentions had sent this.

"Let's put it out for the guests!" Sheri Jean found a tray of dried chocolate-dipped apricots and a tin of chocolate-covered cherries and made a nummy sound.

Kellen looked up at the gathering crowd: Sheri Jean and her receptionists, Mara and her spa workers, the newlyweds and the Shivering Sherlocks. She could hardly say she feared poison or some other mischief. Unless she wanted to explain herself, and she did not, that could be construed as paranoia. In fact, it might *be* paranoia. "Help yourselves," she said and stepped back.

Frances slid the foil off a ripe pear and took a bite, and her eyes slid closed in unadulterated pleasure.

Mara took the tray of chocolate-dipped glazed apricots and danced around to the employees and guests, offering and teasing.

Carson Lennex arrived and watched from the outskirts, arms crossed over his manly chest and a slight, charming smile lifting his lips.

Chad Griffin hid in the lobby bar and sulked.

As the staff and guests passed the chocolate-covered fruits, the tight knot of worry inside Kellen relaxed. This was the kind of treat the troops had loved receiving overseas, luxurious tidbits that reminded them of home and holidays—and so far, no one had dropped dead.

Frances ran her finger around the edge of the bowl. "I wonder if this is really a Japanese Awaji piece. If it is, you've got a secret admirer with expensive taste."

The whole secret admirer thing gave Kellen the willies. "I hate that crackle glaze." The decorative bowls at the Greenleaf mansion had sparkled with that glaze, and Erin and Gregory had both adored them. Looking back, Kellen thought it was because they enjoyed the idea of something that was prebroken. Like them. "You take it," she told Frances.

"Really? Okay, I will. Thank you!"

Kellen went back to work unpacking the fruit. Tiny tangerines with their zipper skin smelled like sunshine, summer and citrus. The prickly skin of a fresh pineapple gave off the scent of faraway tropical plantations. Only people who lived where the continual rain bleached the world gray could understand. Kellen lifted one of the last tangerines to her nose, took a long sniff—and something long and slim and alive and colorful slithered out of the bowl.

Guests squeaked and screamed and scattered.

By some trick of levitation, Kellen found herself ten feet back from where she'd been.

The snake, ten inches long, with black, gray and red stripes running the length of its body, slid off the table and onto the floor. It moved rapidly across the cool marble toward the front door.

Sheri Jean moved with intelligence and speed. She dumped the last of the fruit out of the bowl and inverted it over the snake, stopping its escape and the burgeoning panic. "It's nothing more than a garter snake," she announced in a loud, firm voice. Then more quietly she said, "Although I've never seen one like that."

"I have," Debbie said faintly. "In our garden in Maine."

Maine. Kellen stared at the familiar-looking bowl. She thought about the snake writhing underneath, trying to find a way out. *Maine.* Her concerns about smuggling, murder and the Librarian changed, and for one moment she reverted to Cecilia, afraid of cruelty, broken bones and violence committed to satisfy a petty despot. She dropped the tangerine and pressed that hand against a marble column. She closed her eyes and breathed in, and banished the memories… They were not Kellen's memories…

She felt a man's arm around her waist. Chad Griffin… Or Gregory Lykke?

No! Her eyes snapped open. She turned and…it wasn't either one of them. Not even close.

A tall man in a dark business suit bent over her in concern. "Are you all right?"

"I'm fine." She recognized him from her research the day before. "You must be Maximilian Di Luca."

MAXIMILIAN DI LUCA:
MALE, 30S, 6'5", 220 LBS., ITALIAN AMERICAN. FORMER FOOTBALL PLAYER. CURRENTLY WORKS FOR DI LUCA WINES. ~~STERN FACE,~~ HANDSOME, TANNED SKIN, BLACK SHADOW OF A BEARD, CURLY BLACK HAIR ~~CROPPED INTO A BUSINESSMAN'S LENGTH~~, A LITTLE

LONG AND DISHEVELED. BROWN EYES WITH LONG BLACK LASHES. GOOD CHEST. RUMBLY VOICE. EYES, VOICE FAMILIAR?

He smiled, a slow signal of delight. "You know me?"

Too much delight. Too much anticipation. She briskly freed herself and stepped away. "You look like your uncle." Or like Leo had looked fifty years before.

"Of course. You're right. I do." He said, "You turned white when you saw that snake. Are you sure you're all right?"

"I don't like snakes. But who does?" A quick glance around the lobby showed all the guests and all the staff standing close to the wall, staring at that bowl as if the snake could somehow escape. "I'm fine. Really, fine."

Sheri Jean was glaring at her, head tilted, wanting her to snap out of it.

Kellen did. One didn't refuse Sheri Jean's demands, spoken or otherwise. In a loud, firm voice, she said, "Let's all go into the lounge, shall we? We'll send the fruit to the kitchen to be well washed and our unwelcome visitor can be taken elsewhere. As fast as he was moving toward the door, he must have been late for an appointment."

A little ripple of laughter.

But no one moved.

"Come on, we'll pour some refreshments and give ourselves a chance to relax again." Kellen made a surreptitious shooing gesture to Mara Philippi and did the head-tilt glare at Frances.

Mara walked to Max Di Luca, took his arm and smiled into his face. "And you are...?"

Frances walked toward the lounge, calling, "This calls for a giant bottle of champagne and some fresh-squeezed orange juice. Any excuse for mimosas, I say!"

Carson Lennex offered his arm to Patty and Rita, two of the Shivering Sherlocks who were indeed shivering. "Let me help you to a seat."

Now Sheri Jean flashed her evil-supervisor-look at her own

staff. Desk personnel began to smile, be the kind of hospitality team that helped guests move beyond their shock and back into a vacation state of mind. Soon the lounge was crowded and buzzing with excitement.

The noise died down when a rumpled Nils Brooks stepped into the doorway, pushed his glasses up on his nose and in a bewildered tone asked, "Did I miss something?"

28

The laughter this time was loud and prolonged, leaving Nils looking confused and the other guests in a much better frame of mind.

Mara returned and took the opportunity to push Kellen around the corner into the lobby. Sheri Jean had disappeared. The snake had disappeared. The bowl sat on the concierge desk.

"Thank God for Sheri Jean," Kellen said. "Where do you suppose she took that thing?"

"I don't know and I don't care." In a low, furious voice, Mara said, "That fruit trick was deliberate!"

Brilliant deduction, Mara. "Why do you say that?"

"The doorman didn't recognize the delivery car or driver. There was no card. The fruit was refrigerated, which would have made the snake lethargic until it warmed up and out it popped! Deliberate!"

"I didn't know that. About the doorman." Kellen still felt a little queasy. "Was it Russell? He knows everybody."

"Yes, it was Russell!" Mara's eyes sparked. "Someone has it in for you!"

"The whole setup was not very nice," Kellen acknowledged.

"Not nice! It was awful. Are you having problems with a man?"

"No. Honestly, I don't know who did that." *My dead husband.*

"You don't have to tell me anything. I understand it's embarrassing to be the victim of harassment." Mara glared at Nils Brooks's back. "But listen. My girls and I are glad to help handle any man problems. You say the word."

"Huh? No, it's not him." At once, Kellen realized she had incriminated herself. "I mean, he's not likely. He's a gentle nerd." And Kellen was a big fat liar.

"Then who is it?" Mara wanted an answer, and she wanted it now.

Not my dead husband, that's for sure! "Probably a disgruntled guest. We've had some winners over the past few months. Remember the weight lifter who decided he could drop the dumbbell bar and grope your boobs while you spotted him? When you banned him from the gym, he was going to sue for you damaging his marriage."

"No one has sent me a snake!"

"It wasn't poisonous."

"Get real. Snake. Snake!" Mara flickered her tongue.

Kellen groped in her mind for another memory. "How about this golden oldie? Remember the first week I was here? Remember the drunk lady who didn't chew her food, got a giant piece of steak stuck in her windpipe? I gave her the Heimlich maneuver, dislodged the steak into her boyfriend's soup, and she slammed me against the wall for trying to steal her boy toy?"

Mara relaxed a little. She eyed the now-empty bowl. "That snake trick does seem like more of a female's mean prank than a man's, doesn't it?"

"Yes." *Hmm.* "Yes, it does."

Mara looked over Kellen's shoulder. "Your new security man wants to speak with you. Did you know Max is a Di Luca?"

"Annie told me, and yes, when he introduced himself, it was pretty obvious."

"I looked him up. He's one of the important Di Lucas—and he *likes* you."

Kellen wanted to moan. She didn't know which was worse, Mara thinking that Max was attracted to her and being wrong, or Mara thinking that Max was attracted to her and being right. Either way was uncomfortable. "That's ridiculous. He just met me."

"Instant attraction." Mara rubbed her fingertips together. "The Di Lucas have a lot of money."

"Then you go after him!"

"He doesn't like me."

Right now, I don't much like you, either. "Use your wiles."

Mara batted her eyelashes. "Wiles? Why, darling, I don't have wiles. I'm sincere clear to the bone."

Kellen snorted most unattractively.

Mara grinned, then sobered. "Remember—if you figure out who did that snake stunt, I'll help you make them sorry. No one comes to my resort and gets away with that kind of stunt." She skipped away toward the lounge, as sparkly and charming as ever, and just as irritating.

Maximilian Di Luca moved to take her place. He did not skip; his feet were so absurdly large, seeing him approach was akin to watching Godzilla crush Tokyo.

Kellen smiled, extended her hand. "We didn't meet properly before. Mr. Di Luca, I'm glad you're here."

He took her hand, cupped it between both of his and looked into her face. "Call me Max."

Those eyes. Not brown, as she had first thought, but golden and intense.

So intense he made her uneasy. She withdrew her hand from his grasp. "Max, then. You came very quickly."

"I would do anything for Annie and Leo." He had a nice voice, rumbly and warm. "When Annie said there was a crisis here, I grabbed that pilot, Chad Griffin, and had him fly me up. He was just mooching around Bella Terra, anyway."

She shot Max a disgusted glance.

Without her saying a word, he caught her drift. "Yes, he's annoying. Say the word, and I'll send him away."

"I already did. Now, will he do as he's told?"

"Not unless he leaves quickly. Snow is predicted for tonight."

"I suppose we should keep him here." She walked across the lobby, toward the stairway to Annie's office.

"Why?" Max answered his own question. "Because you're suspicious of him. For murder? Or smuggling?" He followed, not too closely, and he moved quietly.

But she knew he was there. He had a presence, and she wanted to put her desk between them. She took the stairs. "Leo and Annie filled you in on all the details?"

"What there are of them. I suspect we're looking at the tip of an iceberg."

"I hate being on the *Titanic*," she muttered.

"Full speed ahead," he said, proving he had good hearing. "And no way to make a sharp turn away from the peril. You don't mind if *I* play the Kate Winslet role, do you? I don't even like to *walk* in the rain."

She couldn't help it. She turned and laughed at him. "You're our new security man!"

He was two steps down, smiling faintly, looking fine in the suit, the white shirt, the blue tie. One didn't see many suits in casual Washington State. "A good security man knows when to duck and run. I was a linebacker. I'm very good at running."

"So…you're fast?" She winced. That sounded faintly sexual.

He sobered, and suddenly he was no longer big and handsome, but rather sad and lonely. "Not always fast enough."

The transformation made her vaguely uneasy. Not only Carson Lennex wore a mask. Everyone at the resort wore a mask of some kind, and trying to peel them away to see the face underneath was more dangerous than she could have imagined.

As soon as they entered the office, he went to the window. "Such a view. I don't know how Annie gets any work done."

"It is amazing, isn't it?" Kellen seated herself and looked at him across the room, silhouetted against a pale blue winter sky and a murky sun that skipped behind the dark gray clouds. Of all the people in the resort, Max Di Luca was the only one she fully trusted. He wasn't the Librarian, he wasn't a smuggler, he was the man Annie and Leo had sent to help her. But where to start, what to say about security? How to explain, to warn, without betraying the information Nils Brooks had given her? For she didn't know how Max would react, whether he would use those big feet to stomp all over Nils Brooks's plan. He might say, and rightly, that his concern wasn't solving a crime, but protecting the resort. At last, she began, "Max…"

He faced her. "Kellen."

"If you would shut the door, we need to talk."

"Indeed we do." He moved toward the door.

Kellen wondered if she'd made a mistake.

Her phone chirped. "Hold on," she said.

Russell texted.

The sheriff is here.

29

Sheriff Kateri Kwinault was in no way what Kellen expected. She was female, tall, Native American and beautiful, regal in the way of a New World princess, and yet she looked and moved as if she had been broken and put back together. Later, Kellen discovered that was true, but for the moment, she concentrated not on the tracery of scars on Sheriff Kwinault's hands or the walking stick she carried, but on the information she imparted.

The sheriff thanked Russell for bringing her to the office. She shook hands with Kellen and exchanged grins with Max.

Kellen blinked at the two of them. They knew each other. She supposed that made sense. After all, Max was a Di Luca and had visited before.

He offered coffee and described Annie's superautomatic coffee maker in a worshipful tone.

Sheriff Kwinault requested an *espresso con panna*, then leaned her stick against the coatrack and sat across the desk from Kellen. As she accepted the tiny cup from Max, she said, "We found Lloyd Magnuson. His car was hidden in the foliage at one of the pocket parks along the highway. We *think* from the way it was positioned he pulled into the lot, tried to park, hit the gas instead of the brake and slammed out of the paved area and into the underbrush. Damage done by the last storm, by the winds and the rain, hid the evidence, and it was only this morning that one of my officers found him."

"He's dead," Kellen said.

Sheriff Kwinault paused, her cup halfway to her mouth. "Definitely."

"He hit a tree?" Without asking, Max brought Kellen a mug of hazelnut coffee with sugar.

"An overdose," Sheriff Kwinault answered.

"An overdose!" Kellen gestured to Max.

He closed the office door, then got himself a bottle of water and pulled up another chair.

"Of what?" Kellen asked.

"Before Lloyd Magnuson came to Cape Charade, he was a heroin addict. He got clean, he moved to Cape Charade, he's been clean ever since." Sheriff Kwinault took a sip. "But he had the paraphernalia in the car and there were needle tracks on his arm."

"When I saw him, he was fine," Kellen assured her. "Out of his depth as a law officer, but not impaired."

"What about Priscilla's body?" Max asked.

Sheriff Kwinault put her cup on the desk. "There was no body in the car with him."

"So some kind of foul play," Max said.

Kellen found she needed the coffee; the heat, the caffeine, the sugar alleviated, a little, the chill of death.

"Definitely foul play. No one forced Lloyd to take heroin, but someone had it to offer," Sheriff Kwinault said.

"Your officers couldn't find him, but someone managed to steal Priscilla's body." Kellen hitched forward in her chair. "How?"

Max reached into his pocket, pulled out a key chain and pushed a button.

His phone squawked.

"I lose my keys all the time," he said. "My wallet, too."

Kellen imagined him coming in from outside and flinging his keys and wallet wherever, and not remembering where they had landed. That evening, he would cook dinner, talk about his day, sing, play cards, laugh…

The next morning, when he got ready to leave for work, he couldn't find his keys and wallet, and he roared and fussed as if someone had stolen his belongings, when it was his own carelessness at fault…

It was almost as if she had been there.

He continued, "I've got a finder on them, and it's the least sophisticated of the electronics. All the killer had to do was tape a finder on the lid of the plastic box, and he or she could find the body in no time flat."

"Law enforcement gets easier and harder all the time," Sheriff Kwinault said. "Who saw him last?"

"Temo." Kellen knew Temo; with his mother's history, he didn't use, sell or tolerate drug use, but he did recognize it when he saw it. While she made the call on speakerphone, Sheriff Kwinault gestured to Max to be quiet.

He stood and paced over to the window.

Temo answered, sounding tired and distracted.

"I have the sheriff here," Kellen said. "They found Lloyd Magnuson."

Temo's voice changed to wary. "He's dead?"

"Very dead." Sheriff Kwinault tinkered with her cup. "Kellen Adams says you were the last person to see him. Can you tell me about it?"

"Start at when I left you with him and the body," Kellen said.

Temo waited a moment, maybe to gather his thoughts. "I told Kellen I'd clean up the girl's bones, so Kellen left. The policeman, he didn't want to touch anything. He really didn't want to touch the girl, so he got in contact with the resort and asked for a plastic box to put her in, then he left in an ATV to get it. He was gone for a while—"

"How long a while?" Sheriff Kwinault asked.

"I had collected the bones, all the bits of cloth, and I said a prayer for the repose of her soul. So...half an hour? A little more?"

"Thank you. That helps," Sheriff Kwinault said. "When Lloyd Magnuson returned...?"

"He was driving his toy car. He had a big square plastic bin, like a storage bin where you keep a child's toys. I put the girl's bones in there."

"How was Lloyd?" Sheriff Kwinault's tone was carefully neutral.

Temo's tone matched hers. "I don't know what you mean."

"Was he sad for the death?" Kellen asked. "Did he seem frightened of the remains?" The caffeine and sugar helped her remember the scene, to get past her own horror and focus on the memory of Lloyd Magnuson at that moment.

"Frightened?" Temo still used that cautious voice.

"Most people don't like the idea of driving with a corpse," Kellen said.

A pause that went on long enough to make Kellen start to speak, and Sheriff Kwinault decisively signaled that she should not.

Finally, Temo said, "He was singing."

"Singing?" Sheriff Kwinault exchanged glances with Kellen and Max. "Happy songs?"

"Yes. Rap songs. From *Hamilton.* He... Like maybe he had a drink while he was at the resort. Liquid courage, maybe?" Temo was verbally squirming.

"Something more than liquor?" Sheriff Kwinault asked. "Maybe drugs?"

"Um..."

Kellen leaned forward and stared at the phone as if she could make eye contact, convince him. "It's okay, Temo. Tell her."

"*Sí.* Yes. He was high on something."

"Do you know what?" Kellen asked.

"I do not *know*. I didn't ask." In a fierce and bitter tone, Temo said, "He was a cop."

Sheriff Kwinault said, "I understand."

At her mild tone, Temo calmed a little. "I knew he shouldn't be on the road, but I'm brown. I've got an accent. I'm not from around here and I didn't try to stop him."

Sheriff Kwinault nodded. "I do understand. I promise I do. Please go on."

"I asked if he was okay. He said he was *great*, but his skin was flushed red and his eyes were very bright for a man who was going to take a corpse on a drive."

"All right. Then what happened?" Sheriff Kwinault asked.

"Then...nothing. I loaded the plastic box into the back of his toy car, and he drove away."

"*You* loaded the box into the car," Kellen repeated back at him.

"Yes. He almost forgot, so I did it." Now Temo let his curiosity take over. "Why?"

"That's all. Thank you. If I need to talk to you again, I'll call. Is that all right?" Sheriff Kwinault asked.

"*Sí*. As you wish. I will be here. He was a very weird man, but no matter. He didn't deserve death." Temo hung up.

For the first time since they'd started the call, Max returned to the desk and pulled up a chair. "We know that Lloyd was fine when Kellen left the scene. We know Lloyd was pumped full of heroin when he crashed his car. In between those two truths, we have some possibilities."

"He came back to the resort and, faced with driving a corpse to Virtue Falls, gave in to his addiction," Sheriff Kwinault said.

"Where'd he get the heroin?" Kellen asked.

"From his car?" Max suggested. "He'd already bought it offsite and had been fighting the need to use it? Alternately, someone at the resort offered it to him."

Kellen felt sick. "Who?"

Both Max and Sheriff Kwinault looked at her.

Kellen answered their unspoken question. "None of the current guests seem likely—" a lie, she thought Carson Lennex was very likely, but she wasn't ready to accuse him "—and I don't believe any of the employees are users. They're all functioning at a strong level. Right now, we don't have enough staff that anyone can slack off."

"They don't have to be users to distribute," Sheriff Kwinault said. "Assuming Temo was telling the truth—"

"He isn't a seller," Kellen said fiercely.

"—Lloyd Magnuson came back to get Priscilla Carter's body and he was already stoned. As he drove, he got progressively less able to operate the car, tried to stop somewhere, drove into the brush and out of sight. He died there, and at some point, someone took the plastic container with the corpse out of the vehicle." Sheriff Kwinault leaned forward. "Why was there a corpse with no hands? Why was Lloyd Magnuson given drugs? Why was the body stolen? What is going on here?"

Max answered, "Someone is using the Yearning Sands dock for smuggling."

Good. Kellen hadn't had to anguish over how much to tell Sheriff Kwinault. Max had taken the issue out of her hands.

Sheriff Kwinault was patently not surprised. "Do we know what? Or who?"

"We don't know what is being smuggled," Max said.

Kellen didn't correct him.

Max continued, "But we do think the head of smuggling is someone here at the resort."

"Very likely it's drugs, and whoever gave Lloyd the heroin is our felon." Sheriff Kwinault looked at Kellen. "You say not Temo?"

"No." Yet he needed to support his sister, and he'd do anything for her. Kellen feared he could be desperate enough to join a ruthless smuggler. Why not suspect him of distributing heroin, too? "Maybe."

"Any other suspects?" Sheriff Kwinault asked.

"I think too many?" Max looked at Kellen for confirmation.

She nodded.

Sheriff Kwinault sighed. "Have you called the Coast Guard?"

"Yes," Kellen said. "That is, not me, but yes, they've been contacted."

"Then they're keeping an eye on things here in between other duties." Sheriff Kwinault tapped her fingers on the desk. "Let me talk to them. The fact we've got a mutilated body that's missing and a dead law officer should get their attention."

"Will they listen to *you*?" Kellen asked.

"Yes. I'm the former Virtue Falls Coast Guard commander." Sheriff Kwinault gestured at the star on her chest. "And I have this nifty badge."

Max indicated Kellen. "*She's* a veteran of a war zone."

"Really?" Sheriff Kwinault looked Kellen over. "I wouldn't have guessed. Keeping up with your fitness?"

Kellen thought of Mara and their daily sparrings. "Yes." Like she had a choice.

"With any luck, our smugglers will underestimate you." Sheriff Kwinault stood. "I'll send officers to check in every few hours. Call us for any reason, no matter how small. Max, you're working security for the duration?"

"I am."

"Good. You look big. You look scary. Maybe that'll keep the bad guys at bay until the Coast Guard can scoop them up."

"I'll do my best Incredible Hulk imitation," Max promised.

Sheriff Kwinault smirked at him. "You're closer to the giant Marshmallow Man."

Yes. They had obviously met before.

Kellen and Sheriff Kwinault shook hands again. "Can I offer you dinner in our restaurant before you go?" Kellen asked.

"Thank you, I'd be delighted to take you up on it, but the weather folks are predicting a big storm and I'm on duty." Sheriff Kwinault shrugged her way into her coat. "Not that the weather folks have been right very often this winter."

"Dinner to go?" Kellen asked.

"That would be much appreciated," Sheriff Kwinault conceded.

"I'll set her up," Max said and took Sheriff Kwinault to the elevator and the lobby.

While he was gone, Kellen texted Mr. Gilfilen the news of Lloyd Magnuson's death and ended with a plea that he cease his operation.

His text came back. Acknowledged.

By which he meant he had received her news, and he would continue to do what he thought right.

When Max came back, Kellen was staring out the big window, where the everlasting gray clouds churned and threatened. "I gave Frances instructions to give Kateri anything she wanted as a to-go meal."

"Thank you."

"I called Annie and Leo to tell them about Lloyd Magnuson."

"Thank you again." She hadn't even thought to do that. "I informed Mr. Gilfilen… You do know about Mr. Gilfilen?"

"Leo told me. I think it's a stupid idea, but Vince Gilfilen is a force to be reckoned with." Max watched her watch the sky and asked, "Are you okay?"

"Somehow, that was worse than I expected." Kellen found she was sitting ramrod straight, her fists clenched at her sides. "I don't want to think of Lloyd being tempted by a devil. It's cruel and callous, and whoever it is, whatever it is, is here at the resort."

"At your refuge."

"Yes."

"And whoever did this could be your friend."

"Yes." The word was no more than a sigh.

He came around the desk and knelt beside her chair, and made his offer with every evidence of sincerity. "It's dangerous here. If you'd like to go away, I can assume control."

Shocked, she looked him square in the face. "What? What are you talking about?"

"I'll talk to Annie. I'm capable of being resort assistant manager. You can go on vacation, take a leave of absence. No one would think the worst of you. This situation is dangerous and—"

She pushed her chair away from him. "I can't leave. Run away? The resort is my responsibility. The people here are my responsibility. If one of my friends is guilty of these heinous acts—well, I recommended them to Annie and Leo. What kind of person would I be if I ran away?" She would be Cecilia, running away from her own cousin's death.

"I thought—"

"Stop thinking. You're security until Mr. Gilfilen returns to his regular duties, that's all. I'm in charge of the resort. I'll stay in charge of the resort." She stood up. "Now if you'll excuse me, I need to make rounds, talk to the guests and employees, assure them everything is being handled to the best of our abilities and their safety is our first concern. I suggest you do the same thing—go meet your security team, and after that, see if you can talk Mr. Gilfilen in before he gets killed, too."

Max watched Kellen stride out of the office.

This was not going at all like he expected.

30

Kellen arrived in the guest lounge in time to see the Shivering Sherlocks off to their last evening with Carson Lennex in his suite. Tonight, they assured her, they would discover who was guilty of...whatever silly mystery murder had occurred.

Kellen scolded herself. Guests had the right to come to Yearning Sands Resort and enact whatever frivolous drama they wished. These women deserved their vacation. They never expected to arrive when real murders and real terrors abounded. But Kellen did know she didn't have the patience, not tonight, to serve appetizers and drinks, and so she commissioned Sheri Jean. Then Kellen toured the rest of the resort: the kitchens, the spa, the housekeeping services. She did not visit the maintenance building. She knew she should show herself, but she feared her friends. She feared what she would have to do if one of them was guilty.

Instead, she went to her cottage, walked in, shut the door behind her and took a moment to breathe. In. And out. In. And out.

Xander would be proud.

She needed a moment alone in a place of her own, no guests, no staff, no noise. Just a meal eaten in peace without the constant yammer and the faces and the fear and the drama. She owed that to herself. She wandered through the kitchen, looking in cupboards. She had everything to put together Niçoise salad. That sounded good and easy, and—

Who did this Max think he was? Suggesting she flake out in the middle of multiple murders and a smuggling investigation?

She put water on to boil, assembled olive oil, vinegar, garlic and Dijon mustard for the dressing.

She was not that person. That was not her. Not since… Not since she woke up…

Cecilia woke in a panic of terror.

She didn't know where she was.

She didn't remember how she got here.

But someone wanted to kill her.

She didn't dare open her eyes for fear that whatever had trapped her was watching, waiting for a hint of life to pounce and slash and destroy.

Blindly, she tried to take survey of her surroundings.

The air around her was cool, fresh. So…she was inside a building. Her fingers twitched, feeling…a sheet below and a sheet above. She rested on a bed, her head slightly elevated on a firm mattress. Everything smelled clean. Music played, soothing music, meditation music.

Other than that…silence. No voices.

Her toes twitched.

She wanted to sit up, to get up, to run away. But she forced herself to remain still, quiescent, until that moment when she knew either she was alone…or she wasn't.

No way to tell except… She opened her eyes the thinnest slit. Without moving her head, she looked left. She looked right. Pale green walls. A window that looked out to a leafy tree and, beyond that, a gloomy gray sky. That ridiculous plinky-plunky music continued to play, music to soothe a restless mind. She opened her eyes all the way. She was alone in a hospital room. The door was open into a corridor. On one side of the bed, she saw a metal end table; against the wall, a tall metal cabinet, a chair with an open book facedown on the seat, and on a tray hooked to the chair's arm was an open cup of applesauce.

On the other side of the bed, she saw a shiny chrome IV stand that fed her fluids...and God knew what else.

Drugs. Someone was keeping her drugged. Gregory...

She froze. No. She remembered Kellen, Gregory, the murder, the explosion. She remembered Kellen's apartment. She remembered fleeing New York... But she remembered nothing else. She didn't know how she got into this room. Now she was trapped here, tied to an IV tube.

In an adrenaline-fueled fury, she tore away the tape that held the needle and pulled it out of her arm. Blood ran. Pain made her gasp. She used the corner of the sheet like a cotton pad, wrapping it over her wound. She closed her elbow to put pressure on the wound.

Her elbow moved rustily. Her neck was stiff. She felt weak. Every muscle ached, as if she hadn't moved in days.

God. What had they been doing to her?

And who were they?

Two monitors were attached to her chest with adhesive. She peeled them off with fingernails that were long and—too weird—manicured and painted with a clear lacquer.

Taking a breath, she worked her elbows under her and lifted herself off the pillows. The sheet slid down; she wore a pretty pajama top. She raised herself into a sitting position and pushed the sheet away. On the bottom, she wore matching soft cotton pajama pants.

Nothing made sense. This didn't make sense.

She was drugged. Yet she was cared for.

Why did she feel as if she'd been sick and in bed a long time? Why couldn't she remember? The burden of fear and panic was only increasing. She didn't know why, but she knew she didn't have much time.

She swung her legs over the edge of the bed. Pins and needles of pain rolled from her toes to her knees, and her head buzzed as if she was going to faint.

She was going to faint.

No! She needed to get out of here. Fast. Now.

She slid off the mattress, put her bare feet on the cool linoleum. The temperature woke her up, erased some of the cobwebs. She put more weight on her legs, pushed off and stood, slid back and rested. Stood again. Rested again. Stood sideways to the mattress and took one step, then another. Rested. Within one minute, she could walk the length of the bed, but as soon as she let go, her knees buckled.

She sat down in the bedside chair and ate the applesauce.

It tasted marvelous, and the half cup filled her up. How long since she had eaten real food?

She stood again, felt steadier and set her sights on the metal cabinet. It looked like a locker or a closet, and she needed clothes.

The IV stand had wheels. Perfect.

Taking it in both hands, she leaned and pushed, leaned and pushed, until she reached the cabinet. Standing there, she stared at the combination lock and wondered—could it be? ECKC. Earle, Cora, Kellen, Cecilia—3, 2, 5, 2. She took her time, rolled through the numbers.

The locker opened.

She stared at the partially open door and realized—she must have set the code. Who else would know about the code?

From somewhere down the corridor, she heard a raucous burst of laughter, hastily muffled.

Hurry. Hurry.

She flung open the door and examined the contents. Clothes: underwear, bra, jeans, a soft button-up shirt, belt, socks, shoes. On the shelf: the same travel wallet Cecilia had worn when she fled Greenleaf. A quick check showed nothing had changed. She had Kellen's driver's license, diplomas, passport. She stared at them in her hands, memory stirring. She had taken them from Kellen's apartment because she was afraid and wanted to get away to…to where?

She didn't know. Was this a mental institution? Was she committed? Was she crazy?

Get me out.

She had money. A couple of hundreds, a handful of twenties, miscellaneous small bills. If she got away, she could survive. She had survived on less…before…although she didn't remember when…

She gathered the clothes in one arm. Held the IV pole with one tight hand and pushed it into the bathroom. Locked the door, sat on the toilet and changed.

Her legs and arms were without muscle. The shirt was loose; the jeans required that the belt be fastened, not in the well-worn hole, but one notch tighter. But the shoes fit perfectly.

That made sense of a sort. Her clothes and shoes were hers, kept in a locker that opened with her combination.

If only she remembered.

When she finished dressing, she ran her shaking hands over her face. It was at that moment she found the scar on her forehead. With increasing alarm, she circled it with her fingers, exploring. It didn't hurt. There was bone under the skin. But when she pressed on it, it felt...weak on the inside. This time she stood easily, without thinking of the effort. She leaned over the sink and looked. Beneath her carefully trimmed bangs, a hard, one-inch round scar shone pink and shiny.

She pulled back and looked at her whole self. She was too gaunt and pale. Her eyes were frightened, sad. At some point, someone had cut her hair into short stylish wisps that framed her face and hid that scar from view.

She had been sick for a long time. Someone had carefully cared for her. The only scenario she could imagine was that Gregory's sister had somehow tracked her down and...and what? Been nice? Nothing about this made sense.

Except that she needed to escape.

She pulled the travel wallet over her head and tucked it under her shirt. Making as little noise as possible, she left the bathroom and went to the door that led to the corridor. She poked her head out. One glance told her all she needed to know.

The laughter came from the nurses' station at one end of the corridor. A dozen people in scrubs: the staff in this wing of a medical center. A man in dark blue scrubs knelt on one knee before a woman in pink patterned scrubs, and as Cecilia watched, the woman wiped a tear off her cheek, smiled and nodded.

More laughter, swiftly muffled.

A tired-looking man in a distinguished business suit walked toward the group, frowning.

Cecilia turned the other way, taking one careful step after another toward the exit sign. She passed two patients, one making the rounds on her walker, one seated in a wheelchair. They looked curiously at her, her IV stand and the dangling tubes, but made no comment.

She pushed on the exit door, stepped onto the landing.

A flight of stairs went up and down.

She looked at the number on the wall. She was on the second floor.

She could do this.

She pushed the IV pole into the corner, grasped the handrail and, taking her time, descended to street level. The exit door warned, "Security alarm will sound if door is opened."

She stopped, took several long breaths, gave the door a push and sprinted outside—onto a sidewalk beside a busy city street. Thank God. Thank God. She could quickly vanish. Straightening her shoulders, she joined the stream of people and disappeared into the city.

She would never be Cecilia again.

In her cottage kitchen, Kellen assembled her salad on her plate and sat down at the eating bar. She picked up her fork, put it down and rubbed the scar on her forehead.

Ceecee. Ceecee. Where are you? Come back to me...

Max Di Luca reminded her of the man in the corridor. The suit. The size. He didn't look tired anymore. And she wasn't sure, anyway. She'd been intent on escape. She'd only glanced.

But if that was the truth, she had known him before.

In Philadelphia.

31

That day, Kellen didn't return to the resort. If they had needed her, she would have gone, of course. But with a skeleton crew and few guests, she was able to handle the couple of crises from her phone. She wasn't avoiding Max; she was taking some much needed downtime.

Besides, a new memory was nudging itself up from the depths of her brain…

A park, trees bare of leaves, openmouthed pedestrians running. A man with a thin, familiar face who spoke with an Italian accent. He held a Beretta Pico to her forehead…

In the background, a man raced toward them and…

And nothing. Whatever happened then…was gone.

But that explained her scar, and why she woke up in the hospital that was maybe a mental ward and maybe not, and why when she woke, she was afraid someone was trying to hurt her. Maybe she wasn't crazy. Maybe if she knew all the facts, she would at least understand what had happened.

Maybe Max could tell her.

She should ask him.

Instead, Kellen pulled up her laptop and went to work, approving menus, viewing the employee roster with an eye to who might be the biggest baddest importer/murderer in the world, studying the resort's blueprints and wondering where Priscilla could have stashed the tomb art. The architect had designed the resort for visual impact, not working efficiency. Storage closets hid in absurdly inconvenient locations, narrow maids' stairways twisted and turned behind the walls, old-fashioned dumbwaiters that had once lifted and lowered linens and plates from level to level... Even if Priscilla Carter had hidden the tomb art somewhere in the resort, one of the housekeepers could have found that gross figure of a man with his massive penis, shrieked in horror and tossed it all in the garbage.

Kellen sighed.

The phone rang.

It was Annie. Her warm voice asked, "How are things going?"

My friends are mad at me.

I'm being haunted by a ghost or tormented by someone who knows my past, and I'm not sure which is worse.

Nils Brooks wants to kiss me.

Your stupid nephew thinks I'm a delicate flower. Or a quitter. I don't know which is more insulting.

"As well as can be expected. Employees are jumping ship at an alarming rate. I hope you're all right with this, but I'm approving every unexpected request for vacation and leave, and offering a bonus when they return."

Annie's voice grew somber. "You're doing exactly the right thing. They're nervous about the murders?"

"Add to that the weather." Kellen glanced at the radar. "We've got another big storm coming in. It's four in the afternoon and like midnight out there. You know. The darkness is difficult even without finding a corpse or two."

"When I get back, I'll send you on vacation whether you want it or not!"

"I wasn't hinting!" Kellen remembered Birdie, and no matter what Kellen felt right now, Birdie needed time off. "But Birdie and I would like to go somewhere sunny."

"I'm glad to hear you've relented at last. Do we have enough employees to keep the resort running?"

"Yes, but only because we have so few guests."

"I never thought I would say that's a good thing." Pause. "Did Max make it?"

"Yes." Kellen inserted a pause of her own. "He's gone to acquaint himself with his security team, for what they're worth."

"What did you think of him?" Annie sounded anxious and nervous.

"I barely met him." Already she'd spent too much time with him. "He seems fine. He knows the sheriff, and that's good." *I knew him before, didn't I?*

"Max is a Renaissance man. He knows about security and resort management, and wineries and… Well, he's very accomplished."

"So you've said."

"Am I overselling him?"

"A little." *And that makes me wonder why.*

"I simply want you to feel as if you can trust him to do his job."

That was a good reason why. "Thank you, Annie. I'm glad to turn security over to him." In the background, Kellen heard a burst of noise, children's voices shrieking in wild delight as they ran through. "You need to go and enjoy *your* vacation. I'll talk to you later!" She hung up before Annie could say goodbye, sat and looked at the telephone. She should be asking probing questions, asking for honesty.

Maybe later, when the murders were solved, the Librarian arrested, winter had ended, world peace had been declared…

She wanted to know, but she didn't. Ignorance was comfortable, safe, without challenge. She was, in fact, tired of standing tall and facing all confrontations with her chin up. She wanted to slump for a while.

Although she and Max did sort of click. Until he thought she'd be glad to run away from her responsibilities. Damn him. Until that moment, he was doing so well.

That evening, she sat with all the lights in her cottage dimmed and watched out her bedroom loft window, watched to the west and the way leading up from the dock.

She saw nothing.

That meant nothing.

The smugglers could be out there with special lights and drones that allowed them to see in the dark, with guns and bombs and traps, and all to bring a few bloodstained relics to a greedy smuggler and his wealthy, grasping collector of illegal goods. Kellen thought about Afghanistan, the battles she had fought, the deaths and destruction she'd seen, and fury held her in its grasp. She hadn't carried a rifle through the treacherous mountains so Americans at home could break the law and fund the very terrorists she'd fought.

Fate led Cecilia in a straight line from the hospital to stand in front of an Army Recruiting Station. She looked in the window at the two people in uniform seated at desks inside. She looked back in the direction of the hospital, looked around at the busy streets, the indifferent people. Danger stalked her here. She didn't know what danger, but she knew something terrible had happened and she needed to get out of this town. What better way to disappear than into the massive organization called the US military?

Pushing open the door, she walked in. Her mind immediately assembled a catalog of data on the officers:

ARMY RECRUITERS:
ONE MALE, ONE FEMALE, PLEASANT AND BRISK, SKEPTICAL WHEN LOOKING ME OVER, DISCOURAGING ABOUT MY CONDITION AND ABILITY TO PASS THE STRINGENT PHYSICAL. PRODUCE STERN WARNINGS ABOUT DRUG USE. IMPRESSED BY KELLEN'S DEGREES, SATISFIED BY PHOTO ID.

The male recruiter, Sergeant Barnes, said, "With these credentials, we'll send you to Officer Candidate School."

"If you pass the physical," Sergeant Rehberger snapped. She was more realistic, less hopeful of Cecilia's chances.

Cecilia nodded at her. "I'm good with numbers, data structure, patterns." As she spoke, her mind was collecting more information about the recruiters, this station, how to turn the details of this situation to her advantage. She could give answers that they wanted to hear, because by their body language and by logic, she could anticipate their needs.

She had never had this gift before, but she knew how to use it now.

They put the paperwork in front of her. She filled it all in without hesitation, using Kellen's New York address, Kellen's birthday, Kellen's degrees. She was, she realized, being Kellen Rae Adams in every way. She got ready to sign and date the forms. "What day is this?" she asked.

Sergeant Barnes said, "May twelfth."

Then she scrawled Kellen's signature and passed over the paperwork.

The recruiter ran through it all, asked a few questions, got to the end and laughed, scratched out the date and passed it back. "I know—I still get the year wrong, too. Initial the change, then we're on to the next stage."

That was when she discovered she'd lost more than a year of her life.

Lost it, apparently, forever.

Someone knocked on her front door.

She clutched the arms of her chair. She knew who was there.

Another knock. The bell rang.

"Bastard." She stood and clattered down the spiral stairs. She looked through the peephole, then flung open the door. "What a surprise," she said in a voice heavily laden with irony.

Nils Brooks stood on the porch. "May I come in?" Like a vampire who had to be invited to cross the threshold.

"If you must." She backed away.

He dusted a few flakes of snow off his shoulders. There, in the porch light, his disguise was stripped away. He looked like a dangerous man, strong, wiry, with a determined jaw and a fake pair of eyeglasses in his pocket. He came in, flung off his Burberry coat and hung it on the rack. "The weathercasters got it wrong again. The main thrust of the storm went south to Oregon."

She didn't answer, and she didn't turn up her lights.

His conversational tone changed. "What do you know?" He demanded information as if he was in charge.

"Lloyd Magnuson is dead."

He dismissed the information with a wave of the hand. "We already had that figured out. What else do you know?"

"You don't give a damn, do you?" She looked at him in the dim light and saw a man driven by ambition. "Someone trapped Lloyd Magnuson by using his own weakness and now he's dead."

He seated himself in the easy chair beside her front door. "Gossip at the resort says he used heroin."

"Exactly."

"Then why was he trapped? He was simply weak." Nils couldn't have sounded more indifferent.

"I don't like you." She had never meant anything so much. "Do you have no weaknesses?"

"Yes." He came to his feet, caught her shoulders and kissed her.

She didn't punch him in the ribs or use the serrated edge of her flashlight on his face. She let him kiss her, mouth to mouth, breath to breath, and as the moment stretched out, she relaxed, accepted the sensation, lived in the moment...and when he lifted his mouth from hers, she said, "I'd give it a B plus."

"Are you frigid?"

She laughed in his face. "Because I don't want to sleep with you? I suspect if you looked around this world, you could find a great many people, both women and men, who don't want to sleep with you."

"I'm only interested in the one."

Most of the time, she didn't like him. Then he was charming and self-deprecating, and she did. "You can leave now."

He pulled on his winter gear. "Let me know if you remember anything I need to know." At the door, he turned and asked, "Who's the guy with the big feet?"

Your competition. But he wasn't. She didn't want to kiss him, either. "Max Di Luca. He's come to handle security. He's smart, he's tough and he's fast. You'd better figure out this investigation quickly, or he'll figure it out for you."

Nils took a step toward her.

For the first time since that first night, she pulled her pistol and pointed it at his chest. "Don't."

"This is not a game," he said. "Let's end this before it gets deadly."

"Priscilla Carter is dead. Lloyd Magnuson is dead. Your Jessica is dead." She slapped him with words, with truth. "How much more deadly do you want it to be?"

"I want it to end with the good guys alive."

"Then you'd better go out there and see that they do."

Kellen barricaded herself in her cottage, set a trap beneath every window and in front of the door and slept the sleep of the pure.

In the wee hours of the morning, her phone vibrated and lit up, and she woke from a dream of something about sex and Max and…sex.

Caller ID placed the number inside the resort, and for one moment she couldn't imagine who among the guests would have her number, and who among the staff would call her when they could text.

Then she knew. She leaped to her feet, swayed as she fought for her equilibrium. "Mr. Gilfilen?"

No sound. Only the faintest breathing.

"Mr. Gilfilen?"

His voice was almost nonexistent. "Depend…you."

"I'm coming," she said. "Hang on. I'll be there as fast as I can."

32

Kellen's ATV swayed as she leaped in. She drove through a blistering cold wind and past the occasional snowflake toward the west wing, toward the suite Vincent Gilfilen had appropriated for his investigation, and all the time she prayed she was in time. Mr. Gilfilen had undertaken this mission because he believed he could make a difference. He should not die for his efforts.

She parked and grabbed the first aid kit. She used her pass card to open the outer door, pulled her pistol and proceeded cautiously into the empty living room. Across the eating bar, a light shone over the range top in the kitchen.

She listened but heard nothing, only her own breath, harsh and broken.

She looked but saw nothing. Then…a dark blot on the rug. A trail of wet crimson into the bedroom, into the bathroom. She followed that trail, pistol clutched in one hand, first aid kit in the other. The bathroom light was on. She stepped into the doorway. And saw him—Vincent Gilfilen, smeared with blood, unconscious, stretched out on his back. The throw rug was rolled and thrust under his neck, tilting his head back, revealing a dark throat bruised darker in a long thin line. Someone had used a garrote on him.

The cat, the mangy cat he had rescued, sat on the counter and growled at her.

"It's all right," she told it. "I'll help him." She stepped over his prone body, faced the door, dropped on her knees beside him. "Mr. Gilfilen!" She touched his cheek.

His eyelids flickered. He twitched as if fighting for breath, but his chest didn't move. She adjusted his head, pinched his nose, put her mouth to his and tried to fill his lungs. No luck.

The swelling in his throat had obstructed his airway.

She had no time, and she had no choice. If he didn't get oxygen soon, he would die, another victim of the Librarian.

Kellen would not stand for that. She understood the procedure for an emergency tracheotomy. She knew how…in theory.

She'd learn on the job. Right now. As she opened the first aid kit, she called Max. He answered, she said, "Nine-one-one to the west wing. STAT."

"On my way." He hung up.

She searched the first aid kit, found gauze, tape, a tube. Nothing to cut with. Very well. She popped open her pocketknife. It was sharp; she always made sure of that. But she had no time to sterilize. Hell, she didn't have time to think.

The cat growled again.

"I'm hurrying," she said. With her fingers, she located Mr. Gilfilen's Adam's apple, found the spot between it and the next hard ring, and without pausing for courage—he had no time left—she cut a slit through his skin and into the tough gristle of his trachea. Blood welled. She wiped it with the gauze, pinched the hole open and inserted the tube. "Okay, breathe."

Nothing happened.

She pressed on his chest. "You're supposed to start breathing."

Nothing.

"You're not going to die like this." She took a hard, deep breath, leaned down and exhaled forcefully into the tube. Once. Twice.

His chest expanded.

"Mr. Gilfilen! Breathe!" she said firmly. She exhaled into the tube again.

His chest rose again.

"On your own this time!" She leaned down to do it again.

The cat yowled and jumped off the counter, landed close to his head.

Kellen jumped and gasped.

The cat raced out of the bathroom.

Mr. Gilfilen's chest gave a great heave. And another. And another.

She wanted to collapse with relief.

He was breathing, but his rapid pulse and cool, clammy skin told her he was in shock. Shock would kill him.

She had no time for tears, but they trickled down her cheeks as she wrapped him in the second bath mat, then ran to strip the blankets off the bed. When she returned, his eyes were open. He couldn't speak, but his eyes flicked at her.

"Honestly," she scolded as she flung the blankets over his legs and went looking for the source of all that blood. "I tried to tell you. Let the big boys handle this. Did you listen? No, you did not. Now look what they did to you."

He closed his eyes.

"Look what they did to—" she faltered "—your hand." His left hand was half severed. He'd wrapped it in his handkerchief. How he had not bled to death, she didn't know.

Outside in the suite, she heard a tumult as people crowded through the door, as Max called her name.

"In the bathroom," she shouted.

He got there first, filled the doorway with his mass, took in the situation. He moved in and took over, pushed her gently out of the way. He wrapped Mr. Gilfilen more tightly in the blankets, called for warm packs, pressed the hand firmly onto the arm, said to Kellen, "They'll try to reattach." Then to the resort's assembled first aid team, "Get ice packs for the hand."

In moments, the team had stabilized Mr. Gilfilen, loaded him onto a gurney and wheeled him away.

When he was gone, Kellen sat on the toilet and did what she'd told Mr. Gilfilen to do. She breathed.

Max returned with a throw. He flung it around her shoulders, knelt and hugged her.

She let him. Philadelphia or not, she needed a hug.

"Helicopter is on its way," he said. "You saved his life."

"I hope so. Did you find the cat?" she asked.

"What cat?"

The one that saved Mr. Gilfilen's life.

She turned to him. She had wondered what she should say when next she saw Max Di Luca, the questions she should ask, the explanations she should demand. But her private nightmares didn't matter now. Instead, she said, "We've got to evacuate the guests."

"And all personnel."

She shook her head. "No. One of them is a killer. We have to find out who and end this thing."

33

In the morning, Mr. Gilfilen was still alive in the ICU in a Portland, Oregon, hospital, Kellen had donned her Kevlar vest under her shirt and was carrying her pistol and the Yearning Sands guests were being kindly ushered out the door. Finding guests accommodations elsewhere was easy enough in the off-season and with such a reduced guest list. The official story was that a structural problem had been uncovered in the recent construction. Most of them had heard some version of the real story and were more than willing to accept a voucher or better accommodations elsewhere.

No one could find Nils Brooks to ask him to leave—dark and suspicious mutterings were heard—and Kellen felt her suspicions of him rise once more.

Carson Lennex flatly refused to go. The resort was, he said, his home, and no killer was going to chase him away. Which in the circumstances was damned shady, to say the least.

As people came and went, Max made himself useful, carrying bags, helping Frances and Sheri Jean contact the other resorts, reassuring the guests. More than that, he was the security manager, he was clearly packing a firearm and he was *visible.* His size alone, packaged nicely in that dark suit, seemed to reassure everyone and keep terror at bay.

Kellen personally arranged transportation for those headed to the airstrip and organized the farewell appetizers and beverages in the lobby for every departing guest. Finding the necessary staff to handle the workload proved the real challenge; most of the spa staff called in sick or scared, some of the maids and desk staff simply didn't come to work and the security center was unmanned. Chef Reinhart and Chef Norbert arrived separately, both bearing well-sharpened butcher knives in their belts; the sous chef for each was a no-show. That created a great kerfuffle in the kitchen as they shouted commands at each other, until Gabriella got tired of listening and made them chop for her.

Birdie drove the first group to the airstrip to catch Chad Griffin's plane to Seattle, but when Kellen tried to locate Temo for the second shift, he was unreachable, and she wanted to find him, shake him, make him be the Temo she believed him to be.

The last group out the door was the Shivering Sherlocks; they were scheduled to check out today anyway, but Kellen gave them a voucher for one night free on their next visit and got into the driver's seat to take them to the airstrip. Mitch came along to serve the food and drink, and to charm the women with his good looks and flattery.

That was fine with Kellen. Her focus kept wandering, running through the suspects in her mind. To pick up a gun and shoot someone required a cold purpose—or a hot temper. But to deliberately attempt to strangle a man, to watch him kick and struggle, then when he was subdued, to take a sharp blade and try to sever his hand…that was cold. That was vicious.

Mr. Gilfilen had lived, but what had he done to his attacker to escape? He couldn't tell her. He couldn't tell anyone. He was unconscious, recovering from surgery, fighting for his life. She would figure this out, and she would get her revenge. For Mr. Gilfilen, and for all of the victims who had died for this deadly game of smuggling. She would get revenge for herself, too. She'd come back to the United States determined to work hard, play hard, be strong, be brave for all the days that were left to her.

Not to witness more pain. Not to fight an unseen foe who lived for blood and cruelty.

Who was it?

She glanced at Mitch, half-turned toward the back, asking the Shivering Sherlocks about their mystery weekend, asking what they would remember when they got home.

"I'll tell you what I'll remember." Candy sat directly behind the driver's seat, and she leaned forward and spoke right in Kellen's ear. "The guest bath in Carson Lennex's penthouse was busy, so I hustled upstairs to his suite to use the potty up there. Guess what I found?"

"Tell me you didn't dig through his nightstand and find his porn," Rita said.

"Not porn." In the rearview mirror, Kellen saw Candy frown. "I don't think. It certainly wasn't hidden away."

Nancy leaned forward out of the very back seat. "What was it?"

Candy said, "He had these stone statues on glass shelves with lights under each one, and I'm telling you, girls—"

Kellen found herself breathing slowly, steadily, listening intently.

"—if we ever met a man with a package like that," Candy continued, "we'd run for the hills."

"What was it?" Tammy asked.

"Some kind of fertility god, I suppose. Gross, this little guy holding this penis twice his size." Candy must have made a gesture, because the women whooped with laughter.

Abruptly, Mitch turned around and faced front.

Because the Shivering Sherlocks were giving him the very information he needed? Or because he was embarrassed by a group of elderly women hooting about a man's genitals?

"Sounds like an Inuit fertility god," Rita suggested.

"Exactly." Candy sounded pleased with the idea. "There was

a female statue, too, all fat and pregnant, an exaggeration of fertility. Carson Lennex collects some pretty weird stuff."

"Probably he didn't think anyone would see it," Patty said.

"He wasn't too worried about it. There was *backlighting.*" Candy sounded as if she had settled back against the seat. "Those things were the grossest statues I ever saw. Art! Heaven preserve me."

"Come on. Don't you remember the toilet paper cover my grandmother crocheted? The one with the Barbie doll standing in the middle of the cardboard tube, and the crocheted part hung over the toilet paper and looked like a skirt?"

Kellen glanced in the rearview mirror.

Candy waggled her head. "You're right—that was worse. But only because it was so tacky. I'm pretty sure *this* was art."

Mitch was frowning, his cheeks flushed, his elbow on the window ledge, his hand over his mouth.

Kellen had to get these ladies out of here and to safety.

A charter plane waited for the Shivering Sherlocks. Kellen and Mitch loaded them and their luggage and waved them goodbye, then piled into the van. Kellen got behind the wheel and they headed for the resort. "Mitch, what are you thinking?"

He pulled a wad of dollar bills out of his pocket. "I'm thinking that, for as much trouble as they were, those old ladies didn't tip very well."

"I mean...what are you thinking about the situation we have here at the resort? About the violence. What do you think is happening?"

"Have you seen Temo?" He sounded tense, terse, intent.

"I haven't seen much of him, no." She'd heard him in the maintenance garage. She'd heard him on the phone. But other than the brief chat in the resort kitchen, she hadn't seen him.

"I'll be frank with you. He's got me worried. Working weird hours, mad at the world, talking about family. His mother recently went to prison, and did you hear about the stepfather?"

"I… No. I didn't hear anything about his stepfather."

"Temo told me he's going to kill him."

Kellen put it together. "Because of his sister?"

"He said he put the girl with relatives, but he hasn't called her and he won't say anything about her. I don't know." Mitch seemed bewildered. "When Temo lost his leg, he went violent. And that poor fellow who died—"

"Lloyd Magnuson?"

"Yes, him. Temo was the last one to see him. What is he thinking? Why would he kill him?"

Kellen's doubts twisted and changed. Was Mitch deliberately misleading her, turning the evidence toward Temo? But he wasn't, really. Only reminding her of Temo's odd and disturbing actions. Even so, it was Mitch she mistrusted. Mitch had never done anything Kellen could put her finger on, yet he smiled when he should frown, moved when he should be still. When he spoke of his parents, he did so with reverence, but to her knowledge, in all the time he'd been here, he never contacted them and not once had he passed on family news or anecdotes. Not that Kellen trusted Temo, but more than that, the way Mitch looked at his own hands made her think she should get a message to Nils Brooks about the statues in Carson Lennex's care.

She projected a mix of worry and urgency—and she wasn't acting. "Do we have other guests to be transported?"

"I didn't think you ever forgot anything like guests and their comings and goings." But he didn't seem unduly suspicious. He seemed preoccupied. "The newlyweds were fighting and they didn't get ready in time to go with the Shivering Sherlocks. They should be in the lobby now."

"Please take them to the airstrip while I search for any remaining guests and the employees who haven't checked in." She stopped the van under the portico and grasped Mitch's hands. "Thank you for warning me about Temo. I swear, when this is over, you'll get your reward."

Mitch looked as if he didn't know if he'd been praised or threatened, and for sure he didn't want to take the newlyweds anywhere. But he didn't challenge Kellen, and as she fled into the lobby and up the stairs to Annie's office, he was rounding up the newlyweds and loading them into the van.

Kellen hoped he would stop at the kitchen for their appetizers, but she was willing to bet the fighting newlyweds were getting the Shivering Sherlocks' leftovers. In the meantime, she needed to track down Nils Brooks. She called him, left a message. Texted him that she knew where the stolen tomb artifacts were. Got no response.

She got a text from Max. Can you come to security?

She hurried.

He sat alone in the room, facing the wall of monitors. He beckoned her over. "Look at this."

She joined Max and watched as Mr. Lennex walked along an empty fifth-floor corridor, holding something that looked like a big flat book. He looked around to make sure he was alone, then disappeared into the housekeepers' storage closet. He came out with another big flat book, a little larger, but he was holding it by the corners, looking at it and smiling.

He was holding a painting of some kind.

"What the hell?" Max said.

Light dawned in a slow, warm sunshine. "That's it. That's what he's been doing." Kellen kissed Max on the cheek. "Thank you. You're brilliant!" She ran toward the door, turned back. "Have you seen Nils Brooks?"

"Not at all." Max had his hand on his cheek and he watched her like…like Hagrid viewed a new dragon egg.

Damn it. Mara was right. As if things weren't complicated enough, Max was interested. She backed toward the door and out. "If you see him, I really need to speak to him."

As the door shut, she heard him say, "Hmm."

What did that mean? Nothing good, she was sure.

She beat Carson Lennex back to his suite. She knocked, and when he didn't answer, she let herself in, left the door open behind her and went up the spiral stairs to the bedroom. Exactly as Candy had said, the sculptures were displayed against a lighted backdrop that underscored the skill of the artists who had created them.

From downstairs, she heard Carson call, "Hello?"

"I'm up here, Mr. Lennex."

He ran lightly up the stairs, and at the sight of her, he lifted his eyebrows. "I've had a lot of women trick their way into my bedroom, but I never imagined you'd be one of them. Aren't I lucky!" His Irish accent gave the words a sardonic quality, and he joined her to look at the sculptures. "But I suspect I'm mistaken in your intentions."

"None of the housekeeping staff came in today. I could *make* your bed while I'm here." She took the painting out of his hands. "May I?" Splatters and squares made up the image. "Is it good?"

"Very good. It's an original Jacie Merideth. I imagine when she did the painting for the resort, she was an unknown. Now this is worth tens of thousands."

Kellen shook her head and handed it back to him. "*I* thought you were stealing toilet paper."

Carson threw back his head and laughed loud and long. "Now you know. You wouldn't believe the decorations hidden away in storerooms here. No one ever goes through it. No one ever throws anything away."

Kellen thought of the car manuals Birdie was tossing. "I would believe it."

"Searching through the junk—and it is mostly junk—satisfies the archaeologist in me, because every once in a while, I find a treasure. Two years ago, I decorated my suite in 1950s kitsch."

"Annie knows you're doing this?"

"Of course. Miss Adams, I'm not a thief. Nothing ever leaves the premises. It simply gets redistributed."

"What about these?" She gestured at the stone statues, fierce, sexual, powerful.

"Those are an anomaly. I can't imagine who brought them to the resort in the first place." He propped the painting on his dresser. "It's not standard hotel room decoration, not in any era. All I can figure is one of the suite residents was a wealthy collector and died either without heirs or with heirs who cared for nothing but the money, and these got stashed and lost forever."

"Then you do know what they are."

"Absolutely. It's looted Central American tomb art. Probably been gathering dust for years." He lost his patina of sophisticated amusement and became, for a few minutes, serious and a little impatient. "Don't worry, Miss Adams, I wasn't going to keep them. After I admired them for a few months, I was going to take them to Annie and have her donate them to the appropriate museum. I didn't play Indiana Jones, but I agree with him. These belong in a museum."

"Actually, these have only been at the resort since September."

Carson must have caught a whiff of ominous, because his voice grew sharp. "How do you know that?"

"Are you aware of smuggling activities along the coast?"

"Right out there." He gestured toward the dock. "I have the wraparound deck, I'm eight stories off the ground and I'm not blind. But I assumed...drugs?" He looked at the art. "Of course not. Why bother with drugs when you can make more with artifacts looted from World Treasure sites?" He swung to face her. "Why September?"

"Priscilla..."

"That girl? She was smuggling? No." He was very certain. "She didn't want to do the work to get rich. She wanted to sleep her way into it."

"We speculate that she stole those items from the smugglers and—"

He caught on at once and finished the sentence for her. "They murdered her."

"And drugged Lloyd Magnuson when he was to drive her body to the coroner and took the body before it could be examined."

He looked again at the art and said in an astonished tone, "Damn. I could be in trouble. It's all the fault of the tablet."

34

"Tablet?" Kellen counted the pieces on the shelf. They were missing one.

"The last piece of the collection is a tablet chiseled from the tomb wall. Very rare find." Carson's enthusiasm began to rise. "Most Mayans wrote on paper called amate, made from the wild fig tree."

Kellen widened her eyes at him.

"And...you don't care." He sighed and got back on the subject. "I don't read Mayan hieroglyphs well, so I brought it back here with the others and used my college textbook to translate the symbols. It's a curse, and I'm superstitious enough to not want to be tormented by a long-dead Mayan lord, so I returned it to the storage room."

"The way things are going, I don't know if you replaced it quickly enough." She gestured at the statues. "Can we package these up? I'll take them to Max for safekeeping. That'll be one worry relieved."

"Of course. I've got the parcel they came in." He went to his closet and came out with an oblong box filled with Bubble Wrap.

Together they wrapped the tomb art.

"I would think the last piece is safe enough in storage. We'll get it when we've secured the situation." She offered her hand. "Thank you, Mr. Lennex, you've solved half the crime."

He took her hand and held it. "What's the other half?"

"Who's doing this."

"One scary bastard."

"We need something a little more definite than that, but I believe we're getting close. Let me get these off your hands, and we'll move on to the next step." The box was heavy for its size, and knowing what was inside, she used both hands to carry it.

He escorted her to the elevator, pushed the button to summon it and said with some humor, "Next time I find you in my bedroom, can I assume you've come on a less deadly quest?"

"Of course, Mr. Lennex. Please be careful. I'm not the only one who knows you had the artifacts."

"Who else?"

"Mitch Nyugen."

"He works in maintenance and he drives for the resort. He's a friend of yours." Carson was very well-informed. "Are we suspicious of him?"

"*Suspicious* is a strong word. Let's say wary."

"He's been here less time than you have."

"He could be working for the scary bastard, and if that's the truth..." She took a breath. "Mitch was a good soldier. He's trained to survive, and he's trained to kill."

"He's the real deal."

"Precisely." The doors opened and she got in. "To get him out of the way, I sent him to the airstrip with the last of the guests, but if he works for or with someone, he could have contacted them."

"Someone who cuts off people's hands? I'll be careful. You, too." He saluted as the doors closed.

Kellen exited near the security center, and as she walked the empty corridor, she glanced around. The sense of being watched crawled up her spine.

And apparently she was being watched, for when she got close, Max opened the door. "What have you got?" he asked.

"Smuggled art."

She entered and he shut the door behind her. "You liberated smuggled art." Now he looked at her as if she was Wonder Woman.

According to Birdie's fictitious account, she was a superhero, and right now, she was feeling pretty smug. "Think it will fit in the vault?"

"We'll make it work." He ran through the code, then pressed his finger to the identifier. It figured that he was one of the privileged few who could access the safe.

The big old bank vault with the new locking system creaked open.

He cleared off a shelf and they placed the box inside.

When the vault door shut with a solid sound, she relaxed against it and grinned. "We're doing good. Any sign of Nils Brooks yet?"

"None."

"Any trouble in sight?"

With some humor, he said, "*You're* here."

She remembered that hungry look he'd given her earlier. Now his interest seemed businesslike.

"Who is Nils Brooks?" he asked. "Who is he *really*?"

Should she tell him? Annie had sent her trusted nephew as security for the resort. But death stalked the dim corridors and windswept grounds. Kellen needed help and Max could give it, and so in the plainest, fastest way she could, she outlined her history with Nils.

When she finished, Max said, "The CIA? The MFAA? He's *undercover*? Come on! You do realize how absurd that all sounds?"

"I do, especially in light of his disappearance. But, Max, right now, I only trust me and thee, and I'm not so sure about thee. Or me, for that matter." She meant that more than she could say. About both of them.

But he chuckled, a nice, rich, warm sound. "I'll help you search. You think he's here—"

"He is not leaving now, not when things are coming to a head."

"Where can he be that we can't see him?"

Her annoyance with Nils fought with her fear for him. "Dead under a rock on the beach."

"Kellen, with all due respect, I can hardly believe he's former CIA and undercover with a newly re-formed government agency that is concerned with, of all things, antiquities."

Everything Max said fed into her own doubts, made her feel foolish and resentful. "If there's a chance that he's telling the truth—"

"I know. You're right. Re-forming the MFAA is a good idea. I simply don't know that I believe the government ever follows through on good ideas." Max pushed his hair off his forehead. "Where is he if he's not dead under a rock?"

"In the spa. In the restrooms. In one of the guest rooms. Because of privacy issues, there are no security cameras in those locations."

"I'll check the spa first," Max said in heavy irony.

"I'm going to check his cottage. He didn't answer the house phone this morning when we wanted him to evacuate. He didn't respond when Frances knocked on his door. She said she went in and called for him and searched. But she's frightened. I can't see her poking into every corner."

"You think he hid in the closet or behind the shower curtain?" Max's tone started out incredulous and ended in a brief, humorous laugh.

"Or he was out beating the bushes."

"Or he's dead somewhere." Max said that in a matter-of-fact tone.

"Yes. That's possible, too. I texted him and he never answered."

"Be careful out there," Max said.

"Be careful in here," Kellen replied.

"No problem. I'm the Incredible Hulk, remember?"

"And I'm Wonder Woman."

As she started to walk out, he caught her arm. "After this is over, we'll need to talk."

She took a breath. "Philadelphia?"

"You remember?"

Her heartbeat sped up. *Confirmation.* He was part, maybe all, of her forgotten past. "Not really."

Heat shimmered in the air between them. They looked at each other, each searching for some remnant of the past, of passion remembered and passion forgotten.

"Later," he said and let her go.

Later? There might not be a later. And she wanted to *know.*

She leaned into him, settled against his big body, absorbed the heat and the muscled strength.

If he'd known her before—and she did believe him—he'd known her as a woman to be protected, to be handled with care. So he waited, his chest rising and falling with each desperate breath.

She slid her hands up his arms, around his neck, went on her tiptoes and pressed her lips to his.

Still he waited.

So she turned a touch into a kiss and a kiss into sunshine and shadow, nuance and blatant lust. The long dark of the Washington winter disintegrated and became summer on a restless ocean where they drowned without breath, without care, without self.

She pulled back with a gasp—some parts of her body didn't care if she drowned, but her lungs finally objected—and her hands trembled as she let them drop out of his hair.

At some point in the kiss, he had wrapped one arm around her waist, the other…

"Um, can you let go of my butt?" She looked everywhere but at his face. "I really need to go and, um..."

"Right." The rumble of his voice was harsh, scratchy, and he released her reluctantly.

Well, sure. He was ready to go all the way. No mistaking that.

She slipped out of the security office and then the resort. She didn't need this distraction. Not now. All these years...

She had never seen the grounds so deserted. The bitterly cold wind whipped through the grass, swirled chips of ground cover into the air like tiny wood shards aimed at the eyes. To the west, tall gray clouds sped toward her; the storm the weather people had predicted was arriving at last. Desolation hung over the resort, waiting for that moment when the tempest broke, when the blood spilled, when death or justice claimed the land.

Since when had Kellen become a fanciful idiot?

She didn't know, and she didn't like it, but as she drove the ATV toward Nils's cottage, she felt exposed and hunched down to make herself a smaller target. Her Kevlar vest didn't cover nearly enough flesh.

She parked and clattered up the stairs; no point in sneaking up on him, the man had a gun. She knocked loudly and yelled, "Nils!" then inserted her pass card and swung the door wide.

"Come in," he called from the shadowy depths.

She texted Max, Found him, stashed her phone and walked into the cottage. She took one look at Nils stretched out in the easy chair, his feet elevated on the ottoman, and shut the door behind her. "You look worse for wear."

He had a black eye that extended down to his jaw and an ice bag strapped to his left elbow.

"Did you try to kiss somebody else?" she asked.

"Ha." He wore a leather holster strapped to his chest with the grip of his Beretta M9 protruding.

"Why didn't you answer my text?"

"Last night, I lost my phone."

She looked him over again. He had a fighting knife and a Ruger LCP .380 ultracompact resting on the end table close to his right hand. Somehow, he'd been involved in a fight. With Vincent Gilfilen? Against Vincent Gilfilen? "Tell me about last night."

"After I left you—"

She went to the refrigerator and got them both bottles of water.

"—I stepped out of your house, and I couldn't see any lights down at the dock, but the wind wasn't blowing, the clouds were low and I could sure hear that big boat engine roaring toward shore."

"You said you didn't want to interfere, that that wasn't going to help capture the Librarian."

"I was tired of sitting around." He accepted the bottle and pressed it to his black eye. "I needed some action. I was horny."

She laughed. "Oh, Nils. You romantic devil."

"Do you want to know what happened or not?"

She thought maybe she knew now, but she perched on a chair arm and got ready to listen.

"I couldn't take the ATV. They make too much noise. So I started running, keeping my head down, doing bursts, zigzags, stopping suddenly. If the smugglers had some kind of night vision, I figured—confuse them."

"Talk about luck. If they'd had *thermal* night vision—"

"Right. I know. They would have seen me. But they didn't, so I managed to get to that give-everybody-the-finger tree and not get shot—I was pleased about that—and I stood there next to the trunk. One person was standing off to the side on a rock."

"The Librarian."

"He was directing the operation, so yes." Nils held up one hand. "Before you ask, no, I couldn't see him. It was *dark*. Two guys carried a box up from the beach. Heavy box, took them both to lift it. No, I couldn't identify them, either."

"But you could see them."

"I had my night vision by then, and I was wondering what the hell I was doing there, because this was a suicide mission. I had my pistol, but no doubt they had more firepower than I did and sooner or later they were going to look at me and register that I wasn't a tree trunk and I was going to be dead."

"Not so horny anymore?" Not that it wasn't an appalling story, but he was obviously still alive, so she could make jokes.

"All of a sudden, the dude on the rock signaled, and the two with the box put it down and all three vanished into the stack of boulders like cockroaches in the light."

"They spotted you? No, couldn't have. They wouldn't have vanished. They would have shot you."

"Right. Something else was going on, but at that moment, I didn't care what. The box was right there, and their ATV was right there, and I thought…make a little trouble."

"What were you *thinking*?" Before he could answer, she gestured him to silence. "I know—you were horny and that precludes thinking."

"I was thinking with the small brain. It happens. Damned good thing it did, too. I lugged the box over to the ATV, unhinged the seat, damned near ruptured a vertebra lifting it up and into the storage bin and dropped the seat over it right about the time the shouting started." He watched her for a few moments. "You don't want to say a word about what could have happened next, do you? You're afraid to feed me information, lead the witness."

"Correct."

"I made a good choice when I picked you."

His phrasing made her want to slap him. But right now, she wanted to slap a lot of people. Or shoot. Whatever. "Why did they disappear?"

"They'd spotted the resort's security chief, Vince Gilfilen."

"How did you know about him?"

"I didn't. I only knew he was in those rocks fighting for his life—the bad guys had him in a stranglehold, so he must be on my side." Nils looked her in the eyes. "We introduced ourselves afterward."

She shook her head and half laughed. Guys.

"So Vince, that son of a bitch is skinny and he slipped down and out. He's strong and wiry. He likes to fight, and he got his licks in, but they got a cord around his neck and the Librarian slashed at his wrists and..." Nils sat there and shook his head.

"What did you do, Nils?"

"I couldn't watch anymore. I couldn't be safe anymore. I couldn't do the smart thing anymore. I got one of the ATVs, one without the box inside, started it, put it into gear, gave it the gas and bailed out right before it hit the boulders."

"My God." She wavered between horror and laughter at the description of the scene, of the evidence of Nils's mad innovative fighting skills.

He painfully sat straight up in his chair. "They scattered. I slammed one guy with a rock to the head. The other guy smashed me with a rock to the arm." Nils lifted his elbow. "Want to refill my ice pack?"

She took it and headed for the freezer. "Keep talking."

"The guy lifted the rock again. I saw it over my head, figured I was a goner, and by God, Vince Gilfilen comes roaring out of those boulders. His hand is half-off, so he *kicks* the shit out of the guy's head. Guy goes down, they're fighting, I'm trying to scramble around and get into it before the third guy jumps in on the action. That was one helluva brawl, three against two, and Vince throwing punches and flinging blood everywhere. And then—"

"And then what?" Kellen stood, hand half in the freezer, totally involved in the action.

"And then nothing." Nils flopped back in the chair, winced and held his arm. "The guy Vince is fighting takes off."

Quickly, she shoveled ice cubes into the bag. "Running away?"

"No, chasing the ATV that the third guy is driving."

"The third guy—was that the Librarian?" She slammed the freezer door.

"I have no idea. The way we were mixing it up, I couldn't tell. I couldn't chase them, because then Vince collapsed. My God, that hand of his." Nils accepted the ice bag and placed it on his elbow. "Is he still alive?"

"Critical, but stable." This explained a lot, like how Vincent Gilfilen had survived at all. "What did you do? How did you get him back to the resort?"

"I took off my shirt, wrapped up his hand, had him put that over my shoulder, and we walked back to his suite." Nils shook his head in amazement. "Toughest man ever."

"Yes. He really is." She groped her way back to her chair, never taking her gaze from Nils. "But you're not too bad, either. What happened to your face?"

"I *think* Vince stepped on it, but I'm not sure. You know how it is. You're fighting, you get hurt, it's dark, might be the enemy, might be friendly fire."

"Why didn't you stay with him? He almost expired before I got there."

"He called you, then he had me stretch him out on the bathroom floor with that rug under his neck. He was pretty pissed, and so was I, and I thought he would be fine until you got there. So I went out searching for the bad guys. I figured they had to be somewhere on the resort grounds." Nils grinned savagely. "I didn't find them, but I found the right ATV. Still warm, and the box was still under the seat. They drove those artifacts back to the resort for me."

35

Kellen laughed in delight. "Did you get the box out and put it somewhere safe?"

He lifted his elbow. "Couldn't."

"So we don't know what's in it or where it is now?"

"Not really, but unless by sheer chance they figured out where I hid it, it's still somewhere on the property in an ATV."

She stared at him in admiration. "You have balls of steel."

Without an ounce of modesty, he said, "I do, don't I?"

"Where was the ATV parked?"

"By the maintenance garage."

Kellen felt the blood drain from her face, felt the clammy chill cover her skin. "So maybe one of my people."

"Not proof. But likely."

Temo? Mitch? Adrian?… Birdie? Tears pricked at her eyes. She didn't want to know one of her friends, her team, had joined the dark side. She wanted to believe in them. Now she doubted all of them.

Nils watched her, analyzed her. "You face every challenge with your chin up until you lose faith with the people you've cautiously taken into your inner circle. It's not a crime to get it wrong in a friendship. The crime is to guard yourself so closely you have no one."

Her tears dried. She stared incredulously at him.

He looked sheepish. "Sorry. It's my mom. She's always saying stuff like that and sometimes I couldn't help listening."

"Your mom is pretty smart." She brushed at her wet eyes and got back to business. "Your phone is out there somewhere. Let's hope the Librarian doesn't find it." She stood and walked over to Nils. "Let me see your elbow."

He pushed off the ice bag, rolled up his sleeve and showed her the swelling.

She didn't like the way the bone was sitting or the color of his skin. "It's broken." She pressed the ice bag back on it.

He agreed. "Cracked, anyway."

Kellen looked around, saw Nils's plaid Burberry scarf hanging beside his coat and brought it over. "Too bad. I have news I thought you'd like to investigate."

"So you didn't come to throw me out of the resort for my own safety?"

"Don't be silly. I don't give a shit about your safety." A patent lie, but he grinned as if he was flattered. "I found Priscilla's tomb art."

He sat up fast. He groaned and grabbed his elbow. "Where?"

"Everyone kept saying Priscilla wasn't that smart, but this was genius. She hid them in a storeroom filled with hotel room decorations." Kellen folded the scarf into a triangle, made a sling and slid it around Nils's arm.

Nils let her do what she could to make him comfortable. "And you found them?"

"Not me. Carson Lennex. He's had them on display. I took them into safekeeping, but the cursed tablet is still unsecured." She tied the sling around Nils's neck and stepped back. "The problem is—Mitch knows, too."

"Maintenance. That's not good." Nils came slowly to his feet, tested the sling and nodded in satisfaction. He slid his knife into a hidden wrist holster, picked up his compact pistol, weighed it, made a decision, then put it down. "I'm betting on your other friend,

Temo. He's got one of the cottages farthest from the resort, and he's hiding something. His friend's in on it, too. What's his name?"

"Adrian. In terms of character, he's a little doubtful. But not Temo. He saved my life many times. I saved his. I can't believe—"

"Depends on what his current motivation is. He might be one of the rare people in this world who doesn't want money just to have more money. But does he *need* money? Is he desperate for money? That's what you've got to ask yourself."

"Is the Librarian desperate enough at the loss of this latest shipment to start making mistakes?"

"I think so. We just have to be in the right place at the right time, and right now, that's in the penthouse." Nils checked his Beretta M9 to make sure it was functioning. "I'll go to Carson Lennex and get him to tell me the location of that last piece of art. You take Big Foot with you to check out Temo."

"Big Foot? Max?"

"If that's his name."

"He's trying for the Incredible Hulk, and he's busy searching the resort for you. Not surprisingly, he hasn't found you." She texted Max again, slipped her phone into her pocket. "Nils, be careful. We've narrowed the number of suspects, but the suspects have narrowed the opposition to us. With you taking last night's shipment, they have to be somehow injured, they're going to be livid and they don't care who they kill. They don't care if they kill every person in the resort. In fact, that would enhance the Librarian's fearsome reputation." What an ugly realization that was. "My guess is all they want to do is get the artifacts and escape to set up their base somewhere else. Watch your back."

"You, too." He hooked his good arm around her neck and pulled her close. "One kiss for a man going into battle?"

"How about if I don't punch you in the elbow?"

"Almost as good." He kissed her nevertheless, a brief press on the lips, and they both headed out into the blistering cold, dark and miserable afternoon.

36

Kellen released the safety on her pistol and cautiously approached the cottage Temo shared with Adrian. She climbed the stairs, put her head to the door…

Inside, she heard a burst of sound: men shouting, a girl crying.

She used her pass card and slammed into the room to find four pairs of eyes fixed on her: Adrian; a Hispanic guy with dyed blond hair who was writhing on the floor, holding his bleeding thigh; Temo himself, hard-eyed and furious, pointing his pistol at the door…and a preteen Hispanic girl who had to be Temo's sister.

Whatever Kellen had expected, this wasn't it.

Without hesitation, Temo lowered his pistol. "What are you doing here?"

"What are *you* doing?"

"My sister… I brought her back here to live with me. My mother went to prison for drug use, and this bastard was planning to sell Regina to work the streets."

"I'm her stepfather!" Mr. Dyed Hair shouted.

Temo pointed his pistol at him. "*Chulo!* Pimp! You never married my mother. You've got no rights to my sister as a parent or guardian."

"No!" Regina screamed. "Don't make me go back with him!"

Temo paced toward the guy on the floor. "If I killed you and dumped you off the cliff, no one here would know or care."

The tense situation explained so much about Temo and Adrian and their recent suspicious activities—but this had nothing to do with smuggling and murder. "Why didn't you tell me?" Kellen asked.

Temo struggled for words. He gestured. He looked hopeless and defiant. "I can't work all the time, take care of the resort like I promised. Regina's eleven. She's been abused and neglected. And…she's eleven."

He gave her age twice, as if it should tell Kellen everything—and in a way, it did.

He said, "She needs me. I have to be here for her."

"Temo, I understand. Annie will understand." Kellen was incredulous. "I told you I'd talk to her. Why would you think keeping your sister here would be a problem?"

"Mitch said—"

"That lousy bastard." Mitch had misled Temo—and Kellen. Sucker and lousy, distrustful friend that she was, she had fallen for it. Mitch hadn't been around long enough to be the Librarian, but he certainly could be one of the assistants. Had he been involved in the fight the night before? He showed no obvious signs of damage, but that meant nothing. He was a good fighter and an excellent survivor. Maybe all his injuries were hidden beneath his clothes.

"I told you so, Temo," Adrian said. "I told you Mitch was full of shit."

"Thank you, Adrian, for the testimonial." She holstered her pistol. "Guys, don't worry—we'll deal about Regina." She looked at Regina. "You'll be fine, I promise."

The girl trembled and nodded.

"As for him—" Kellen gestured at Mr. Dyed Hair and his bloody leg "—I don't care if you shoot him and drop him off the cliff. But clean up the mess afterward."

The pimp gave a howl of objection.

Like she cared. "Guys, when you can, I need help at the resort."

"We'll be there as soon as we handle him." Temo waved his gun at the pimp. "Shouldn't take too long."

Adrian focused on Kellen. "What kind of problems are we talking, Captain?"

She said, "Be prepared for ambush, deadly force, sabotage. Trust no one."

"Captain, you might put a cap on." Adrian removed his and tossed it to her.

She pulled it on, nodded at Temo's sister, whirled and ran for her ATV.

Behind her, someone slammed the door closed.

She liked to think they were going to kill the pimp. Probably not, but a guy who preyed on desperate women and little girls would be no loss to the world.

And talk about no loss to the world... Mitch Nyugen and his boss, the Librarian, Nils Brooks. From the start, she had been suspicious of Nils: his art degree, his CIA connections, the reformation of the MFAA. Yet she'd done her research, knowing full well he could have the capacity to change internet reality.

Nils Brooks was the leader who had organized the destruction of world archaeology sites for profit. Wealthy collectors paid him to destroy history and sell it to them. He made money. He killed his people to assure their cooperation. He cut off their hands. She had believed that Nils Brooks had been hurt helping Mr. Gilfilen. What a joke. He'd been hurt attacking Mr. Gilfilen. *Nils Brooks* was the Librarian.

As she drove toward the resort, she called the security center.

The connection crackled and failed.

She didn't believe this was a natural outage. Not tonight. Rain fell, but this wasn't a big storm; this wasn't numbing cold, blasting wind or sleet. This was far too convenient. Someone had sabotaged the resort's communications network. The CB radio in Annie's office would work to call in outside help—but she didn't have time to wait.

As she drove, she planned her rescue of Carson Lennex. She needed help. She needed someone at her back, so she veered for the maintenance garage. She used her pass card to open the door and stuck her head in. Lights were on, but dim. So the electricity was out and everything was running on generator. One of the resort's working pickup trucks, a Ford F-250 crew cab, sat over the hydraulic lift, waiting to be raised and its oil changed. From the back of the shop, she heard the clink of tools. "Birdie!" she called. "Grab your pistol and your Kevlar vest. I need your help!"

No answer.

She frowned and stepped inside. "Birdie?"

Someone gave a muffled scream. A warning.

Kellen dived to the floor, aiming for the pickup, skidding along the concrete.

A bullet slammed into the door where she'd been standing. She'd walked into an ambush.

She low-crawled to the pickup and took cover under it.

Silence.

Where was Birdie? That was her scream, Kellen knew.

Who was shooting?

Who was capable of disabling the communications network?

The same guy who had *fixed* the last outage. Mitch. Mitch was working for the Librarian.

She unsnapped her side holster, click-released the safety on her pistol, slid it back in place.

What had he done to Birdie? She was hurt, maybe dying. She needed help, and only Kellen could get it for her.

"Mitch, this is stupid." Kellen spoke calmly, persuasively, while with all her stealth, she slid along the floor, keeping well under the protection of the vehicle, moving from her current position to one closer to the back of the shop, trying to figure out a strategy. A tool chest stood there, great for defensive positioning. Lots of metal, lots of tools inside. On wheels, but nobody ever moved a filled tool chest easily. "This can't end well for you."

From the back wall, she heard Mitch's soft laugh. "No, Captain, it can't end well for *you.* I've got orders to eliminate you. You know too much. You see too much." Reflectively, he added, "I did say you would be a problem."

He walked forward, his boots smacking the concrete and echoing around the steel-frame structure. She knew without looking he had his firearm out, grasped in both hands, pointed at the pickup. She also knew where he was headed—for the hydraulic lift controls. All he had to do was raise that vehicle and she would be revealed. The man was a warrior, trained by the US Army; a Kevlar vest wasn't going to save her.

But she was a warrior, too, trained by the same fighting force, and she wouldn't die here with so much undone, so much of her past life to reveal and so much of her future to live. Beneath her, metal plates covered the old, no-longer-in-use grease pit. Painstakingly, she dragged one aside, careful to make only the barest of noises.

He heard, of course. She'd meant him to. "Climbing in there's not going to save you." He sounded so smugly superior. "What are you thinking, Captain?"

She was thinking that for one vital second after he activated the lift and started lifting the vehicle, he'd be looking down at the pit instead of up at the truck. She reached up into the body of the pickup and slid her right elbow around the drive train. She braced both feet on the rear axel and pulled herself up flat against the undercarriage.

He found the controls.

With a high metallic moan, the lift started up, slowly, dragging power from the generator.

Two feet.

With her left hand, she fumbled for her pistol. She was a good shot—with her right hand. But the pickup faced into the garage and the controls were on the right wall. No choice.

Four feet.

She would do what she had to do. Shoot with her left hand. Make each shot count. She held herself up against the vehicle and perfectly still. She saw Mitch's feet, legs, waist. He walked toward the grease pit, his pistol and his gaze pointed down. Like her, he would be wearing a Kevlar vest. So—his belly and his head: her targets. She swung her weight onto her right elbow. Aimed at his abdomen.

Six feet.

Her motion caught his attention. He looked up, realized he'd been suckered, lifted his pistol.

Kellen shot. Missed. Damn that left hand!

Seven feet.

At its full extension, the lift ground to a halt.

She was exposed, hanging above him like a piñata.

He aimed.

She shot again. Blew a hole in his thigh.

His shot went wide. He screamed in agony, crumpled to his knee.

She shot, hit his chest.

The impact caught him square on the Kevlar vest, knocking him onto his back. In one smooth motion, he rolled and flipped, raised furious red-rimmed eyes to her, supported his gun hand with his other hand and aimed.

She prepared to drop, knowing she could never outrun a bullet shot by a master marksman.

From above, something large and square slammed down on his head, knocking him flat. Knocking him unconscious.

What? A cardboard box. He'd been hit by a cardboard box. Car manuals spilled out, dozens of them, thick, heavy, leather and paper and *weight.*

From the loft above, Birdie said, "Take that, you bastard." Her voice was no more than a croak.

Kellen stashed her pistol, supported herself with both hands and swung her feet down. She landed flat-footed and ready to fight.

Mitch was unmoving, a pool of blood beneath his thigh.

With her pistol in her right hand and her left hand supporting her aim, she approached him.

None of her guys should ever be underestimated.

Still in that hoarse voice, Birdie said, "The box was full of old car manuals. Probably weighed forty pounds. He's not getting up."

With her foot, Kellen pushed the box off Mitch's back.

His neck was crooked sideways.

Kellen felt for his carotid artery.

No pulse.

"You broke his neck." Kellen looked up at Birdie.

"Good for me." Birdie used the handrail to lower herself to the loft's metal mesh floor. "Because he damned near killed me."

A drop of blood splatted on the floor beside Kellen.

The right side of Birdie's face was split open, bruised and shiny like a ripe eggplant.

Kellen holstered her pistol, grabbed the first aid kit off the wall and ran up the stairs. She knelt beside Birdie. "What did he do?"

"Came in all friendly. I turned my back. He smacked me on the side of the head with a tire iron." Birdie's cheek was swelling so fast one eye was shut and she spoke out of the corner of her mouth. "Dragged me up here while I was half-conscious. I fought. He gagged me, tied me up. He knew you'd be coming for help, but you got here too soon, before he thoroughly secured me. Thank God. He went after you and I screamed through the gag. I spent too much time getting myself free. I'm sorry, Captain. Dropping that box on him was the best I could do."

Kellen supported Birdie and helped her recline, inch by inch. "You killed him. What else do you want to do to him?"

"Torture. Hot needles under his fingernails." Birdie closed her one eye. "Did you call 911?"

"I can't. Mitch cut us off from the world." Kellen pressed a gauze pad to Birdie's head to staunch the bleeding and used a roll of gauze to hold it in place.

Birdie's eye opened. "Then I will attempt to survive this night. Wrap me warm. Put a pillow under my head."

"I know what I'm doing!" Kellen snapped, but she wasn't really snapping at Birdie. She was trying to explain...

"You've got to leave me. You've got to go finish this." Birdie took a breath. "Blanket. Pillow. Go."

Kellen had never abandoned a fallen comrade before. Not on any tour of any place in the world. But she had to leave Birdie. She stripped the blankets off Birdie's cot and gently wrapped her, rolled her so she was cocooned in warmth. She lifted Birdie's head and deftly slid the pillow beneath her. She pressed a kiss on the least-swollen side of Birdie's head and whispered, "Stay alive. I'll be back. Stay alive."

"I'll try." But Birdie's voice was less than a wheeze, and she didn't move.

Kellen ran down the stairs, stopped by Mitch and touched his cheek. He was already cooling. It had been the fast, brutal passing that he deserved. But damn. He'd been her comrade in battle. She died a little inside to know he was gone.

Then, ruthlessly practical, she reloaded her pistol, placed it in her holster. As backup, she found his firearm, reloaded it and stored it in her boot.

She had no way to call for help, no time to find Max for help. She was alone.

37

Kellen ran out into the silent night, where black streamers of clouds clawed across the sky, grasping the stars, then releasing them. She climbed into her ATV and drove toward the castle, toward Carson Lennex's tower room, where light radiated like a beacon. Time and worry oppressed her, and the taste of grim fear filled her mouth.

After such a delay, after so much time spent suffering under Nils Brooks's hands, was Carson Lennex even alive?

She let herself in a side entrance, ran the dim, silent corridors toward the elevators that led to the private suites. She pushed the up button.

Nothing moved. Nothing lit.

A step behind her had her pulling her pistol and spinning around.

Sheri Jean stood like a disconsolate ghost. "Everything's broken. The elevators, the intercoms, the house phones. Some of the lights are running on generator. Some are not working at all. I can't call or text on my cell phone. Kellen, what's happening?"

Kellen had included Sheri Jean on her list of possible candidates for the Librarian. She was so smart, with an edge that marked her as a possible predator. But this Sheri Jean was frightened, seeking direction. "We're in a deep pile of trouble with the guy who killed Lloyd Magnuson and cut off Priscilla's hands."

Sheri Jean whimpered. "Can you fix this?" She gestured at the elevators.

In Kellen's mind, she paced off the electrical schematic and shook her head. "I don't know enough about wiring to guarantee I won't electrocute myself in a spectacular way, and I need to handle this situation in an unfried manner. Are any of your staff here?"

"Russell's at the front door. He won't leave. Frances is manning the front desk. She won't leave. I convinced her to take cover underneath. They're the only ones of my crew that I know of. If anyone else is here, they're hiding."

"That's probably best. Listen, I need your help." Reluctantly, Kellen said, "Mitch Nyugen tried to kill my friend Birdie."

Sheri Jean knew Kellen had recommended Mitch as an employee. She didn't try to shame her. Bless Sheri Jean for that. "Birdie's alive?" she asked. "Can I help her?"

"She's in the loft in the maintenance building. She's bleeding. Use the CB radio in Annie's office to call for help."

Sheri Jean's eyes widened. "A CB radio? What am I, a trucker? I have no idea how to use a CB radio!"

"It's not hard, you just..."

Sheri Jean got that old Sheri Jean scowl of disdain.

"All right, who knows?"

"Annie!"

"And me." And no doubt Max, and he could be anywhere.

Sheri Jean snapped to attention. "I *can* stabilize Birdie long enough for someone to get her to the hospital. My first aid training is up-to-date."

"Thank you!" Impulsively, Kellen grabbed Sheri Jean and kissed her cheek. "Run now, be careful, and if you find anybody who can use the CB, get them to Annie's office. We need emergency services. We need law enforcement."

"Right!" Sheri Jean left Kellen standing in front of the sabotaged elevators.

Kellen checked her phone. No messages from anyone. Certainly no message from Max.

She couldn't warn him. She couldn't get his help.

In her mind, Kellen re-created the resort's floor plan, each corner, each line, each lettered word and carefully created detail. Only one stairway led to Carson Lennex's tower, and that dumped her in the suite's entry. Nils would have that covered. But the old dumbwaiter shaft was still there and hopefully the dumbwaiter mechanism itself. Maybe she could make that work.

Scrub that. She had to make that work.

For access, she went to the first-floor hospitality storeroom. It was dark; the generator's power didn't extend beyond the necessities. She pulled her tactical flashlight and shone it at the wall and found herself staring at...nothing. When use of the dumbwaiter had been discontinued, the resort had walled off the entrance.

She rubbed the scar on her forehead and again concentrated on seeing the resort's floor plan. In the past, the dumbwaiter also could be accessed from the fourth-story linen closet. Maybe she'd have better luck there.

She shed her coat; she didn't want the weight, the bulk or the warmth. She made sure the fastenings on her Kevlar vest were secure, then secured the buttons on her white button-up shirt and tucked the tails into her jeans. She started up the first stairway she found and ran up three flights of stairs.

Thank God for Mara and her pitiless step-climbing workouts.

On the fourth floor, Kellen used her pass card to enter the dark linen closet and shone her flashlight around. Bracketed shelves loaded with linens covered the place where the dumbwaiter access should be. She threw out her hands. "Could it ever once be easy?" she asked the folded sheets and towels. She placed the flashlight pointed straight up on the floor and set to work shoving the linens onto the floor. When the housekeepers returned, they'd curse her name, but in her head a chorus sang, *Hurry. Hurry. No time. No time.*

When the top shelf was empty, she repeated with the second shelf, then the third…and there it was, a cabinet, thirty inches by thirty-six inches, with a handle at the bottom to lift the panel up and out of sight. She removed the fourth shelf, shoved the door up and looked into a narrow wooden box that had once discreetly carried food and dishes up and down from the eighth-floor suite. In fact…reaching in, she pulled out a single stained white plate festooned with an ancient bread stick and a tarnished silver fork and placed them on the floor.

She released the brake and tried the electrical controls; they were useless in the blackout and perhaps broken with age. So she pushed down on the bottom of the dumbwaiter. It slid down, and four stories above, the old iron wheel that supported the cart squealed in ungreased anguish.

She froze.

To rescue Carson Lennex, she needed the element of surprise.

Slowly, delicately, she pushed the dumbwaiter down again. Again the wheel squalled.

The wheel was attached at the eighth-floor ceiling outside Carson's suite. She was so screwed, and yet—even with the noise, an archaic and discontinued dumbwaiter was her best bet. Inch by inch, she pushed the cart down, grinding her teeth at each metallic wail. At last, she could see the top of the box and the steel cables that supported it. They ran up to the wheel and down again; one raised it, one lowered it. On this end, things looked sturdy enough. She stuck her head in the shaft, pulled out her tactical flashlight and shone it up into the darkness. She couldn't see twenty feet up, much less view the ceiling where the wheel was secured. *Well* secured. She hoped. If it wasn't, during the fall, she'd have a long time to think before she landed in the resort's basement and all the equipment from above came hurdling onto her head.

When the top of the dumbwaiter was even with the bottom of the cabinet door, she set the brake and checked her equipment. Her pistol rested in her side holster. She reloaded Mitch's pistol and slid it back into her boot. Her knife's leather holster was buckled on her belt. Beneath her shirt, she wore her Kevlar vest, and she used the clip on her flashlight to connect it to the brim of her hat. Gripping both cables tightly in her fists, she eased her way onto the top of the box.

The wheel moaned in protest.

She stood up and began to work the cables.

The box moved up a few inches.

The wheel squealed, high and shrill.

She stopped. Started again.

More squealing. No matter how gently she moved the cables, the wheel complained.

Nils might not know exactly what was happening, but he had to hear that and he was far too smart not to investigate.

On the other hand, if she grasped both the cables and *climbed* them, she would in theory reach the eighth floor with a minimum of noise.

That idea was a winner.

Okay, it stank, but Carson Lennex didn't have time for her to think of another option.

She had been through basic training. She knew how to climb, and Mara's constant, ruthless full-body training had kept Kellen in practice. She didn't usually ascend four stories without a safety net, but—hey, no guts, no glory, and she didn't want a dead movie actor laid at her guilty doorstep.

Gripping both cables, she leaned into them, wrapped them close, used her shoulders and arms and legs to lift herself into position and began to climb. The mechanical wheel whispered its protests now, a secret squeal every time she gripped and shifted. The metal cable ripped at her palms and caught on her clothes. Thick, sticky old grease clung to her face and hands. The narrow shaft was stuffy; sweat gathered on her face and beneath her Kevlar vest, and little rivulets trickled down her skin and itched like scampering spiders. Or maybe they were scampering spiders…

Climb faster.

She knew when she passed the fifth floor; a cabinet door like the one on the fourth floor marked the spot.

So she could mark her progress.

Sixth floor.

Seventh floor.

She was now thirty feet above the fourth floor and the shelves where she'd started. Her shoulders throbbed, her arms shook, her legs clasped the cables and her hands were bleeding. A sense of urgency overrode the aches and pains, yet she moved slowly and steadily. Her uncle used to tell the story about the two bulls in the field. The young one said, "Let's run down to the pasture and screw some of those cows." And the old one said, "Let's walk and screw them all."

Kellen was close; now wasn't the time to expend all her energy attaining her first goal, the suite itself. Once she was there, she had Nils Brooks to contend with. She knew her opponent, she'd fought her opponent and Nils was a combatant whose skills surpassed her own. She did hope not to do battle with him. She hoped merely to kill him. But she had to be prepared for any eventuality.

She looked up, and at last, the flashlight illuminated the old black iron wheel where her cables looped and held. The closed cabinet door before her led into Carson Lennex's bedroom…if no remodels had been done since the floor plan had been created.

No cabinet hardware existed on the shaft side.

Why would there be? Only a fool would come up the dumbwaiter shaft.

She gripped the cables with her left hand and wound her legs around them, and with her right hand pulled her knife from its holster. Leaning forward, she slid the tip of her knife into the crack between the door and the sill and pried the door up a crack. Light leaked into the shaft. As she killed the flashlight and slid it into her holster, she wondered—when she opened the door, what would she find?

From far inside the suite, she faintly heard a man's muffled scream.

She unsnapped her holster, cleared the pistol's safety, leaned in again and lifted the cabinet door inch by inch. She heard nothing. Then…the faint sound of music. Classical.

Full orchestra. Tchaikovsky's "1812 Overture." Music to torture a man by.

The door was lifted enough for her to see that half of the opening was blocked by a tall piece of furniture—Carson's chest of drawers—and the other half faced a wall three feet away. She knew where she was now—in the short corridor between Carson's bathroom and bedroom.

She faintly smelled cigarette smoke. The overture swelled, and as it did, as cannons blasted, she heard another scream of agony.

In every battle, there came that moment when your mind screamed, *Go! Go! Go!* This was that moment. Kellen shoved the cabinet the rest of the way to the top, holstered her knife and launched herself sideways through the gap.

The cables rocked back and forth.

The wheel squalled in protest.

Kellen got stuck at butt level. This indignity was likely to get her killed. She grasped the forward edge of the chest and dragged herself forward. In some horrible comedic parody, she fell into the room and scrambled to her feet. She pulled her Glock and peered around the chest of drawers.

The bedroom was empty. The glass shelves that had held the statues were smashed.

Violence. Not good.

She needed backup. Did she have it?

She pulled her phone, glanced at it.

Her text to Max hadn't gone through. That was her mistake, one she would dearly rue.

She fought alone.

The scent of burning tobacco was stronger here, wafting up the stairs from the living room.

She recognized her own battle readiness—a strong heartbeat, deep breaths, each sense hyperaware—and the slightest tremble in her fingers.

In a crouch, she moved toward the spiral stairway. She pulled Mitch's pistol out of her boot and placed it, ready to fire, on the top step to use as a backup. Quietly, slowly, she crept down first one step, then another, and as she moved, the living room opened, inch by inch, to her vision. With her pistol raised, she eased sideways to get a greater view of the room. Eased sideways again and saw a shapely leg molded in tight black spandex, and a foot in a lime mesh running shoe propped up on the coffee table.

Something about that was so familiar—and so wrong.

A woman's voice said, "Cigarettes are bad for my health, and good when it comes to making a point. Tell me where the hieroglyphs are."

Carson Lennex's voice was rough and strained, like a man who had been screaming for too long. "You'll kill me and cut off my hands."

In a conversational tone, Mara said, "That's true. But if you don't tell me, I'll cut off your hands and then kill you."

Mara Philippi was the Librarian?

Then who—and where—was Nils Brooks?

Kellen descended another step to get a full view of the room.

38

Max glanced in the spa for signs of life, then checked the restrooms on the first floor. As he ran the stairs to the second floor, the electricity went out. Of course. The dim halls echoed with emptiness. In the second-floor ladies' room, the cleaning crew had abandoned their carts. He checked every stall, and by the third ladies' room, he was feeling ridiculous. Then he met Frances coming out, and while she backed away, he made a fool of himself trying to explain.

That awkwardness made him stop and think sensibly. He did *not* have time to check all the bathrooms and all the guest rooms. He was wasting time away from the security monitors, where he could survey the whole of the resort.

Besides, something was niggling at him. Something about the spa.

For a space that had been hastily abandoned by its staff, it was very tidy. Clean. Almost psychotically so.

He strode back to the spa and entered cautiously. Soothing music played. The aromatherapy diffusers gave off scents of lavender and sweet orange. He stood in the middle of the lounge, among the tan chairs, cotton rugs, bowls of healthy snacks and recently filled pitchers of cucumber-mint water—and he didn't believe it. Something was off here. It seemed as if the staff had prepared for a normal day of pedicures and massages—and then vanished.

He walked through the whole spa again, up and down the corridors, through the steam room and sauna. He looked into each of the treatment rooms, prepped and ready, their doors ajar as if waiting for the next customer. Only one door remained closed; the sign on it was marked Linens.

He stood in front of it and shouted, "Hello!"

At once, someone began releasing muffled screams and slamming against the door.

He opened it and found a female he recognized, bound, gagged and wide-eyed with panic and appeal. Behind her lay a male masseuse, bound, gagged and unconscious.

Max pulled the young woman into the hall, gently peeled the adhesive off her lips and removed a wad of gauze from her mouth.

She tried to speak.

"Wet your lips," he advised. "I've got to check this guy."

"Xander," she croaked. "He's Xander."

Max crawled into the closet and put his hand to Xander's throat. Xander's heart beat, but his breathing was shallow. Max removed his gag, too, and his breathing improved. But blood oozed from somewhere on his head. Possible spinal injury? Max didn't dare move him. For the second time today, he called 911. Or rather—he tried to call 911. He had no cell service. He tried to text. Nothing. "Damn it." When he was running around looking for Nils Brooks, someone had cut the resort's ties to the outside world. Probably Nils Brooks.

In the hallway, he heard the female begin to cry. He crawled out of the closet, and as he untied her, he said, "He's alive. What's your name?"

"I'm Destiny Longacre. I work here."

He remembered her photo from resort records. "As a masseuse, right? Can you tell me what happened?"

"I came in this morning. Came in the outer spa door. It was open a little. I thought, *I didn't do it. Someone's going to get in trouble—I hope it's not me.* I got inside, into the hall for the treatment rooms, and I saw something splattered on the floor. Mara hates when the spa is dirty. She insists we clean everything before we leave. Gets really weird about it, so I thought we'd missed something and I'd clean up before she came in. I got the carpet cleaner and started on the splatter, and the towel came out red and I couldn't figure out what..." She gasped, trying to get a breath between the tears. "Then I thought, *It's blood.* I looked up, and she was standing in the door of one of the treatment rooms."

"She?"

"Mara Philippi. Our boss. She was beat-up, bruises on her face, blood at the corner of her lip—I thought she'd been attacked. I thought whoever was attacking people had attacked her."

Max knew then. He pulled out his phone and tried to text Kellen. Nothing. He tried to call. No connection.

Destiny continued, "I jumped up and said, *Are you okay?* and she pointed a gun at me and said, *Clean it up.* She's said it before, lots of times, but never with a gun. I was like, *Mara, it's Destiny!* She laughed, sort of creaky, and said, *That's for sure.*"

Max freed her hands and feet. He gestured toward Xander, unconscious in the closet. "Did she shoot him?"

"No. But she hit him. Xander came in and she told him to clean, too, and he was, he really was. But he was all Xander-like, talking to her about Karma and nonviolence and the way of the Dalai Lama, and she just up and bonked him on the head with the butt of her gun. He fell down and I screamed and I thought she was going to shoot me, but I couldn't stop screaming." Destiny wiped her nose on the sleeve of her smock. "Then Mitch came in. He's so cute—I like him a lot. I thought he was going to save us. But he went right up to Mara and told her Carson Lennex had the statues."

"The statues?"

"That's what he said. I don't know what it means, but he said Carson Lennex had the statues, and as soon as she was in his suite to let Mitch know and Mitch would cut electricity and communications."

Again Max tried to text and call. Mitch had done as he was told. Communications were down.

While he tried, Destiny babbled, "She…she… Mara told him *Good job* and to tie us up and stash us in the closet, and she left and he did. He told me if I tried to escape he would kill me." She huddled on the floor and rubbed her wrists. "My fingers are tingling. I hope he didn't ruin my hands—I have to work today. I need the money!"

She was in shock. Max threw a blanket around her shoulders. "The resort will reimburse you for lost time. The paramedics will make sure your hands are okay, and Xander, too." Although how he was going to contact them, he didn't know. He stood. "Can you let them in?"

Her teeth were chattering, but she nodded. "What's *wrong* with Mara?" she asked urgently.

He hurried toward the door. "Mara Philippi is the Librarian."

"A librarian? No, she's illiterate."

He swiveled on his heel. *"What?"*

Patiently, Destiny explained, "She can't read."

"She has to be able to read. She runs a very successful business."

"She doesn't tell anybody. I figured it out for myself. She uses the computer accessibility settings as a work-around. She's got it all worked out."

"Holy shit." Somehow, knowing that made Mara, the Librarian, so much creepier. He moved out of the spa and into the stairwell. It was going to have to be a fast run up those eight stories to Carson Lennex's suite, but he had to make it.

He'd been too late once before. He wouldn't be too late now.

39

Kellen saw her, Mara Philippi, standing astride Carson Lennex's bound body, dressed in her mottled black-and-brown fashion hoodie, her hair in a jaunty ponytail and her face… Her face was bruised, battered, swollen. Her blue eyes were angry—and satisfied. She held a cigarette between two fingers, a pistol in both hands, and smoke spiraled into the air.

The Librarian, in person.

On the floor beneath her, a handcuffed Carson Lennex writhed in agony.

Unsurprised, Mara looked up at Kellen. "I'm not surprised he couldn't kill you."

In a smooth motion, Kellen fired her gun.

Mara dived to the side, landed on the coffee table.

Kellen followed the motion, fired again, saw Mara jerk sideways as the bullet smacked her shoulder.

Successful strike, but no blood. The hoodie she wore was body armor.

Mara rolled off the table and fired.

The slug hit Kellen right above the heart.

The Kevlar vest took the impact, but the sheer force drove Kellen backward against the stair railing. She felt the crack of her sternum. *Blinding pain, can't breathe, can't breathe, can't breathe.* She missed her footing, tumbled down the rest of the stairs. Her pistol broke free of her fingers, then disappeared over the edge. Kellen came to rest with her spine on the last three treads, one arm caught in the banister and one foot on the floor.

I can't see. I can't see. I can't breathe. Mara is here. I am going to die.

But she didn't die. When the swirling red motes of agony cleared from her vision, Mara stood with one foot on either side of Kellen's legs. She looked like a high school cheerleader, smiled like a shark, and she held her own pistol pointed at Kellen's head. "You wore Kevlar. You're so goddamn smart. But you didn't know I was the Librarian, did you? You thought it was him." She pointed.

Kellen lifted her head, and through the fog of pain, she saw Nils Brooks sprawled facedown in the entry, unconscious and bleeding. Dead? Not yet, but unless something changed, none of them were long for this world.

She saw something else. She saw her beloved Glock 21 SF lying on the floor on the side of the stairs.

Oh yeah. Things were about to get interesting.

Mara kicked at Kellen's thigh.

Kellen groaned, struggled feebly, grasping at her chest, her ribs...grasping her one accessible weapon and holding it concealed in her palm.

"We are so much alike. But I'm perky and you're grim, and you thought that made you tougher. You thought your war experience made you smarter. But I was always one step ahead of you. I knew you'd finally figure it out. I knew you'd show up, and I knew I'd get to kill you." Arms straight, Mara lifted her pistol.

Kellen rammed the tactical flashlight, jagged side first, into the thin material over Mara's knee.

Mara stumbled, tripped on Kellen's leg, fell sideways.

Kellen yanked her arm free, rolled down the steps, jagged ice crystals of pain tearing into her chest, and reached for her pistol.

Mara rolled, too, with a gymnast's speed and grace.

Kellen's fingertips touched the pistol's grip.

Mara stomped on Kellen's hand.

Kellen screamed. Lifted her hand and looked. Her little finger stuck out sideways.

Mara kicked her in the head, slamming her flat onto the floor.

Kellen couldn't hear. Couldn't see. This was it; the oblivion she feared. She would be bound to that hospital bed until they mercifully let her die...

With a gasp, she was conscious again. She opened her eyes. She could see nothing but Mara's face leaning close, Mara's eyes gleaming with vindictiveness, the barrel of Mara's pistol pointed right between her eyes.

In that moment, something happened in Kellen's brain.

Everything shifted.

A light came on.

An old film played in skips and jumps.

Behind Mara, around Mara, she saw a park, trees bare of leaves, openmouthed pedestrians running. Mara...was no longer Mara. She was a man with a thin, familiar face who spoke with an Italian accent. He held a Beretta Pico and he—

Mara said, "I don't have time to cut your hands off, but breaking your fingers with my heel was almost better."

Kellen blinked. "One finger," she said. Or did she? She didn't have breath. Maybe only her lips moved...

Kellen was here in Carson Lennex's suite. With Mara. Mara was pointing her pistol at Kellen's forehead and—

The man's name was Ettore Fontana and he said, "You'll never interfere with me again."

Mara's voice intruded on the past. "I'm going to finish what someone else started." Taking her time, drawing out Kellen's anguish, she cocked the pistol. Deliberately, she pressed the cold metal to Kellen's forehead.

Out of the corners of her eyes, Kellen saw a man running toward them, roaring in fury and anguish. She knew him.

Max. It was her Max. He had to make it. He had to. She loved him so much! Then—

The present day rushed back in, but everything was blurred, overlapped.

She was in the bustling city park.

She was in the penthouse suite.

Max was moving in slow motion. He wasn't going to make it—

Max was moving in slow motion. He wasn't going to make it—

40

Max tackled Mara, low and hard, knocking her off her feet. The pistol roared, the shot blasting over Kellen's head. Plaster showered from the ceiling. Max and Mara rolled across the room. Max slammed Mara against the floor.

Mara pulled a small, sharp, deadly knife.

He lifted his big fist and punched her in the face.

Her head snapped back, and she went limp.

"Kellen!" he shouted.

"I'm here," she whispered.

Gasping, he looked around at her.

He was the man who had tried to save her.

He was the man who had failed to save her.

He was the man in the hotel.

He was the man who had saved her.

His face was harsh, primitive with fury, with bloodlust, with...passion for her.

She had forgotten him, but now she remembered.

My God, how she'd loved him.

They looked at each other, just looked, a moment of gratitude...and recognition.

Then his head snapped back to look at Mara, the collar of her hoodie clutched in his fist.

Kellen wanted to believe Mara was unconscious. But she

didn't dare trust that even Max's full-fisted punch could take out the Librarian, so in an overly loud, unsteady voice, she said, "Restrain her."

He did. He took Mara's pistol and secured the safety and slid it into his jacket's inside pocket. With a key he found on the coffee table, he went into the living room and came back with handcuffs—those used to bind Carson, she guessed—and dragged Mara to the cast-iron screen set before the unlit gas fireplace and used the cuffs to secure her hands behind her back.

Carson Lennex appeared. On his cheek, a round red burn marred his classic features. His button-up shirt stood open, and three burns dotted his chest, leading in a line to his nipple. He limped into the room. Everything about him was angry. To Max, he said, "Please. Allow me." Kneeling beside Mara's feet, he used the curtain cord to tie her ankles and her knees. To Kellen, he said, "She came up here with a message that you had sent her. I said, *For the hieroglyphic tablet?* She said yes. I invited her in." He sounded outraged when he said, "I fed her her lines!"

"I'm sorry, Mr. Lennex." Kellen spoke through broken gasps. "When I realized what could happen, I did everything I could to save you."

"I'm ashamed to know I'm such a fool," Carson said.

"You didn't tell her where the tablet was."

"No. Damned if I'm going to help an archaeological looter and thief." He had been tortured for his passion, for archaeology, and he had come out the victor.

"When it comes to Mara, you're not the only fool. She played me." Kellen's temper rose, and that seemed to ease her breathing. "I never even suspected…" She turned to Max. "If she wakes up, promise you'll hit her again."

"If she wakes up, this time I get to hit her," Carson said.

Kellen indicated at the body sprawled in the entry. Nils. "Is he alive?"

Max checked for a pulse, lifted his eyelid, slid his fingers along his neck. "He's alive."

She was more than a little angry with Nils, and more than a little worried at his continued unconsciousness. She told Max, "He's not one of the bad guys."

"I know. But he made me think that you and—" Max caught himself in midsentence. Going to the couch, he grabbed a throw and tossed it on Nils. "She hit him a good one. He's out cold. Concussion. When we get the power back, we'll get him to the hospital. They'll check him out. He's going to have a headache tomorrow."

"You sure know a lot about head wounds."

"I learned everything I could about them when you…" He choked.

She saw a tear.

No, don't do that. She eased herself into a more comfortable position against the wall.

Max hurried over and knelt at her side. "Can you move?"

She wiggled her left hand, moved the uninjured fingers of her right hand. The little finger was swelling, throbbing and crooked, and she used her other hand to crunch it back in place. It was still broken, but as the joint slid back into place, the relief was immediate.

"Your legs?" Max insisted.

That took more concentration, but at last she shifted her feet, pulling them toward her, then using them to leverage herself into a sitting position.

He watched, offering no assistance, and if ever a man showed terror, it was him. She knew why. He feared she had survived, only to live a life without dance, without speed, without motion. Unlike hers, his memory of her time spent unconscious and recovering in the hospital would be whole and unbearable. He feared history was repeating itself.

"I'm not paralyzed." She put her bruised and broken hand to

her shattered chest. "I am in a lot of pain. Do you have an aspirin on you?"

He sighed in relief. "Stay still. Stay quiet. We'll get a helicopter here to lift you out." He pulled out his phone, tried to dial and swore virulently. "Someone put some kind of damper on the system."

"Mitch did it." She took a breath. "Birdie killed Mitch. And I did."

Carson said, "I don't know much about electronics, but I know where the server center is and I can try to figure out how Mitch sabotaged it." He moved like a man who'd been bound and tortured, like a man in pain. But his eyes sparked, his forehead scowled, his mouth sneered and, at the same time, gave the tiniest twist of pain. Kellen could see why the man had won his Academy Awards. He knew how to express emotion, and he knew the right emotion to express.

"There's a CB radio in Annie's office," Kellen said.

"Right. Good! CB radio first. Then restore communications."

"Then—" she met his eyes "—my friend Birdie..."

"I know Birdie. She has driven for me." Carson spoke too quickly. "What's wrong with her?"

"She was hurt. Badly. I sent Sheri Jean to her, but...can you check...?"

"I'll check. She's too wonderful to lose." As Carson made his exit, she wanted to clap in appreciation of his ability to show her her own face, her own feelings.

Max disappeared into the bathroom and returned with a roll of gauze. "Let's see what we can do with this." Gently, he wrapped her little finger to her ring finger to hold it in place.

"Better," she whispered.

He fetched a cashmere throw off the couch, and as he wrapped it around her, he whispered, "Do you remember?"

As soon as he spoke, that sense of being in two places returned:

the cool metal of the pistol, the man springing at her assailant, the blank nothingness of…of what?

She broke a sweat, a fine sheen all over her body.

"Kellen?" His tone changed to pleading. "Ceecee?" He tried to embrace her.

"No." Panic swamped her. She wasn't Ceecee. She wasn't Cecilia. She could never be Cecilia again. Those flashes of moments past…they were not memories. They were merely impressions. She held him off with one hand. "Don't. I'm in pain. That shot to the chest…"

"The sound of that shot brought me up here." Abruptly, she could see into his tortured memories, to that moment when he had been too slow to save Ceecee from a bullet to the brain seven years before.

"I'm fine," she said.

At once, he was practical Max. "Oh?"

"Well. Solid hit over my heart." She touched her chest. "Hurts."

"Let me see." Max removed the leather shoulder holster and placed it off to the side. He unbuttoned her shirt, slid it off her shoulders, then off her wrists. He worked the vest's fasteners free, then eased her out of its protective embrace. Reaching behind her, he unhooked her bra and pulled it away.

Great. She was naked from the waist up. She pulled the throw closer around her shoulders.

But he wasn't drooling, and she found herself with mixed feelings about that. Why she cared, she didn't know. Yet it seemed unfair to strip down and not have the guy notice. It made her half-remembered erotic dreams seem pitiful, the imaginings of a desperate woman.

He winced as the bullet site was revealed. "Oh, Ceecee…"

She corrected him. "Kellen." She looked down at herself. A two-inch black bruise radiated from the center of her chest, and it was growing. If she hadn't worn the vest, Mara would have shot her through the heart. She would be dead, lost to this world, and all her struggles to regain her dignity, her strength, herself would be for naught.

She looked at Mara, cuffed and slumped against the iron grill, and she considered turning on the gas fire and letting her roast.

"I thought the vest would stop injury," Max said.

"It stops death. The force of the bullet has to be dissipated, and it was dissipated on my sternum." She wet her dry lips. "Can you call for help yet?"

Max checked his phone. "Not yet. As soon as Carson gets the damper removed, we'll take you to the hospital."

She reached for her shirt. "You can't leave with me."

"I can." He held her shirt while she put first one arm in, then the other.

Okay, *now* he was looking at her boobs. She had mixed feelings about that, too. She was one big mixed feeling poured over a very confused woman. "You're in charge of the resort."

He started to button the shirt, got it wrong, had to start over.

Good to know her boobs still functioned as a secret weapon.

He said, "I'm not in charge."

"Who else? Now?" She gestured around her and winced at the pain the unrestrained motion caused her.

He stood, went to the bar, brought her a bottle of water and waited while she sipped.

When she'd wet her mouth enough to speak a little more clearly, she said, "Someone has to call the cops and wait for them to show up. Someone has to reassure the staff. Someone has to…fix everything. You're the only one capable. You know that. Annie needs you."

She might have only just acknowledged that she knew him, but she remembered that scowl when he didn't get his way. She drove her point home. "If you insist on coming to the hospital with me, then I can't go to the hospital. Annie left me in charge. Someone has to be in charge."

"Fine." Max set his jaw and never had he looked so much like an Italian thug. "I'll get someone to drive you to the airstrip."

"Birdie, too. And Nils."

"Yes, Birdie, too. And... Nils." He finished buttoning her shirt. "But when you wake, I'll be at your bedside."

She thought that was a vow he had made before. "Don't worry. I'm okay." She thought she'd said that to him before, too.

His phone rang.

Kellen sagged with relief.

He answered and gave her the thumbs-up. "Carson, good work. You did it."

She checked for her knife; it was still safe at her belt. She reached for her shoulder holster and laboriously strapped it on. Because Mara was still here. This wasn't over yet. All she needed now was her pistol.

She looked around, didn't see it, leaned back and took a few laborious breaths.

Across the room, Nils sluggishly lifted his head. Blood from the wound on the back of his head had trickled onto his face. He seemed to be having trouble focusing, but eventually he zeroed in on her. "Kellen..." he whispered. "You shouldn't have come."

Kellen had to get herself on her feet. She had to. She couldn't sit here and gasp like a beached fish or soon she'd be flat on her back, Max would be at her bedside and she'd be...she'd be panicked. She had to give herself a chance to remember...everything. She had to think about how she wanted to proceed in this situation with Max.

Things were complicated.

Understatement.

She crawled to the coffee table, and using it as a support, she got to her knees, then more slowly to her feet.

Max watched, poised on the balls of his feet, ready to catch her if she fell.

She smiled toothily at him. "There. That wasn't so bad." She lied. Her hand hurt. The bones in her chest felt as if they were moving, grinding.

"Here." He presented her with her Glock 21 SF. "You dropped this."

Using her left hand, she took it by the grip and found it fit not awkwardly, but like an old friend. She holstered it, looked up at him, and the magnitude of the recent events overwhelmed her. "Thank you. Thank you for saving my life."

He reached for her, gripped her arms, and his hands had a fine tremor. "I prayed to God for a second chance, and for speed, and for you."

He was so intense she wanted to look away. She couldn't. In his amber eyes, she could see a man stripped to the bone by emotions she could only imagine.

Then Nils called, "Kellen, I need you."

41

Nils's voice caught her by surprise. Kellen looked toward the entry, then back at Max. "I, um, need to talk to him."

"It's not so easy," Max said and released her.

She told herself she didn't know what he meant. But she did. As she made her unsteady way to Nils's side, Max took out his phone and made another call, and another, to emergency services and to the staff left in the resort, and all the while he watched Kellen.

Kellen meant to kneel beside Nils's prostrate form; she got half-way down, collapsed onto her knees. That hurt; she'd have bruises tomorrow. But what were a few more bruises? She leaned close to Nils's bloody head. "After I got to Temo's and saw what was happening with him and his sister—I thought *you* were the Librarian."

"I know."

"How did you know about Temo?"

"I investigated everyone, especially the people close to you. He was acting suspicious, so I kept an eye on him and, sure enough, realized he had his kid sister living with him."

"Why did you lie to me? Why did you send me on a wild-goose chase?"

"I read the report from the Army. I know why they discharged you."

Kellen sat up straight. She'd been afraid of that, that if he'd hacked into her military records to discover her fighting skills, he would also have read all the details of her hospital stay.

"I didn't want you to be hurt even more," he said. "I believed I could handle it."

"Of course you believed you could handle it. Now you know better." At least in the Army, her men knew she could fight, and would fight to the death. "I'm conscious. That's good enough for now." She looked at Mara, bruised and unconscious. Or maybe just bruised; Kellen thought she could see the glint of her eyes beneath those lids. "How dangerous is she?"

Nils slid his hand up until it reached his chin, then propped his chin up under his hand. "Judged against Hitler? Or simply judged against greedy, ruthless female serial killers who happen to be narcissist psychopaths?"

He chilled her with his detached evaluation. She gestured Max over. "Did you call Sheriff Kwinault?"

"She's on her way." Max loomed, unmoving.

Nils ignored him. "A local sheriff will probably be outmatched. Mara will attempt to escape without a care to who or what she hurts." He didn't sound ominous. He sounded matter-of-fact, and that made it all the more chilling. "She is the Librarian."

"She's illiterate," Max added.

Both Nils and Kellen started and stared.

Nils grunted. "That could explain a lot."

Max radiated a solid satisfaction.

But all this information sent chills up Kellen's neck. Annie had left her in charge of the resort, and Kellen had visions of explosions and flames. Urgently, she said, "We've got to get Mara out of here. You said it yourself. She's a serial killer. That makes her the responsibility of the FBI. Get her out of here." Kellen sounded excessively pleasant, and she put her hand on her knife. "Get her out of here or I'll neutralize her myself."

Mara was definitely conscious, for at Kellen's threat she flinched a little.

Good. She was smart enough to fear Kellen.

"Get me a phone," Nils said. "I'll make some calls."

Someone rang the suite's doorbell.

"I called for a first aid kit," Max told them and looked through the peephole. "I thought Nils would like to stop bleeding on the carpet."

Kellen felt foolish for thinking Max needed to be defended, for reacting like a Victorian maiden to Max's embrace and, most of all, for caring whether Nils noticed she had a thing for Max. Nils had kissed her a couple of times. He'd gone out and gotten into a fight because he was horny. So what? What happened between her and Max was nobody's business but theirs, and furthermore, what had happened in the past was…

She slid down the wall. Everything in her future hinged on the past. Maybe that was always true, but at least now she knew. Didn't she?

Max answered the door. Frances stood there, wide-eyed. She looked at the guns, looked at the knife, looked at the blood, handed Max the first aid kit, and in a slow, graceful slither, she fainted. Max caught her in one arm, handed Nils the kit and lowered her to the floor.

Kellen got up—rising was easier this time—and walked over to Mara.

MARA PHILIPPI:
FEMALE, WHITE, TANNED. HEALTHY, 5'6", 130 LBS. EMPLOYED 8 YRS. SPA MANAGER. AGGRESSIVELY PHYSICALLY FIT. ~~EAST COAST STREAKED-BLONDE PREPPIE.~~ BLUE EYES. ~~DORIAN GRAY PERFECTION OF SKIN TONE.~~ BATTERED, BRUISED. UNCLEAR ON DIFFERENCE BETWEEN WAR ZONE AND GYMNASIUM. SMUGGLER. SERIAL KILLER. LIAR. ACTRESS. MASSIVE EGO. DO NOT LIKE. ~~NO GOOD REASON.~~ EVERY REASON.

Kellen should have trusted her instincts.

She knelt beside her, close enough to speak quietly, close enough to get in Mara's face. "Your nose is broken."

Mara pretended to be unconscious.

"That's going to ruin your chances for the International Ninja Challenge."

As Kellen had known she would, Mara opened her eyes. They snapped and sparked with fury. "You think I'm done? I'll never be done."

"You gave Lloyd Magnuson that heroin."

Mara's lips curled in a smile, and her lashes fluttered. "The poor dear man simply needed a bit of seduction and a push in the right direction. He was an addict through and through."

Kellen had never seen the truth behind the mask Mara wore, because Mara believed she was justified in every cruelty, in every murder. "How did you find Priscilla's body? Where did you take it?"

Mara's smile disappeared. "We didn't *find* it. I'm not so sloppy. I put a tracker on Lloyd. Mitch followed the signal and retrieved Priscilla's body. I didn't need any surprises popping out of her other shoe." Mara's eyes narrowed. "Who knew that bitch could be so devious?"

"You just confessed to killing her." Mara wasn't stupid; did she consider herself above the law? Or, more likely, that she would never go to trial?

"There's no corpse to be found," Mara said. "Not this time."

"Let me unlock your handcuffs." Kellen smiled invitingly. "You run really well. Let's see you run now."

"Run so you could find the nerve to shoot me? You can't shoot me in cold blood? I chose you as my opponent because I thought we were alike, that you were worthy. But you're weak." Mara raised her head. "Yes, go ahead and free me. I'll kill you all and I won't run—I'll walk away with your hands in my pocket."

Her vitriol wiped the smile from Kellen's face. "Then I'll leave you bound. Because, by my count, you've now lost *two* shipments of Central American tomb art." She waited a beat to see if Mara corrected her, if Mara said she had recovered the second shipment. But she didn't, so she hadn't, and that meant it was still somewhere on the property stored in an ATV. Kellen continued, "At best, you're done as a smuggler. At worst, your twice-disappointed buyer is going to kill you."

"I have allies in powerful places. Tell your Nils Brooks that one of those allies killed his MFAA bitch. He's still out there, and he knows who to hunt."

"Your cruelty makes you a target to be destroyed. Your position leaves you weak. Allies abandon the weak." Kellen turned the taunt back on her. "You're weak." The trouble was, Kellen didn't completely believe what she said. Something about Mara lured and attracted, and she feared Mara's allies would try to save her.

As Kellen returned to the entry, Mara muttered, "Snakes and phantom faces, indeed." A small frisson slithered down Kellen's spine.

When and how had Mara found out about her husband, about Gregory Lykke? That face outside the window had been his, and Mara had been so convincing in her indignation about the snake in the fruit bowl, the snake that had been native to Maine...

Nils was holding an ice bag to the back of his neck. She looked into his eyes and said, "Listen to me. You find that stone tablet with the hieroglyphic curse and you take it, and all the Mayan carvings, out of the resort. Get the curse out. This resort needs to be curse-free now. Today. Do you understand me?"

As if he was surprised at her forcefulness, he leaned away from her. "A curse-free resort. Right. I've got it."

She glanced at Mara.

Mara's smile was all barbed wire lips and bared white teeth.

Kellen said, "And I don't care what it takes, you put that bitch behind bars."

42

With that, Kellen's flush of energy faded. She began to breathe laboriously again, and she leaned her head against the wall.

At once, Max walked over and slid his arm around her waist. "I've got a town car waiting." He lifted her to her feet. "You need an experienced trauma center. I talked to Sheri Jean—Birdie's alive, but she needs trauma care, too. A helicopter is on its way to take you to Seattle."

Kellen nodded.

"After law enforcement gets here, I'll send Nils to the emergency room, too."

Kellen nodded again.

"No argument?" He assisted her as she walked slowly to the elevator. "That's worrisome."

The trip down the elevator wore her out; she couldn't breathe deeply and wasn't getting the oxygen she needed. Russell held the resort's exterior door; she touched him lightly on the shoulder and he burst into tears. Outside, under the portico, the town car waited.

Max opened the back door and assisted Kellen into the seat, helped her lie down, covered her with the cashmere throw and turned on the seat heater. He said to the driver, "Pick up Birdie at the maintenance garage. Take the women to the airstrip. Wait for the helicopter, get them on board and come back. I might need you."

"Of course, sir, I'll do whatever you bid."

Kellen frowned. She didn't recognize the driver's voice, but she certainly recognized her attitude. This woman was sarcastic and amused, and something about her set Kellen's teeth on edge.

Before she could puzzle out that unpleasantness, Max rested his hands on her shoulders. Kellen opened her eyes. He was upside down, looking at her in exasperation and joy. "Listen to me. I see you. I know you. You know more than you want to admit. So in reply to your unspoken thoughts, let me say this." Leaning over, he kissed her.

If Kellen had had time to think about it, she would have suspected that inept little Ceecee had fallen for Max because he was kind, protective, able to keep her safe.

Not so. When he kissed, nothing about Max Di Luca was safe. He was a daredevil who leaped with her into a free fall. He was a beast who dared her to take him in the roughest way possible. He was a dark lover, consuming her in wicked ways she had never imagined.

When he lifted his head, his lips slid across her cheek and rested against her ear. "Now we make more memories."

Then he was gone. The car door shut. And despite the cashmere throw and the heated seat, she was cold.

The driver put the car in gear. The wheels rolled over the pavement in a soft, rhythmic hiss and Kellen drifted in a sea of pain and the past.

What did she know? What did she remember?

Nothing in Cecilia's life had prepared her for the months on the Philadelphia streets. With no resources, no defenses, she drifted from one underpass to another, from an abandoned building to a homeless shelter to that place by the river where a gentleman in an Armani suit tried to rape her. She stabbed him in the neck with rusty scissors and ran again.

The only things she had, the only things she treasured, were Kellen's identification papers carried in the worn travel wallet beneath her clothes. Keeping them safe obsessed her. They were her link to her cousin, the proof that Kellen had existed, the honored preservation of her memory.

She trudged along the streets, wrapped in rags and her own misery, until the day she saw that man dragging the little girl behind him. The child looked like him, like his daughter, but she was screaming, "No. No! I want my mommy. I live with my mommy. The judge says you can't have me. I want my mommy!"

He turned and slapped her, one hard blow across the cheek.

The girl staggered and would have fallen, but he held her up by her arm and said, "Shut up, Annabella. Your mommy will pay to get you back."

In that moment, Cecilia saw herself in the child and Gregory in the man, and she was livid. She couldn't recall when she'd last eaten. Last night, she had slept on a pile of trash behind a restaurant. But from somewhere inside, strength born of injustice rose up in her, and she attacked. She ran, jumped on the man's back, wrapped her legs around his waist. She pulled his hair, clawed at his face.

He let go of Annabella's arm. He whirled in circles, cursing in languages she didn't know.

People on the sidewalk gaped. She didn't care. In a frenzy, she dug her filthy nails into his neck, smashed her fist into his nose. She screamed, "Run, Annabella!"

He pried her legs off and dropped her to the sidewalk.

She smacked hard.

He took a moment to kick at her, then raced after the child.

Cecilia shrieked like a banshee. "Stop him. He's kidnapping that child!" She didn't know for sure if it was true; she only knew he was abusing that little girl and she would not stand for it.

From down the block, another man was shouting, "Stop him. Stop him!"

"Save the child," Cecilia yelled. She staggered to her feet.

The father captured the little girl again, picked her up by the waist and flung her over his shoulder. His face was bleeding, his pristine tie askew; his dark eyes were murderous.

Cecilia jumped between him and his town car.

He tried to block her with the flat of his hand.

She ducked beneath and butted him with her head. She nailed him, too, because he released Annabella and leaned over, holding his family jewels.

The kid knew what to do this time. She took off down the sidewalk, veered into traffic, dodging cars, using them as blockades and concealment.

Her daring stopped Cecilia's breath in her throat.

The father ran after her.

Cecilia flung her weight into his back.

An oncoming car slammed on its brakes, struck him with the right front bumper, spun him into the street.

Cecilia hit the still-moving car on the passenger door, whirled backward and fell facedown on the asphalt. She knew she had to get up. She had to help that child, but the best she could do was crawl… Vaguely, she heard sirens and a man's rumbling voice she now knew to be Max's said, "You saved Annabella. You saved my niece."

Cecilia relaxed, slid toward unconsciousness, then tensed again. Desperately, she groped for the travel wallet hidden under her clothes. Kellen's documents. She couldn't lose them.

"What's wrong?" the man's voice asked. "What can I help you with?"

She wrapped her fingers around the string, tugged the wallet out so she could grasp it. She opened her swollen eyes, and for the first time, she looked into Max's strong, grave face.

"Do you want me to keep that for you?" he asked.

At the thought, terror gripped her.

"I'll keep them safe. I'll return them as soon as you wish."

Behind him, she could see policemen and EMTs advancing on her. They would take Kellen's wallet. They'd ask questions she couldn't answer.

She offered the wallet to Annabella's uncle.

He grasped it.

"Don't look," she said.

"I won't."

"Promise you won't look."

"I promise."

Cecilia spent a week in the hospital. She'd cracked her tailbone and fractured her cheek. She was dehydrated and undernourished. More than that, the physicians had expressed concern about the old burns around her hairline and on her shoulders. She heard one doctor tell Max that at some point in her life she'd suffered physical and mental trauma, and that no doubt accounted for her overly violent defense of Annabella. He also told Max that she should be confined to an institution until they could ascertain that she was stable.

An hour later, when Max came in, she was out of bed and scavenging for clothing.

He flung a small overnight case on the bed and opened it. "Here. Pick out what you want to wear. I'm taking you home."

"To the home?" Kellen's travel wallet was on top. She snatched it up, pulled it over her head, settled it on her chest. "To hell with you."

"My home," he said. "You saved my niece. Her father is Ettore Fontana, a desperate man without honor. He intended to kidnap Annabella and hold her for ransom. You saved her. The Di Luca family owes you a debt. We always pay our debts. No more fears. You're safe with us."

"I'll never be confined again." Imprisoned, abused, married. Never again. She turned her back to him, stripped off the hospital gown and started to dress. The guy had good taste in underwear, she'd say that for him.

His voice rumbled with patience. "In my home, you can rest, recuperate, and then when you wish, I'll help you go somewhere safe. I'll help you find a job. I don't know what misfortune put you on the streets, but I will protect you."

Cecilia had listened to another man once say pleasant things in a con-

vincing voice, and Gregory had murdered her cousin and almost killed her. "Why should I believe you?" she asked hoarsely.

When she had donned one layer of clothes and started on a second, he gently turned her to face him, and his eyes, golden brown and warm, met hers. "Because I'm Maximilian Di Luca. I always keep my word."

As the town car rumbled along the asphalt, Kellen touched her wet cheeks. Tears. She remembered so well what Max said, what he did, how she had loved him…

The first time she woke in the hospital, he asked her what her name was.

"Ceecee." Funny. She hadn't thought about what she should say. She just said it. Ceecee, her family nickname. That was what he called her.

She groped along the leather seat, pulled herself into a sitting position, asked, "Birdie? Where's Birdie? We were supposed to stop for Birdie."

"Someone else is bringing her to the airstrip."

"Carson Lennex is bringing her?"

"Right. Carson Lennex."

"That's nice." Kellen took a few more careful breaths. "I think he likes her."

The driver gave a soft snort.

Kellen tried to remember this driver. She knew everyone at the resort. But she couldn't remember this woman.

She touched the scar on her forehead.

Had these new memories crowded out the old ones?

Or was the explanation for this memory loss as simple as a concussion?

Her head spun, and she slowly reclined.

43

The Di Luca estate in Pennsylvania's Brandywine Valley consisted of forty acres of rolling hills planted in vines, a Tuscan-style tasting room and Max's home. As winter began its first sweep across Lake Erie, Cecilia huddled under a heated throw on the wide porch overlooking the vineyards and watched Max drive his battered pickup in from the blending barn. For the first time in more than two years, since her marriage to Gregory, she believed that, somehow, her life was worth living. More than that—she believed she was worthy of life, and with that revelation, she'd fallen in love with Max. After her marriage, it seemed impossible, but Max made her smile. He made her feel special.

She didn't expect that he love her back. After all, he made Annabella smile, too. Same with his sister. Same with his mother. He was the kind of guy who cared for his people, and Cecilia had earned her place as one of his people. Still, after Gregory, it was interesting to feel a warm glow in the region of her heart—and other parts.

He ran up the porch stairs and grinned at the sight of her. "If you're so cold, why don't you go in?"

"I don't like to be confined."

"Right. I knew that. Scoot over." He crowded her into one corner of the swing, pulled her into his arms and held her.

Slowly, she relaxed and allowed her head to sink onto his chest. "How do you stay so warm?" she asked.

"I've always been like this. I sleep naked in the winter."

"Um." Her apparently sex-starved mind constructed a glorious naked Max out of internet cowboys and James Bond movies. But Max didn't deserve to have her using him for her own titillation, and hastily, she deconstructed the image.

"I'm not particularly hairy," he said, "but I don't wax and I'm not about to start. Is that okay?"

Naked Max was back, with a light dusting of body hair.

Her mouth was dry. She must be dehydrated. "Sure?"

"Do you have body hair?"

"Um. Parts of me. Since I'm blonde, there's not actually...much."

"Ah." The sound was no more than a slow, soft exhale. He ran his fingers over her cropped head. "Blond all over."

She broke a sweat. When she'd come out to the porch, the temperature had hovered at thirty-seven degrees. When had summer arrived?

"Whatever you do doesn't matter to me. I like you the way you are."

When had his voice grown so deep? Rumbly? "I don't think that we should...talk about..."

"True. We shouldn't talk." He loosened his grip on her, stood up and offered her his hand. "Shall we go in and explore?"

She stared at that hand. She memorized the shape of the palm, broad and square, the length of the fingers, long and blunt, the nimble thumb, the sweeping lines, the scar under the index finger. She stared because she needed to think, but something about the stability and strength of that hand convinced her that thinking was overrated.

Putting her hand in his, she let him lift her to her feet. She didn't know why he was doing this, but she followed him inside to his bedroom and watched him take off his clothes. When his clothes were off, then she knew why. He looked at her, still skinny, skittish, scarred and scared and broken, and he wanted her.

Taking a long breath, she dropped the heated throw, pulled off her headband, her gloves, her boots, socks, sweatshirt, jeans.

Max started to chuckle when she got to her winter underwear, and he came to help her. The man was efficient; he got her naked in no time. Then she was naked and he was naked and they were naked together, and she was very warm, and for the first time since seeing Gregory kill her cousin, she could sleep without nightmares.

She was safe.

Max's family had gathered Ceecee into their collective bosom and smothered her with loving care. Yet as winter turned to a cold, wet spring, Max watched over her, gave her everything: food, drink, heat, love, laughter and sex, not necessarily in that order. It was, for Ceecee, a happy time…within reason. Someday soon, Max was going to want more from her. He would want to know where she came from, what her real name was, why she was hiding from her past.

She wasn't ready to tell him. When she remembered her cousin, her soul shriveled with sorrow and guilt. Kellen Rae had had so much to live for, and she had died saving Cecilia. When Cecilia tried to look into the future, she couldn't see herself ever telling Max the truth. When she did, Max would turn away and she would be alone and unloved. She did deserve that, but she couldn't throw away what she had. Not yet.

But as she grew stronger, the old Cecilia, the person she had been before she met Gregory, the person who had gone off on her own to travel the United States, reasserted herself. She loved Max so much she couldn't live without him, and that frightened her. She grew impatient with his care, then irritable. She started feeling tired, not really ill, but queasy and irritable. She looked for something to occupy her mind, and he was always working, so she offered to help him.

That was when Max made his fatal mistake.

He ran his hand through his dark hair and agreed. He said, "Sure. You've got a business degree. That would be great."

He didn't realize what he'd admitted.

At some point, he had looked at the documents Cecilia so vigilantly guarded. He believed she was Kellen Rae Adams. He thought she had a business degree. He probably knew the police wanted to talk to her in conjunction with the explosion at the Lykke house in Maine.

He had looked.

He had lied.

She was so sickened by the betrayal she threw up. Then while he was at work, she called his car service, took Kellen's papers and ran away to Philadelphia. She didn't have a plan, or money, or even good sense. What she had was a terrifying sense of panic. Max knew her secret, he'd never said a word about it to her—and the secret was a lie.

She had the car drop her off at Rittenhouse Square. She wandered the walks under budding trees and through cold sunshine. How could she explain to him her marriage, her cousin Kellen's death, her own cowardice and deception?

Beneath Cecilia's fear was a lurking anger.

Why had he looked at the papers she so carefully guarded? How dare he invade her privacy! Why had he broken his word? He had ruined everything.

A man, rough, unpolished, walked the path toward her. He had pulled the collar of his coat up around his ears and kept his hands plunged deep in his pockets. He had a desperate air about him, a reckless attitude she identified from her time on the streets.

She veered to avoid him.

He walked to intercept her, and she recognized him: Annabella's father, Ettore Fontana, his face a death mask.

How had he found her so quickly?

Probably an informant on Max's staff.

Across the wet, brown lawn, she saw a man running toward them. Running as fast as a linebacker could run. Max!

How had Max *found her so quickly?*

Probably through his credit card, the one that paid for the town car.

She tried to run.

Ettore grabbed her by one arm, pushed her up against a tree trunk and pulled a pistol out of his pocket. He touched it to her forehead.

She froze, afraid to move, afraid not to move. She felt the cool metal, saw the black barrel, smelled her own fear.

Max raced toward them, his mouth open as if he was yelling, but she heard no sound except the heavy beat of blood in her ears.

Then…then nothing.

Nothing, until the moment when she woke in the hospital from her coma.

She remembered so much. Almost everything. But nothing would ever bring back that year after the bullet had entered her brain.

That didn't matter, did it?

What mattered was that in the years since, she'd lived and grown and become the woman the real Kellen Rae Adams would be proud to know.

And maybe what mattered was that Max Di Luca seemed to think they had unfinished business.

Perhaps they did.

44

The town car slid to a stop.

Kellen sat up, groggy, her chest aching, her breath a struggle, her little finger so hot and swollen it felt as if it was a fat sausage roasting on a fire. She half laughed. Her chest, her fingers were the least of her problems. She would get on a helicopter, fly to the hospital and be made well. That was easy. That was clear. It was the welter of emotions connected to Max and their past that was difficult.

The chauffeur opened the back door, grasped Kellen by the waist and forcefully helped her out.

Wait. The car had stopped at the airstrip, but the runway lights were on. A small corporate jet waited, stairs down, engine idling. That made no sense. They didn't need an airplane to get her to the hospital.

"Where's the helicopter?" she asked.

The chauffeur put her arm around Kellen's shoulders, pulled her tight and said, "We're taking the plane."

"Max said there would be a helicopter."

"Max does not command *me*."

Kellen looked up at the woman who held her so tightly. In the reflected light of the runway, that face looked like a horror mask from around the campfire. But Kellen recognized the hazel eyes, the unkempt blond hair, the wide mouth, the high, aristocratic forehead. Erin Lykke.

Then Kellen looked again at the plane. A twelve-passenger Gulfstream with a corporate insignia painted on its tail.

Erin intended to kidnap her.

Kellen rammed her elbow into Erin's ribs.

Erin grunted, let her go, then grabbed and, with one hand behind Kellen's head, placed a cloth over Kellen's nose. As the world spun in circles, Erin cooed, "Did you think you could run forever... Cecilia?"

Max was damned well going to get the resort under control so he could get to the hospital and sit with... Ceecee. Cecilia. Kellen. Whatever name she wanted him to call her, he would. She was the woman of his dreams. She was the love of his life.

He organized the resort's staff, what few were left, as they came out of hiding, and visited Carson Lennex's suite for the pure joy of viewing the damaged and now-conscious Mara Philippi, who sported two black eyes, a broken nose and a cool demeanor.

No, not cool. Cold. She didn't speak. She didn't move. Frost rimmed her vigilant eyes.

Nils Brooks was sitting up against a wall, holding an ice bag on the back of his neck and a pistol in his other hand. He kept the gun pointed at Mara and he gave terse instructions to the visitors. "Stay back. She's not to be trusted." If the way he held that gun was any indication, he didn't trust anyone in the room. And if he was to be believed, the US government would be removing Mara from their custody very soon.

Max didn't care if the FBI took her away or Sheriff Kwinault handled the arrest. His only concern was that it happened sooner rather than later. Without a doubt, this was a dangerous woman.

Nils didn't relax until Temo and Adrian appeared. Those two he apparently trusted, and as they took up their positions around Mara, she finally seemed to accept she could not escape.

As soon as the arrest was made, he would have to send Nils to the hospital.

He called Annie and Leo and gave them the update, and while he was on the phone with them, Carson Lennex rang in.

Max hurriedly finished briefing Annie and Leo and answered, "Carson, what's your report?"

"It's good, I guess. Birdie's not good. Sheri Jean stabilized her condition. Somehow, we got her down the spiral staircase and waited for the car, but—" Carson sounded frankly peeved "—nothing."

Max frowned. "The car didn't show up?"

"No, so we loaded Birdie into my car and right now we're headed toward the airstrip. We'd damned well better get Birdie on the same helicopter that's taking Kellen to the hospital."

"I don't know how the driver got it wrong," Max said. "I'm sorry, Carson. Keep me up-to-date."

At the time Max put Kellen into the car, he had thought nothing of the driver's attitude. He had had more important things on his mind. But now, the memory of her tone grated at him. Annie and Leo would never put up with an insolent driver.

Before his unease blossomed, Carson called in again. "Max, why are people loading Kellen onto an airplane?"

"What are you talking about?"

"They're carrying her up the steps into a corporate jet."

Max found himself on his feet. "Who is? What kind of corporate jet?"

"This woman. This guy in a pilot's uniform. Big jet. She's unconscious."

"Stop them!"

"They carried her inside. They shut the door. The logo on the plane says Lykke Industries. Does that mean anything to you?"

"Yes." Max's heart stopped. This wasn't possible. Not after he'd just found her again. Not when they'd come so close. "It means Kellen is about to die."

45

Kellen woke to the drone of an airplane in flight.

She knew where she was before she opened her eyes. Under her nose, she smelled expensive carpet, so she was sprawled face-down in the airplane aisle. But something close at hand emitted another odor, the reek of something burned and rotting. The stench made her want to vomit.

Her fear made her want to cry.

The truth made her want to hide.

She remembered everything. Every damned Cecilia thing.

She wished she didn't. She wished she could forget she had ever been Cecilia, weak, broken and guilty. For years now, she had pretended to be Kellen, to be strong, fearless. But here, on the floor of the Lykke Industries jet, the only thing that seemed real was—she was an impostor.

She pulled her hands to her chest, used them to lever herself up.

Everything hurt. Her shattered sternum robbed her of breath. Her broken hand throbbed. The chemical used to drug her gave her a relentless headache.

At her first movement, Erin cackled.

Of course. This night had shone a light on Kellen's past and in the process stripped away her future. She didn't glance around, but she said, “Erin, you need a better air freshener to hang on the rearview mirror of your fancy corporate jet.”

Erin stopped laughing. “How could you? Make a joke? When he is sitting here like this…” She choked on tears.

Kellen froze. The hairs rose on the back of her head. *Something not quite human was watching her.* Slowly, inch by inch, she turned her head and looked, past Erin, who was crouched in the aisle, to the back row where a blackened hulk of a decaying human sat propped against the window. “Is that…?” she whispered.

“My brother.” Erin’s voice throbbed with devotion. “My darling.”

His teeth shone in a face devoid of flesh, smiling death’s smile at Kellen.

He had come for her at last.

Erin petted his hand.

Kellen gagged at the thought of touching that burned, flaking flesh. “How did you locate—” she nodded toward Gregory “—the corpse?”

“He wasn’t dead!”

Kellen remembered the force of the blast, the heat of the fire. “I can hardly believe that.”

“When the police didn’t find his body, I searched. I searched and I found him on the boulders by the sea. He’d been blown out of the house by the explosion and he rested there, burned, broken, the salty waves battering his rocky bed. He was alive.” Erin stood and stepped closer. “Do you hear me? Alive. I brought him home. We cared for him, Mother and I. We loved him.”

Kellen faintly heard the rhetoric, the melodrama, over the ringing in her ears. “How did you get him on the plane?”

“I carried him myself. He weighs so little now…” Tears trickled down Erin’s cheeks. “Do you not even recognize your own husband?”

Kellen muttered, “He was less crispy last time I saw him.”

Erin kicked her in the chin.

Kellen blacked out again.

When she came to, she was facedown in the aisle, her ear against the floor. The plane droned on. She heard no other movement. Yet she knew, she knew, Erin was somewhere behind her, waiting to hurt her, maim her. Her partner was a man, dead and rotting for seven years.

Foolish Cecilia feared them both.

With eyes closed she considered her situation. At the front of the plane was a small galley. A door protected the crew, whoever they were. They knew Erin had brought this rotting piece of flesh aboard. So were they crazy? Zombies? Extremely well paid? They wouldn't help her. She needed to defend herself, to bring this to a different conclusion than Erin imagined and hoped for. Yet she was badly injured and her weapons were gone; Erin had stripped them away. Erin was taller, big-boned, sturdy—and uninjured. So what to do? How to survive?

She thought about the real Kellen, about how bravely her relative had come to the rescue of her young, terrified cousin. Would she betray the woman who had sacrificed her life by giving in to fear? No. God help her, no.

She rolled onto her side, slowly gathered herself and sat up.

As she suspected, a grinning Erin again crouched in the aisle beside her brother's decomposing body. Their smiles were eerily alike.

Kellen needed time to get herself into position. Erin wanted to talk. Kellen was glad to oblige. "Where are we going?"

"Back to Maine. Back to the Lykke mansion, where I'll do as Gregory wished. I'll see that you die as he did—slowly and in agony."

Kellen shifted to sit cross-legged. She used the knuckles of her good hand to massage her thighs, get the blood flowing again. "Did he die slowly and in agony?" Kellen knew what to say now. Knew what to do. Coolly, she said, "Good!"

Erin kicked out again.

Kellen turned her shoulder.

Erin missed.

Kellen caught Erin's leg at the top of her kick and flung herself forward, toppling Erin off her feet.

Erin crashed backward across the seats. Her head hit the airplane's window and Kellen heard a satisfying thumping sound like a ripe watermelon on a hot Nevada summer day. That almost made up for the slashing pain in her chest and head and... Damn it, she was supposed to be on her way to the hospital, not fighting for her life with a dead man as a witness.

God bless Mara for one thing. She'd made Kellen stronger than she had ever been in her life, taught her kickboxing, and now Kellen brought a kick around from the side and slammed Erin in the ribs.

Erin struggled to turn, fell into a seat, sat there and stared into the distance as if looking into the past. "During the whole long week when Gregory struggled to die, he said only one thing. He said you were still alive."

Kellen had suffered nightmares about witnessing her cousin's murder—and the look Gregory gave Cecilia when he looked up and realized his mistake. "Before the explosion, he saw me."

"Yes. He made me swear I would do what he failed to do." Erin lifted her head. "I'm going to fulfill my brother's final wish. I'm going to send you to join him."

Kellen had to finish this, and she had to do it while she had the breath and the strength. "You're as mean and crazy as your brother. You know that?"

Erin came off the seat as if she'd been stung and swung her fist at Kellen.

Kellen leaped backward down the narrow aisle and into the galley. "You're the one who sent the snake!"

"As a warning."

"Gregory's face in the window—that was your doing."

"You went to a man's rooms to betray your husband!"

"First of all, I didn't—" Kellen stopped herself. "I can't betray Gregory. He's dead. Look at him." She gestured at that grotesque, blackened, grinning body. "He's dead. He has no wife. He has no life. He's *dead*."

"Every time you look at another man, you betray Gregory's memory. He loved you. He loved you so much that when he realized you were going to leave him, he wanted death at your side."

"Do you approve of his love for me?"

Erin glanced away.

Kellen saw the crack in Erin's devotion, and she pressed her advantage. "You approved of everything he did. You had to approve of me."

Bitterly now, Erin said, "You didn't deserve him."

"That's for sure. No one deserves to be hurt, humiliated, killed. He was a murderer, but you're not. Not yet!"

Erin laughed. She laughed, all merry and amused. "My mother wanted to warn you I was coming for you."

Kellen stood still for a critical moment. "Your mother wanted to warn me?"

"I couldn't let her do that."

"So you...killed Sylvia? You killed your mother?"

Erin smacked Kellen with a roundhouse to the jaw.

Kellen dropped to her knees, her head ringing. Every time she inhaled, pain knifed her lungs. Every time she lifted her hand, the swelling intensified.

"I smothered her with a pillow. She was senile, babbling about how she had bred monsters by a monster. She was talking about me and Gregory, and about our father!" Erin swayed back and forth like a charmed cobra. "She said she loved us, but she called us monsters."

Kellen cradled her aching jaw and collected bits and pieces of consciousness. She opened her swollen eyes and with her left hand pulled herself to her feet. "Erin Lykke, you're going to hell."

"No." Erin had the audacity to look hurt. "She deserved it. She was going to betray Gregory!" She started toward Kellen.

Kellen backed up, drawing Erin farther into the galley.

Erin laughed. "You're puffing like a freight train gasping its way up a mountain. What good do you think retreat will do you? You're almost at the crew quarters. You've got your back to the wall."

"And you, my dear Erin, are a sucker." Kellen leaned her left hand on a counter, lifted herself and flung her legs in a circle in the roundhouse flying kick that Mara had taught her. The flying kick she'd never been able to perfect before.

Her foot caught Erin on the side of the neck. Erin gagged. Her eyes rolled back in her head. She stumbled backward down the aisle, then fell on her rear next to Gregory's charred remains. When she opened her eyes, she stared at Kellen in round-eyed wonder. The Cecilia she remembered had been weak, feeble, a weeping wimp of a girl who Gregory abused in body and mind.

This Cecilia had fused with her cousin, Kellen. They were one, and they were strong.

Head outthrust, eyes intent, Kellen advanced down the aisle. "If your own mother said you were a monster, if she said Gregory was a monster, that tells you everything. He was barely a human being. He was a demon."

"Then we were monsters together!" Erin surged out of her seat and right at Kellen.

Kellen used her elbow under Erin's jaw to snap her head back. "I'm not going back to Maine, and you're not, either. I'm not going to die on this plane, and you're not, either. I'm going to survive, and you're going to go to prison."

Erin collapsed onto the floor again. Her nose was bleeding, her cheek bruising. She crawled backward, her eyes fixed on Kellen. "They'll know who you are... *Cecilia.*"

"Then it's time the world knows. Most certainly, it's time the pilot understands what's at stake." Kellen started for the front.

"Cecilia..." Erin sang the name in a horror-movie voice.

Kellen swung around, ready to defend herself.

Erin was on her knees. She pulled Kellen's Glock from the seat pocket in front of Gregory. She held it in both shaking hands, released the safety and pointed it at Kellen.

No. Kellen had done so much, come so far. It couldn't end like this. "Look." She held both her hands up. "You don't want to shoot at me. If you hit any of the electrical or the hydraulics, the plane could go down."

Erin hoisted herself into the seat beside Gregory, leaned her head against his charred shoulder and touched the barrel to the window beside him. "I won't hit the electrical," she promised.

"This is a pressurized cabin. If you put a bullet through the window, all the air inside here will blast out of the plane like a giant explosion." Kellen spoke slowly and gestured, trying to convey the scope of the calamity. "You'd be in big trouble. You'd go shooting out into the upper atmosphere, never to be seen again. Your pilot probably wouldn't be able to control the plane, and he'll die, too."

Erin laughed, and she sounded so much like Gregory a chill rippled up Kellen's spine. "You'll die, Cecilia, and somewhere, Gregory will be happy." Erin's finger squeezed the trigger.

The bullet shattered the window.

Kellen threw herself to the floor, grabbed the metal legs of a seat and held on. Air pressure blasted out the window, peeling away a two-foot-wide chunk of the plane's fuselage from ceiling to floor.

Erin disappeared into the void. The reeking wreck of Gregory's body vanished out the hole with Erin.

The plane rocked, out of control.

Kellen careened back and forth, helpless, caught in forces beyond her control. Her injured hand slipped and slipped again. She clutched with her good hand, but…

No air.

No gravity.

No strength.

She fought to again grasp the metal leg with her swollen fingertips.

The plane spiraled downward.

She couldn't breathe. She was losing consciousness.

She was going to die.

46

As dawn faintly lit the eastern sky, the plane touched down... somewhere.

Kellen sat buckled into a seat as close to the cockpit as she could get. With her injured hand, she held a yellow oxygen mask over her face. With her uninjured hand, she clutched the arm of the chair. With every fiber of her being, she prayed.

All too clearly through the puncture in the fuselage, she could hear the squeal of the brakes, the roar of the reverse thrusters. She felt the pressure that slammed her against the seat and the skid and crash as the plane lurched to a halt, crooked in a ditch.

She looked out of the hole in the plane. Seven feet down, she could see asphalt. A two-lane road with a yellow dotted line down the middle. She could jump the distance.

She did.

She stumbled, fell onto her hands and knees. Sheer blinding pain from her hand made her rest her head on the cool pavement, but as the agony retreated, she lifted her head and laughed.

She had to. She was alive.

More than alive. She was free. The fears that had lurked within her had vanished. No, not vanished—been vanquished. By her. All those years, she'd been afraid of Gregory's ghost. She'd been afraid of Gregory's family. She'd been afraid that somehow, somewhere they would find her, that a wave of corrosive acid Lykke family craziness would crash over her and she would again be helpless, belittled, broken.

Well, Erin, cruel and crazy Erin, had found her. She had done everything to break Kellen. She had used the name Cecilia against her as if it was an insult. And today Kellen had discovered Cecilia was smarter, braver, funnier than she had ever imagined. It hadn't really been Kellen who escaped from the horror of Gregory's murder/suicide, survived the Philadelphia streets, saved a child, learned to love... It hadn't really been Kellen who joined the Army, learned hand-to-hand combat, to carry a weapon, to fight in battles against an unseen enemy, to save her comrades from death, to be wounded and live.

Cecilia had stood alone and defeated Gregory's ghost and the terror that tainted her days and nights.

Cecilia had become the person her cousin, Kellen, had wanted her to be. At long last, she was worthy of the sacrifice Kellen had made.

She looked around. The world was flat here, a great plain of prairie dotted with farmhouses surrounded by mountains and covered by a grand, wide sky. A breeze whipped up and brought a crackling sound and the scent of something burning. That brought her to her feet. Behind her, the plane's wheel was buried in a roadside ditch, the plane's wing pointed toward the vanishing northern stars...and smoke curled from the engine.

A quarter mile away, a man stood on the porch of a farmhouse, filming the scene with his phone. She walked toward him, staggering from pain and shock. When she got close, she looked up at him—he was still filming—and she asked, "Where are we?"

"Montana."

"Can you call 911? Because there's a pilot on that plane and the plane's about to explode."

She spent one day in a small Montana hospital while they stabilized her, gave her oxygen and ascertained the hairline fractures in her sternum would heal with much pain, but no lasting effects. She was transferred to a moderately sized Montana hospital with a skilled orthopedic surgeon, who operated on her shattered finger. Her cast reached to her elbow, her fingertips were the only things showing and they were bruised and swollen, and learning to do anything with her left hand made every waking moment a challenge and sometimes a humiliation.

While she was recovering, she heard from everyone—Annie and Leo, who reported the resort had survived, Mr. Gilfilen, who reported he had survived, Birdie, who reported she had survived and that Mr. Lennex was a very nice man. Sheri Jean, who was aggravated that not only was Mara a villain, but her absence left a gap in the guest services lineup and how was Sheri Jean supposed to deal with that? Temo, whose sister was settling in nicely, and Adrian, who assured Kellen that the son of a bitch who had wanted to sell Regina had been shown a cliff that plunged into the ocean but had been allowed to limp away.

Nils Brooks did not call, but he did message to let her know Mara Philippi, aka the Librarian, was in federal custody without incident.

Max sent flowers but no word. After that kiss...well, she didn't know what she wanted from him. She only knew they would have to talk and decisions would have to be made. Yes, she'd loved him once, but she'd made a new life apart from Max. Things had happened to her. No doubt things had happened to him. Could they find a neutral meeting ground? Did they even want to?

Now, two weeks later, the plane landed on the Yearning Sands airstrip and skidded toward the ocean. Just like the first time, it stopped short. The pilot lowered the stairs and Kellen limped her way out into a rare sunny day. The cold wind took her breath away, and clouds ripped across the sky, tearing like tissue paper.

A town car waited; Kellen slid inside the front passenger seat and smiled at the chauffeur. Wrapping her arms around Birdie's neck, she hugged cautiously and was cautiously hugged in return. "They sent you."

"I volunteered."

Kellen teared up. Mitch had betrayed them. Mara had proved to be a killer. Birdie... Birdie was tried-and-true. "How do you feel?" Kellen asked.

"Pretty good." She turned to show Kellen a face still disfigured with bruises and stitches and a droop that was possibly nerve damage. "I'm disillusioned about Mitch, but life can do that."

"Tell me about it." The week in the Montana hospital had returned Kellen to the most fragile of health, but Kellen didn't care—she was alive. *They* were alive.

Birdie put the car in gear and started toward the resort.

Kellen turned on the seat heater, struggled out of her winter coat and settled back to watch the road as it wound through groves and over hills toward the resort. "I heard from Nils."

"Which is more than we have," Birdie said in exasperation. "When the government took Mara away, he disappeared in a hurry."

"He's got a job. An important job." All Kellen's doubts had been set at rest. Nils Brooks really was MFAA. "He said she's in custody."

Birdie hesitated. "I hope so. I hope she doesn't escape. I don't know why I think she can, but I do, and I'm more afraid of her than I ever was of anyone in Afghanistan."

Kellen put her hand on Birdie's shoulder. "I know. I used to think that gleam in her eyes was competitiveness. Now I think it's ego and rabid lunacy."

"Did you hear when the Feds went into her cottage to search for evidence, her bedroom closet was locked, and when they got it open, it was full of books?" Birdie glanced at Kellen. "I mean—*books*. First editions, autographed editions and part of a genuine Gutenberg Bible. The stash is worth millions."

"She was illiterate and locked her books in a closet? Isn't *that* symbolic?"

"And—" Birdie looked vaguely ill.

"What else?"

"Hands. Mummified."

"Birdie." Kellen pressed her back against the seat as if trying to get away from the vision. "That's..."

"Yeah. It is." Birdie took a breath. "There's speculation she used a dehydrator."

Kellen leaped to a horrifying conclusion. "Not a dehydrator in our kitchens!"

"No! At least, the chefs said no, but they're buying new ones."

"Ugh." Kellen could only imagine the chefs tossing the resort's commercial-sized dehydrators out the windows. "Mara is all things twisted and warped. Does anybody know who she really is?"

"You mean her background? No. She just appeared out of nowhere."

Like me. Kellen shrugged the thought away. "She corrupted Mitch. I swear he was our man until she got her claws in him."

The car swerved as Birdie half turned toward Kellen. "You can't blame her for Mitch!"

"I guess not. I just feel less stupid about trusting him if I have her to blame."

"He tried to kill us. He almost succeeded. For money and maybe for sex with her? I feel for his family, but he hurt me and he hurt you. He was responsible for his actions, and I don't mourn him." Birdie was angry, vehement.

"Okay. You don't have to." As badly as Birdie had been injured, Kellen didn't blame her a bit.

Birdie asked, "Guess what else? Guess what washed in on the beach the day after they took Mara away?"

"If you tell me more artifacts, I'll tell you I don't give a damn."

Birdie grinned and shook her head. "Guess again."

"My God." This time Kellen knew she had guessed right. "Priscilla's body?"

"In the plastic container," Birdie affirmed. "She didn't have any family, so she's buried in the Cape Charade cemetery. Annie and Leo paid for the gravestone. We all chipped in for some nice flowers. She deserved that."

"What about her ring?"

"We put that in the coffin with her."

"Good. Good. I hope she knows the good she did by stashing that ring in her shoe. I'm glad she's at rest, and I hope she's at peace."

"Amen," Birdie said.

They fell silent. The miles rolled past. Kellen kept stumbling on the memories she had recovered along the way. Nils was gone from the resort. Maybe Max was gone, too? But she didn't want to ask—it revealed more than she wanted, so instead she said, "Are Annie and Leo back?"

"Got here last week." Birdie was a little too terse.

"They're upset?"

"What do you think? It's Annie's resort. She feels like she left it to be destroyed." Birdie glanced at Kellen. "You saved it."

"You saved it, too."

"Leo says I have a job for the rest of my life. I'd be more flattered if I thought they could ever find someone to take my place."

Kellen chuckled. "You're irreplaceable. But should you be back on the job? You look tired and as if you're in pain."

"Other than driving you to the resort, I'm not doing much. As soon as all the kinks have been worked out, I'm going on vacation someplace warm."

"I thought we were going on vacation together." Then, "What kinks?"

Birdie drove carefully around the curves. "Things are changing at the resort, you know. Mr. Gilfilen's injuries have left him with limited mobility, so he can't manage security anymore. A replacement must be found."

Kellen had already thought of this. "I'll do it. I'd rather be in charge of security than be broadsided by another management crisis involving a missing shipment of nail polish with a name like Orgasm."

Birdie made a doubtful sound. "When all is said and done, I don't know that you as the head of security is such a good idea."

Kellen's attention swerved toward Birdie. "When what's said and done?"

Something was out of whack in this conversation. Birdie kept glancing at Kellen, smiling and frowning, then smiling again, and every once in a while, she shook her head.

It must have to do with Max. Taking the bull by the horns, Kellen asked, "Where's Max? Is he still here? Is he going to take over security?"

"Max is at the resort. No, I don't think he's considered a permanent position at Yearning Sands."

"Oh. Well, that would be too much to..." Kellen caught her first glimpse of Yearning Sands, of the stone castle-like edifice that grew out of the sand and scrub, that faced storms and murders, that had accepted the passage of time with such grace. Home. Kellen's friends were here, and here she felt at home.

She was glad to be home.

"I knew Max before." Saying the words made Kellen feel light-headed.

"I know," Birdie said.

"He...told you?"

"It was a surprise."

"Does everybody know?"

"Pretty much. Kind of." Birdie verbally squirmed. "Yes. But he didn't blab anything! Things just...got around."

Kellen's return got more complicated all the time. "When I knew Max before," she said again, "he lived on the East Coast.

I did a little more research on him—" very little, looking him up online made her feel like a Peeping Tom "—and now he lives in Oregon full-time."

"That's not too far. That'll make things easier."

That was odd. "What things?"

Birdie tried to say something. Tried again.

"What's happening?" Kellen persisted.

In a voice vibrant with worry and encouragement, Birdie said, "Sweetheart. Your life is about to change."

47

Nothing about this was making sense. "Birdie, you're scaring me."

"Don't be scared. Be excited." Birdie pulled the town car under the portico.

Russell opened the front door, and Carson Lennex and Max stepped out, Carson in slacks and a sweater, Max in his trademark dark suit and blue tie.

Carson walked around the front of the car, opened the door for Birdie and helped her out.

Even in his sixties, even with bruising and burns, he was straight and tall and movie-star handsome.

Birdie was not yet thirty, dark-skinned, bony, with bandages on four knuckles and swelling that unevenly reshaped her face.

Yet as they stood together, they smiled at each other, and they looked so sweet.

Max stood, legs braced, hand crossed behind his back, waiting outside the hotel door. He looked good. Strong. Stable. Stern. He came to the car, opened the passenger door, offered his hand.

She looked at his hand and flashed back to that moment on his porch in Pennsylvania. *The shape of the palm, broad and square, the length of the fingers, long and blunt, the nimble thumb, the sweeping lines, the scar under the index finger.* She put her hand in his and used his support to climb out. "Hi there." Wow. Eloquent.

He looked into her face without smiling and without speaking.

She had wondered, with a rapidly beating heart, whether he'd take one look at her and sweep her off her feet in a massive reaffirmation of their passion.

She guessed not.

Really. Not.

She looked past him into the lobby.

People were standing around. Front desk staff, mostly, as they should be, but...why were the spa employees there? Why were the chefs lingering close? Temo and his sister and Adrian lurked by the concierge desk, too.

"What's going on?" Kellen looked right at Max. "What's wrong?"

Like Birdie, he tried to speak, then sighed. "Nothing's wrong. But...let's go in and up to Annie's office."

A brief moment of alarm made her ask, "Is it Annie? Did she...?"

"She's fine, I swear."

Russell rushed to hold the door for them.

What kind of surprise did the resort hold for her? Not a party welcoming her home, that was for sure. Because no matter what Birdie or Max said, some momentous thing had occurred, and it wasn't a laughing matter.

Max put his hand at the small of her back and guided her inside.

She was pleased to see she was a little wrong about the party. A giant gold banner read "Welcome back, Kellen!"

But this wasn't a cheering throng, not by any means. Sheri Jean, Frances, Destiny, Xander, Daisy, Ellen, the housekeepers, the guests: when they met her eyes, they smiled, but they watched her in silence. The atmosphere was claustrophobic with interest. Yes, they definitely knew about her and Max.

Kellen and Max climbed the stairs to Annie's office. She glanced back at him; he kept taking a breath like he wanted to say something, then letting it out. And if he was happy to see her, he hid it well.

In the office, Annie and Leo waited in the seating area beside the fireplace; they were holding hands and looking anxious. Hammett rested beside them, his head on his paws, watching the scene with as much interest as the people below. "You're looking one thousand percent better," Annie called. "Welcome back!"

At last somebody had said it. "Thank you!"

An older woman, handsome and imperious, sat beside Annie in an easy chair, and a little girl, about six or seven, leaned against the arm. As Kellen walked in, the girl stared and smiled a smile that showed two missing front teeth. The child started hopping, first one foot, then the other. It was all too obvious she wanted to run toward them, but the older lady kept her tethered with a hand on her wrist.

Max sighed as he viewed the little gathering. "Could Kellen and I have a few moments alone with Rae? Mama? Annie and Leo?"

"Leo and I wanted Kellen to know she had support from us." Annie turned her wheelchair and started for the door. "And we do support you, dear, no matter what you decide."

The woman Max called mama stood, also. "She does not need support, Annie. No one here is against her."

Kellen felt like the elephant in the room. But she was so sure she recognized the little girl, she couldn't speak.

Had the child been a guest at the resort?

No, Kellen didn't have a profile in her brain.

Leo and Hammett followed Annie, and Leo in a low, masculine conspiratorial voice said to Max, "It was her idea."

Max nodded.

His mother leaned down and spoke to the little girl. To Rae.

Rae stopped hopping and stood very still, arms stiff at her sides, but she beamed at Kellen and Kellen had to smile back.

Max's mother walked toward him but asked repressively, "Are you sure, Maximilian?"

"We need time to get matters cleared up," Max said.

What things? Kellen wanted to ask. *What did they need to clear up? Who was the child?*

Max pushed his relatives out of the room and shut the door behind them.

The profile Kellen was attempting to produce kept getting scrambled by that smile, that excitement, that blond hair, those dimples. "Who is she?" she asked Max.

"You don't know?" His voice sounded as if it was coming up from a deep well.

"I swear I've never seen her before." Kellen chuckled. "Except, well...she's the spitting image of my cousin at that age."

"Yes," he said, which was a very odd answer.

"Funny that her name is Rae. That was my cousin's middle name. What a coincidence that that little girl—" Kellen's mind, her heart, her words, all stammered to a halt, yet her steps irrepressibly carried her toward the child. She couldn't stop herself. She was on a collision course with fate, and with the year she couldn't remember.

Max kept pace with Kellen and said quietly, "When you were shot, you were pregnant."

The child couldn't stand it any longer. She ran at Kellen full tilt, wrapped her arms around her hips and looked up at her. "Did you know that you're my mama?"

I have three confessions:

1. I've got the scar of a gunshot on my forehead.

2. ~~I don't remember an entire year of my life.~~ I still don't remember, but I know what happened now. I had a baby, and that changes everything.

3. My name is Kellen Adams…and that's half a lie.

★★★★★

Acknowledgments

The journey to create and write *Dead Girl Running* and the Cape Charade series has been by turns complex and challenging, funny and romantic, intricate and interesting. I couldn't have done it without the advice and support of the publishing professionals at HQN.

Allison Carroll is unmatched in her editorial direction, as well as her bravery and humor, and her ideas and her tact inspired and guided me.

Sean Kapitain thrilled me with the evocative *Dead Girl Running* cover. Thank you, Sean. And thank you to the whole trade and hardcover art team, led by Erin Craig.

Thanks to Lisa Wray, manager, publicity and events, who sees *Dead Girl Running* in terms of a publishing event and generates excitement every day.

Dead Girl Running owes its speed and legs to Sales—always, always a huge thanks to Fritz Servatius!

Thank you to Tahra Seplowin, editorial assistant, for explaining the details of publishing with HQN and keeping me on track.

A most important thank-you to Craig Swinwood, president and CEO; Loriana Sacilotto, executive vice president; and to

Susan Swinwood, HQN editorial director, for the opportunity to publish with HQN. A special thank-you to Dianne Moggy, vice president of editorial, who has consistently been enthusiastic about my work. I am so glad we were able to come together to create a story that speaks to the heart.